JONATHAN STRONG

QUIT THE RACE

A NOVEL

PRESSED WAFER

for Jim and Wendy

ISBN: 978-1-940396-25-5
FIRST EDITION
PRINTED IN THE UNITED STATES OF AMERICA

PRESSED WAFER
375 PARKSIDE AVENUE, BROOKLYN, NY 11226
WWW.PRESSEDWAFER.COM

PART ONE

1 All that hot evening, Joel had been out in the front room trying to set to music "The Fire of Driftwood" by Longfellow. He always relied on Sean to find poems he'd like to set, poems with regular meters and rhymes to mess around with. Joel was never much of a reader, but Sean had read a lot over his sixty-five years and had a sharp sense of what Joel might respond to. It couldn't be sentimental or pretty and must have "inner symmetries" and "concealed dissonances" for Joel to uncover. That night, his composing sounded particularly excruciating. He was at the far end of the apartment, smudging chords on the piano and croaking along in his off-key baritone. The notes bounced off the walls of their under-furnished front room and echoed down the hall and through the bedroom door. Sean trusted that coherent lines would begin to emerge and then some recognizable form and that, when the piece was finally rehearsed and sung by the choral group at Foxridge Academy, it would prove not only perfect for the words but also sound surprisingly beautiful, even to Sean.

That hot July night with no breeze off the lake, waiting for Joel to come join him in bed, Sean found it harder than usual to convince himself that those awful sounds out there were moving confidently along in the process of becoming music. Joel kept going over and over one single line: "We spake of many a vanished scene." The series of slight alterations was driving Sean a little nuts. His undershirt was damp with sweat, so he peeled it off. He had to switch his lower pillow with the top one to rest his cheek on cooler cotton. Finally, he kicked the sheet all the way off and lay there on their high four-poster in his red plaid boxers, too tired to get up and close the bedroom door or turn on the window fan.

This was what he heard: "We spake of many—no!—we spake—no!—spake of many a van—shit!—many a vanished—yes!—scene, we spake of many—oh, Jesus Christ!" and then again and again. The air lay heavy on Sean's skin, and the reverberating chords were pressing into his ears. Gradually, he found himself taking refuge behind closed eyelids and drifting into a vanished scene of his own. He began by picturing his Gramma Tyson sitting on a blanket on the grassy terrace at the farm. She was shelling peas from her garden with his mom beside her like a dutiful daughter-in-law, and he was up in a canvas chair, fifteen years old, with a small dark-green book in his lap. He pictured exactly how Gramma had reached across the shabby old blanket and given an approving pat to the back of Mom's hand, and he heard her voice again saying, "He's reading local history, Eileen." Sean's sister Mary and little brother Sandy were down in the pool, splashing and screaming in a game of water polo with the cousins. Dad and big brother Danny were setting up fireworks for when it got dark. Sean had discovered, a few months earlier, the muscleman magazines in his dad's file cabinet back at home, but on that Fourth of July at the farm, he didn't yet know what they meant.

Now, suddenly, Joel's hypnotic pounding ceased, and the lid over the keys snapped shut, his way to stop obsessing. Sean waited for him to wash up in the bathroom. Then, Joel flicked the hall light off and the window fan on and climbed up onto the far side of the bed. Sean started telling him how all those chords on the piano had somehow carried him back to a summer night fifty years ago when Danny and Dad were setting up Roman candles at the pool's deep end and the Catherine wheel on the end of the diving board. Joel said, "Please, I'm about to fade," but Sean kept talking because the picture was so sharp and was making him feel things he hadn't felt in a long while. Joel only growled, "You know that I get one chance for sleep. Now you've ruined my one chance! Why do you keep doing this to me?" He pounded his pillow. "You never think," he grumbled and turned away, slamming his other pillow over his head.

6

There was no point in having it out at that time of night. Sean knew it was stupid of him to persist in things that made for discord. After more than three decades together, he assumed too often that what was on his mind must also be on Joel's. It puzzled him that couples got into ruts like that. When his dad had left the family, he thought it meant that people could change their lives, but it turned out they really couldn't. His dad was only being who he'd always been. You just learned more about yourself as your life went on.

Joel tossed the hot pillow off his head and onto the floor. In ten minutes, his snuffling breaths were coming in a steady rhythm. Sean was left lying on his back, feeling his heart beating under his ribs. He stared up at the ceiling, which was lit a faint gray by the streetlamp. Occasionally, a wash of yellow streaked across it from a slow-passing car in search of a parking space.

《 》

The next morning, half dressed for work in khaki slacks and an as-yet-unbuttoned shirt, and still barefoot, Sean was eating his oat bran and rye toast when he heard violent throat clearings in the hall. Soon, a bleary-eyed Joel staggered into the kitchen in camouflage boxers. His pale hairy belly and gray chest hairs were wet from a wake-up splash that dripped off his chin. Joel put his toast in the toaster, his cream of wheat in the microwave, and took his seat at the enamel-top table with a glass of pomegranate juice.

"I've been up since six," Sean said. "I tried reading out on the balcony till the sun was up over the roofs, but I couldn't concentrate."

"Poor Shaw-awn," Joel whined with an "aw" for the "ah" that Sean's mom used to insist on. In his childhood, before all the Shawns and Shauns, he was the only Sean he knew.

They ate in silence till Joel announced, "I made it to 'the first slight swerving of the heart.' I'll play it for you tonight. I'm not sure how to set 'swerving' without being pictorial." Joel had always been against scene-painting in music.

"You have a whole free summer," Sean reminded him.

Joel savored a large spoonful of cream of wheat with brown sugar and complained, "We really need to get out of Chicago. Jesus, two weeks in the UP won't be nearly enough of an escape! Gustav Mahler only composed in the summer, but he had a little composing shack up in the Alps."

Lately, Sean had been hearing versions of this too often. He got up to rinse his dishes and fetch his shoes and socks, glad to be going to his air-conditioned office. He knew that Joel, shut in and alone in their sticky apartment, would be agonizing all day over his music. He might take a break to run through his viola part for quartet night and he'd certainly procrastinate by doing the laundry and going out for groceries, but he'd be grumpy about it.

"Hey, when you get off work," Joel called from the kitchen, "let's meet at the lake for a picnic. You can change into shorts at the office. I'll bring towels and food. Five-thirty by the tree. I'll be scoping out the sunbather boys for you." He always claimed he never took note of young men on his own behalf.

Heading to the El, shorts packed in his shoulder bag, Sean grew sweatier with each block. He kept trying to recall lines from the Longfellow poem. "The first slight swerving of the heart" and then something about lives having separate ends. He was sorry he'd picked that poem for Joel. It was about growing old and finding how much you must keep to yourself. When you're young, you say things that mean what you think they mean, but later you can't quite, because it's all much too elusive and private and more than you'd ever thought it could be.

As the train rattled along into town, lines of the poem did come back to him. "All that fills the hearts of men—" no, "of friends—when first they feel—" something, something. "Their lives thenceforth have separate ends." That was it. Back on that Fourth of July at Gramma's farm, when she touched Mom's hand while Sean read the history of the Black Hawk wars, there had been nobody and no place he had yet been separated from, nothing important he had yet lost. He had thought he came from a happy family.

« »

He located Joel, Cubs cap protecting his balding scalp, lying back on the pale-blue blanket spread out in the shade of their usual ash tree on the grass above the sand. They were both careful of the sun. In Sean's younger days, he'd bake in it and turn himself brown, but now he went annually to a dermatologist to have small skin cancers frozen off, and Joel filled their medicine cabinet with moisturizers, salves, and "Age Shield" sunblock for his fair skin. When Sean had unbuttoned and draped his shirt over his shoulders, his chest looked downright lizardy and the skin appreciably looser than it once was.

"There's one for you," Joel said, pointing to an oiled body on the bright sand, a well-built young fellow in baggy red shorts leaning on an elbow and reading a fat hardback through reflective sunglasses. Sean glanced at the bicep bulging in his angled arm but met Joel's suggestive squint with an indifferent shrug. They unpacked their insulated bag of two Jamaican ginger beers, two thick tomato-mozzarella-and-pesto panini from the deli down their block, and paper napkins, a pepper grinder, and pickles in waxed paper.

Sean told Joel about his day at the North Side Housing Collective. A recalcitrant landlord was stalling on repairs, a developer was out of compliance with city ordinances, and certain state subsidies had gotten all tangled up in Springfield. Sean generally had plenty to be distressed about, but Joel's days were always worse. He had made no progress on his piece and hated the whole damn thing. "So I played some of the *Kinderszenen*," he said.

"That usually helps," said Sean.

"Schumann makes me feel inadequate. So does that boy over there."

"You picked him, Joel, not me." The young man had stretched out on his back and, with muscular forearms, was holding up the book, revealing the author to be David Foster Wallace.

Joel whispered, "And the boy's an intellectual, too."

"That poor writer recently committed suicide," Sean said. "I'm afraid I haven't read him." For once, he wasn't going to play along with Joel's game.

More and more people just off work were traipsing down to Lake Michigan. The red shorts and biceps were eventually obscured by a trio of fortyish male joggers who flung themselves exhaustedly under the lengthening shade of the ash tree. Joel proposed shifting the blanket to improve the view since none of the panting runners removing their shoes was an attraction. Sean said it wasn't worth it, so Joel lifted his cap to run a napkin over his sweating brow then reversed the brim to shade the back of his neck from the sun. Soon, the tree's shadow would miss them entirely, the sun would fall behind the city, and it would be time to saunter home. They didn't have the energy to take even a quick dip.

From the joggers' point of view, or from that of the sleek young man, if he'd noticed them at all, Joel and Sean were anonymous scrawny old men, one pale and hairy, the other dried out and leathery with white bangs tossed up by the rising breeze. They were probably a couple, but perhaps not—who cared anymore? Along the lake, Chicago was a happy place of bright sun and sparkling blue water. Bodies of every shape and hue conversed, talked on cell phones or Bluetooths, or texted, or plugged music into their ears. Some read from books or phones or pads or simply stared at the silvery horizon from the edge of the monstrously huge city.

《 》

Their building was the first on a block of brown-brick three-deckers. Brick-pillared balconies rose on either side of the heavy glass entry door. Similar facades receded north up the street with patches of green grass out front and a random spindly tree. The row across the street to the east was now reddish in the low sunlight, but their row was deep in shade. Sean and Joel liked having a southern exposure on the cross-street side, but it meant a steeper mortgage and twice the traffic.

They trudged up the stairs in their solid old building. The Filipino family in 1-B below and the young lawyer couple in 3-B above had never complained about Joel's piano, nor had any residents on the A side. Perhaps they enjoyed free concerts. Sean unlocked and Joel slung the insulated bag to the kitchen then brought out second ginger beers to the balcony. The breeze off the lake had reached them. Joel plopped into one of the canvas sling chairs and said, "Too damn many people around here. I can never get away from them, street after street. Christ!"

Sean took a long swallow from his bottle. "You shouldn't mind people, Joel. We're people, too."

"But where I grew up, there was hardly anyone." A bus hissed to a stop on the main drag down the cross street. "Listen to that fucking noise! If we lived up in the Ocooch Mountains, I could play my music without all that interference. I could hear it in the silence of nature. Cows would moo, birds would sing, but that's all."

"You and your Ocooch Mountains! You grew up in a town."

"But I'd go out walking in the country and make up music in my head. Unless I was meeting a farm boy for some more experimentation in his hayloft."

"Yeah, yeah, Joel."

"Hey, what were you going on about last night when I was half awake?"

"I've lost it now," Sean said, though he remembered well enough what he had been trying to say.

"Something about your dad and fireworks?"

Joel had heard all of Sean's stories, and Sean Joel's, so how many times could they go over their past lives? "It was only a picture," Sean said. "That poem got me thinking about what's vanished."

"There's two kinds of sherbets, orange and lemon," Joel said. "Which do you want?" He had hauled himself out of the canvas chair and was already inside when Sean called after for just the lemon.

Sean liked the city's sounds. He liked being a block away from stores. He liked riding the El to work. At nineteen, when he'd refused his dad's money and transferred to Northern Illinois from Kenyon College, he found he liked being at a big state school. He met new people he felt at home with who'd never known his suburban self. Joel called him a stick-in-the-mud, but Sean had made that one huge change in his life and that was enough. He couldn't do it again.

When Joel reappeared with two bowls, he was still on his latest toot. "We could actually leave the city behind, Sean. There's amazing deals in my part of Wisconsin. On our vacation, we should look around a bit before prices start going up."

"Our agreed-upon plan for my measly two weeks off," Sean reminded him, "is to go hiking in the Upper Peninsula. We put a deposit on that cabin."

"Here's your sherbet. I'd gladly forfeit—"

"But you reserved it."

"Jesus Christ!" Joel snapped. "This is what I mean about you." He stomped back inside. "I'm going online just to see what's out there. I'm not saying we have to buy, but it can't hurt to look. You always squelch my ideas."

Sean heard the door to the middle room slam. That was where they had their desks, their old desktops, and the plain pine shelves crammed with books and CDs, so their living room could remain uncluttered, just a comfy couch and a wooden rocker and music

12

posters on the walls. Joel's upright and his chair and music stand for practicing the viola were all he needed, but sometimes Sean would stretch out on the couch and read and listen to him playing his Schumann or something else with melodies and harmonies Sean could follow. He had long ago stopped asking why Joel didn't compose music like that.

How Sean explained Joel to himself was that Dr. Nathan and Annie Greenwood had never given their son a sense of proportion. His parents told him he was like no other kid in Richland County, Wisconsin. They'd continued to say so, well into their eighties. "He's remarkable, isn't he, Sean?" Annie would say. Joel expected Sean to be more like his parents, and Sean had to say, "But you want everything your way" or "You can never be wrong about anything!" And when Joel got an obsession, as he seemed to have now, there was no deflecting him. His idea of retiring to the so-called Ocooch Mountains had been cropping up a lot. "We only have so much time left," he kept saying. Sean pointed out that, at sixty-five, they were still happily employed, they were both healthy and likely to live another quarter century. He and Joel had different concepts of time.

Sean scooped a spoonful, half lemon and half orange though he'd asked for plain lemon. He enjoyed the iciness in his throat and accepted the fact that Joel would spend all evening searching the Internet for some dump of a farmhouse in a lost valley in the land of his youth. It was a way of avoiding going back to composing.

When the sun finally left the top balcony across the street, Sean went inside to the middle room and carefully twisted the doorknob. Joel didn't look up but kept clicking away at his desk. As Sean stepped closer, Joel stared up with his wide brown eyes, enviable for their near-perfect vision, and said, "What!"

"I thought you wanted to play me your new piece tonight."

"After the mess I made of it? Forget it." He turned back to the screen, which showed a county map pinpointed with available properties and prices as low as "40K." "It wouldn't mean anything to you yet," Joel said. "You wouldn't see where it's going."

« »

Sean climbed onto their bed and lay there, uncovered and hot, in a fresh pair of boxers. He put on his drugstore reading glasses and picked up his dog-eared *Sister Carrie* but soon returned it and the glasses to the bedside table. It was too hard to concentrate on reading. He'd like to blame Joel, but it was really his own lack of purpose. Why did he let Joel go on so? For over thirty years, it had been a question of who did what for whom. Joel depended on him to take care of practical things, to organize and keep track, to insulate him from the world outside. That was what had attracted Sean in the first place. He'd needed someone to look after. Sometimes, even now, it was like having a teenager in his life. Yet Joel was so musically gifted and such a beloved teacher. In fact, everybody loved Joel. And there was always something big in Joel's life besides the two of them. Despite fits and starts, after all those years, he had kept writing music. In a generous mood, he'd give Sean credit for keeping him going, but Sean knew Joel would compose music no matter what. He'd composed the class anthem in high school and improvised piano interludes for his parents. They loved him so much and believed in his art. They never took vacations. Dr. Nathan was filling teeth far into his seventies, and only arthritis made Annie stop being his hygienist. Sean never heard a complaint from either of them. They left it to their son to supply the ups and downs.

He could hear him now, around the corner, grousing at the computer. It was making Sean sleepy. He flipped his pillow to the cooler side and closed his eyes. He didn't want to keep thinking about their problems. Sometimes they would flare up, but it was never anything new. Sean always balked when Joel suggested they see a counselor because, for someone working at the Housing Collective, therapy

14

seemed such a bourgeois suburban thing. And Joel claimed he himself didn't need any help but Sean sure could use some so he'd get off his back. "Except in bed," Joel took care to add, and they'd be again where they started. The issue seldom came up anymore.

Still, when Sean was tired, or nervous, or feeling far from wherever Joel was, such as right then, he couldn't stop himself from mulling over the past. He saw himself again at fifteen, alone in the old family house on Cedar Street, walking into Dad's study to snoop once more. He was opening the file cabinet and shuffling through the folders. He always took careful note of which documents each magazine was tucked between. He told himself they were for body-building because Dad and Danny were the athletic ones, not Sean. By snooping, maybe he could learn to be more like his dad. That was the explanation he gave himself at the time. But his heart had begun beating in his chest, and he'd wanted to look longer and closer but also didn't want to. With shaking fingers, he'd leaf through the shiny pages of handsome men in jockstraps or loincloths like Indians or wearing cowboy hats and chaps and boots with only some sort of bulging pouch for concealment.

Suddenly it was several years later, and Sean saw himself back home for spring break from Kenyon. He had turned nineteen and was feeling depressed. Nothing felt quite right in the house. Danny was in Cleveland, Mary and Sandy were out doing schoolkid things. Dad was away on some case. And just as Sean was lying now on his own bed in his and Joel's apartment, he had been lying then, on his side, on the lumpy green corduroy couch in the family living room, half asleep. His mom had come in. At first, he hadn't looked up past her nylon-stockinged feet pacing the carpet in front of him. He had never seen Mom act like that, going back and forth and sometimes gulping a few quick breaths. He had a fearful notion that she might be having a nervous breakdown. He'd read articles about suburban moms having breakdowns, and even before she said a word, the thought of those muscleman magazines in his dad's file cabinet came to him as if he already knew what was coming. "I don't know how to tell you, Sean," she finally said, "but I found out that your father has a man friend." Sean could hear her exact tone of voice from so many years ago: "Your father has a man friend." For a second, he thought she'd said "a Manfred" and what could that possibly mean? But she repeated it. "A man friend, Sean!" And he did know what it meant from the pictures in those magazines and from what he had worried about, all by himself, when he snuck in to look at them.

Mom couldn't bring herself to explain anything further, but in a very steady voice, she said that Dad was moving down to Hyde Park to live with that man and she didn't know yet if she'd let him have a divorce. And then she got talking faster and more upset. Sean couldn't remember all she said, but it was about never having fit in with the damn Tyson family or the fucking North Shore. She never used words like that and her voice had never sounded so furious, but they were alone in the house and no one else would hear. It was as if she wasn't even talking to Sean now but cursing herself for having left the Church to marry that god-damned Daniel Tyson and aggravating her parents and her whole clan—and why had she ever moved up out of the city! Sean had tried to say it wasn't her fault. Mom was almost angrier at herself than at Dad, and something in him had wanted to tell her about the magazines, though it wouldn't make her feel any better, and if she didn't already know about them, he'd feel guilty for not having told her sooner.

He had scrunched his legs up so she could squeeze down next to him on the couch. "And poor you!" she said while steadying herself by holding onto his bent-up knees. Danny was named after his dad, she told him, because boys often got named for their dads away in the war, and afterwards, she had insisted on naming her second son Sean. "Gramma Tyson remarked that it sounded awfully Irish! For Christ's sake, I only wanted to name you after my big brother who died when I was three!" Sean heard her trembling voice and again saw her burst into tears.

He opened his eyes and felt his forearm on the warm pillow and the hot sweat on his skin. There he was, on their high four-poster. Joel was still out there looking at pictures of sagging old farmhouses on country roads. He never looked at Internet porn the way Sean sometimes did. "Up in my small Wisconsin town," Joel would say, "I never got to see photos of naked men. That's why I'm so normal!" And now this thought of Joel and him having separate ends was haunting Sean terribly.

2 Joel had suggested he come to the Lilienthals' after supper to hear some of the Mozart they were working on, the "Dissonant" quartet. "Dissonant by eighteenth-century standards," he explained. So after working late and grabbing two pizza slices on the corner, Sean took the train up to Rogers Park and walked along to the imposing brick house where Joel's old professors lived. The open windows were sending music out to the sidewalk. He listened and waited for a concluding cadence.

Art and Rebecca Lilienthal had mentored Joel at Northwestern, and he'd been playing quartets with them ever since. Their daughter Clara had gone to teach in California, and her friend Sheila Bowden had taken her place. Sean discerned her cello warmly undergirding the Lilienthals' upper registers. Joel's viola was in there somewhere. When they stopped to make corrections, Sean rang the bell. Art's "Come right in!" prompted him to step inside the paneled vestibule and pass the broad oak staircase toward the dark living room. The musicians sat on folding chairs behind lit-up music stands, instruments and faces aglow. Extension cords ran over velvet-lined leather cases and twisted between chair legs to reach wall plugs. There were stacks of solo parts and full scores on the armchairs and couch. A rotating fan blew Joel's viola part up at the corners each time the breeze swept across the room.

"It sounded good from outside," Sean told the room.

"It's coming around," Art said. "Take a seat. Move that pile of Shostakoviches off the cushion. We won't be getting to him tonight."

"Nice to see you, Sean," Rebecca said, reaching out a sharp-knuckled hand to squeeze his. "You've met Sheila, I think. We have to run through this last movement once more."

So he leaned back and listened. Watching Joel play always pleased him. The composing Joel was in either a fury or despair or so absorbed in his work that Sean ceased to exist. But the viola-playing Joel was transmuted into Mozart. If he got it wrong, he'd merely grimace and throw himself back in. Joel, the Lilienthals, and that small round person, Sheila Bowden, were a team intent on making each instrument sing properly with the other three.

After a quiet bit, the movement ended with a cheerful kick. "And that's that," said Art. Satisfied, they eyed each other then turned to Sean, so he clapped his hands. From outside the window came echoing applause. A couple with a stroller was standing under the streetlamp. The woman called a thanks, the man gave a thumbs-up, and they pushed their baby down the block.

"Most of our neighbors appreciate us," Art said.

"Could we do the Adagio intro once for Sean?" Joel asked. "I want him to hear how amazing it is."

They quickly turned their parts around, paused for a breath, and on eye contact plunged in again. Sheila's cello was the pulse, and the others were piling on notes above it that began to sound like the chords Joel had been hunting for on the piano. Finally, there came a silent moment, and then Rebecca swept into a quick little tune but cut it short and said, "And the Allegro goes on from there."

"If it wasn't for the cello," Sean ventured to say, "I couldn't have followed it."

"That's because I'm the organizing principle," Sheila said. "I allow everyone else to stray from the ordained path." She gave Sean a more intimate wink than he might have expected from a new acquaintance.

"Amazing, wasn't it, Sean?" Joel leaned over to give him, at last, a welcoming hug.

"Let's light the lamps and have a drink," said Art. He stood, remarkably tall and straight-shouldered for seventy-five. Rebecca, with her mass of gray hair pulled back, was equally impressive. Sean had always been a bit intimidated by them. They may have been American born, but they seemed European. It made him somehow uncomfortable, though they were always so kind to him. When Joel studied under them in college, they couldn't have been much more than thirty, but Sean had met them when they were already turning gray. He'd never kept up with his own old professors. He hadn't particularly wanted to know adults back then. He had new friends his age, and they were all getting political.

Joel and Sheila had begun folding up the chairs and music stands while Art went to the kitchen and Rebecca stowed the sheet music on shelves behind the grand piano. Cooler air was moving through the long living room from front windows to back. It was drying the sweat that had formed on Sean's forehead during that last strange music.

« »

Art Lilienthal handed around daiquiris, even to Sean, who seldom drank. Rebecca had placed herself on the couch between him and Joel, so Sheila claimed an armchair and explained how Art had just wangled her an adjunct position in the Music Department. "I'm still writing my beastly thesis, Sean," she said. "It's on chamber works of the Viennese fin de siècle, the next-to-last siècle, that is. I'm fascinated by decadence."

Sean didn't see how chamber music could be decadent but felt it wisest not to ask.

"I like watching things break down," Sheila went on, "societies, the visual arts, tonalities, language. I find it all so fascinating and can't bring myself to finish." Despite her rotundity, she was delicately

19

built. She had narrow wrists for a cellist and small elegant hands. She might've been in her forties, but it was hard for Sean to tell. "And my cats keep messing up my notes," she added with a piping shriek of a little laugh.

From the other armchair by the piano, Art made his familiar guffaw. Joel could imitate it perfectly when reporting his evenings with the Lilienthals. "Tell Sean their names," Art said.

"Uday and Qusay. They're spoiled dumb thugs. I adopted them when we were going after Saddam Hussein's sons." She gave a second piping shriek and Art a briefer guffaw. Sean managed to laugh along.

He found Sheila odder than Joel had let on. He'd met her only once before, at Joel's spring concert at Foxridge Academy. She had given him a chubby person's soft hug and said she was glad to meet Joel Greenwood's beloved. No one had ever called him that.

The talk moved to Clara Lilienthal's new life in California, and soon Sheila was raising her nearly empty glass to send Art back to the kitchen for the pitcher. When everyone's drink was refreshed, even Sean's scarcely sipped one, Sheila turned to him with an inquisitive gaze. "I hope I'm not being too nosy," she waited for Sean's friendly nod, "but I've been dying to ask you about—well, Joel's told me some of it, but that's secondhand. I'm fascinated by this sort of thing—I mean, about your family."

Rebecca laid her hand on Sean's elbow and said, "Don't let her grill you. She tends to do that."

"It's okay. You mean about my parents, about my dad?"

Sheila's wide-eyed smirk seemed to say, "Well, obviously!"

"What would you like to know?"

"You see, Joel has told me some, but what I'm more intrigued by is if you see yourself as part of a pattern."

"You mean if it's genetic?"

"Genetic? No, no, it's the breaking apart, I mean, the breaking of the harmonious family."

"Really, Sheila!" said Rebecca.

"Because Joel told me you never saw your father again, though you lived in the same city."

"Chicago's big enough," Sean said to joke it off, but he threw Joel a quick glare. Art was leaning back in his armchair, aloof and apparently amused.

"Because I'm studying how decadence happens," Sheila went on. "I'm not talking about sexuality, for heaven's sake. It's more about how one thing leads to another. When something breaks apart it encourages the breaking of something next in line, like the tonal shift from Strauss's *Elektra* to Schoenberg's *Pierrot Lunaire*. It's how our sense of discord changes. It's not necessarily a bad thing. It's simply what happens. It may reach such a chaotic state, though, that someone decides to invent a fresh system to put things into some new form of order, but that's not what interests me. It's the process of breaking things apart. For instance, Joel has told me how your father had his secret, and that you knew it, stumbled on it, and kept it, and then it came out, but then you went on to keep your own secret." Sheila had a quizzical expression on her soft round face. "And when it, too, came out," she said, "it broke your mother's heart all over again."

"Sheila, it's not really your business," Rebecca said. Art was sipping his daiquiri and observing thoughtfully through his trifocals.

"I'm simply attempting to trace things," said Sheila. "It's not a criticism of Sean."

"I didn't break my mother's heart," he said with a slight quaver in his voice. If he hadn't been sipping that drink, he might not have been able to say anything. But somehow he didn't object to Sheila. She had, it seemed, a scientific interest in him.

Then Joel said, "Well, you pretty much did break your mother's heart, Shaw-awn. By the time I came into the picture—"

Sean was going to ignore Joel. That was who he was mad at. "Maybe you're too young, Sheila," he said, "but it was a very different time. I didn't even know who I was yet. Dad's leaving had set me back years."

"I'd already figured myself out in high school," said Joel.

"Because you were so normal!" Sean said.

"Joel, you shut up," Rebecca added. "Sean was speaking."

"That's all," he said. "But maybe the notion of a harmonious family is wrong from the start."

Sheila was leaning forward, fleshy elbows on chubby knees. "Yes," she said, "the musical analogy is misleading. It's just that as the ear attunes itself to discord—as in *Elektra*—further discord becomes possible. If your father kept a secret and then left his family, then so could you."

"But I tried to stick by my mom," Sean said. He was beginning to feel choky in the throat. "I would've stuck by her, but the Church—"

"See, his mom," Joel started to explain, "went all Catholic on him."

"Let's not get into religion," Rebecca said. She stood up, brushed the wrinkles out of her skirt, and went behind the piano. "Why don't we decide which Shostakovich we'll work on next week."

Decisively, Sheila plunked down her glass on the coffee table and said, "I didn't intend to rile everyone up. We'll discuss this calmly between ourselves, Sean, another time. I mustn't sow dissension between you and your beloved."

"Oh, I'm used to it," Sean said, though he was feeling quite annoyed with Joel and dreaded the train ride home.

"The Fourth, in D major," Art declared, and no one dissented.

Sheila leaned back in her chair, her delicate hands resting on the puffy upholstery. She didn't have much of a lap. Her white blouse bulged over where her khaki slacks began. Her round knees, with which she had embraced her cello, bumped out like small brown hills. It was just as well that Sean didn't have to say anything more.

"I'll play it through as far as I've got," Joel said when they'd come in the front door.

"You always feel encouraged about your own music on quartet night."

"Because I've been making good music for a change. And I'm with my pals. You get to work with people all day, while I'm sitting here alone all summer."

"But when you do get with people, you blurt out my secrets."

On the train home, they had already hashed it out, so they let it go and Sean was just as glad. Joel set his viola case on top of the old upright and sat down on the bench. Sean came and stood behind him so he could attempt to decipher the jottings on the music paper, all scribbled over in soft pencil with numerous erasures. A xerox of the poem was taped onto the rack, but ever since cataract surgery had given Sean far sight, he needed glasses to see up close.

"So I played you up to 'our voices only broke the gloom.' Here goes!" Joel half-sang, half-hummed "what we once had thought and said" and "what had been and might have been" and then, to the gentlest thought-filled strange chords: "and who was changed and who was dead." The last word sounded to unmusical Sean like a resolution of all dissonance. But when Joel got to "the first slight swerving of the heart," he stopped and tried it three different ways. "Which do you like best?"

"Depends on what follows," was the evasion Sean came up with.

So Joel played on through each version to an additional measure and then looked up and said, "Just imagine my choral group kids' teenage voices singing about growing old."

"They'll feel very sophisticated."

"So which one, Sean?"

"You're the composer."

"I still favor the first. It's the least obvious."

Sean nodded, but there had seemed nothing obvious about any of them. Joel played on, croaking out "and leave it still unsaid in part," but all Sean heard were smudgy chords in an irregular rhythm. He couldn't tap along the way he did when Joel played his favorite *Kinderszenen.*

Then Joel got stumped. "'The very tones in which we spake...' How can I set 'tones' to actual tones! Sean, why did you make me do this? It's the hardest poem you've ever foisted on me. And I thought those Carl Sandburgs were rough."

"I didn't foist it."

"You chose it because it's about friends forgetting their memories and dying alone. Jesus Christ!"

"That's not all it's about. You said it was perfect when I read it to you."

Joel pushed back the piano bench and plopped his forehead onto the keys. "What did you get me into, Quimby!" he moaned, smooshing notes with his skull. He had called Sean by his middle name to convey a certain affectionate irony.

"You always find your way, Joel. Art's daiquiris threw you off track. And our own little contretemps."

Sean could tell Joel was in need of some physical attention. Lately, it had been hard to give it to him, but now he felt the need welling up also in himself. Their fights often led to that. Maybe it was Sean's way of taking back control of things. He grabbed Joel's hand and gave it a tug, then tugged harder. Reluctantly, Joel got up from the piano and followed him to bed for one of their increasingly rare bouts of intimacy.

« »

At breakfast, they spent some time speculating about Sheila Bowden. Sean was well past the discomfort of the previous evening and now felt somewhat sorry for her. Joel said she put on that icon-oclastic act. He figured she was pretty lonely.

"Is she a cat lady?" Sean asked. "Does she go out with men?"

Joel didn't think so, but she wasn't a lesbian as far as he knew. The Lilienthals had taken her under their wings as they had done years ago with Joel. Sheila had been playing in a North Side community orchestra beside Clara Lilienthal's first chair cello.

"I'm wary of her decadence thing," Sean said. "Now she expects me to talk to her privately. I don't want to be an exhibit in her thesis."

"But you're so fascinating," Joel quipped. He gulped the last of his pomegranate juice and stood up from the table to go launch into his stretches. He was in shorts and running shoes and planned to take a jog in the cooler morning air. Such resolutions never lasted long. It was too embarrassing trying to keep in shape amongst all the young. In fact, Joel was as disinclined to exercise as Sean was, but he claimed, if they lived in the country, he'd willingly go out running down the gravel roads and into the peaceful hills.

But that morning off he went, and Sean soon followed in his office clothes. He was glad to work where a button-down shirt and khakis were as formal as it got. He took the shadier side of the cross street. For years now, the city around him had been speeding up while he was going slower. Down the block, he saw the train pulling out, but he made it in good time for the next one.

The car was packed with sweaty bodies like his own. Joel had once invented a game in which Sean had to select the man he'd take to bed, given the choices presented within a designated area. It could be played on a train, in a restaurant or store, at the beach, on a walk, but Sean had to choose. Joel himself claimed to have no eyes for beauty, only ears.

Down the car, there was one pale young man in a sleeveless undershirt and clinging nylon shorts holding onto a pole with an open paperback in the other hand. He would let go of the pole to turn a page and quickly grab on again. Most everyone else was staring into an electronic device, and a few older men were reading the *Sun-Times*. Sean glanced at the young man and noted the sweat glistening on his skinny hairless arms. He'd be good to take to bed, but those days were long past.

Sean often saw himself as two distinct creatures. It was hard to align his outward older self with the younger one in his head. Besides, he didn't creak in the joints, his bones didn't ache, he needed glasses only to see up close, he hadn't gotten fat or lost much hair, he breathed easily enough for a childhood asthmatic—but it wasn't so much a physical matter. It was more about the increasing space of time separating his two selves. Actually, perhaps he wasn't slowing down. Perhaps he was speeding up now, and all the younger people were taking their own sweet time. Sean couldn't decide which it was. He was standing still in the fast-moving train, and no one was looking at him, but in his head, if he closed his eyes, he was very close to that fifteen year old who had stared at the bare bodies in his dad's magazines, who had read the history of the Black Hawk wars and, one night out in Gramma's meadow, had pretended he was an Indian warrior with the moon glistening off his nakedness.

The train rumbled along, and at each stop a reconfiguration of riders provided a glimpse of the appealing rear end or slender shoulder of the paperback reader. At his own stop, Sean managed to pass him closely by, curious what the book was. He caught the author's name: Jonathan Safran Foer. What was with those three-named writers that kids were reading now?

Soon he was out on the platform, the strong scent of the boy's sweat lingering in his nose.

3 Halfway through the afternoon, an elderly gentleman arrived for his appointment. He'd been denied an affordable unit in a new building because of his spotty history of paying rent. He wore

shiny black pants, a yellowed white shirt with a narrow tie, and a thrift-shop Madras jacket.

"Come in, Mr. Thorp," Sean said. "I'm Mr. Tyson."

The old man hesitated in the doorway. "Usually, I see Mr. Malik, but they sent me in here."

"I'm covering Mr. Malik's folks while he's on vacation. Have a seat, sir."

Sean went over the tattered application forms and collated them with the online file. Meanwhile, the man was peering at the plastic nameplate on the desk and mouthing "Ty-son" as if to remember where he'd heard the name. He pointed a crooked finger at Sean and then at the nameplate and nodded knowingly across the desk. "I imagine I may have known your mother," he said.

"Oh?"

"I once knew a lovely woman by the name of Eileen Tyson. I imagine she may have been your mother."

Sean looked more closely at the unshaven old man. Had he known Mom on the North Shore before falling on bad times? "Yes, my mother was Eileen Tyson," Sean said and immediately wished he hadn't.

"I knew her when she first came to St. Joachim's," said Mr. Thorp. "She had a son who was a great worry to her. She used to serve coffee and sandwiches after Mass to fellows like me. That was many years ago, but I remember her because of certain things she confided in me. I imagine she's passed on."

"Nearly twenty years now," Sean said.

"I can see you're her son. There's a similarity about the flat upper lip. Typical Irish. She told me how she'd come back to the Church because," he declared with sudden vehemence, "your father had betrayed her with a South American fairy."

Sean knew not to let the man continue like that, so he said, "But now you need a new place to live. That's what I'm here for."

"After he abandoned her, she came back to St. Jo's. She'd grown

27

up in the parish, as you know. She helped me get off drink. I've been off and on ever since, of course, but she did all she could, poor dear lady. I clearly recall her face. And now you're looking after others. I know you had your own troubles with drugs and you were such a worry to her, but I imagine you're a good Catholic now."

Sean shook his head in regret, though he felt none, and said, "I wasn't brought up Catholic, Mr. Thorp. By the way, that was my younger brother with the drug problems." Why had he bothered to clear that up?

"But I distinctly recall her talking about a son named Sean because she corrected my inauthentic pronunciation. She was a true angel. It's my belief she's still guiding you to the right path."

"I merely do my job, Mr. Thorp. Now, we should get on with your application. We'll try to find you a suitable place. How do you feel about sharing bath and kitchen facilities, more of a rooming-house arrangement?"

"But I don't wish to be thrown in with any foreign-born."

"I'm afraid that may not be avoidable."

"And there's another thing, young Mr. Tyson," Thorp said, fixing his sharp eyes on Sean. "I will never share quarters with fairies."

"I can't actually consider that, Mr. Thorp," Sean said as crisply as he could. "My sole job is to find something you can afford."

"Your job!" the old man huffed. "It's a modest request. I have the right. No fairies or foreign-born."

Sean stiffened. "Franklin Malik will be back next week, so you might want to talk to him. Given your restrictions, I can't be of help. I doubt if he can be either. I'm sorry, sir, but we'll keep your application on file, and you're welcome to contact Mr. Malik on Monday."

Thorp gave Sean another fixed stare then slowly began pulling himself together. Finally he stood up with much effort and said, "And I thought I'd found a friend from the past. Eileen Tyson would be ashamed of you. She was a good Catholic." He made his way slowly out to the hall muttering, "She'd have understood, after what she went through."

Sean wanted to yell after him, "A good Catholic wouldn't shun others in need," but he knew never to talk back to a client. It had been pleasanter in the old storefront days when applicants were more grateful for their services. And he'd been just "Sean" to them, not "Mr. Tyson." By the eighties, when they moved into their new offices, the city began to offer help, and by the nineties they were qualifying for federal funds and working with HUD. The communal effort was lost on most of the current clientele, but the Collective was still its old nonprofit self, and they shared the load equally between them.

« »

Heading home, Sean didn't have to think about other people's problems—except for Joel's. What if he wanted to take an equity loan on their apartment or sink what was left of his Greenwood inheritance into a Wisconsin retreat? Joel's salary at Foxridge was even lower than Sean's.

He met the young black businesswoman in 2-A on her way out. "Hello, Mr. Tyson," she said, and he said, "Hello, Mia." They lived across the hall from each other but were barely acquainted.

Sean found a shirtless and sweaty Joel at his computer in the messy middle room. "All right, Quimby, we're going to the UP but only for one week now. The fellow at Camp Mishe-Mokwa has people who'll take the second week, so we just pay a twenty-buck cancellation fee."

"And?" Sean held back his annoyance by pulling off his shoes and socks and wiggling his toes. He pretended to scan the bookshelves for something to read.

"So then," Joel went on, "the second week I've reserved us a motel down by the Kickapoo River."

Sean unbuckled his belt and dropped his khakis to air himself out.

"We can check out some properties. I'm not committing us, but it can't hurt to look. There's all sorts of amazing deals, but it'd only piss you off if I showed you, so I'll wait till we get there. I hooked us up with a realtor in Richland Center and got a good deal on the smaller Chevy for the two weeks."

Sean unbuttoned his shirt and fanned the shirttails by the window, staring out at the converted primary school across the street. "You do know it's my only vacation," he said.

"You always have to be negative," said Joel, and then his voice rose, "before we even start!" But his expression softened, and a hopeful glimmer came into his brown eyes. "You'll still get your week on Lake Superior, and then I'll get a week in the Ocooch Mountains." He'd taken hold of Sean's hand and was pulling him toward his desk to show him the Google map. "See how green and empty it is. It's nature, Shaw-awn," he added with a wheedling whine.

As kindly as he could, Sean said, "I'm afraid that driftwood fire poem started all this."

"Well, it was your choice. I'm just thinking of our future. We only have so much time to enjoy it."

"I've got to take a cool shower," Sean said, pivoting on his bare heels and padding across the hall.

That evening, Joel was full of energy. Sean's reluctance to keep up with him didn't slow him down. He kept clicking on things and printing things out and humming to himself melodies that were sometimes familiar to Sean, sometimes not.

So Sean went to sit out on the balcony and listen to the traffic passing below and the people strolling along chatting to each other. There was no point in resisting when Joel got going. A few years back, Joel had been the one to propose taking Amtrak across the Mississippi to what he called "the free state of Iowa" to get married. Sean had obliged because Joel was so insistent, though if left to himself he would as soon have had institutional marriage abolished for everyone. But for decades, they'd been as good as married anyway, so Sean had decided not to risk intensifying their different views with his stick-in-the-mud stubbornness.

The apartments across the street had lit their lights. Neighbors were out on their balconies taking the cooler night air. Sean knew none of them more than to say hello to, but he had come to recognize most, as they must have recognized him. It was remarkable how so many people, moving in and moving out, could coexist at peace on such a small stretch of what was once a swamp. He didn't find people as oppressive as Joel did. He liked being surrounded by them. He was afraid now that Joel wanted to get away from the life they'd made there together for over thirty years. Sean loved being just where he was.

« »

It rained heavily all that Saturday, and the heat broke. After dinner, Joel returned to the piano as if having totally forgotten yesterday's obsession. He played, over and over, all he'd written so far. Several passages were becoming familiar enough so that Sean, trying to read in bed, almost had to hum along. Once he'd discerned the semblance of a tune, he even began to catch on to the irregular rhythms.

Of all Joel's works, his viola sonatas were Sean's favorites. They also continued to supply the only modest royalties Joel had ever received for his compositions. Art Lilienthal had recommended him to an educational music publisher, who then commissioned a set of six sonatas, from easy to difficult, so young violists wouldn't have to learn on transcriptions of violin or cello pieces. Joel set the teacher's piano accompaniments in the lowest and highest octaves to leave the middle range free for the student to shine. Sean liked to picture young violists all over the world practicing the Greenwood sonatas, but Joel never took the compliment and only said he was a tediously slow composer and music didn't pour out of him the way it did from geniuses.

Sean didn't know what words from the poem went to the chords he heard out there now, but Joel was surely hearing words in his head. Then, suddenly, he broke off, scraped aside the bench, and came thumping back into the bedroom. "I see the way to end now! I don't dare touch it anymore tonight. You don't know what this is like!" He hopped onto his side of the bed and stretched out with a long yawn. "So it hasn't been a complete waste! Jesus, why can't I remember that when I get stuck?"

"Because you live in the present, Joel, and it's enough to drive me crazy."

"But that's what composers have to do. Everything's linear. We move a measure at a time. Notes follow notes. I have to hear each beat. It's how I think about everything." He looked pleased to have figured himself out, though Sean had been hearing versions of this self-analysis for years. New insights were rare and, if they came, they came only in imperceptible increments. Joel scratched at his chest hairs then leaned over to smooch Sean's cheek and flop an arm around his waist. "Now, you sleep," he said.

"What do you think I've been trying to do?"

Sean remembered how Dr. Nathan Greenwood would formally shake their hands before sending them up to Joel's childhood room with the twin beds under Milwaukee Braves bedspreads intended for sleepovers with school friends. As they climbed the creaky stairs, Annie Greenwood would call after them, "I know there's not much for you boys to do up here in our little town, but we sure like having you come see us."

The Greenwoods had become Sean's substitute parents, though being fastidious, they never mentioned sexuality. Sean had gone from being their son's friend from Chicago to being his roommate and, finally, his companion. They had found the way to be entirely contented with Joel's life, and Joel blithely assumed that his steady little family had made up for all the damage done by the Tysons. He'd never quite grasped what Sean had gone through.

4 On Monday, his sister Mary called him at work to ask if he could meet her in the Loop for supper. It meant going downtown, but Sean agreed because something seemed to be on her mind. He called home and interrupted Joel just when he'd lain down to nap. "Then you should've turned off the phone," Sean told him, and Joel said, "But what if it was an emergency?" So it was still Sean's fault for keeping him from sleep. Joel said he might as well go back to the piano now. It wasn't worth arguing about.

On the El, he mulled over their squabbles and wondered what other patterns might have emerged if he'd ended up with someone else. Any other man would simply have different peculiarities, and who wanted to be free but lonesome? That was how Joel put it. He was referring to some old German violinist saying he was *"frei aber einsam."* Joel was full of musical anecdotes like that. Sean's present train car certainly held no likely alternatives to Joel Greenwood. The few men of their generation were thick and dumpy, and the one slightly younger one was too groomed and businesslike for Sean's taste, so his eyes settled on a young brown-skinned man staring into his iPad. Long lashes obscured his downcast glance, and his blue jeans fit tightly around his thighs. These might entice someone into a love that finally would have little to do with thighs and eyelashes.

Mary wasn't yet at the café, so Sean asked the hostess for a two-person booth and sat down to wait. A second brown-skinned man filled the water glasses and handed over two menus. He introduced himself as Osberto, slightly flirtatiously, which made for a sustained interchange. Osberto thought it was nice for a brother and sister to meet for dinner. He missed his own sisters in the D.R. but must wait till January for time to fly down. He wished his sisters could visit Chicago in the hot months to see the bright blue lake. "I go sometimes to the beach to pretend it's my old sea at home," he said.

The café was nearly empty, so nothing moved Osberto along before Mary pushed through the revolving door, bumping her several shopping bags. She looked about frantically until she caught Sean's wave, and Osberto stepped silently aside.

"Sean, Sean, Sean, oh lord, I'm sorry, I'm sorry. It's so damn hot. I'm not used to the city. I never get down here anymore. The Art Institute was jammed because it's cool inside. It was all too much. I'm exhausted." She threw her bags and herself into the booth and leaned over the table to press her hot cheek to her brother's, which had chilled in the air-conditioning. Mary shook her short mop, now a shiny auburn, and collapsed against the back cushion.

"Slow it down, grandma," Sean said.

"Oh please! I'm the only person you can call 'sister,' so make the most of it. Have you ordered?" Attentive Osberto reappeared. "I desperately need a tall cold G and T," she told him.

"Diet Pepsi for me."

"Oh please," Mary said again, "come on, brother, this is too special an occasion." She gave Osberto a determined stare and said, "We see each other so seldom, he can at least have a real drink with me." Osberto turned encouragingly to Sean.

"It'll only make me sleepy."

"That's fine, two G and T's," Mary said, and Osberto slipped away before Sean could retract her order. "So what are we hungry for? My treat, of course, being the well-heeled suburban grandma. But why am I a grandma when Gramma Tyson was a gramma?"

Sean shrugged. He'd been studying her unfamiliar hair color, her bright red-and-gold African-print blouse, and the large gold hoops weighing down her earlobes and making her look all the sweatier.

"I'm going for the scallops putanesca. You?" she asked.

34

When Osberto showed up with their drinks, Sean ordered for her and said he'd have the same. "For brother, for sister, good," Osberto said.

Unlike his two brothers, Mary had always been quietly loyal to Sean despite their mother's dismay over him. It was good to be together again. She caught him watching their waiter retreating through the swinging kitchen door, so he said nonchalantly, "In the D.R. he has three sisters."

"Ah, you've been chatting him up. You flirt with waiters the way Trevor does with waitresses. The older a man gets, the more he flirts. It gives Trev a little boost. He'll say, 'Mare, you should see the cute black girl waiting on me at the Club.' I tell him I don't need to because I can imagine the whole scene. Here's to you, brother!" She raised her glass for a clink. "Lord, do I need this!"

"You and Trevor are doing okay?" Sean asked. "You sounded rattled on the phone."

"Look, Trevor Ahern's the same old big shot he always was. What else is new! I'm rattled because I'm down here in the Loop. How do you city dwellers do it?"

The tang of juniper and the bubbles tingled pleasantly in Sean's throat. He'd forgotten that taste.

Mary was leaning on her elbows, her gold earrings dangling against her flushed cheeks. "But Mom liked city living," she said. "She had her cozy nest in Lincoln Park and that old Monsignor and the nuns and her parish work. You got out of that whole scene, Sean."

"I would've helped her more, if she'd wanted me to."

"And I'm sure Joel Greenwood would've appreciated that. Sorry that Mom never quite took to him."

Osberto reappeared with their putanescas, so Mary dropped the subject and Sean was relieved to turn to their meals.

Well into her second drink, Mary was again complaining about all the hours she'd spent listening to Mom go on about the North Shore Tysons, and Danny never coming home from Cleveland, and dealing with Sandy all by herself—no thanks to Dad—and Sean and that high-school music teacher, but Mary finally moved on to her older daughter-in-law Polly's fortieth birthday party. She had come downtown to shop because Devin didn't know what to get for his own wife. Besides, Mary had a stake in keeping Polly happy for the sake of the grandkids. "Now that they're older," she said, "maybe you'd invite them to come visit Great Uncle Sean in the city? They always ask about you. They think it's cool you and Joel went to Iowa to get married. They wish they'd been there. I know, you don't like parties, but never fear, you're not expected at Polly's, it's for her crowd. I thought Seurat napkins and *Blue Guitarist* place cards from the Art Institute shop would be fun. And I was up and down North Michigan looking for something Devin could claim he'd chosen all by himself. It couldn't be too elegant or she'd know I had a hand in it. But let me show you—where did I—which bag is it in?" She pulled out a flat velvety box containing a silver necklace set with large turquoises, Southwestern style. It must've taken a chunk out of Trevor's credit card. "See, it's the folksy choice Dev would make. And from me I got her a fun sun dress for evenings on their new terrace, but I won't bother showing you because you never notice clothes. I haven't planned a menu yet. See the hassles you miss not having dependents!" She flung herself into the back cushion with an exasperated sigh. "It's chilly in here."

"But are they still dependents?"

"They still depend on me!" Mary said. "Devin makes enough money, and so does Polly despite the current slump in real estate. As for Keith, he already makes more than the both of them, but then Charlotte doesn't work. But it's emotional dependence, Sean. We Aherns are a tight unit."

"I don't doubt it."

Sean could feel his sister edging toward some deeper complaint that might have caused her to call him at work. Not that it didn't make sense for them to meet the one time she'd come downtown in months, but he was sure there was something more on her mind. She had drained her glass and was clanking the ice cubes with her swizzle stick.

"People depend on me, too," Sean said.

Mary gave a noncommittal humph. Then in a cheerier mood, she looked up at him and said, "Did you see the obituary in yesterday's *Tribune*?"

"We don't take a paper anymore. Joel gets it online."

"The obituary for Carlos Villalba?"

"Oh," Sean said. There was a thump somewhere between his throat and stomach. "That was his name, wasn't it?" He hadn't thought of him in years. He'd never met him, but way back he'd found one particular loose photo tucked inside one of Dad's magazines. It was of a bare-chested stocky muscular young man in white tennis shorts. He had an American Indian's nose and cheekbones and shining brown skin.

"He was eighty-one," Mary said. "That makes him thirteen years younger than Dad. I'd never been sure of their age difference. Anyhow, it's not as shocking as I'd thought. I used to imagine he was closer in age to us kids."

"You happened on it in the paper?"

"I always check the Irish sports pages, as Mom used to call them. It was one of those small paid notices. It said he was preceded in death—what a phrase!—by his life partner, Daniel Tyson of Hyde Park and Fort Lauderdale, who passed in 2002. I hate how they say 'passed'—'passed away' is bad enough, but just plain 'passed' sounds gross."

"You don't know anything more? You have the clipping?"

Her eyes brightened. "I fucking crumpled it up and threw it in the trash."

"Mary! Why?"

"Oh shit," she whispered and the brightness suddenly flooded her eyes with tears. Then, she burbled out what Sean heard as "their happy life" and something like "their many dear friends."

He slid out of his side of the booth and squeezed in beside her to give her a tight hug. He'd noticed Osberto by the kitchen door looking their way then quickly averting his eyes. The place was filling up, so he was busier now.

« »

It was typical of Mary to leave her news to the last minute, as if she'd only just remembered it. Perhaps that was the case. But it was significant news for both of them. Now no one was left from that time. Riding home drowsily on the El, Sean began enumerating his genealogy. Too much had been coming back to him. It started with that poem about the past, then it was Sheila Bowden's curiosity, then old Mr. Thorp, and now Mary and the obituary. Chance had collected it all into the week when Joel was pushing for a place in the country—he didn't want to have to think about that, too.

On the train, still fuzzy from the G and T, he looked about for a choice as required by Joel's game. He had to settle for a pimply Cubs fan in all the apparel, who was too stupid-looking to be of any continuing interest. So he turned his thoughts back to his sister. He'd left her, in better spirits, at the Grant Park garage. He was glad to have seen her but more so once she had disappeared underground. Mary took things harder than he did. After Dad left, she nearly hadn't finished high school. When Mom moved down to Lincoln Park, she'd stayed at their uncle's so she wouldn't have to switch schools. Mom put Sandy into Foxridge Academy, of all places, and on Dad's dime. It was where his troubles began. Mary had gone on to DePaul and Danny had managed to finish up at Case and head to business school, but Sean was the only one who cut off his support from Dad. "You're so stubborn it scares me," Mom had told him back then.

Sean looked across at the pimply Cubs fan, but what came to his eyes was the handsome Indian face of Carlos Villalba, his tight-muscled body in white tennis shorts. That young man had lived all those years with Dad and died an old man of eighty-one, well taken care of. Sean had long ago acknowledged to himself that, as a form of punishment, he hadn't allowed his dad to take care of him. That was how much angrier he had been than his sister and brothers, but he still didn't quite know why.

The city lights were flashing by the windows as if the train car was standing still and everything out there was moving very fast, but Sean was heading home.

《 》

"The viola is the basis of all the other strings," Sean heard when he came in the door. On phones Joel always talked too loudly, as if he was on a party line in the country in the old days and couldn't believe anyone could hear his voice from miles away. "See, everybody assumes it's the violin," he went on, "and my parents did make me take violin because who wants to be serenaded by a viola? It wasn't till college—oh, hi, Sean. It's Sheila Bowden, I'm telling her why I chose the viola."

Sean went into the bedroom to change out of his work clothes but couldn't escape this repeat of one of Joel's familiar lectures.

"I ran into these excellent violinists at Northwestern and decided I'd never be a Heifetz or a Milstein and mostly wanted to compose anyway, so I switched to viola. After all, Hindemith was a violist. What? Lug a cello around? No way. Besides, as I was saying, the

39

viola is the standard stringed instrument. In Italian, a *violino* is a little viola, a double bass is a *violone*, a big viola. You play a little big viola, a *violoncello*. Come on, you never thought of that? Yes, he just got home. Want to talk to him? Quimby!"

Sean padded back into the middle room and winced at Joel.

"I warn you, Sheila," Joel said, "he's already down to his boxers. He's been out on the town and who knows what mischief he's gotten into." He pressed the speaker button, so Sean heard Sheila's shrieky little laugh.

He grabbed the phone and said, "I trust you don't believe everything Joel says."

"Hello there, Sean, it's Sheila. How does one shut Joel up?"

"She wants you to get together for brunch," Joel shouted from his desk.

"Without Joel Thomas Greenwood," Sheila added.

Sean took a breath and said, "That'd be nice."

He was soon committed to Saturday morning at the local deli and signed off with a cheery "See you there." Turning to Joel, he said, "I'm not ready for another grilling. Dealing with Mary was enough for one week. She'd seen an obituary for Carlos Villalba. Do you remember who that was?"

"So he's dead?"

"And it seems he and Dad had a place in Fort Lauderdale for the winters."

"They had two places? Hey, we could end up just like your dad!"

"Are there no other thoughts in that one-track brain of yours? You know, comparing me to my father isn't the most effective pitch."

Sean stalked off into the bedroom to finish *Sister Carrie*, but once again his thoughts went elsewhere. Joel wanted them to retreat north. Chicago would merely provide a southern respite from icy gravel roads and snow-deep hills till the countryside called them back. The grass up there would turn green. The cows would come out to fresh pastures. The windows of the old farmhouse—the one, despite himself, Sean had conjured up through Joel's dreamings—those windows would be flung open and songbirds would chirp in the branches of the blossoming fruit trees and nest under the eaves of the front porch. Or was that a memory of the house his great-great-grandfather Erastus Quimby had built after coming home from the Civil War, the house of all Sean's happy youthful summers? In his mind, he was sitting on a wooden swing that hung from that front porch ceiling. With bare feet, he was pushing himself off from the worn floorboards, and he could hear his gramma in the kitchen, shouting into the phone that connected them and their nearest neighbors to the town. She was asking desperately for something she had lost.

Sean looked over at Joel, who had appeared in the doorway. "I was thinking how lucky it was that Gramma died before the family fell apart," Sean said. He put the book he'd stopped reading on the bedside table and propped himself higher up on his pillows.

"Where did that come from?" Joel asked. Then he looked closer and said, "Oh, you and your sister. I get it. Poor old Sean."

5 It was quiet at the North Side Housing Collective the next day. July tended to be slow. Homeless people could sleep in the open and fear only muggers and thugs. Single moms did show up in a steady stream because they never got an off-season. Since the crash, Sean had also been counseling men once comfortably employed but now overextended shame-filled breadwinners. Still, the summer-job kids they were obliged not to turn away were all temporarily stuffed in somewhere, so that chore was over.

After updating his files, Sean wandered down to the break room and found Franklin Malik and Elise Ilg with coffees and the jelly donuts Andrew Stone liked to bring in. He and Sean were the leftovers from the Northern Illinois grads who had founded the Collective in 1968. Andrew's nervous metabolism kept him trim though he'd lost most of his hair and shaved off the rest. He was Sean's first black friend. Another of their group, Davey Nussbaum, was still working but came in only twice a week now. Soon enough, the three of them would be on their way out completely.

"I've been boring Elise with my vacation on the Thumb of Michigan," Franklin said. "There's nothing like flopping down on the sand with sunglasses and a trashy thriller."

"Why does he take his vacation in July when it's so nice here?" Elise asked.

"Well, Joel and I are going to the UP in August," Sean said. "Lake Superior's cold, but the bugs will be gone."

"You two always go to the UP," said Franklin. "We prefer the Thumb. It's as dull as a place can be. Total nothing. But we get Leila's parents' cottage for free. With the kids grown, we have it all to ourselves. I've returned completely rejuvenated."

"You guys are so unadventurous," Elise said.

Sean took a seat but ignored the donuts and decided to wait on coffee for when he needed it later. "Who's Andrew got in there?" he asked.

"The old gent who complained about me—and about you," Franklin said.

"Andrew can handle him," said Sean. Then, he went into a story of how, when they started out, there were plenty of old-school Mr. Thorps around. "Think of Mayor Daley—my Mayor Daley," he made clear, "and think of him at the Democratic Convention. Yet, believe it or not, only a few years earlier, my mom and sister and I had marched behind that Major Daley with Martin Luther King himself, and everyone was singing freedom songs. Daley hadn't yet realized that one little brotherhood show wasn't going to shut up the black folks. My mom got the giggles when the singing started sounding like 'Dum-free, Dum-free.' After we got home, she had us all sing the 'dumfree song' to my dad."

Andrew popped in for his second donut and announced that Mr. Thorp had been placed. "I'm not as intolerant as you three," he said. "I stuck him in that rooming house in Andersonville, Mrs. Markovich's, the fat old Croatian bigot." He poured himself more coffee and joined his colleagues at the table.

"Hey, Andrew," Franklin said, "did you know that Sean here and his mom marched with Martin Luther King?"

"All the way to Soldier Field," Sean said.

"First thing he ever told me," said Andrew. "Tyson was trying so hard. You had to love him. My own mom never let me go on those marches. She made me stay away from trouble. Her idea was that a nice boy like me should never leave the South Side. When I used to see planes taking off from Midway, I'd imagine them all full of white people looking down at me from the sky, and I'd feel so small."

"Andrew," said Elise, "when you met him, did you know Sean was gay?"

"Did Sean know Sean was gay?" Andrew countered.

"Yes, Sean did," said Sean, "but he wasn't letting on yet. He wasn't sure how Stone and Nussbaum and Company would take it. You forty-somethings have no notion what our world was like, do they, Andrew?"

"And they can't help it," Andrew said.

"Aw, you pair of old lefties," said Elise, "you should be going part-time like Davey Nussbaum and let in some new blood."

"Maybe we need the income," said Sean, "such as it is."

"Look," said Elise, "you get Medicare now and next year you can start Social. It works for Davey."

"Because Beth's got him on her supplemental. Besides, I like to work."

"I'd retire so quick," said Andrew, "if I could live off my daughter, but my ex already got that deal."

"You're stuck with us," Sean said, and went to prepare for his next applicant.

Elise walked him to the train. Her girlfriend was a lawyer at Northwestern Legal Aid, and they lived grandly in one of the Marina Towers. Sean liked to rib her about their high-rise life, and she pretended to condescend to his downward mobility.

When they crossed into the shade of a tall warehouse, it was much cooler. Sean began to tell her how he never knew what he'd find at home these days. Joel could either be in some musical ecstasy or grumping around like a total failure. Or he'd be obsessing at his computer about country properties Sean had no intention of letting them buy.

"You've been looking a bit worn out lately, Tyson," Elise said. "Seriously, think about going part-time."

They were nearing the station where Sean would be heading up the northbound stairs and Elise the southbound. Neither train was coming yet, so they paused by her entrance.

"That Joel of yours," she said, "his artistic temperament would do me in. Thankfully, Patsy's a fucking lawyer. You should put Joel on a leash. Hey, that could be a turn-on!"

"Don't give me ideas," Sean joked, though he'd never been easy with suggestive remarks from women, lesbian or otherwise.

"Aha, you're blushing," said Elise.

He heard his train approaching and made a run for it. They yelled goodbyes, and just in time Sean slipped through the car doors and grabbed onto a pole right above a nicely veined hand. Then he saw a thick wrist and muscled forearm that led to a bicep straining at a tight powder-blue sleeve with each swerve of the train. When they got up to speed, the broad shoulders swung around and Sean was given a bright-toothed smile from a young man. He had irregular features, sort of goofy-looking, but he was handsome enough. Sean would probably have selected him in Joel's game after reviewing the entire male contents of the car.

The young man said, "Hi," so Sean nodded, and the young man said, "You're usually on this train." Sean said he was. How had he ever missed this fellow? "You going home from work?" Before Sean could answer, the friendly young man said, "I am, too. I've seen you before. I remember you because I had this idea you look how my dad might look now if he was alive."

Sean didn't know what to say. What came out was, "I'm sorry." He couldn't think of anything else.

"My dad died when I was a little kid," said the young man, "so I'm only hypothesizing from old pictures. I like hypothesizing about people riding the El." He gave Sean a crooked grin. Because he was young and attractive, sort of, didn't mean he wasn't also somewhat peculiar. After pausing during a squeal of the brakes, he added, "Oh, so I'm Owen."

Sean told him he was "Sean," but since it was Owen's stop, he grasped Sean's hand firmly, said he'd see him next trip, and squeezed into the departing crowd. Even though their commutes overlapped for only one short leg, it seemed odd that Sean had never before picked him out.

《 》

When he got home, he didn't mention the encounter on the train. Joel would only replace the David Foster Wallace reader with the father-fixated commuter. "Perfect for you," he'd say, "typical Tyson." Sean was "Tyson" when Joel wanted to portray him as a horndog-ger—Joel's term—and "Shaw-awn" when he was annoyed with him.

He found Joel sitting before the old oak music stand on the matching oak chair practicing his Shostakovich for quartet night. He put down his viola for a hug, and Sean did tell him what Elise had suggested about putting him on a leash.

"I knew it," said Joel. "It's what you've always wanted. There's plenty of boys out there who'd be into it, you know."

45

"Somehow it wouldn't be the same," Sean said and went to change out of his sweaty clothes.

Joel followed him down the hall. "But I've always wanted an actual dog," he said. "We could have a dog in the country. You never even wanted us to have a cat."

"I don't warm up to cats. Go back and practice. I need a shower."

"A big furry shepherd kind of dog," he heard Joel say as he closed the bathroom door. He inspected himself in the medicine-cabinet mirror. How might he look like Owen's father preserved to sixty-five? "Hypothesize" was a strange word to come from that young man's mouth. It must have been something in Sean's eyes or the expression of his lips that matched the old photograph. Or nose, or ears—or eyebrows? Mr. Thorp had said something about a flat Irish lip.

Sean seldom looked himself over in the mirror. Joel, who claimed not to care so much about a man's exterior, was always checking himself out. He worried about his complexion, his thinning and receding hair, his hardly noticeable gut. "I was never truly your type," he would whine when he felt underappreciated, but it wasn't true. He had always been Sean's type, if he could be said to have a type. Owen, despite his impressive build, did have some of Joel's manner, the eager grin and wide brown eyes and no shyness in talking to strangers. It was what had struck Sean when he first met Joel.

Sean's former boyfriend, Floyd Griffin, had insisted on dragging him to a birthday party for a pal of his where he hoped Sean would meet someone new. It was a Third of a Century party, four months after the birthday boy turned thirty-three. Everyone was supposed to bring an LP; in 1979, CDs hadn't come in yet. Floyd said this Joel guy was a musician, which Sean assumed meant he played in a rock band, so he got him the new album by The Police and set it on the pile of flat twelve-inch-square presents. Joel looked adorable with his brown crop of curly hair and his big eyes. When he unwrapped Floyd's present, Joel's face lit up. He said something like, "Wow!

I didn't know Zwillingsbruder had written a sixth symphony!" That record was still on their shelf of old LPs, and Sean got embarrassed when he noticed it. Back then, he'd felt like an idiot. But why hadn't Floyd clued him in? It was the sort of thing that had caused their breakup. Floyd was a morose sort who didn't take others much into account. He wore his limp blond hair long and was world-weary about everything. And then that bouncy enthusiastic Joel Greenwood opened Sean's present and exclaimed, "Jesus Christ! What the hell is this? *Outlandos d'Amour*? There's a group called The Police? Thanks, Tyson." He'd only caught the "Tyson" when they were introduced. Then he admitted he hadn't really been following current rock music since college but was grateful to Floyd's friend for expanding his horizons.

It wasn't long before Joel discovered Sean was more comfortable pulling his horizons closer in. After they moved in together, Joel took to saying, "Don't be so quimby." It was the friendly sound of the word that distinguished it from the more annoyed "Shaw-awn." But to Sean, Joel was never anything but "Joel." He wasn't even "Greenwood." He never had given Joel a nickname, fond or not, because "Joel" was entirely who he was.

Standing under the cool shower, Sean saw that first meeting as clearly as his meeting with peculiar Owen on his commute that night. But he assumed he would never see Owen again except in a fading memory while young Joel was still always there with him, no matter what.

« »

A few nights later, when Joel came home from the Lilienthals, he seemed in a low mood. "It's from playing Shostakovich," he said. "That man had it rough."

"It should make you feel better about yourself then," Sean said.

But Joel stormed off into the middle room yelling, "And yet he

47

managed to write fifteen amazing quartets! See what I mean about geniuses?"

It was best not to argue. Sean gently shut the bedroom door and got in bed to read. He chose not to think about what Joel was looking for in there at his computer. Having finally finished *Sister Carrie*, which he'd not exactly enjoyed but felt moved by, he had ordered online cheap used paperbacks of *An American Tragedy* and *Jennie Gerhardt*, and they had come in the day's mail. He was making up for having guiltily skipped Theodore Dreiser on his American Lit syllabus back in college. He'd come to appreciate how novels had a way of drawing him out from whatever was hanging over his head. He'd find himself believing everything in a novel as if it were happening before his eyes, even when it was told by someone recalling past events in precise detail, such as no one could possibly do. He was more skeptical about actual history books. They made unreliable conjectures while novels always seemed entirely true.

Lying there in bed with those two old paperbacks, Sean remembered that, after Dad left, he'd found Mom in their old double bed reading a play by Tennessee Williams, purported to be about a homosexual. Later, when she moved to the city and went back to St. Jo's, she tried reading *Sexual Behavior in the Human Male* to make more sense of the man she'd been married to for twenty-five years. But Kinsey only made it worse. Even before learning about Sean, she'd blurted out, "Why is it always the mother's fault? That's what these therapists say!" and stormed into her bedroom and slammed the door. Sean had yelled after her, "It's no one's fault, Mom," but soon it was only Monsignor Hildebrand she would talk to about such things because he, supposedly, had no sexual desires. All other men she could no longer trust, and she said so to her own second son, who had his own deep secrets.

He had been reading now in bed for an hour and a half. He'd started *Jennie Gerhardt* because *An American Tragedy* looked so long. At last, Joel gingerly turned the doorknob and said, "Oh! You're still up."

"Feeling any better?"

"What do you mean?"

"From your Shostakovich depression."

"It wasn't Shostakovich. It was all the talk after." Before Sean could ask what that was about, Joel said, "You know, Sheila's looking forward to meeting up with you Saturday."

"Oh dear."

"No, but she can be good to talk to. You can trust her. Art and Rebecca wouldn't have taken her in merely for being a good cellist. A quartet's chemistry isn't only musical, Quimby." He was pulling off his sticky T-shirt and then dropping his baggy shorts to the floor. He did some creaky knee bends and stretches to touch the ceiling, barely, but soon came around to his side and collapsed on the sheet. "So now what're you reading?"

"Listen to this," Sean said. "It's from exactly a hundred years ago, 1911."

"If you insist," said Joel, whose mind tended to drift whenever Sean read him things he thought he might like.

"But it's practically about our life today," Sean said and began the following paragraph from Chapter Seventeen:

"'The tremendous and complicated development of our material civilization, the multiplicity, and variety of our social forms, the depth, subtlety, and sophistry of our imaginative impressions, gathered, remultiplied, and disseminated by such agents as'—get this!—'the railroad, the express and the post office, the telephone, the telegraph, the newspaper, and, in short, the whole machinery of social intercourse—these elements of existence combine to produce what may be termed a kaleidoscopic glitter, a dazzling and confusing phantasmagoria of life that wearies and stultifies the mental and moral nature. It induces a sort of intellectual fatigue through which

49

we see the ranks of the victims of insomnia, melancholia, and insanity constantly recruited. Our modern brain-pan does not seem capable as yet'—see what I mean?—'of receiving, sorting, and storing the vast array of facts and impressions which present themselves daily.'"

"Jesus Christ!" said Joel. "That poor man wouldn't even make it out of bed today."

"But it gets me wondering," Sean said, "if things have always only appeared to be speeding up. Does it seem faster only because we got used to the speed it was before? The next generation takes the new speed as normal. The last generation naturally falls behind. It's a race where the older ones run too slowly."

"It's like a stretto in music," Joel said, "as in Rossini. But it does get objectively faster, Sean. The author's right. If he couldn't store it back then, who can store it now? There's only so many beats you can make in a bar before it becomes mush—or Charles Ives."

But Joel did cuddle up close to reassure him, Sean thought, and said in a seductive voice, "That's why we should get a place in the Ocooch Mountains. We can be two old goats together up there and quit the race."

Since it was too hot for further cuddling, Joel rolled back to his side of the bed and Sean flipped his sweaty pillow over one more time.

6 On Saturday at eleven, Sean showed up as agreed. There was Sheila Bowden at a narrow two-person table against the back wall. She was nibbling one of Lo Grasso's famous cinnamon buns and taking gulps from a large mug of coffee to wash it down. Before Sean could greet her, she looked up as if startled and said, "They don't call this place The Fat Man's for nothing."

He took the other chair and got out a hearty "Good morning."

"I arrived early," Sheila said. "I didn't know how often trains ran on the weekend."

"Where is it you live? You shouldn't have had to come all the way down here. We could've met halfway."

"I roped you into this, Sean Tyson, so it's only fair I come to you. I live up in Evanston."

Sean's regular waitress took their orders, and he tried to keep the conversation general. Sheila talked about Clara Lilienthal, who was missing her parents far too much but was determined to stick it out in California. She was thirty-seven, after all, and out there on her own she might be more inclined to meet men. "But there are some women who live happily by themselves," Sheila said. "Some don't even yearn for kids. Look at me!"

"It never occurred to us to want a kid," Sean said, "but it wasn't much of a possibility back then."

"Didn't stop your father," Sheila said with one of her piping laughs.

Sean's café au lait arrived along with a coffee refill for Sheila. To set her off in another direction, he asked after Uday and Qusay, which kept her going till their omelets arrived.

"But now, Sean," she said firmly, "I don't, in fact, intend to delve into the fascinating disintegration of your family. Not this time, anyway. I've brought you here under false pretenses."

Sean looked up from his eggs. That short, twinkly-eyed woman was holding a forkful delicately in her small hand. He should have felt relief, but her tone had him worried.

"It's about your beloved," she said.

"Joel?"

"Actually, it's about the Lilienthals. They're so dear to me. Where would a perpetual grad student and journeyman cellist be without Art and Rebecca? And they're getting on. First, their daughter flits off to the West, then the nice Jewish boy of their dreams is rhapsodizing about living in Wisconsin without noticing what it's doing to them. Rebecca tried an encouraging smile, and Art put on an expression of mentorly concern, but inside they were coming apart,

Sean. I love Joel Thomas Greenwood, but he doesn't have the proper sensitivity to other people's feelings. It's one thing to disappear for a summer month, but he's been yapping about moving to the boonies for good. What's the quartet to do? It's easy enough to scrounge up another violist but not an honorary son who composes pieces especially for you. I don't mean to put you on the spot, Sean, and now you're way ahead with your breakfast because I'm doing all the talking—"

She dug quickly into her hash browns, and Sean could see she was rather upset and wouldn't raise her eyes to his. "I should've known," he said.

"They love you, too," said Sheila. "It's not that they want Joel all to themselves. Only Thursday nights! In fact, Rebecca often says she doesn't know how Joel would manage if it wasn't for you."

As glad as he was for the compliment, it also bothered Sean. "I'm the steady one," he said. "It can get exhausting."

Sheila considered this awhile then said, "Good. Then you don't want this move either. But you must clue Joel in about the Lilienthals."

"It's that he wants more quiet, Sheila, more space, more time. For me, our two weeks in the UP is plenty. Moving to the country feels so lonely. I could maybe handle a month."

"And he was telling us about downsizing to a pied-à-terre here for you and quitting his job and moving himself up permanently. It may be the moment to lay down the law, Sean Tyson."

Sean swallowed the last of his café au lait and realized he had found an ally. He was strangely contented, sitting there in his neighborhood deli surrounded by people he didn't know, though he recognized some, and staring into the round sympathetic face of this Sheila Bowden.

"Arnold Schoenberg," she said and looked at him as if he should know what she was getting at. "Well, Arnold Schoenberg was Jewish, and after he found himself guilty of destroying traditional tonality, he simply had to invent some new Tables of the Law to pull back his disoriented art from the abyss. So there you are yourself, Sean. Schoenberg spent many years struggling with his opera about Moses and Aaron. Moses is trying to hold it all together and stop Aaron from leading the dance around the Golden Calf. Aaron's the musical one, and Moses is the man of the Word."

"I thought Moses was trying to reach the Promised Land."

"I guess that's true," Sheila said, only momentarily thrown off her metaphors. "But he was leading his people home. Home, Sean, that's what you're about, domesticity, not some crazy dancing with cows. Now, in World War One, Schoenberg was quite the Austrian patriot, and he saw the old Empire breaking up and old Kaiser Franz Josef dying. He had to make order out of the fragments, no more random atonality. I'm speaking psychosocially here."

She went on half whimsically, theorizing about music and history and her own lack of fascination with orderly systems, and all Sean could contribute was, "I guess Grandfather Gruenwald made it to Wisconsin just in time."

"And if he'd stayed to fight for his Kaiser," said Sheila, "there might never have been a Joel."

"So it worked out for me," Sean said. Sheila piped a tiny shriek. On the spot, Sean decided to say, "Why don't you come back with me and see where we live?"

《 》

They agreed to say nothing about the Lilienthals' distress and to pretend they'd had a deep discussion of Tyson family psychology. "But let me ask you one thing first," Sheila threw out casually as they walked up the block. "When did your father find out about you?"

"I'd confided in my sister, but she had to go tell our crazy little brother, who went and told Mom, and then Sandy thought he'd do me another favor and tell Dad, too."

53

"And you wouldn't tell him yourself? What if you'd bumped into him out at the bars?"

"I don't think he was much of a barfly."

"Were you?"

"At first, yes, sometimes." Sean had forgotten that his new ally was still on his case. She seemed to be taking preliminary notes for a future inquisition. She never revealed anything about herself, so he decided to throw a question back at her. "Where did you grow up, Sheila?"

"My father was forever getting transferred. My cello always traveled with me. It got its own seat on planes."

"And your father was—"

"A foreign policy wonk. Think tanks in Vienna and Paris. It's how I grew up so worldly."

"There, that's us." Sean pointed across to the balcony where Joel's Cubs cap was all to be seen of him, stretched out on a canvas chair taking the noon sun. Sheila shushed Sean before he could call out and then, in a swooping voice, half sang something in German. Joel later explained it was Pierrot's Serenade by her favorite, Schoenberg. Now, he popped his head and bare shoulders over the brick pediment and said, "Uh-oh!" then hurried back inside.

"You shouldn't be sunning," Sean said when Joel greeted them at the door, tying his seersucker bathrobe.

"I'm slathered with Age Shield," he said. "So, Sheila, you figured him out yet?"

"I have all the information I need. Nice bright apartment! A little sparse. I thought your sort decorated. You should have more *objets*. You should give the place some color. White walls, really! Ravinia posters!"

"This is basically Joel's music room," Sean said, "and I like to read on the couch while he plays."

"You should see my underground den," Sheila said. "All my stuff is crammed into two dark basement rooms and trimmed with cat hair." She inspected the oak music stand and chair and noted the scratched finish on the upright. She wanted to leaf through Joel's manuscripts, but he swiped aside "The Fire of Driftwood" and only let her see his recent Suite for Unaccompanied Viola and that quartet for the Lilienthals where he'd given Clara's cello a prominent role. "So now," Sheila said, "you must write a quintet with a second cello, like Schubert's, so when Clara visits her parents, we can all five play."

"I'll just run and dash one off," said Joel.

Sean could tell he wanted to go put clothes on. Under the robe, he was probably wearing only his sky-blue skimpies, so Sean said, "You go get decent and make some iced tea, and I'll show her the balcony."

On the concrete floor between the chairs, a half-empty mug of coffee was holding down a folded-out map of Richland County with red-penciled circles at certain points on back country roads. Sheila noticed it but made a dismissive shrug and went to the corner pillar to lean out and look up and down the street.

"You have trees!" she said.

"A few."

She sniffed the air. "You have a breeze!"

"You don't?"

"I have air-conditioning. I have no idea what's blowing above in the sublunary world." Sean gestured to a chair, but she said, "I'd never extricate myself from one of those. I'm rather short of leg and broad of hip and don't have much upper body strength."

Sean brought out the viola-practicing chair and then lowered himself into his designated canvas sling. "But when you play the cello—"

"It's remarkable how an instrument transforms one. As soon as I grasp the bow, I'm endowed with a force I don't understand. You must sense it in your beloved when he gets behind his viola."

Sean recognized the effect. When Joel played, he seemed surrounded by an impenetrable aura. Sean couldn't imagine himself having that level of concentration. Joel's music was something mysterious.

It was peaceful enough listening to Joel and Sheila talk about the quartets they'd played, and she managed to slip in some hints about how much it all mattered to Art and Rebecca at their age. "I have this idea," Joel said at one point, "that when you get older, it's only music that keeps you going anymore." Sean didn't like the sound of that. He glanced over at the Wisconsin map he'd folded up and tucked between the geranium pots on the windowsill. He told himself that their ten-by-twelve concrete balcony with its potted plants and canvas chairs was country enough for him.

The afternoon dragged on. Sean could tell that Sheila didn't want to return to her basement and her thuggy cats. Around two o'clock, she offered to bash out the piano parts of the Greenwood Viola Sonatas. She claimed to be a sketchy pianist, but she really wanted to hear what they sounded like off the page. Art had always made a big deal of them. So they went inside while Sean returned to *Jennie Gerhardt*. The sun was too high to reach beyond his sandaled toes. The sonatas floated out through the porch door. He was glad to hear them again, though they distracted him from reading. Sheila played perfectly well, the somber chords in the base, the twiddling bits in the treble.

The first sonata was singable enough, the second started tossing in wrong notes, and by the third the rhythms had moved a bit off-kilter. Sean closed his eyes and imagined an earnest high-school boy practicing the Greenwood sonatas with his teacher, working up to number four, which was soon wafting out to the balcony. It was quite dissonant with rhythms changing every couple of bars, but since he'd heard it often in the past, it must've lodged in some permanent fold of Sean's brain and he anticipated each phrase and could almost hum along.

That morning, he had feared having to recount his past to Sheila, but the afternoon was bringing him up against his present instead.

The music was reminding him of how Joel lived in another world from the one they shared, maybe even two other worlds. The earliest was Richland County, that map he'd been mulling over, the gravel roads winding through valleys and into the hills he called the Ocooch Mountains. His next world was music. It existed in measures of time in some omnipresent space. It didn't need words because the singing of Joel's viola and the shapes formed by Sheila's hands on the keys had meanings beyond words. Those two in there understood why each note moved forward to the next in a logic Sean couldn't grasp.

He had never accomplished anything that those two couldn't learn to do after a brief training session. In a few weeks, they'd be expert at finding affordable housing for victims of the so-called free market. Sean did allow himself some credit for his personal sensitivity, but hearing those musicians in there playing so perfectly together, he couldn't credit himself much.

This mood passed when they reached that part in the fifth sonata with the pizzicato. Sheila was laughing squeakily, and Sean could almost hear Joel smiling. He closed his eyes. If Joel was happy, he was happy. But he knew it didn't always work the other way around.

Soon, they had begun the sixth sonata, the difficult one for advanced violists. At the piano Sheila was getting a workout. Sean could hear her heavy breathing.

« »

"All right, Tyson, let's hear it," Joel said after she'd left.

"I didn't mind. Sheila's insightful. You're right, she was good to talk to. But she has to get out of that basement."

"You're not going to tell me what she got out of you?"

"I couldn't possibly go through it again."

"What did she say about me?"

"It wasn't about you, Joel." Sean took a seat on the couch, but Joel kept pacing around the room Sheila had found so undecorated.

"Anyway, she's an excellent sight reader," he said. "She easily picked up the piano part."

"I loved hearing those pieces again," Sean said.

"You could play the CD anytime, you know," Joel said and huffed off into the kitchen with the tea glasses.

The recording had come out with the published scores back in 1993. Art Lilienthal was the pianist. It was even listed in the Schwann catalog. Joel had hoped it might attract attention to his other works, but the CD of his first two quartets never made it beyond the local record shops. Joel had no instinct for marketing. He was always on to the next thing. But the Lilienthals did sell discs at their concerts and now they could be downloaded online.

Sean got up and followed Joel into the hall. "But hearing them live," he said at the kitchen door, "is different."

Joel turned around impatiently. "Because a performance is a single event, Shaw-awn. That's the whole point of music. Even that book you're reading—the words on the page are like notes on a score you're performing in your head. Reading it again later can never be exactly the same."

Once in a while, Joel said things that got Sean thinking. He imagined him teaching his students like that. Sean knew Joel was good at it and that the kids adored him. Then he thought of the look that came into Joel's eyes when the music he was playing reached the top of a crescendo, the same look they had when Sean made love to him. That must be how Joel's three worlds came together—the countryside, the music, and the two of them.

Unfortunately, later that afternoon, Sean went into the middle room to hunt for the CD so he could hear the sonatas again on earphones while reading on the couch.

"I was going through my new piece," Joel said, "and I was hearing it so beautifully in my head when you just barged in. Thanks a pile! Now I have to clear out my ears and start all over. The door was shut, Sean. I don't barge in when you're looking at porn."

"I thought you were still checking out real estate."

"It's such a crucial stage, getting the notes away from the piano and hearing them sung." He hung his head a moment and said, as if only to himself, "It's going to be rough going with the kids to get this right."

"But you like it?" Sean had slipped the CD off the shelf and was heading back toward the door.

"As Vaughan Williams said of his Fourth Symphony, 'I don't know if I like it, but it's what I meant,' or something like that. And don't ever mention to Sheila Bowden that I'm a Vaughan Williams man. She's a true modernist. She scorns the folksy Brits. She's so fucking sophisticated, that Sheila!"

Sean's hand was on the doorknob, and he should have left and gone back to *Jennie Gerhardt*, but he decided to say a word for the Lilienthals before judging he'd better not. "How would you ever make music up in your mountains, Joel?"

"There's music in Wisconsin, Shaw-awn."

"I meant for quartet nights."

Joel straightened the manuscript pages carefully then swiveled his desk chair to look Sean straight in the eyes. "I'm sure I can find a quartet in Madison. Violists are always in demand."

"I meant for the Lilienthals."

"It's not as though I'd never drive down and see them. We'll have a car at last, and you can stay at our new place and take care of the dog."

"The dog," Sean said flatly.

"Are you using Art and Rebecca to guilt trip me out of my plans? But they're my friends, it's my quartet, it's my business."

"They've also been my friends for some thirty-two years."

"But you don't play with them!"

"Joel, I was only asking a question."

"You really can't stand it, can you!" Joel shouted. "You can't look into our future. We're sixty-five years old. At best, we've got a couple of decades. We're squeezed into this white-walled shoebox with no space to run and breathe. We can't see the stars or touch the dirt or smell nature. It's gotten to me. I only put up with it all because of you. We bought into this place so cheap—"

"But it's our home. And your students—"

"Aw, none of those little hip-hoppers gives a shit about my music."

"All I meant to say was how much I loved hearing your music, and Sheila loved playing it, and the Lilienthals—"

"I'll write better music in the country." Joel stood up and came toward Sean with a hurt scowl on his lips. He was getting angry at the world and sorry for himself at the same time.

Sean knew how it went. If he stepped closer to hug Joel, it might calm him down, but at such moments Sean was more likely to shy away. "Joel," he began.

"I'll write better up there because no one will have to hear it. I'll compose only because I have to." His voice was rising, unmindful of the open window. "It goes back to high school. It goes back even before that. I played piano interludes for my mom and dad. They sat and listened. It was in my blood. I never cared if it didn't matter to anyone else."

"It matters to me," Sean said.

Joel was right up against him, almost touching. "It matters to you that it keeps me busy. That's not the same as understanding it."

Sean grabbed his shoulders and gave him a shake. "I'm going to go listen to your CD, Joel. I'm sorry if I don't understand everything in your music. But I do have ears, I do listen, it does mean something to me." Sean let go of him and left the room with a slam of the door.

« »

He felt his heartbeat. He did slip the CD into the portable player and stuck in his earphones and lay back on the couch and thought back to the year Joel was writing those sonatas. It was before researchers

60

had figured out how to treat HIV. At the Collective, Sean had volunteered to run a program to find safe housing for sick men. At times it seemed that entire neighborhoods and even the city itself were against them. Landlords ignored his inquiries. No one would say it outright, but the tone had changed. Joel had wanted to title his sixth sonata "Music for the Plague Years" but knew the educational publisher wouldn't approve. He had put such sounds of mourning into the viola part. *"Trauermusik,"* he called it, like Hindemith's, Sean remembered. Their friend Floyd Griffin had just lost his partner, Mick. Though Joel wouldn't say so, because he didn't want to be pictorial in his music, Sean knew that the last movement depicted how, after Mick's funeral, the congregation had promenaded down to the beach and let hundreds of balloons go sailing up eastward over Lake Michigan into the night. The viola notes kept disappearing into the twinkling stars of the piano's right hand over the low solemn chords of the lake in the left.

Sean realized he couldn't bear to hear that sonata after his fight with Joel, so he paused the machine. He couldn't make himself read, either. He couldn't even quite think. It had been a long time since he'd thought of those years when he and Joel were so lucky to have each other. They and their closest friends had felt apart from the rest of the world. Sean's mother was very ill then, too, but she didn't want him to bring Joel over. She'd decided, under her morphine, that he must have the virus and would infect her son. She even told Mary she was sure their father was spreading the virus to innocent young men at the University of Chicago. Sandy had reported the mad things she said. He might have spared Sean, but Sandy was too caught up in Mom's dying. She was now on drugs like him. She was always angry but claimed that her little Alexander was the only man she still loved and made him stay over at night on a cot by her bed to spell the hospice workers, who were all women. And Mary came as often as she could, but Danny only came back once from Ohio. Besides, he drank too much and Mom was certain he had a woman on the side, and Sean had taken after his dad, but with a Jew instead of a Latin, and she even suspected old Monsignor Hildebrand now of secret perversions. Her Sandy was the only good man left.

Back then, Sean was furious at the Church for outlawing condoms and sex ed, and he went on sit-ins and protests. When he told Mom what he was doing, they got to yelling at each other. It was his last visit that she was fully conscious. He couldn't stay to hear her ranting at him. He knew the drugs let her say things that had always lurked inside. As he stomped out the door, the last thing he heard was, "I never want to see you with that Jewish boy again."

When Sean was growing up, Eileen Tyson had been a polite North Shore mom. She'd gone with Dad to the Episcopal Church. She'd tried to fit into his Tyson world. Gramma had loved her and even preferred her to Uncle Albert's wife because Aunt Susan was a vegetarian. Gramma almost preferred Mom to her own daughter, nutty Aunt Elizabeth, who embarrassed her with off-color jokes and sloppy manners. Mom had loved sitting with Gramma and talking about the family, helping her prepare meals or arrange flowers, and Gramma loved Sean for the way he'd sit with them, reading a book like a scholar. She had considerable power over them all. Dad had to wait for her to die before he could finally have what he'd always desired.

《 》

"Are you all right?" said Joel's voice.

Sean opened his eyes to find him standing there, offering a bottle of ginger beer with a bottle for himself. "I fell asleep," Sean said.

"Are you still pissed?"

"I wasn't the pissed one."

"Oh, Quimby, you must rue the day that Floyd Griffin brought you to my long-playing birthday party."

"I was thinking exactly the opposite," Sean told him and pulled himself up to lean against the armrest. He took the bottle. Joel was watching him hopefully. "Because your sonatas got me remembering the year you wrote them and how lucky I felt to have you."

Joel took a seat at the other end of the couch, swigged from his bottle, and said, "How many violists does it take to screw in a lightbulb?"

"Not another violist joke."

"Sheila's full of them. So how many?" Sean shook his head. "None," Joel said. "They expect the violinists and the cellist to do it."

Sean shook his head again, this time as if to say, "Not funny."

"So a string quartet walks into a bar."

"Oh, no."

"The first violinist orders a dry martini, the second violinist orders a gin and tonic, and the cellist orders a rum and Coke."

"And the violist?" Sean said on cue.

"He says he'll have what they're having." Sean poked Joel's side with his bare foot. "Come on, Shaw-awn, it's just another dumb violist joke. I'm sorry I'm a dumb violist."

"Well, it's a dumb joke." Sean knew Joel was trying to coax him back to a cheerful mood, so he drank his ginger beer and stretched out his legs and rested them on Joel's lap.

"You really think I'm dumb?" Joel said in fake earnestness.

"Sometimes."

"Good. Then you'll have to look after me. But why does Sheila Bowden think our sort has to decorate?'"

They sat awhile longer in silence. It was how they'd made it through the years. Sean couldn't imagine more than a day or two with them not in the same place, sleeping in the same bed and waking up side by side. His mother had ended up alone for years, but his father had had Carlos Villalba to the end. Poor Mom, he thought. She'd wanted to do good. She'd taken Sean to march with Martin Luther King. She'd tried to fit in with Gramma Tyson at the Quimby farm. Life had been unfair to her.

7 When quartet night came around again, Sean figured he'd call up Floyd Griffin. "Come on and swing by," Floyd said, "before I forget what you look like." He still lived in Boys Town and didn't mind being an old man there. He'd complain about the vapid youngsters while delighting in their tight T-shirts and skinny retro jeans. Sean admired youthful beauty just as much but felt pathetic talking about it. Maybe he didn't admire it in the same way. Floyd's admiration was mixed with a degree of nostalgia.

On his block, Sean did see plenty of summery thighs and torsos, but with white hair and office clothes, he went largely unnoticed. Two tank-topped boys from Floyd's building were sitting on the stoop by the open front door. "Mr. Griffin expects you," said one. "He told us you were his old lover," said the other. Sean wouldn't have used the term now, but it was what they'd said back in those days.

Floyd had the top floor with a roof deck. At the door, Sean heard his languorous voice calling him out back. "Good evening, laddie," said Floyd, leaning up from a rattan recliner for a cheek kiss. "You met my welcoming committee?"

"Very nice, Floyd."

"They're innocent little lads—just out of U of I and planning to stay together for life. Good thing we don't have marriage in this state or they'd be tying the knot."

Sean pulled a wicker chair over and sat down. Floyd had a gin and tonic and, pointing weakly, directed Sean back inside for a glass of lemonade. "Still fearing the Irish propensity?" he called after him.

When they had settled down to talk, Sean found himself telling what he'd intended to lead up to more slowly. "So, Floyd, Joel and I are at some kind of crossroads. All these years, we've been so stable, but now he's got this idea of getting us out of the city, or at least him, and me part of the time."

In the light of three fat candles flaming on the tabletop between them, Floyd's parchment-pale skin looked ghostly. His lids hung heavily over his pale buggy eyes. Sean could perceive his cranium

64

under those scant gray hairs. Floyd was only two years older, but Sean doubted he looked as tired himself.

"Joel Greenwood's been having ideas ever since I met him," Floyd said, shaking his bare skull in the candlelight. "Remember how quickly he got ideas about you? He thought you were so hip and unavailable. What was I thinking, introducing you two! And he wouldn't stop pestering me about you. I didn't get it then, and I still don't. Before he met you, he'd only gone out with musical types and no one for long. Who can understand anyone else's attractions? But just because you and I had bad chemistry didn't mean you wouldn't suit him. That professor couple at the party, the violinists, what's their name, they saw immediately what was happening."

"The Lilienthals, Art and Rebecca. He's there tonight, practicing their Shostakovich."

"They were watching their protégé like hawks that night. Joel was such a volatile young fag. Sean, you've been far too stable for him. That's your problem."

"But what he wants is for us to get a place in Wisconsin where he grew up."

"In Governor Walker's police state? Doesn't he read the papers?"

"He remembers his childhood there. He wants us to slow ourselves down."

"Joel Greenwood slow down?"

"He's thinking of quitting his job."

"Well, laddie," said Floyd contemplating the ice floating in his glass, "do you want to be two old duffers in a walk-up apartment forever? I may be a single old duffer, but at least I've got a roof deck and a welcoming committee that comes up for drinks. It's a decent enough way to start fading out."

Sean felt a little sorry he'd brought all that up, so he said, "I know there are worse problems than fussing over whether to buy a 'second home.' I'm in the business of finding people a first one, well, not to buy, but—"

65

"Me, I'm a contented old duffer," Floyd went on. "Retirement's relaxing. Four decades in middle management? Now I sleep in, go out for late breakfasts, see my old pals—even you, when you care to swing by. I go to the Lyric and the Friday afternoon concerts. I take in some theater. And I'm surrounded by such delectable young flesh. I even have the occasional trick, if it isn't too much bother. Don't indulge that Joel of yours, and good heavens, stop feeling guilty. I know how you cling to your old griefs, Sean. I know how you hated your queer father and dearly wanted your saintly mother to forgive you, but they're dead, for God's sake!"

"I didn't hate my father."

"Oh, I knew you when, laddie. But that poor man was the victim of his times. We have no right to judge our predecessors. Now, be sweet and get me a refill."

In the kitchen, Sean heard a soft voice from the hall say, "May we intrude?" The committee introduced themselves as Jake and Gene.

"My young lads!" Floyd exclaimed from the deck. "Mix them two more!"

"We have beer," said Gene, the heftier one. It was Jake who'd called Sean "the old lover."

"Then it's a party," Floyd said when they'd pulled two more wicker chairs from under the awning out into a semicircle around his recliner. The conversation turned to who had been seen down on the street that evening and who was wearing what. Sean noticed in the candlelight that slenderly boyish Jake gripped his beer with surprisingly hairy hands.

« »

He didn't stay long. The boys did ask him what Floyd had been like back in the day. They were sure he used to be hot. "They've seen the graphic evidence," Floyd said. "Remember those art shots some old dude took of me in the buff? Art shots, my ass!"

66

"I'd have done you," said Gene, so Jake gave his chunky thigh a swat.

"Save that for bedtime, laddies." And when Sean got up to go, Floyd said, as if the committee couldn't hear, "Call me if Joel keeps acting up. I'll read him the riot act."

Heading down the stairs, Sean didn't know whether he felt happy or sad for Floyd. He supposed he'd found what he wanted, but he must still miss Mick every day. Not that they hadn't fought like crazy before Mick got sick.

Sean decided to walk around a block or two in the cooler evening before catching a bus. On a quiet street, with his thoughts off at Gramma's farm on a summer night in the long-lost past, he heard a panting voice call, "Hey, Sean!"

He turned to see a young man catching up to him at a jog trot. It was getting dark, and with a street lamp between them, Sean couldn't be sure who it was.

"Hey, Sean, it's Owen. Remember, from the train?" Owen stepped around so the light was shadowing only half his face, and Sean recognized the angular profile, the crooked nose and sharp jaw. He had exaggerated his appeal in his imaginings, and he warned himself that Owen's peculiarities, though delightful in fantasy, might be problematic in life.

"Oh, yes," said Sean. "I haven't seen you since."

"I'm on a new schedule. They're always switching me."

"I'm sorry," Sean said, which was what had come out when he didn't know what to say about Owen's dad's death.

"You don't live around here, do you?"

"I was visiting an old friend."

"I didn't think you lived here. I don't either," said Owen. "I was just cruising around. I worked late and didn't want to go home."

"I have to get home myself. My partner's there." That sounded like the old days: You got a place?—No, I have a lover—And I've got straight roommates—Well, uh—. The whole business with Owen was pulling Sean back in time.

67

"What's his name?" Owen asked. He hadn't said anything yet about his own inclinations, but by that point Sean had no doubts.

"Joel."

"Joe?"

"Joel."

"Oh, Joel. Cool name. Is he younger than you?"

"By a few months."

"Nice," said Owen. He was leaning nervously on one leg and then the other, as if he'd only paused in his run. "I could tell it was you from down the block. I hope you don't mind. I miss not being on your train."

"Yeah, I never saw you again."

"Because of the stupid schedule change."

"Where do you work, Owen?"

"This health club on North Michigan, but I'm taking accounting." He kept blinking his big brown eyes. He seemed too nervous for such a solidly built fellow. "I'll walk you to the train," he offered.

"I'm taking a bus."

"I'll walk you to the stop," he said even more eagerly. Tonight, his polo shirt was green but equally tight around the biceps. As they passed each street lamp, his face went lopsided one way then the other. Sean decided he was not really handsome, but his bounciness put him in a separate category from Floyd's young friends. When they stopped to wait for the bus, Owen said, "Remember how I hypothesized the way my dad might look today?"

"'Hypothesized' is a good word."

"I hypothesize lots of things." Owen gave Sean a wink, or was he only still blinking nervously? "You have your phone?"

Tapping his pocket, Sean realized he'd left it at home.

"Bummer. I'll write my number down. We could get coffee sometime?"

"Actually, pretty soon Joel and I are going to the Upper Peninsula on vacation. It'd have to wait till late August."

"That's no problem." But since neither of them had paper or pencil, Owen punched Sean's cell number into his phone so he could call it and leave him his, and then they'd have each other's.

Owen waited with Sean for the bus. He looked like a son seeing his dad off. He had gone silent, staring down at his running shoes, but he did give Sean one of those masculine public hugs when the bus finally pulled up.

« »

Sean came home to a message on the machine from Joel saying he'd be in by ten and a text on his cell that read: "its owen, hi." He quickly entered him in his directory then thought it wiser to write the number down and delete it there. "Who's Owen?" Joel would ask. He could say he was an intern at work and begin a string of lies, or he could say he was a young man he'd met on the El, which would be fodder for Joel's teasing. Instead, Sean wrote the number in a neutral hand inside the back cover of *Jennie Gerhardt*, where it appeared to be a jotting by the book's previous owner.

He had a full hour then to dream up a session with this now more visually accurate Owen, but remembering the way the young man's muscular rear end filled out his loose-fitting slacks brought it to an end in only five minutes. So Sean lay on the couch and couldn't stop rethinking the whole evening. First, to have put Floyd on the defensive about living alone and then to have been chased down by the goofy-faced young Owen and appear indifferent, only to creep home and imagine him spread out naked on a bed—Sean reassured himself that Floyd was actually doing fine and Owen would never have to know. He turned to the back of the book to check the phone number. It was still there. Calm down, Sean Quimby Tyson, he told himself, you're sixty-five fucking years old.

When Joel got home, he was full of Shostakovich. The opening of the Fourth Quartet, where he and Sheila played a drone and

69

the Lilienthals soared above, higher and higher, more and more intensely—it got to him every time they ran through it. "It's so passionate, so sweeping, so orgasmic," he said. And he also loved his solo in the third movement. They would play the piece on their fall program at Northwestern, along with the "Dissonant" and a Brahms quartet they hadn't rehearsed yet. Sheila had kept pushing for Schoenberg's Second despite Rebecca's point that they shouldn't play two twentieth-century works. Besides, the Schoenberg added a soprano solo, but Sheila suggested Irene Wilson because she was Joel's old classmate and also her voice students would swell the audience. Joel liked the idea but felt Sheila was intruding on Art and Rebecca's territory. He said he tried to mediate the controversy, but they'd only agreed to put off deciding.

"I went to see Floyd Griffin tonight," Sean said.

"Oh, that's where you were. How was the old sot?"

"He's got two boys downstairs devoted to him for now."

"That's what you need, Tyson, or even just one David Foster Wallace kid."

"I haven't given him a second thought. You think about him more than I do."

Joel set down his viola case and opened the piano to strike a strange-sounding chord. "That's Dmitri Shostakovich for you! If only I could reach heights like that."

"You know what Floyd said about Wisconsin? He couldn't believe you'd go live in a land of Republican reactionaries."

"You discussed our plans?"

"They're *our* plans now?"

But Joel was searching for other strange chords and shaking his head when he got them wrong. Sean snatched up his book and went back to the bedroom.

He could tell when Joel was not to be disturbed, but if Sean was reading some old paperback, Joel considered him entirely interrupt-ible, even in the middle of a dramatic scene. Someone might be dying or declaring love or bursting into a fit of rage. He would hold up his palm like a traffic cop, but Joel never got it. He didn't understand that reading did for Sean what music did for him. But that wasn't quite true. Music was Joel's whole self, while Sean didn't write the books he read. Reading was his way of observing other people, but in playing those Shostakovich chords out there, Joel was communing with a comrade. He was one with him, with all of his dead masters. They all wrote music, played music, listened to others playing music. Joel wasn't the audience, like Sean, but part of the music itself. Of course, he did quickly turn back into cranky, bothersome Joel again. Sean couldn't love one without loving the other.

8 On Friday night, Sean stood outside the door to 2-B, wondering why Joel was in there banging out old Bob Dylan songs. He quietly turned the knob while Joel was crooning "Lay, lady, lay" and saw his brother Sandy draped across the couch. Joel noticed him in the doorway. Sandy twisted himself around and gave a casual wave as if he'd seen his brother only yesterday. For a warm day, he was bundled up in a hooded Blackhawks sweatshirt and saggy raggedy jeans. Sean could tell Joel had been trying to keep him entertained. With his face shadowed by the hood, his dangly loose limbs looked like a disaffected teenager's, even though Sandy was now past sixty.

"It's been awhile," Sean said.

"Well, there's some news," Sandy said in a slow, low voice.

"There's big news," Joel said, closing up the piano and grabbing off the music rack a fat business envelope, which he rushed over to Sean.

"I got one, too," said Sandy.

Sean slit the seal and pulled out a packet with a cover letter, he realized, from a lawyer in Dad's old firm. With each sentence he realized more. Then, he backtracked to read it all again. The remaining principal of the trust Dad had left to support Carlos Villalba, worth some four hundred thousand dollars, was now to be divided between his children: Daniel Erastus Tyson, junior; Sean Quimby Tyson; Mary Elizabeth Tyson Ahern; and Alexander Dermot Tyson.

"Pretty awesome, huh?"

"It's in stocks and bonds," Joel said, "so there'll be capital gains if you cash in, but still it's lots more than you thought you had when you walked in that door."

Sean took a seat beside his brother. Sandy seldom showed enthusiasm unless he was off his medications and then he hardly shut up. It had been months since he'd stopped by, and lately he didn't have a phone or even a permanent address. "How did the lawyer find you, Sandy?"

"He found Mary."

"How did she know where you live?"

"Sometimes I call her."

"So she already knew about this?"

"Danny knew, too. They googled Erie Shore Enterprises. You never even gave Dad your home address. You were such a shit to him."

Joel was standing by the open window, looking across the street at the old school that now housed the elderly, as if to avoid coming between the brothers.

"I wasn't a shit," Sean said. "I didn't want him in my life anymore."

"Because of you both being gay."

Patiently, Sean shook his head. "Because I was mad at him, all right? Maybe I was wrong, but can't you understand?"

"Don't put it on me," Sandy said and pulled his hood closer so no more than the tip of his nose showed.

"Dad always looked after you, Sandy. This money could help you a lot now." Sandy shrugged. "You'll have to manage it some safe way."

"I'll manage it." He pulled the hood off what was left of his tangled graying once-blond hair. He looked like the more hopeless

72

applicants at the Collective. Sean had tried before to find him better housing, but it had never worked out. "I bet you don't even take Dad's money," Sandy said, his voice still low and slow. "You never would when he was alive. Can't you get over your bullshit, Sean? You won't take it, will you!"

"He'd better," Joel said, not turning around. "We're legally married in Iowa. I have a right to it, too."

Sean hadn't begun to think what he'd decide. It was only a lawyer's letter. He supposed he'd have to sign documents and set things up at the AmTrust bank. What if he didn't take it? The others could then get thirds.

"Joel was singing me some Dylan from the old days," Sandy said in a livelier tone. "He did 'Maggie's Farm' and 'It's All Over Now, Baby Blue' and whatever. He can play anything."

"I didn't know you even knew those songs, Joel."

"I was in college once, Quimby." He came over and lay an arm across Sean's shoulders. "I even remember those songs by The Police. Words always come back when I get the tune in my head. Now, what about this letter?"

"Don't bug me. It'll take some time to think it through."

"Remember, we're a married couple. Sandy," Joel said, "I need your help here. Want to stay for dinner?"

"Definitely."

"Let's talk about something else," said Sean.

« »

As if he hadn't eaten in days, Sandy scarfed down two fat hamburgers with cheese and a big salad. He shied away from the ginger beer but swallowed two tall glasses of 1 percent milk and went into an endless discourse about how it should be called 99 percent milk or else 1 percent fat. That led to other critiques of the current world: labeling, regulations, the cops, the city, Mayor

Emmanuel, the erosion of his freedoms. His meds seemed to be wearing off.

Sandy was a combination of sloppy kid and batty old man. When Sean squinted across at him, he could almost see the silent recluse curled up on Mom's sleeping porch in Lincoln Park, huddled under blankets, skinny and acne-ridden, reading his *Zarathustra*. Sandy had hated his fancy private school. He was one of those weird smart teenagers that fall easily off track. Mom had let him do whatever he wanted—skip classes, come and go at all hours, leave his mess around for her to clean up. At last, when he wouldn't get out of bed, she'd consulted Monsignor Hildebrand, who had the sense to make her call a doctor because the Church wasn't equipped to help in such cases.

While Sandy rambled on and Joel pretended to take an interest, Sean couldn't help but recall his brother's first big depression when Mom got him into a hospital day program, where he told his shrink he'd grown up happy on his family's farm and maintained that his mom had dragged him to Chicago after his father abandoned them. He didn't even let on he'd been attending a school like Foxridge. At the hospital, he idolized one druggy new friend named Jamie, but Mom mostly distrusted the older male patients for chumming up with her sixteen-year-old son. "He's so delicate and fair-skinned, the sort those types go for," she told Sean, who pretended not to know what she meant because he didn't want her to suspect him, too. It was such an awful in-between time, and he hated to think of it now.

Anyway, Sandy's friendships didn't outlast his hospital days, and soon he was back on the streets and into drugs again. When Sean stopped squinting at him across the kitchen table, it was a scraggly old man he saw. He'd clerked at a shop or two, pumped gas, waited tables, and now and then Mary took him up to the North Shore and cleaned him up. Jamie was long gone. None of the women he went with stuck around. Sometimes, he'd go with Mom back to St. Joachim's but not after he got into a big blow-up with the Monsignor

74

over Kierkegaard. Sean didn't think a hundred thousand dollars would help him get any better.

Joel was scooping out bowls of chocolate ice cream to break off Sandy's monologue. Cautiously, Sean asked if maybe the Housing Collective could help find him a more permanent place to live. They could set up electronic payments so he wouldn't have to worry. "There's decent studio apartments near the El," he said.

Sandy tilted his head to one side. The hood fell back and now lay across his scrawny neck. Sandy was the least likely Blackhawks fan. He'd probably picked up his sweatshirt at a shelter. "I've got a place, Sean," he said.

"But I don't even know where."

"Ask Mary."

"Come on, Sandy."

He raised his pale eyes for the first time all evening, but his low voice returned to its slow pace when he said, "You never told Dad where you lived. You didn't want him to know when you got together with Joel. You wouldn't even give Dad that much!"

Joel was washing up at the sink, pretending not to listen. Sandy had lowered his eyes again to observe each spoonful he lifted to his thin lips.

"I've explained a thousand times," Sean said. "When Dad left, I didn't yet know who I was. The point is, Sandy, all that was suddenly his big deal, not mine. It stopped me dead."

"You don't make any sense," his little brother said, wiping the brown smear off his face with a faded black sleeve. The ceiling light made the old acne scars stand out on his sunken cheeks.

"And then you had to go and tell Mom about me."

"Whatever," Sandy said. "It's old news. You turned out all right. I'm the one that didn't."

"Brothers!" Joel yelped. He turned off the water and came and spread his hands on the table as if to separate them. "Look, I never even got to have a brother! Jesus Christ, be glad you have each other. Now, more ice cream?" Sandy nodded, so Joel scraped the rest of the

75

carton into his bowl and said, "A hundred thousand apiece makes up for a lot."

"When Mary told me about that obituary," Sean said, "it didn't occur to me we'd get a thing. I'd always supposed some Venezuelan family would get it all. Well, probably they get the Hyde Park condo and the place in Florida."

"Shit!" Sandy spluttered. "You mean we could've got them, too?" He dug his spoon angrily back into the ice cream.

« »

In bed that night, Sean set his glasses and the book with Owen's number in it on the table, and soon Joel's head was resting on his chest, a hand reaching up to his shoulders. They both seemed surprisingly contented, so Sean asked, "How have we, with all the world's miseries, gotten so fortunate?"

"Your mom would see God's hand in it."

"It's unlikely that her God would dole out a stock portfolio to us two Sodomites."

"Your dad would say it's from him being a Tyson, working hard and making a living and all those years suppressing his own lusts for your sake."

"But Gramma claimed me for more of a Quimby, like her, but with a touch of the Irish, of course. I took it for affection back then. Those were my harmonious family days."

"I don't mean to sound selfish," Joel whispered into Sean's chest, "but don't forget that my piddling Greenwood inheritance did help pay off one of our equity loans."

"I haven't forgotten."

"So whatever you do, please, please, don't throw anything away on your messed-up brother. Promise me it's all for us."

"I promise it's for us."

"You'll sign the papers?"

76

"It would make us safer," Sean said.

"Christ, Quimby, it changes everything! I couldn't figure out how we'd swing it otherwise." He gave Sean some tight squeezes around the waist as if it was already a done deal.

"You keep pushing for this 'it' of yours."

"Because with you, everything has to be a push or you'd never budge."

"I'm not likely to budge on this one," Sean said in an attempt at firmness. Joel only hummed something lively right into Sean's ribcage so it tickled. He hadn't surrendered.

In the dark of their bedroom, with the occasional passing car interrupting the night's silence, Sean did feel especially near to Joel. Then he imagined Sandy sleeping alone in some dreary place and, again, knew he was luckier than he had a right to be.

Joel's humming had stopped. He must have been thinking hard about something because his hand on Sean's shoulder was gripping him harder. "It's such a sad poem you chose for me," he said. "'The long-lost ventures of the heart.' It's what makes me want to go back home. I might've been going along here with no fear of the future, but the more I tried to set those words, the more I knew—see, when I got to 'the long-lost ventures,' I recapitulated 'the first slight swerving' but in retrograde. Never mind, you wouldn't be able to tell. I've only got to finish the last stanza before we go up north, but endings are the hardest."

"You'll finish," Sean assured him. "You always do. In the middle, you just forget you've always found an ending."

"In tonal music," Joel said, "endings move toward the home key. But that was a hundred years ago."

9 After a heavy Monday at work, Sean had slid into a low mood. It came from having interviewed one after another victim of the unfree market, and that got him thinking again about his little

brother's lonesome life, and he had to consider seriously the possibilities his father's money had presented him with. It didn't cheer him up. It disrupted his whole concept of himself. If it was up to him, assuming he accepted the inheritance at all, he would pay off the mortgage and put the rest in the bank, not buy an old farmhouse with it, but when he called Mary to discuss the whole thing, she'd said, "Welcome to marriage, brother."

After Davey locked up out front, he peeked in Sean's door and said, "Hey, Tyson," who answered with "Hey, Nussbaum," as in their college days. Their friendship had neither lost nor gained. They'd shared a group house when they first came to Chicago and Davey was with Beth and Andrew with Maxine and there were several other casual pairs while Sean was with nobody. They never talked about what went on in their emotional lives, though the girls surely did. Back then, hippie men had a lot to learn. Eventually, Sean had found a one-room apartment of his own so he could bring bed partners back.

Now, there was Davey, flopped into the applicant's chair, still part of his life. Davey and Beth had been together all those years, and as far as Sean knew, their marriage had no rough patches. As far as Davey knew, neither did Sean's. "I have to come in all five days for you? And the week after? You owe me, Tyson." He ran his long fingers over his sparse hair, and Sean tried to picture thick blond waves to his shoulders and his once pinkish skin, now blotchy red. Davey still wore his blue work shirts and jeans, still kept the trim mustache and beard he'd grown after graduation when he stopped being the baby-faced kid Sean had had a pointless crush on. It was hard to imagine that old feeling now.

"On my gradual way out of here," Davey said, "I've been thinking a lot about us back then and all that was going down. We were so into it. You, me, and Andrew, we're the ones who stuck with it. Lucky the draft numbers we drew or who knows where we'd be. Dead like Schoener? You could've checked the box like your future boyfriend did, but all you claimed was your asthma. We'd needle you about your sex life, and you'd clam up and say you were putting it all into work. What did we know where you went after dark!"

"It wasn't all that exciting, Nussbaum."

"You know," Davey went on, "I've been trying to assess how much worse off people actually were in the sixties. No women's rights yet. Civil rights? Working on it. Shit, gay rights not even mentionable. I was such a pig. I maintain they went into Vietnam to get people's minds off poverty. But, fuck, back then no one had to have all this crap! Wi-Fi in every room? What did a decent meal once cost in relation to what you'd earn sweeping floors? Get real!" Davey leaned closer, and Sean knew the lecture had only begun. "What we didn't count on, Tyson, was how financial interests would replace production. We didn't realize electronics would eventually tip the scales. Even service jobs we're losing to Asia. Or to robots. And the powers-that-be exploit the undocumented folks doing the shit jobs."

"You're depressing me, Davey."

"We didn't realize how entertainment would be at our fingertips all the fucking time and be so goddam stupid. Worse opiate than religion!" He flung his hands up with a disgusted exhalation. "It's our fault, of course. We're the dopes who believed in everyone's right to have all this crap."

It was his favorite theme. He used to have the sharpest mind of the three of them, but now he'd get going on a rant and repeat everything he'd ranted about the week before. It was simply a more left-wing version of Sandy's self-absorption. But Sean agreed with what Davey professed. Joel dubbed him "your Marxist buddy, Comrade Nussbaum," and Sean would say he, too, was a Marxist, at least in spirit. And ever since communism was declared dead, Sean had actually become even more of a communist at heart. Joel told him that was all bullshit.

Finally, Davey went off to his western suburb, and Sean was left to sit at his desk and ponder. His father had made lots of money lawyering for the University of Chicago, and Carlos had coached tennis in Hyde Park. According to Mary, they lived quite well. Dad had to keep rescuing Sandy, and he put Danny through business school and Mary through college and cosigned loans for them. He'd bought Mom her apartment and sent Sandy to Foxridge Academy and paid alimony, too. He'd wanted to contribute something, if not to Sean himself then to the North Side Housing Collective. Dad wrote him at the office, the old storefront, and Sean wrote him back on their new stationery, saying thanks but they were doing fine on their own. It was the meanest thing he'd ever done.

And the hundred thousand? He should think of it as having been left to Joel. Dr. Nathan hadn't made that kind of money. Whatever he could do, he'd done for his son, and he never charged his patients more than they could afford. He was an old Wisconsin socialist, and Grandfather Gruenwald had been a Wobbly. Somehow, Sean had inherited Joel's family's politics and Joel a bit of the Tysons'.

Andrew Stone passed the open door, stopped, and looked in with an analytic stare. "Are you just pooped," he tapped his shiny shaved head, "or is something dreadfully wrong in there? I heard Nussbaum yammering at you. Is that it?"

"Andrew," Sean said, trying to pull something up from deep inside, "shouldn't it be possible to see the mess the world's in and still be deserving of what you've got?"

"Don't be such a Roman Catholic, Sean. Your mother did some kind of number on you. I knew it from the day we started rooming together."

"And, Andrew," something else was coming to him, "why, when Joel says he wants to go back home, doesn't he mean to our own place and not to where he grew up?"

"I see." Andrew came around the desk to pat Sean on the back. "You never tell me these things. Believe me, no one actually wants to go back to where he grew up. That home doesn't exist anymore."

"And he expects me to want to go with him."

Andrew sat up on Sean's desk and shook his head. "What do I know about relationships! Mine all went to shit."

"Do you think I'm a psychological Catholic, Andrew?"

"Don't ask me, I was raised Baptist. But your mom had to pass unworthiness on to one of her kids. Now, let's close up shop for the day. Be glad you've got someone to go home to. It's only if my ex dies first that maybe my daughter will come and take care of feeble old forgotten me."

"Now you're making me feel guilty again," said Sean, half seriously.

Andrew hopped off the desk and sauntered out and down the hall. "There's no place in this business for guilt, Tyson," he called back. "We'd never get anything done."

But Sean sat awhile longer and pondered.

PART TWO

1 Last night in their cabin, they'd found a heavy old illustrated volume of *The Song of Hiawatha*. Joel was soon obsessed with it. "That Longfellow! Talk about a regular meter to mess around with!" he said when they were sitting on their porch the next morning, looking out over the shining Big-Sea-Water, as Joel now called it. Sean had read the poem, most of it anyway, in tenth grade. Mr. Gault, his English teacher, had made them recite it, one by one or all in chorus. It came back to him when Joel began to declaim a passage he particularly liked:

> *Honor be to Mudjekeewis!*
> *He had stolen the Belt of Wampum*
> *From the neck of Mishe-Mokwa,*
> *From the Great Bear of the Mountains,*
> *From the terror of the nations*
> *As he lay asleep and cumbrous*
> *On the summit of the mountains,*
> *Like a rock with mosses on it,*
> *Spotted brown and gray with mosses.*

The small resort where they were staying had one of those huge bears carved from a tree trunk, standing before the main lodge. It was supposed to represent Mishe-Mokwa, the place's namesake. Between his giant raised paws, he held a wooden WELCOME sign, but he looked as if he'd been roused from his winter sleep, hungry and eager to avenge himself on Mudjekeewis. Each of the ten cabins bore a character's name from the poem. Theirs was Chibiabos, to

83

Joel's delight, "the sweetest of all singers." Next door was Iagoo, the Great Boaster.

In high school, Sean had been puzzled that Mishe-Mokwa had been slain and yet, in the story, lived on. Mr. Gault had tried to make him understand that legends existed outside of time. They forever reenacted themselves and forever revived. The great bear may have been slain, the nations may have taken his land, but nonetheless he still lived and threatened them. His thunder still rolled. Hunting in his mountains, the danger never left them. Mythic time ran at a different pace alongside mortal time, Mr. Gault had explained. It was continually re-creating its creation.

Sean remembered those school lessons from age fifteen. It was why, that summer, he had taken Gramma's *History of Illinois* from her shelf and read about Chief Black Hawk. The militia had chased the Sac people up into Joel's Wisconsin. On that long march, many of the tribe had starved to death and only a remnant made it safe across the Mississippi. Sean wondered if Joel had been taught the story in the Richland County schools.

It was so peaceful, looking out through the tall pines on the carpet of soft needles that sloped down to the narrow sand and the cold, shining lake. Sean saw nothing man-made, only what Hiawatha himself might have seen many years ago. He had lived to face the arrival of the whites, but he also persisted in an ancient lost time at the origin of nations. Sean wanted to explain all of that to Joel but decided to let him discover it in his reading.

Phil Kimbley, with his stiff-legged old dog Cinder trailing behind, stopped by to ask if they'd slept well on their first night. He was a hefty bearded man of forty who had taken the place over from his parents when they retired to a warmer climate. Sean told him it was the nicest place they'd ever stayed on the Upper Peninsula. "Gonna be fine weather all week," Phil said. "You picked it right. Good hiking time for the Porkies. Been in the lake yet? Take out a canoe.

Too bad you fellas can't stay a second week now you see how good the life is up here."

Joel told him they were sorry, but they had people to see down in Wisconsin.

"Gonna lose our late sunsets," Phil said. "You'll be back in Central Time. We're the farthest west that's still in Eastern. Midnight sun, practically, and when she does go down over the lake—" He put on an ecstatic smile and clutched his hands together, as if in prayer.

Clearly, Phil liked talking to his guests. He did get lonely in the long winters, but having grown up in the UP he couldn't ever settle anywhere else. They'd heard it all last night when they drove in from Green Bay. Phil said he'd once visited his aunt and uncle out in Boston but couldn't take all the people. It seemed he'd never married, but he made a point of liking women. He went into Ontonagon or Ironwood for the bars when it got too quiet in the late fall, but in summer he had his guests. Sean and Joel both liked Phil. For all his talk, he seemed something of a crushed soul.

Cinder led them over to be outfitted with paddles and a canoe. Joel took the bow because he couldn't grasp the steering principle, and Phil pushed them off. The sun was high above the piney shore to the east, and to the west they could see the silhouette of the Porcupine Mountains. Sean hadn't seen them since a summer camp trip when he was eleven. Lake Superior, edged by forests and high hills, and with a foreign country out beyond the horizon, wasn't like Lake Michigan. The water was deeper, colder, and not as sandy-bright blue. If they didn't look too closely, they couldn't even make out the cabins of Mishe-Mokwa between the trees.

"Are you still angry, Sean?" Joel asked.

"Why would I be angry?"

"For making you leave here next week."

"I'll take what I can get," Sean said, stroking hard and ruddering to compensate for Joel's meager dippings. From behind, he didn't look his age. He could almost have been a wimpy teenager in a Cubs cap.

« »

At breakfast, they'd met Sylvie, the short fat cook who lived beyond Nokomis Lodge in Minnehaha. She moved out from Ontonagon for the season, she told them, and had worked for the Kimbleys ever since they bought the place forty years ago. She pointed out a framed photo on the wall of chubby seven-year-old Phil holding a two-foot muskie. His mom and dad, long-haired hippies, were standing proudly beside him.

For lunch, Sylvie brought in thick turkey clubs and her famous coleslaw. She sold it all over the county, along with her famous German potato salad and pasties. She corrected them when they said "pastries." "Not like paste but like the past! See, it's one of my sidelines up here. You have to do a variety to get by," she said. "I got hired to watch little Phil, but the Kimbleys kept me on. I never met folks like them. That's a made-up name—Kimbley. They didn't approve of the wife taking the husband's. I'm surprised they even bothered to get married. I never understood why they chose to settle down in this godforsaken place."

"It's so beautiful here," Sean said.

"Can't live on beauty, Mr. Tyson. Young folks don't realize. And they eventually got pretty tired of it. She went to give piano lessons over in Ironwood just to see people. He got more like a hermit, reading all the time and taking up weird ideas. Well, they send me a card now and again from down south. Phil won't ever leave, though, not so long as I'm around looking after him. Now, I'll let you have your lunch in peace. I gotta make the next ones for those Wisconsin folks."

A thirty-ish couple was coming across the lawn. When they stepped inside, they each gave a nod and went to sit by the other lakeside window. In past summers, on Trout Lake or Whitefish Bay,

86

Sean and Joel had gotten on pleasant terms with other guests, but at first everyone was reserved. These two looked shy and awkward, even with each other. It could be a new marriage or an old one that had run out of things to say. He was hearty and fresh-faced, and she looked timid and frail.

Against the back wall stood an upright piano, even shabbier than Joel's. Phil's mother must've played it. After finishing off Sylvie's custard pie, Joel went over to see if it was in tune. The shy couple looked his way. "Oh, do you play?" the woman asked.

"Some," said Joel. "I'm more of a violist."

"A what?"

"I play viola, you know, in a string quartet."

The man gave the woman a subtly admonishing twitch of his head, so she simply smiled at Joel and returned to her sandwich. Soon other guests arrived, and Sean and Joel went back out into the sunlight.

"All I want to do this afternoon, Quimby, is sit on our porch and read *Hiawatha*. It's exactly what I need, living in a long-ago world with everything in its place, man and nature. It's very musical."

"I suspect the old Indians around here actually had quite a miserable existence," Sean said, "freezing, starving, fighting, always afraid."

"But they knew the meaning of it all. They had stories to explain it."

"If they believed the stories."

"But they did! Their stories are much truer than the ones the old Hebrews made up about the vengeful father in the sky or in a burning bush or wherever else he'd show up." He eased himself into an Adirondack chair, opened the large book he'd left lying there, and recited:

> *Gitche Manito, the mighty,*
> *The creator of the nations,*

87

Looked upon them with compassion,
With paternal love and pity;
Looked upon their wrath and wrangling
But as quarrels among children—

He read on till the warriors had smoked the peace pipe and the Master of Life ascended into the clouds, smiling on his helpless people.

"I don't know how a modern Indian would take that, Joel. They've got their casino down in Lac du Flambeau. We saw the billboards."

"You reduce everything to the evils of capitalism, Shaw-awn."

"But it's true."

"I'd rather live in the old magical world, if you don't mind, so stop being such an asshole."

Sean patted Joel's Cubs-capped head and went inside to find his own book, all nine hundred pages of *An American Tragedy*. He didn't know why he had to keep bringing Joel back to reality when he, too, loved those magical stories from his youth.

« »

They nerved themselves for a dip in the lake. All afternoon, reading in the Adirondack chairs, their legs and chests coated with Age Shield, their faces shaded by broad brims and the porch roof, they had heated themselves up enough to need cooling off. They grabbed towels, slipped into flip-flops, and padded down to the sand.

"After dark, we can skinny dip," Joel said with a suggestive glance.

"And we'll be asleep by ten," said Sean.

In sunlight, they soon got used to the water and didn't want to get out. Sean floated about, pushing his feet off the sandy bottom, gazing up into the blue. Gitche Manito was everywhere. If mythic time was all time, then that afternoon was also mythical, all myths, all times and places. What was the difference between metaphor and reality? Sean never had such thoughts splashing in Lake Michigan among so many fellow human beings, but he was having them there in the Big-Sea-Water.

He was still floating when Joel got out and toweled off his goose bumps. Sean had to remind himself that he was no old Indian but a sixty-five-year-old white man and that there could not possibly be a Master of Life smiling down at him from those passing clouds.

When they had warmed up and dressed, they strode over to Nokomis to pump some coffee from what Phil called his samovar. They went to sit in the rocking chairs on the wide veranda, and soon enough, Phil came out of his office and took the Adirondack chair beside them. They greeted him as an old friend, though they had yet to spend a full day at Mishe-Mokwa. Joel reported on the canoeing and the sunny swim, and Phil happily took credit for it all. Cinder came out and lay in a patch of light on the pine boards.

"So how did you fellas hear about us?" Phil asked, reaching down to scratch the dog's gray head.

"I searched online for lakeside cabins," said Joel. "The photo of your big bear did it."

"Ugly old rotten thing," Phil said. "My father chain-sawed him from a tall pine he felled the summer I was three. My earliest memory, that tree falling and watching the stump turn into a bear." He tugged at his grizzled beard and chuckled like an old prospector in a Western movie.

"You put up the site yourself?"

"This place?"

"I meant your website."

"Oh, I took you to mean this site here. There isn't a better one for watching the summer sunset. We're just enough off the road and close to the state park. Of course, that fancy motel had to come in up the way, but it can't offer what we can. The website? No, I hired a gal in Ironwood. I use it easy now. She's got me trained. In this business, you gotta have these things. What sorta business you fellas in?"

Sean had assumed Phil only wanted them to listen to his own

tales, but he seemed genuinely curious about theirs. Some of his mother's music books were still in the piano bench, he said, so maybe Joel could play a little after supper. He missed hearing his mother play. And when Sean told him about the North Side Housing Collective and all his years doing poverty work, getting by on stingy commissions from landlords and grants and fundraising from rich donors, Phil declared he was glad to live out in the wilds where he could do for himself. His cabins, one after another, had been built by his father with some local men, and when Phil got older, he'd helped out with the last two. "Ten cabins and the lodge," he said, "all hand-hewn from these woods, and enough chopped and split logs to keep me warm all winter."

"You're out here alone?" Sean asked, though he'd already been told so.

"Sure am. Sylvie goes back to town, so I get my own grub. There's plenty to keep me busy, shutting things down, doing repairs, opening up again. I do go see the old folks in Georgia, but I don't like it much down there. Not my kinda land, all scrub and clay. This here's my home. What else did I ever know? A guest once called me a prime example of autodidact, if you know what that is."

"That's a fine thing to be," Sean said.

"You bet it is," said Phil Kimbley. "Why should anyone else tell me what I should know? Well, I'll go give Sylvie a hand, so you fellas rock in your chairs and breathe easy." His dog followed him to the kitchen.

« »

Sean had begun to wonder if Phil didn't somewhat put on his folksiness. His parents had been sixties hippies, back-to-the-landers. They'd given their son a world completely apart from their own. He'd never known the comforts they'd grown up with, never had their advantages.

90

At supper, Joel got talking to the older couple from Wayzata, Minnesota, who'd been coming to Mishe-Mokwa for two dozen summers. They'd known the Kimbleys and adored them, the wife said, and they could remember Phil as a wild little teenager. Then the husband urged Joel to play something for them if the Moores, the shy couple, didn't mind. A lone guest, a man who came for the fishing, said, "Don't mind me, I'm hitting the sack."

When Phil came in to clear off and refill their decafs, Joel went to inspect the piano bench. "Schubert's B-flat!" he announced. "Phil, your mom must be a real pianist. Schumann's Symphonic Etudes! That's way too difficult for me. Maybe I can manage the slow movement of the Schubert. I'm not really a pianist. I'm a violist."

"You're a what?" Phil asked.

"I play the fatter kind of violin."

The shy woman added, "He plays in a string quartet, Mr. Kimbley. We're music lovers, Bill and I, but we don't play, just listen." Bill was looking into his lap. Perhaps he'd rather be alone with his new wife or, if they'd been together for years, go off somewhere by himself.

Joel spread the music on the rack of the old upright and tried a few chords. "It'll do," he said.

"She's a sturdy old piano," said Phil, "but she goes in and out of tune with the weather. Having a good day, I reckon."

In Nokomis Lodge, with the setting sun turning the blue lake pinkish, they began to hear lovely music from two centuries ago. Sean hadn't grown up with classical music. His dad preferred musical comedies, and Mom liked folk music. But having lived with Joel for so long, his kind of music had slowly worked its way into Sean's ears. Joel played now with tightened lips and sharp eyes shifting from the rack to the keys. He seemed so close to a beautiful inexplicable thing. Sean did start to feel each turn of the melody, each changing chord, as if the music was inside him, too. He couldn't say what it meant. The notes had sad and gentle meanings of their own he could not find words for.

Sean looked at young Mrs. Moore from Wisconsin, her mouth pursed in the shape of a kiss, as if to keep her from speaking. Her husband had turned to gaze out at the darkening sky. The elderly Minnesotans were sitting up straight in their chairs like attentive pupils. Phil Kimbley had stopped to lean in the kitchen doorway, holding a stack of smeary dessert plates, no doubt remembering his mom at her piano.

« »

On the excuse that the night had grown too cold, they didn't skinny dip. But they did sit out on their porch with several bug candles burning while Joel read aloud. "*On the shores of Gitche Gumee,*" he began in that hypnotic rhythm,

> *Of the shining Big-Sea-Water,*
> *Stood Nokomis, the old woman,*
> *Pointing with her finger westward,*
> *O'er the water pointing westward,*
> *To the purple clouds of sunset.*

It was the same sunset they had seen while Joel played his slow beautiful music.

Now, holding the heavy book up to the candlelight, he read Sean the story of the Manito of Wampum who sent the fiery fever, sent disease and death, and was at last slain by Hiawatha. "*All the trophies of the battle, he divided with his people, shared it equally among them.*" Joel set the book down in his lap and said, "See, Sean, a white man would've kept the loot for himself."

"Not only that," said Sean, "but the white man would've sided with the Manito of Wampum all along. I never wanted to be white, anyway."

"I know, I know, you used to run around like a naked Indian in your grandmother's meadow. You were such a little horndogger, Tyson. I wish I'd known you in your naked Indian days."

"I wouldn't have known what to do with you yet."

"I could've helped you with that," said Joel. "I'd figured it out all by my country-boy self."

They sat awhile, thinking back. Joel always kidded Sean for being so slow catching onto things. After they met, it had taken him weeks to realize that Joel's enthusiasm went deeper than for a mere affair. He simply couldn't believe that such an adorable curly-headed fellow would be that serious about him. When he found himself feeling things he'd never felt before, it was a huge surprise that Joel felt them, too.

"So am I right about your Indian thing being adolescent horniness not knowing what to do with itself?"

"Come on, Joel," Sean said. "I was a super-serious kid. I was worried about the Quimby farmland not being rightfully ours."

"That sounds more like Davey Nussbaum. Right on, comrade! Now, why don't you come inside and go all Ojibway on me!"

"Oh, shut up, Joel."

They saw a light switch on in Iagoo next door where the Moores were staying. Had they heard and taken offense? Sean felt sorry for the wife, who had followed Joel's playing so intently while her handsome husband looked out the window. But he couldn't know what another couple was like. Sometimes, he hardly knew what went on between him and Joel. Suddenly, he thought of Owen, which had a certain stimulating effect.

"All right, young man," he said in a stern whisper. "Get your ass in there and take off your clothes."

"Cowabunga!" said Joel.

That almost spoiled it, but Sean quickly conjured up Owen wandering lonesomely around Boys Town after dark. He blew out the bug candles and followed the shadowy male figure through the screen door that shut behind him with a click.

93

2 "Today you hike the Porkies?" Phil asked, taking a chair at the neighboring table while they finished their coffees and Sylvie's breakfast pasties. "Perfect day for it."

"I was there on my camp's trip when I was eleven," Sean said, though he'd mentioned it the night they arrived.

"Even before my folks were here," Phil noted. "I'd like to have seen things then. I bet there weren't all those marked trails. It was wilderness pretty much when my folks came. I was a baby. By the time I can recollect, most of the cabins were up. I helped a little on Osseo and Oweenee. They're booked today, along with Pau-Puk-Keewis."

He'd told them so yesterday, but when you didn't really know people and probably wouldn't be seeing them again, the conversation didn't have to go anywhere. Phil said the same sorts of things to the elderly couple that had known him as a boy, his way of playing host.

"When you fellas get back this afternoon, the place'll be filling up," he warned them now. "Big family from Iowa—grandmothers, kids, grandkids. They're the ones that want your cabin next week for more cousins. August's always booked."

"So it'll get lively around here," Sean said, trying not to sound apprehensive.

"Don't worry, Mr. Tyson. Sylvie's good with little ones. She'll keep the grandkids from screaming too much. That's how she raised me, isn't it?" He stood and turned his chair around to move it closer, straddle it, and lean on the backrest. Old Cinder's pale eyes were watching from the kitchen. "Now, you got your trail maps?"

"We've been studying them," Joel said. "I come from the Ocooch Mountains myself, down in Wisconsin."

"They're not really mountains," said Sean, "and he comes from Chicago."

"They are so mountains! Geologically, they're ancient mountains eroded over millennia. The glaciers had to go around them."

94

"The Porkies are mountains, too," Phil said. "Not your Western mountains, not even your Eastern mountains, but plain old Midwestern mountains, that's all. Hey, I see you been reading your *Hiawatha*. My dad collected those books, put them in every cabin instead of Bibles. You know how Henry Wadsworth Longfellow got those stories? There was a man named Schoolcraft who studied the Indian languages. He came out here and married this Ojibway girl on Madeline Island." Phil pointed out over the lake. "That's where she told him those stories. But he heads back east and tells 'em to his poet friend and then goes and marries himself a white woman. Michigan even named a county after him. The Ojibway girl sure didn't get no county! Yep, my dad used to put me to bed with that old poem. You see how he named all the cabins? My folks had Hiawatha back then, and I slept over in Minnehaha with Sylvie. Later, I got my own room off the kitchen where my office is now. I was only nineteen when the folks started taking winters on that Georgia island and left me caring for the place. I don't miss 'em that much up here. I've always been mostly on my own. I got Cinder. And I still got Sylvie, right, old girl?" She had come in to set up for the late-sleeping Moores. The fisherman must have had his breakfast at dawn and driven off to his trout stream.

Sylvie said, "I never thought those wide-eyed rich kids would last as long as they did. When you've actually been raised here, like Phil and me, you don't see much sense in going anywhere else."

"Forest, lake, and sky," Phil said. "Our kinda country."

"I guess everyone has a place he feels he belongs in," said Joel.

Sean quickly added, "I belong in Chicago."

"But you gotta get out now and again, don't you?" Phil asked.

"Man, does he ever!" said Joel.

They parked the little Chevy and took the Escarpment Trail toward the Lake of the Clouds. It was coming back to Sean from being eleven amongst a troop of campers, hiking on their short legs up what they took for a magnificent mountain with their heavy backpacks and their counselor, who was probably twenty-one but seemed like a dad. He'd talk tough if they dawdled. Now it was Joel dawdling, contemplating views of the woods and hills. Sean felt some powerful psychic magnet drawing him back to a spot he'd seen as a boy and expected to recognize from the depths of his memory.

The trail had certainly been improved since 1957. Sean had greater strength in his legs, and the incline seemed less daunting. His lung power had increased since his asthmatic youth. After his father left the family, he never had another attack.

"Slow it down," barked Joel, catching up from behind. "I'm the outdoorsy one. You're the sluggard."

"Not today. Besides, I've been here before." And he added the startling fact: "fifty-four summers ago."

"I wish I'd seen funny little Quimby huffing and puffing and being picked on by the cool kids."

"I wasn't picked on. I was nice to everybody."

"I was a snotty little twerp," said Joel. "If a kid made fun of my fiddle, I'd call him a dumb farmer."

"And he'd pound the crap out of you."

"Hell no! I could wriggle out of any hold."

The trail was ascending more sharply now. They were getting nearer. They heard women's voices ahead, and soon three middle-aged couples were coming down the trail toward them. The wives were chatting, the husbands strolling silently behind. "Oh, it's breathtaking, it's worth the climb," one woman told them. "But don't go near the edge," said another, "it goes right straight down." "But so gorgeous," her heartier friend said. The third woman just smiled and said, "Hi." The men nodded as they passed. They must've been in their sixties, but Sean saw them as an older generation.

Before he made it to the very top, he suddenly stopped on the path. He had to prepare himself for the sight. Joel gave him a nudge and said, "Get the old man up the mountain." He leaned in and started gently pushing. "Now, Mr. Tyson, you can do it, it's your daily regimen."

"Yes, Dr. Greenwood." He let himself be budged forward.

When Joel stopped shoving, he wrapped his arms around Sean's waist and said, "Poor old Quimby."

There was light through the trees, and soon they were out on bare rock. Sean stepped up to a high flat slab and looked down at the pale Lake of the Clouds. It was exactly what he'd seen as a boy, the very angle of the view. He must've stood precisely there. He shut his eyes, waited a moment, looked again, then shut his eyes to imagine being surrounded by shouting little campers.

When he opened his eyes again, Joel said, "So?"

"It was all entirely new to me then," Sean said, "standing on a cliff and looking down at miles of trees and a silvery lake and no people. I was proud of myself. This was the only mountain I'd ever climbed. I stood on this exact spot when I was eleven and not once in between, and I've remembered it."

« »

They had the top to themselves for twenty minutes before some other middle-aged tourists trudged up. The two men came right up and started talking about their trip. They and the gals were on a lakeshore tour, from Duluth all the way to the Soo, where they'd drop off the rental van and fly home to Indianapolis. They were at the big motel past those funky cabins—first-rate suites, nice full bar, clean pool and hot tub, great meals, sandy beach though the lake was too damn cold. The fatter man wore a tightly stretched Porcupine

97

Mountains T-shirt with a bear on it, not a porcupine. Joel interrupted with the information that they were staying at the cabins. "They looked too damn primitive," the fatter man said. "We've just retired. We deserve some luxuries. You guys may like roughing it, but wait till you hit sixty-five!"

Sean and Joel only glanced at each other, not to spoil the flattering effect.

The thinner husband asked, "You guys leave the ladies at home? We had to drag ours along." Their wives clucked their disapproval.

"Well, we've put up with each other for forty years," said the fat husband.

"Forty-one," said his wife.

"Anyways," he went on, "I guess we can make it for a few more."

"We know all about married life," said Joel.

Sean immediately cut in with "We're heading on down to the lake, I guess. Enjoy the view."

"There was a time I could've handled a trail like that," the thin husband said.

"Sure you could," said his wife.

"Now I only want to get back to a beer and that hot tub."

Sean had located the trailhead and beckoned Joel. Once out of sight, he whispered, "I was afraid you were going to make a point. It wouldn't be worth the awkwardness."

"Look, is that bear poop?" Joel asked irrelevantly. "Now, be more careful, Mr. Tyson. You might slip."

A squabble avoided, they didn't say more till they got down to the Lake of the Clouds. On his camp's trip, they had only looked from above and then gone back to their tents where the counselors scared them with tales of tomahawks and scalpings.

There was a patch of moss to sit on. They aired out their feet and cooled them in the lake and ate Sylvie's sandwiches and drank the cans of lemonade. The water was sending off flashes of yellow with the sun approaching noon.

"Are you sure you can make the whole loop?" Joel asked. "It's four miles to Government Peak and another four back to the car."

"You tuckered out already?" Sean said.

"No, but you are."

"Hardly," Sean said.

Joel was studying the park map. "It's eighteen hundred and fifty feet, the peak."

"That's from sea level. We're starting halfway there." He could tell Joel was dreading the long slog, but if Sean was to be dragged around Richland County next week, he was going to force Joel up another mountain.

It began easily enough. Getting to the summit wasn't so bad, and they even thought they could make out the islands to the west, misty blurs on the horizon. That was where Hiawatha came from, that was the land he had to leave when the French priests arrived in their canoes. The end of the poem had made a strong impression in Mr. Gault's class. The Indians had been kind to the Black Robes, who told them stories of the Virgin and her Son. That was when Sean had stopped considering himself a Christian.

Coming down from the peak, there wasn't anything more to look forward to but the little Chevy. Their calves and thighs ached more going down than up, their knees and hips creaked, their shoulders were sore, and even their necks barely held up their hanging heads. When they were getting nearer and saw a fork for the Overlook Trail, Joel said, "Hey, let's go that way. It's only an extra 2.7 miles."

All Sean had to say was "Fuck you!" and on they trudged.

When, at last, they sighted the little gray car in the now quite full lot, they stumbled toward it and collapsed inside. They had passed the age to be making nine-mile treks. The men from Indianapolis needed no excuses for soaking in a hot tub with a beer. Did Sean and Joel think they had to keep hiking, keep climbing, keep moving, if they weren't to come to such a lazy capitulation?

99

Mishe-Mokwa was swarming with Iowans, little ones chasing each other, squealing and giggling, bigger lunky ones hanging out in the pines, moms and dads settling into their cabins, the old ladies rocking and gossiping on the Nokomis porch. Sean and Joel offered no more than friendly waves and dragged themselves to Chibiabos. They dropped their packs, yanked off their dusty boots and socks, and went straight into Gitche Gumee up to their hiking shorts. "Oh, hell," Joel said and plunged in all the way. Sean cupped his hands to splash his face and rub his sore arms then went back to the cabin and flopped on the bed. Soon Joel came inside and stripped to his wet blue skimpies and flopped beside him.

They only woke to the clanging dinner bell and shouts of frazzled parents corralling their young. When they hobbled in late, they found Sylvie had cooked a massive kettle of stew and four big pans of corn bread with deep bowls of her coleslaw alongside. Sean and Joel's usual table by the window had been commandeered by the Iowa grandmothers, so handsome Bill Moore suggested they join them. His wife seemed surprised at his gesture. Sean set down their heaping plates on the checkered oilcloth, and Joel soon returned with glasses of cider. The four of them feasted on the simmering stew and buttered crumbling corn bread and the spicy coleslaw. It was as if Phil Kimbley had invited two dozen total strangers to his private woodland celebration.

"You've been out exploring?" Bill asked.

Joel gave a much too thorough account of their hike. Sean wished he'd keep it short so they could ask the Moores about their day, but Joel was proud of his achievement and had to make a long story of it.

"Molly's afraid of bears in the woods," Bill said.

"I saw what I suspect was bear poop," said Joel. "It could've been coyote, but it had berries in it."

"They sleep during the day, don't they?" Molly asked.

"She's so worried about wild animal life," said her husband.

"I worry about the poor animals themselves, Bill. I'm not afraid. I just want to leave them undisturbed. It's their habitat, not ours."

"Humans intend to inhabit everywhere, honey."

"But it's so presumptuous of us."

"Out there, I wasn't thinking about bears," said Joel. "I was thinking how crazy we were to be taking an all-day hike."

At Sean's prompting, the Moores did explain that they'd gotten married only a month ago but had been living together for ten years. Molly said this was a sort of honeymoon. Then Joel told about them getting married in Iowa as soon as it was legal. One of the moms, hearing Iowa invoked, turned and apologized for their noisy crew. "Oh, no, we love kids," Sean said untruthfully and then turned back to the Moores.

"So you two lived together even longer than we did," said Molly, "not married, I mean."

"They didn't have a choice, honey."

"I was quite content to leave it that way," Sean said.

"We'd been together almost half our lives," Joel said, "and I still had to drag him into it. But he must admit, when we saw our names together on a state document, he got a little tearful. Yes, you did, Shaw-awn."

"Yes, but why?" Sean joked.

"If it's any comfort," said Bill Moore, "for us, marriage was a practical thing. We didn't make it a big deal."

"Yet for you guys," said Molly, "it had to be a bigger deal when you finally could."

"That's what I told Sean," said Joel. "Have you two been reading your *Hiawatha*? Last night, I got to the part where he marries Minnehaha."

"I saw you reading that big old book on your porch," Molly said. "You were reading out loud, but I couldn't quite hear."

"I leafed through our copy," said Bill, "but it seemed to condescend to native culture."

With sudden vehemence, Joel said, "It's not condescending at all! Who else back then took Indians so seriously?"

"The Indians did."

"We should read it and decide, Bill," said Molly.

"I don't mean to argue," he said, "but at UW we're sensitive to these things."

"What I was going to say," said Joel, revving up again, "was that Hiawatha had the kind of wedding Sean and I should've had. Pau-Puk-Keewis danced and Chibiabos sang and old Nokomis cooked sturgeon and wild rice and bison, and Iagoo—"

"That's our cabin," said Molly.

"And Iagoo told the story of poor old ugly Osseo, son of the Evening Star, and the lovely young Oweenee. It could be a cantata, Osseo and Oweenee, for soprano, baritone, chorus, and string quartet."

"This is where his mind goes," Sean explained to the Moores.

3 "Do you think the money's made it to our AmTrust branch yet?" Joel asked, the moment Sean woke to the morning sun.

He stretched his aching joints. "What money?"

"The money, Shaw-awn!"

They had agreed not to discuss the issue after Sean had signed the documents.

Joel was propped, fully awake, on an elbow. "Because then we could actually put cash down when we find the perfect place."

"We?"

Joel leaned over and kissed Sean's forehead. He'd obviously been daydreaming of old farmhouses. "Sorry, I shouldn't have said—"

"Correct." Sean rolled to his other aching side.

"So we're not leaving camp today," Joel said. "Phil promised that the whole Iowa clan is picnicking up at the park, so it'll be quiet.

Molly and Bill turned out to be nice, don't you think? They're from Wisconsin. They could be our new neighbors. Uh-oh."

Sean let it pass. He didn't want to get up yet. Phil had said it might rain. They could sit all day reading on their porch, though Sean was about to give up on *An American Tragedy* before what he feared was going to happen happened. He should've known from the title that it was a disturbing story. At Phil's resort, those boating scenes were all too real.

"I'm going to the lodge to bring you a coffee, tired old Quimby." Joel was pulling on his shorts and Foxridge Academy T-shirt. In the morning light, he looked and acted like a high-school boy. "And a pasty?"

"Just coffee."

Sean was slowly coming into full consciousness when an excited Joel returned. It seemed he had bumped into Molly Moore, who had used Phil's Wi-Fi to search "Hiawatha" and find out what academics said about it, and she'd also come up with a musical setting to download for Joel. "Damn, someone beat me to it," he said. "I never heard of the composer—Samuel Coleridge-Taylor?"

"Samuel Taylor Coleridge," Sean murmured from the bed. "He wrote about Xanadu and the Ancient Mariner."

"No, I'm right—Samuel Coleridge-Taylor. He was half African. Molly read me the Wikipedia entry. See, you can find out anything up here in the woods. She's bringing over her iPad, so I can listen."

"Not now, Joel," Sean pleaded. "Let's listen to the birds."

Joel crawled in beside him and laid his head on Sean's chest while they sipped from their hot mugs. Then there was a footstep on the porch and a tentative knock on the doorframe. Joel leaped up. "That's her already! I asked her to come help me get you out of bed."

Sean pulled the sheet up to his neck, and there came Molly, no longer so timid. "Good morning, Sean. I told Joel I know shiatsu, if that would help."

"He's the one in need of shiatsu," Sean said, not meaning to sound perturbed. "No, I'll be my usual self after breakfast. We overdid yesterday."

"Later, Bill and I are going to paddle along the shore, if you're up to taking out a second canoe."

"Please, all I want is a day of rest." Again, Sean was afraid he was sounding impatient, but Molly only gave a gentle laugh.

She was a slim, tidy young woman. At first, Sean hadn't quite registered her looks, but now, with her smiles and her not being as shy, she seemed rather pretty. It always took him longer to distinguish between women. Men snapped into focus right away, but with women, he needed more time to see them in full.

"Well, come eat while Bill and I are lingering over coffee," she said. Joel followed her out. He had a way of attaching himself to women that sometimes made Sean jealous. He did like the Moores, but he hadn't come up there to make new friends.

« »

He got his wish. The clouds began to gather before noon, and during lunch, with only the old Minnesotans in the lodge, the rain began. Sean and Joel reclaimed their table at the window, and when Bill and Molly came in from an abbreviated canoe trip, they took the closest two-person table. All six of them got to talking like old pals. At the thought of the family picnic in the Porkies, they shared an uncharitable laugh. Phil Kimbley, when he came back from a supply run to Ontonagon, pulled up a chair and reminisced with the old folks he called Scott and Trudy who kept coming back every summer. They didn't seem to do much but sit on the porch of Wenonah and look through the sap-dripping pine trunks at the horizon.

"I was a baby when my parents brought me up here," Phil told the newcomers once again. "All they had was the Grizzly, Dad's old jeep. Mudjekeewis was the one cabin already here. It gave Dad the idea to name all the new ones. We only had an outhouse and a pump before Nokomis got built. Of course, he hired men from town to help. What did he know about homesteading? He'd come up from your neck of the woods, fellas, outside Chicago, I mean. But in those days, college kids like them split for some simple country living."

"Some of us split for the city."

"Sean was once a flaming radical," said Joel.

"I'm just an old-fashioned Midwestern socialist like your grandfather, Joel. I should've lived a hundred years ago."

"My parents are plain working folks," Bill Moore said, "and they tried to give me a better life than they had." The faint lines crinkled around his eyes, and his freckles were reddening. He seemed put off by what Sean had said.

"It's a complex system we're living under," said elderly Scott. "In years to come, I don't know how anyone will ever make it. Trudy and I were sure lucky to make it when we did, right, dear? We're not Tea Partiers or anything, but I'm not too crazy about the way things are going."

"I don't think about politics much up here," said Phil. It seemed his hostly way of avoiding any unpleasantness.

After lunch, Sean went to look over the bookshelves past the piano. He pulled out a novel, *The Real Adventure* by Henry Kitchell Webster. The torn and faded jacket said it was the best-selling novel in America in 1915. It told the story of a young wife in Chicago who leaves her husband and children to go back to school and do something of her own, which sounded advanced for the time.

"Take your pick," said Phil. "Guests leave 'em. Some are what my father found in Mudjekeewis from when an old codger lived here all by himself." He made his way out to join the Moores, now watching the downpour from the front porch.

"Oh, no, you're not reading another one of those," Joel said when he saw Sean leafing through the pages. "Why don't you ever read a book about life today?"

"You play all your old music."

"But my music doesn't go out of date, Shaw-awn."

"I like reading about how it was before the First World War."

They could hear Phil out there telling Bill and Molly how glad he was he'd never married, never had children, but he did have a couple of lady friends in Ontonagon. It was the story he'd told Sean and Joel when they arrived. "I know what works for me," he was saying with a satisfied chuckle.

Sylvie had appeared in the kitchen doorway, muttering, "And I know who's worked for him all these years!"

《 》

They dashed across the squishy grass and pine needles, *The Real Adventure* tucked under Sean's shirttails. He was happily imagining an afternoon by themselves with the rain pattering on the cabin roof. Joel got right into bed and plugged himself into Molly's iPad, and Sean took an Adirondack chair on the porch. The curtain of raindrops off the eaves gave the trees and lake the look of the gray etchings in *The Song of Hiawatha*. Sean pictured some Storm Spirit in the dark clouds and a fleet of birch-bark canoes paddling toward shore. Soon though, the book was taking him back home to old Chicago. It was a more reassuring story than Theodore Dreiser's.

At one point through the falling rain, he heard Phil yell gruffly to Sylvie that he was taking the truck and Cinder up to the park to check on those soaked picnickers. He doubted they had enough sense to come down to the shelter. When the chugging engine had faded away, there came another crunching on the gravel, the fisherman back from his stream. Sylvie called from the kitchen window, and he called back that they'd all be having fresh trout for dinner. Then, all was quiet again.

There was a light on in Iagoo where Bill and Molly were also, perhaps, reading peacefully. The Minnesotans were probably sitting on their porch gazing out through the rain like Sean. In ancient times, weather must've been everyone's first thought. They had to study the habits of the animals and the seasons of the corn and berries and the wild rice that grew in water. They had to fear the other peoples beyond the mountains or farther along the shore. Gitche Manito had taught them to smoke the peace pipe, but they were still his helpless children and kept making terrible mistakes. They envisioned their Great Spirit as a man, a father, because they had need of his strong, protecting arms. Sean knew how, even today, religious people, even the halfhearted ones, even most women, continued to think of "God" as a father. It was total bullshit, as Joel would say.

It was the beating of the rain that was causing Sean's thoughts to go floating off through time and space. He simply didn't want to think about what was coming next week. Joel was inside on the bed, plugged into his dreamy music world. It was the safest place for him.

« »

When the rain let up, Sean set down his book and watched the trees shed the last drops of the storm. Mist was rising off the lake. He felt suspended in a rare atmosphere, both ancient and fresh. Then the creaking of bedsprings alerted him to Joel padding into sight.

"Aren't you cold out here, Quimby?"

"It's invigorating."

"I'm invigorated, too," said Joel, "by this Samuel Coleridge-Taylor guy you didn't think existed."

"It just seemed odd that—"

"You always think you know things, Tyson. Anyway, it's amazing how he got so many different rhythms out of all that regular meter. It's nineteenth-century harmonies, of course, but I didn't expect a composer I never heard of to be this good. I'm such a pathetic miniaturist! I could never sustain anything that long." He slumped into the other chair but perked up when the sun began to break through. "I guess I can feel pathetic and invigorated at the same time," he said, though Sean knew Joel's moods weren't exactly simultaneous; they simply flipped quickly. Soon Joel was sitting up, eager to talk. "It was very sad, the last scene. I haven't read that far yet, but now from the musical setting I know how it's going to end. First, the famine comes, then Minnehaha dies. Then there's nothing left, and the priests get there, and Hiawatha has to paddle away to the land of Ponemah. I started to cry, Sean. And those Frenchmen were fucking anti-Semites! They were preaching the gospel, warning those poor Indians about the Jews. They had to start all that again over here!"

"Maybe we could go canoeing now, Joel. I'm not feeling as stiff."

"Aren't you listening to me?"

"Sorry, but I was noticing the lake's so smooth, and we've been lazing about—"

"And I was talking about crying because of that music and those priests or whatever they were! Jesus Christ! So now you want to go canoeing and you didn't want to with Molly this morning."

"But now, just ourselves."

"You're not so into her. Bill's more your type."

"Come on, Joel. You've been listening and I've been reading, and now we could go out on the lake in the sunshine."

"I was crying over that music! I wasn't just plowing through another old book."

Sean did not apologize again, but at least he didn't quibble.

The gravel crunched louder than usual. Phil must have pulled in fast. "Where's the crowd?" came an old woman's voice from the Wenonah porch.

"They're toughing it out," yelled Phil. "The grandmothers were playing cards in the shelter. The little ones were chasing each other in and out. One kid was singing something godawful with his ukulele. They'd made quite the barbecue. I had to heave Cinder into the truck with all those folks to beg from." Phil's voice was fading as he and the dog headed for their cabin.

"All right," said Joel in a sulky voice, "we'll go canoeing. Maybe the Moores will be up for it again."

To Joel's delight, it was only Molly who wanted to come along. Bill was preparing his paper for a sociology conference. They took the longest canoe and gave Molly the middle seat so the men could do the paddling. It was relaxing, gliding along the still water after the storm with that pretty young woman between them. Joel kept being distracted, pointing things out on the shore, so Sean kept them on course. He aimed for where the mountains came down to the lake. Joel and Molly were talking about what it was like being in a couple with someone so different from yourself. "It was probably what attracted us," she suggested, "but later on it can get to be a serious obstacle to domestic tranquility."

"Are you referring to me?" Sean asked, half humorously.

"I'm talking about Bill," said Molly.

"I'm talking about you, Sean," Joel said.

4 The rain had swept the sky clean. The stars that night, with the occasional Perseid shooting across the blackness over the lake, faintly illuminated Sean and Joel, sitting side by side on the sand at the shore. They held each other's hand and leaned in, their arms encircling them for warmth. No one else was awake, or if anyone was, nothing was heard, no murmurs or shuffles or throat clearings. The lodge's one light seemed to flicker when the pine boughs swayed. Sean could detect the shadowed form of Mishe-Mokwa, the bear, with his upraised arms, threateningly holding the WELCOME sign. Such almost darkness set the seal on the day.

In the morning, they both woke more rested than they'd felt in months. Joel was up first, doing his stretches and puttering about, humming tunes that must've come from that *Hiawatha* music. He could reproduce melodies he'd heard only once. His ear was attuned to notes in a way Sean's eye wasn't to words. As soon as he finished a book, he'd forget the characters' names and most of what they'd done. What remained was an atmosphere the story left behind. These atmospheres, layered book upon book, were what persisted from his years of reading.

But there was Joel, humming music he could call up out of his memory. Sean stretched himself out, toes to the foot of the bed, arms back to touch the wall. "About time," said Joel.

"You go on over. I'll be right there."

When Joel had trotted off, Sean got up and inspected his leathery, sagging chest and arms, puffed himself up to approximate his fifty-year-old self, maybe for a moment himself at forty, if he squinted. He showered quickly in the lukewarm spray, toweled off, pulled on his shorts and striped short-sleeve shirt, and flip-flopped to the lodge. He found Joel sharing a table with the Moores. They were all earlier than the Iowans, who last night had skipped the trout dinner after their rainy picnic and had been remarkably quiet in their cabins.

"Beautiful morning," said Bill with a flashing smile. After yesterday, Sean was a little leery of him. Joel was wrong to see him as Sean's type.

"We've been talking about the four of us doing the Lake Superior trail," Joel said. "It's only two miles to Buckshot Cabin. We could also go on to Lone Rock or partway."

"Well," said Sean, taking the fourth chair with his mug of coffee, "I guess I've loosened up enough to give it a try."

Joel coaxed more enthusiasm from him by promising great views of Gitche Gumee.

« »

The trail went up and down, crossed streams, gave them glimpses and then wider panoramas of lake and sky. It was slow going. Bill dropped back with Sean while Joel and his buddy Molly forged ahead.

"It's good for her, talking to him," Bill said, as if to himself.

"It's good for Joel, too," said Sean. "He can let off steam."

"I'm not the most forthcoming person, Sean," Bill suddenly confessed. "It's getting worse. I'm very busy with my work, but here's the irony: what I'm researching now is whether American men tend to get more silent with age while women need to talk more."

"It must depend on the man and the woman," Sean said, "but maybe there's a general tendency—"

"In our culture," Bill said, "but it's hard to isolate, chicken-and-egg stuff, nature versus nurture. I'm not concerned with biology or psychology. I'm trying to quantify cultural norms."

"Sociologists get to do interesting stuff," Sean said, though he remained skeptical of statistics. He could tell that Bill wanted to explain more, so he listened politely.

"I started with a roomful of a dozen thirty-something straight white men, like myself, and observed them through one-way glass. They almost entirely avoided intimate conversations. Then I tried a dozen such women in the room, and they got right down to it."

"You should try gay men," Sean said. "Put Joel in there."

"Oh, I'm doing a range of groups—gender, age, race, all that, and then mixing it up. I'll definitely include sexual orientation."

"Can't avoid it these days," Sean said, to be funny.

"It's shameful how long we sociologists did," said serious Bill.

"What about you and Molly?"

Bill winced, crinkling the pale skin by his eyes. "We do talk," he said, "but she does most of it."

"When we first met you, she seemed shy."

"Oh, she's not shy," Bill said.

The uneven terrain caused him to be silent for a stretch. Sean could hear Joel and Molly chatting ahead. They had stopped at a rocky ledge to take in what the map noted as a scenic vista. Sean and Bill caught up, and they all took time admiring the silvery blue lake and the sharp clear horizon. Far out there lay Canada.

"So what have you been saying about me?" Joel asked, which drew a gentle giggle from Molly.

"Actually," Bill said, "I've been telling Sean about my research."

"Typical," said Molly. "He's never truly on vacation."

"And I've been letting Molly know how stuck in the mud you are and how I have to force you to go look at old farmhouses."

"For now," Sean said, "let's just look at the lake."

"Molly thinks you could at least give me a chance."

"Yes, but since it's your inheritance," Molly quickly put in, "you should do what you want with it, Sean. I don't want to get between you two."

"Well, thanks to the Iowa Supreme Court, what's his is also mine," Joel proclaimed and gave Sean a long possessive squeeze.

"We keep our own finances separate," Bill said, "because I do make much more and get our health plan through the university, and I put the money down on our condo."

"And I'm fine with that," said Molly. "I like being taken care of."

"From each according to his ability," Sean quoted, "to each according to his—or her—need."

"He gave a book report in seventh grade on *The Communist Manifesto*," Joel told them. "He's so proud of himself."

"Because I already didn't like the idea of some people having so much more than others. Something in my childhood must've—"

"Let's head on," Bill said impatiently.

Soon he and Sean had resumed their man-to-man conversation. Bill confessed that in college he'd been a pretty staunch Republican like his dad. Then he met Molly, who was basically an anti–Iraq War Democrat. "Yeah, I didn't vote for Bush the second time, so I had to vote for Kerry, though he seemed like such a snob. I'll probably vote for Obama again next year. See what love can do for your politics?"

"I wish mine could move Joel back to a little more reality."

The other two were already far ahead. Sean couldn't tell if Bill was going slow for the old gent's sake or if he wanted to keep talking in private. "Molly's even afraid my research will help some corporation improve its marketing," Bill said, as if to enlist Sean's support. "But I'm just trying to see what social settings lead to trust and understanding. My hypothesis is that it gets better the more people mix, that monolithic societies are more defensive. It's counterintuitive."

"A hard thing to prove," Sean said.

"I know. Look at Wisconsin. My parents still have a Scott Walker sign on their lawn. We don't talk about it. If I hadn't been with Molly, I would've been voting for him, too, because I owe my dad my college education. He sent me off to Madison on his savings, so I can't ever come home a Democrat." At last, Bill managed a laugh.

Sean felt his knees beginning to give out. He hoped it wasn't far to Buckshot Cabin, but he was pleased how the talk was going and didn't want it to end. Up ahead, Joel and Molly had stopped at another lake view and were waiting for the stragglers.

Joel yelled out, "Guess what! Molly has friends in Madison who play chamber music!" Sean was huffing his breaths, but he made it up to the rock they were standing on. "So I can go play quartets and stay over at the Moores' condo, if it's too late to drive back to our farm."

"Now it's our farm," Sean said to Bill.

"Molly, don't be encouraging him," Bill said. "It's not our business."

"I already said it's Sean's money."

"That's still meddling."

"Don't worry," Sean said. "We're always like this. Joel loves little dramas."

"Because otherwise he's so quimby."

"What's this 'quimby' thing with you?" Molly wanted to know.

"It's his middle name. His grandmother was a Quimby. They go back before the Civil War. Quimbys think of themselves as the real Illinois folk. Tysons were business upstarts, but it's the Quimby side that makes him want to lie in bed and read old books. Right,

Shaw-awn? That's how I say it when I want to bug him. My grandfather came over from a remote corner of the Austro-Hungarian Empire. It's why I'm the explorer here."

Sean was only half listening. He was thinking about his weakening knees and hoped no one would push for going beyond Buckshot Cabin.

« »

Two young women, with a little girl and boy, had rented the place for the week. They'd come all the way from St. Louis, they said, to escape the heat and get their children away from computer screens. Sean wondered if they were lesbians or just friends, each with her own kid. Bill insisted he didn't want to spoil their solitude, and the moms did seem relieved to see the hikers turn, after admiring the view, and head back down the trail the way they'd come. Everything looked different to Sean now, with the lake on their left.

What the moms had said about computers caused him to ask Bill if he allowed his research subjects to bring their electronic devices.

"I considered that," Bill said, walking ahead on a narrow stretch of path, "but I opted for a more self-contained sample. The Internet introduces too many variables."

"But," Sean risked saying, "nowadays, people always have their devices."

"Look, Sean," Bill said, a little sharply, "I try to account for cultural forces, and the use of electronics is a big one, but there's plenty of studies out there on technology's effects on social behavior. I'm hoping to get at something more essential."

"But aren't all these devices pretty much essential now? They've changed everything. Molly downloaded some old opera for Joel out of the sky, way up here on Gitche Gumee!"

"That's simply not what I'm looking at!" Bill was sounding exasperated, and Sean knew he'd pushed too hard. "I've tried to be clear, Sean. I'm looking at the behaviors various identities impose on us. Like, do straight white American men think they oughtn't to share intimate thoughts with each other? I'm watching how different samples establish acceptable norms. Do you get it now?" He was walking faster, as if to outdistance the argument.

"I get it," Sean said, raising his voice but continuing to make his point. "Still, you can't avoid electronic communication when it comes to how people interact. It's changed the way I work. I don't talk face to face, or even voice to voice, with landlords or inspectors the way I used to, or even with some tenants."

Bill was now so far ahead that Sean started jogging to reach him. Up there, Joel was yelling that it was time to switch partners. Bill shrugged his shoulders, as if he didn't care one way or the other. "And at the next vista," Joel said, "we'll eat our power bars. I'm wearing out fast."

"Maybe we should let the youngsters set their own pace," Sean said breathlessly.

"No way," said Molly, "it's my turn to walk with you. I see enough of my dear spouse."

"We always say 'spouse' to be gender neutral," Bill explained.

It wasn't obvious if he was being earnest or satirical of his own careful terminology, but Sean fell into step with Molly and watched Joel and Bill stride on ahead and out of earshot.

"Joel's very much connected to you," Molly said. "He wouldn't be himself without you."

"Oh?"

"I think he wants to take you away with him and leave everyone else behind."

"Except when he goes to play quartets with your Madison friends and stays over at your place. My version of Joel making music is going to my job."

"A time will come to retire," said Molly. Her voice was calm and confident. Sean could tell why Joel liked her so much. She'd stopped on the trail and was giving him the same pensive purse-mouthed consideration he'd seen her give Joel playing Schubert. She was quite lovely in the light dappling through the boughs of pine. "And here's a thing about Joel," she said. "He tries to experience each moment. I'm somewhat in touch with that, or I try to be. I mean, I do yoga, I do shiatsu. He was telling me about composing, about finding chords."

"You should hear some of his chords, Molly."

"But he meant that each new harmony is a point in time, moving from measure to measure. I'm only a listener, but I feel what he means. It's that it's all moving toward some still point."

"Joel's hardly still."

"But he's taking it in as it's happening."

"And that makes me the stick-in-the-mud," Sean said. They began walking again, slowly, thoughtfully.

"He's just kidding, the way he calls you Quimby."

"And I'm supposed to sit on a farmhouse porch while a herd of cows moos past on the hillside. What he doesn't think about is what comes before or after. It's not just moments. If he wants to be musical about it, what about long beautiful melodies? And he goes on about thematic development and inverted retrograde or whatever. Look at him, charging along ahead with Bill. Anyway, I understand you turned Bill into a Democrat."

Molly laughed, as if she understood Sean wanted a change of subject. She reached across the path and took his hand in hers. It was strange to go along, walking like that. Sean had never felt quite at ease having physical contact with women. "It took us nearly ten years to decide to get married," Molly said. "His politics were only the start of it. But back to you—"

"Must we?"

"It's only that I wonder," she said, "if Joel isn't in touch with something you aren't."

"I'm in touch with things he isn't. That's just his bullshit," Sean said a little harshly then added, "Sorry."

"No worries," said Molly. "All I really know, Sean, is that he truly wants to quit his job, and he wants you to do so, too. He thinks country living is in your blood. After all, your grandmother Quimby had that farm."

"She was a Tyson by then. It was just the place we went in summers."

"Still," said Molly hopefully.

That was all more of Joel's propaganda, Sean figured, but this time he didn't say so.

« »

"He was telling me you had no appreciation of how complex his statistical analyses are," Joel said, as soon as they were sealed back in their rental car. "He said you think it's only a matter of common sense. I thought you liked Bill. I was giving you a chance to be a mentor."

With a heavy sigh, Sean started the engine. "They're both so wet behind the ears, Joel."

"But why would you impugn his professionalism."

"Maybe I was trying to be mentorly."

"You were just being cranky, and you know it."

"Joel," Sean said, "we're going to enjoy our last days here."

They drove out of the entrance to the park, and Joel said in a kindlier tone, "Molly's truly concerned about us."

"Yes, she's the nicer of the two."

"Ah," said Joel, "I see what's happened. Handsome Bill proved a bit disappointing."

"I never said he was handsome."

They made it to Mishe-Mokwa and pulled up beside the Moores' SUV, in time for lunch. The Iowa clan had eaten and was mostly in the lake, splashing and screaming, but one of the grandmothers, rocking on the Nokomis porch, scolded them for being late. Bill and Molly had gone straight to their cabin, so Sean headed toward a two-person table by the window. "You don't want to wait for them?" Joel asked.

"We spent the whole morning together," said Sean.

In fact, the Moores never appeared. Sean and Joel ate their chili and slaw by themselves. Phil came in with Cinder and straddled his usual chair. "You fellas sure are spry for your age, doing all that hiking. When I was a kid, I did lots of hiking up here. Can't be bothered now. Fishing's more my thing and some hunting in the season. Now, tell me," he said, leaning closer, "I don't mean to offend, but would you say fellas like you are likely to stay young longer than your average man? I'm feeling old just starting my forties."

"You work too hard, Phil," said Joel.

"If we had your life," Sean added, "we'd be wrecks. It's not a matter of being gay," he said to put a word to it so Phil wouldn't have to. "We just have easier jobs, and we don't have children."

Phil gave a wink and nodded out the window into the bright sunlight to see what was going on in the lake. "I'll say this, fellas, if I do have any children myself, at least I don't know who they are!" He slapped his palms to each knee. "But they're possibly out there somewhere."

"You're one of those bad boys," Joel said, which caused Phil to tug proudly at his beard.

"I do enjoy hearing you folks talk," he said. "One thing I know from running this joint is you gotta take folks as they come. I don't care about married or not, man or woman or whoever, whether there's kids or black or white—though we don't get many blacks up here. Indians, though. I'm fine with the Indians, except for that casino down in Flambeau. I'm never going down there again, that's for sure."

"My summer camp was near there," Sean said. "Flambeau was a muddy little crossroads. I remember seeing little Indian boys having pissing contests in the street. I felt sort of ashamed to be a white boy going to summer camp."

"No one ever sent me to summer camp," said Joel.

"My motto," said Phil, "is never feel ashamed. Right, Cinder? Most dogs shame easy, but not this old guy. Nope, never feel ashamed, Mr. Tyson. I get the idea, though, Mr. Greenwood here doesn't have that problem."

"Jesus Christ, no!" said Joel.

Phil had been talking to them the way he might not have talked to his other guests. Sean was pleased by that.

« »

He thought it over later, sitting on their porch with *The Real Adventure* half finished. Maybe his shame at seeing those Indian boys waving their little dicks around wasn't as much for having been a rich suburban kid as it was about sex. His big brother Danny had been at the camp the year before and told him about his best buddy Pete he shared a pup tent with on canoe trips and about the jerk-off games in his cabin when the counselors were out, but Sean couldn't imagine Danny doing anything like that. He remembered watching the older campers during skinny dips and wondering when he'd have hair down there, too.

Surprisingly, he felt bad now about Bill Moore. Through the screen, he told Joel he was going next door to Iagoo to check on him. "Thanks. I was almost asleep. Now you've woken me for good." Sean ignored that and stepped quietly along the pine-needle path, intending not to intrude unless the Moores were in evidence.

He did hear soft voices and found them sitting on the pine-log chairs that didn't look nearly as comfortable as their own Adirondacks. "We missed you at lunch," he said.

"We were so beat," said Bill. "Molly gave me a great massage. We've been eating too much up here. We needed to skip a meal."

"Here," Molly said, "take a chair. I'd rather lie in the sun on the

119

deck." She gave a relaxed yawn, lay back, and let her tan legs dangle off the edge.

"Well," Sean began, "I didn't want you to think I was doubting your research, Bill. I was only curious about it."

"He gets anxious when he's starting a new project," Molly said. "Future tenure prospects, you know."

"It's all right," said Bill. "I'm no good on vacations. I should be back at work."

"That's why he has me, Sean." Molly stretched her soft arms over her head. Sean could see she must do yoga from the way she moved. "On our walk, you know," she said, "Joel told me about your father. That must've been tough for a teenage boy."

"Joel told you about that? Why does he do this! He knows it's for me to decide who to tell."

"I told you, honey, not to tell Sean."

"But it's good, knowing," Molly said. "It's important having older friends we can truly know. Our parents never tell us about the things they've gone through."

"But Joel's always doing this. He told the woman who plays cello in his quartet."

"I'm sorry. I shouldn't have said anything."

"See, Molly," said Bill.

What difference did it really make? Sean asked himself. He wouldn't be seeing those two young people again. And he'd come over to apologize to Bill and maybe to reassure Molly that he was feeling fine after their talk. He'd finally put them both in the proper perspective. He was so much older. "Don't worry, Molly," he said. "If I'm not used to Joel by now, I'll never be. He does mean well. We'll see you at dinner?"

He headed back to his book waiting on his chair on the Chibiabos porch, but when Joel woke up, he could either pretend that Molly hadn't said anything or start another squabble and upset the peace of their last days on the shores of Gitche Gumee.

After dinner, Joel played through some old Beatles tunes for the Iowa clan. They gathered around and sang along, getting most of the words, and then at last paraded off to their cabins, leaving an audience of Phil Kimbley and Molly for Joel's attempts at Schubert and Schumann. Phil's mother had surely played those pieces more fluently.

Out on the Nokomis porch, Bill Moore had taken the rocking chair beside Sean, who'd found the Beatles medley somewhat painful. They both rocked softly and said nothing till there came a pause, a shuffling of pages, and a tentative request from their host, seconded by Molly's "Oh, yes!" Then a piece Sean recognized from home began, and Bill leaned closer and said, out of the blue, "Sean, as a gay man, do you believe it's determined biologically or environmentally? I've been wanting to ask, I mean, you might suppose, because of your father—"

"Well, my two brothers and sister are straight."

"I know the science is still out," Bill went on, "but what I'm interested in is more how you think about it."

"Is this one of your studies?" Sean asked, trying not to sound critical again.

"But you must've wondered."

"Do you wonder about yourself?"

"You mean because my father's straight?"

"And a Scott Walker man," Sean said to get off the subject.

Bill was looking at the sky with such a scattering of stars they could never see in the city. "I guess I can't know your generation," he said, rocking gently. "I mean, for me, born in 1980. All we can ever know is what it's like right now because as soon as it's another time, all the variables change."

Sean had identified the music, the Chopin prelude with the raindrop note plinking all the way through while the rest of the piece went on around it. Phil Kimbley must have loved hearing his mother play it. It was one of those pictorial pieces Joel would never write, but he would have to admit, it caught the image perfectly.

When it came to an end, they heard Joel shut the lid over the keys and Phil say, "Thanks for that, Mr. Greenwood. That took me back."

In bed that night and very sleepy, both of them, Joel told Sean that the Moores were going to Ontonagon tomorrow for a break from the wilderness, not that there was much to do in town. "And we'll have a break from them," Sean said. Joel frowned in the faint light coming in the window above the bed. Sean was tempted to get mad at him for telling his secrets but caught himself and said, "So what will we do tomorrow instead?"

It turned out to be a gray day. They were saving their final hike to Mirror Lake for Friday when they'd gotten their strength back, so they stayed around Mishe-Mokwa. They did dip in the lake and took a canoe out for a slow paddle. Sean told Joel of a book he'd loved as a boy, *Paddle-to-the-Sea*, about a toy canoe carved of wood that made its way from Lake Nipigon all the way out the St. Lawrence. It even got detoured down Lake Michigan to Chicago. All those giant bodies of freshwater lay deep in Sean's consciousness, he said, deeper than the house he'd grown up in, deeper than the Quimby farm, deeper than the city he'd escaped to.

While Joel was pulling the canoe back up the sand and then taking the paddles and life jackets to the storage shed, Sean struck up a conversation with one of the Iowa dads standing on the dock. He was from Burlington, where they'd gone by train to get married. Sean decided to mention it. It didn't throw the man off. He said he was proud of his state for being one of the first. "We still have that progressive streak that goes back a hundred years," he said. "To the west, of course, it's another story, all flat and church-going. We don't think much of those Iowans." He introduced himself as Ralph, and he'd heard all about them from Phil Kimbley. "Now, my brother-in-law's from Sioux City," Ralph said. "I wouldn't get talking to him, if I were you. This country's got some bad times coming. I sure wouldn't want to live up here in the UP or down in Wisconsin with that cross-eyed governor of theirs. Maybe Illinois still has a chance?"

5 Friday was to be their last full day. Joel was up doing knee bends when Sean opened his eyes. A quick breakfast and they'd be off, by themselves, on an easy hike, a half-mile up to the Summit Peak observation tower, and then a mile and a half down to Mirror Lake in the heart of the park.

"I don't want to wait for the Moores to wake up," Joel said when they stepped out from an early breakfast with packets of trail mix from Sylvie. Only she and the fisherman had been up before them, and his truck was already out of the drive.

When they drove to the trailhead, there was just one car in the lot. It was a relief to hear no chattering voices through the woods. At the tower, Sean wanted to stand, leaning on the top railing and looking out, not talking, not even touching, just taking in the wilderness. After five minutes of that, Joel did impatiently nuzzle in with his arm around Sean's waist. He kept quiet, though, and they both stared meditatively at a land without humans. Somebody else was surely there, camping or fishing, but the only sign of life was birdsong.

Down they went. On the far side of Mirror Lake, the map said, were three more of those cabins. Joel wanted to go inspect them, but Sean thought there might be renters and he shouldn't disturb them. Joel went off anyway, and Sean found a sunny spot by the water and lay down to rest. From that angle, the lake was a pale gray expanse, smooth as glass. Sean felt, in the quiet there, that he had lain down to say goodbye to something. He had no idea what it was, but that was the feeling that came over him. Long ago, he'd said goodbye to his childhood, his youth, goodbye to the family he barely belonged to anymore. He couldn't be saying goodbye now to the city he'd lived in so long or to the great lake that had always been there, through all his years.

Sean knew it had been hard for Joel to stay silent on the hike. It must have oppressed him, but this Mirror Lake was sunken in the trees in stillness, so it seemed to be part of Sean himself right then. It was quiet and restful and enclosed and safe—as he was.

He heard Joel mucking back along the lakeside path. "We ought to have rented one of those cabins. I peeked inside one. It was cozy and tidy and had a little propane stove. We could've packed in supplies. There's an outhouse and a screened deck. We'd have avoided all those Mishe-Mokwa people and had a total escape."

"We wouldn't have had Phil or Sylvie feeding us, and you wouldn't have met your new best friends."

"I don't need the Moores, Shaw-awn."

"But what'll you do when you have to stay over for quartets?"

Joel gave Sean a fierce scowl. "You just don't want to go off alone with me, here or in an old farmhouse or anywhere! You have to see your boys on the El or the beach and your grimy homeless people and Davey Nussbaum making you feel guilty if you desert the cause."

"Davey's part-time now."

"Then you go part-time, too! Or totally quit before he does. Otherwise, you'll be the last man left." He was looming over Sean, holding his hands out to pull him up. Sean felt himself rising slowly, creakily. He still ached from the exertions of the week, but in a good way. The sun now cast their two shadows darkly on the glassy water. No mirror threw them back at themselves. It was a pale slate they themselves were darkening.

When they headed back up the slope, Joel did his elder-care shove from behind. "There you go, Mr. Tyson, you can make it." Soon he was back in a cheerful mood. Sean had known only to wait. His own moods elevated more gradually.

Up at the tower, which an orderly troop of Boy Scouts was now ascending, Sean tried to say something conciliatory. "That one there, the slumpy one, that's the little Quimby you wish you could've seen back when."

"Aw, funny little Quimby with the knobby knees."

They said their farewells to the park and drove past Mishe-Mokwa to the big motel for Joel to buy souvenirs. Then, back in time for lunch, they were met by Ralph from Burlington in front of Nokomis. He said there had been a big controversy that morning on the dock. It started with who got which canoe but went political. "If you know what I mean," Ralph said.

Inside the lodge, the Iowans had separated into two contingents on opposite sides of the dining room. Ralph's wife had already joined the Moores at their table, so Joel and Sean took the small window-side table they'd claimed their first morning. Sylvie came right over with their club sandwiches and whispered, "You fellas missed quite the set-to. I didn't expect that family reunion to go smooth. They never do. I warned Phil, but he always thinks the best of folks."

« »

That afternoon, they stuck to themselves and took a quick swim before packing up so they could spend a relaxed evening. At dinner, both factions of Iowans were absent. The Sioux City ones had gone to a bar in Ontonagon, and the ones from Burlington went down to Ironwood for a restaurant meal. So the Moores and Scott and Trudy from Minnesota and even the fisherman, whose name no one seemed to know, reminisced about their happy week. "Yeah, there's always a little dust-up," said Phil, "when families get together." He sat there, grinning contentedly into a mug of what might be whiskey.

Bill Moore assured him that none of them minded hearing someone else's family lose it. "That Ralph's a nice guy," he said, "and he didn't have to take that grief."

"He sure let 'em have it," said the fisherman.

125

Scott and Trudy promised to return next summer for the same two weeks and hoped to find the others there. Everyone pretended to hope so, too. It was only Sean and Joel who were leaving the next day, so Phil extracted a distinct promise from them. "I'm penciling you in," he said, "for two perfect weeks."

In that nostalgic atmosphere, Joel proposed a recitation of the closing pages of *The Song of Hiawatha* to accompany the sunset outside. Sylvie brought in a candlestick and lit the wick with a kitchen match. Phil carried over an even larger edition of the poem from atop the piano. Then he turned off the electric lights, and everyone pulled their chairs closer. "I'm not much on poetry," said the fisherman, "but give it a go." Out the windows, the light was sparkling off the Big-Sea-Water and marking a trail to the west.

Joel began at the part where the Black Robes were honored guests of Hiawatha and his people. They were fed a feast in thanks for having come so far to see them. Then the guests told their tales of the Virgin Mary and her blessed Son and were told *"how the Jews, the tribe accursed, mocked him—"* Joel interrupted himself: "It's my people they're talking about. Those nasty priests! What could Hiawatha have cared about Christians hating Jews? His own stories were so much kinder—Gitche Manito and the peace pipe and Osseo descended from the Evening Star. Sorry if I offended anyone."

No one said a thing, so he held up the heavy volume again to the candlelight and read on. When the Frenchmen had safely gone to sleep in their wigwam, Joel read what all of them, at that exact moment, were seeing out the windows through the tall tree trunks:

> Slowly o'er the simmering landscape
> Fell the evening dusk and coolness,
> And the long and level sunbeams
> Shot their spears into the forest ...

Sean felt moisture behind his eyelids and a shiver up his spine. It grew sharper when Hiawatha went to say farewell to old Nokomis, the mother who bore him. He must have known how all he loved and understood of nature, and of his people, and of all he had protected, was soon to be taken from him. Himself, Hiawatha, he could stay no longer.

Joel's voice was rising as passionately as when he sang one of his compositions in his slightly off-key baritone. Everyone but him was now looking out through the panes of glass at the same lake and sunset as in the poem. Sean, and maybe others too, imagined a birch canoe departing on that sparkling trail across the water toward the pink horizon. Even Joel looked up briefly beyond the candlelit page but then read on to the final lines.

That was how they spent their last evening at Phil Kimbley's resort on Lake Superior. Phil gave Joel's shoulder a thankful pat, and the fisherman said, "Yep, that about says it all." Joel blew the candle out, and Phil asked if they could all see well enough in the twilight to get to their cabins because he didn't much feel like switching on the lights right then.

《 》

When Sean awoke, he heard Sylvie and Phil nearby in Kwasind, which had been vacant all week, shoving up stuck windows and shaking out bedding and rugs off the porch. They were joshing back and forth, but he couldn't catch the particulars. Somehow, Sean had overslept. The feuding family had cruised in late from Ontonagon and Ironwood and made a midnight ruckus, and he'd had trouble falling back asleep.

He nudged Joel's side. Joel grumbled then gave a cowlike yawn and sat up, blinking. "It's almost nine," Sean told him.

"Jesus Christ, Tyson! We can't miss our last pasties." He slipped from bed and, without even a stretch, pulled on his jeans and sweater. Sean had to catch up to him on the pine-needle path to the lodge.

Yesterday's fuss had had no apparent aftereffect on the gaggle of kids charging around the parking area between the cars. The grandmothers were rocking lazily with coffee mugs on the wide Nokomis porch. Sean and Joel received disapproving nods but strode right inside to pump from Phil's hot-coffee-all-day samovar, and there were the last pasties with a note: "Reserved for lazy city folk."

"To Sylvie, we'll always be Chicagoans," said Sean.

"But it doesn't matter," Joel said, "because we're leaving." They took the table by the window for the last time. "Then someone's moving into that empty cabin today, and tomorrow people will take over ours. You think you belong with everyone at places like this, but then they're out of your life. That's why I want to stop having these vacations in different places every year."

"Phil wants us back."

"It wouldn't be the same," Joel said.

Sean knew he was right about leaving. They'd felt close to Phil Kimbley and motherly Sylvie, and they'd had their brief friendship with the Moores, but he didn't expect to miss any of them.

And when the time came, nothing of what anyone said was a true farewell. It was all softened with pledges to meet again next year. Joel did give Molly his email, and she gave him hers.

When they'd loaded up the little Chevy, Ralph made a parting crack about them descending into Governor Walker territory. It was the last thing they heard as they pulled out after big hugs from Sylvie and an intent look, straight into the eyes of each of them, from that grizzly-bearded Phil. His pale blue irises seemed to be saying: "You'll remember this place. It's my home year round. It's all you'd ever need—forest and lake and sky."

PART THREE

1 On the drive south, Sean insisted on taking a detour to see his old summer camp. Having passed the huge casino in Lac du Flambeau, they searched outside town and found a newly paved road that led to Fence Lake. Sean remembered arriving, shy and fearful, in a station wagon bringing the Chicago boys from the final stop of his first overnight train ride. It was an old Pullman with fold-down bunks and curtains and a friendly black porter. Sean had never before slept surrounded by so many other boys.

Joel was annoyed by the detour and started arguing about the casino. "But at least they're not so poor anymore," Sean said.

"They're poorer in spirit," said Joel.

"What good is spirit, though, if you live in squalor?"

"But why were they living in squalor, Shaw-awn? Because of people like you with your fancy-shmancy summer camps."

They emerged from the woods and ought to have come upon a row of cabins along the bluff, but instead, broad driveways led to half a dozen suburban split-levels strewn across the old ball fields. One remaining log cabin seemed to serve as a storage barn. Sean pulled the car up beside it. He couldn't orient himself.

"So this is where you finally pubed," said Joel.

"It's where Danny did. He went at twelve, but Mom and Dad sent me at eleven because they figured I was more grown up."

"Yeah, right! Hey, you just said 'Mom and Dad.' You never put them together like that."

Sean peered out the windshield beyond the two closest houses to the expanse of blue water but didn't say anything. "Where's all the people?" he wondered.

"Betting the tables and slots so the Indians can rip them off. You like the idea. Makes up for your fancy camp. I had to work at the hardware store in summers and practice my fiddle."

"Poor underprivileged Joel."

"I'm just reminding you that your politics don't line up with your nostalgia."

"Oh, fuck off. I'm still trying to take this in." But he shifted into reverse and then wheeled quickly away from that painfully unrecognizable scene of his adolescence.

« »

In silence while Joel napped, Sean drove steadily on as the North Woods dwindled away into farm fields. He was thinking how much he'd missed his family when he was at camp. He still had four more years of happy innocence left. Then, when he came upon Dad's secret stash and told himself it was probably for bodybuilding, for normal athletes like his dad and big brother, his uncertainty began. His eyes kept shifting across those perfect bodies before he quickly slipped them out of sight again. He yearned to look longer but also didn't dare to. He tried not to think about them yet couldn't help wondering why Dad had hidden those pictures. Dad wasn't a slouchy little book reader like himself. He was a tall tennis-playing golfing ball-throwing man like the ones in the magazines. Dad loved to compete. He and Danny competed at everything, but they never bothered to compete with Sean.

Joel was snoring now, his head bobbing against the backrest. He'd never had to wonder about Dr. Nathan's secrets. He'd never felt the way Sean did at camp, having to swim naked and hold up another naked boy's hand for buddy call to make sure no one had drowned. The year before, Danny had won awards for batting and sharpshooting, but at his own final banquet, Sean only won "cooperation points." He gripped the steering wheel tighter in a surge of resentment at his brother for having been twelve and bunking in the jerk-off cabin.

At the junction with Route 80, Joel snapped awake and said he was starving and desperately had to pee so they'd better find a diner soon. "But thanks for doing aw-awl the driving."

Sean thought for a few seconds then said, "I prefer to. You're too easily distracted."

« »

Eventually, they made it to the banks of the Kickapoo River and the motel run by a Hindu couple, "The Satyanarayanans, Your Hosts." Down the road was the small town of Viola—*Vy*-ola not *Vee*-ola—which Joel thought was a favorable omen. "We can live in Viola, Wisconsin! It'll be perfect." Sean ignored that and went into the office while Joel waited in the car, having said to make sure of the lower weekly rate he'd arranged online.

Sean settled with Mrs. Satyanarayanan, and soon she was telling him of her cousins with a lovely motel in Kentucky and her eldest son who was preparing the grand opening of his own motel down in Illinois. He'd bought it from a sportsman, and it was all done up in hunting and fishing motifs. "You are from Illinois," she said. "Let me give you his card."

Mr. S. was watching a console television from an overstuffed armchair in the inner office. He grabbed a stack of calling cards from a magazine-covered coffee table and passed it to his wife, who pressed the top one firmly into Sean's palm. She would have gone on chatting if he hadn't begun backing toward the door, thanking her as he went.

"We're in Number Twelve, down at the end." He gave Joel the key on a stiff leather fob and went to unload their bags.

"I'm dog tired," Joel said as he stumbled off with only his day pack. "Too much meatloaf and cherry pie," he groaned. It was growing dark, and without music to play or Wi-Fi to connect him to real estate, Joel was ready for bed while Sean still felt agitated from the long drive.

They were accustomed to a queen-size mattress, but the room had two standard doubles, so after hot showers, they got into separate beds. Sean considered what might be Mrs. S.'s old-world proprieties. What might she be making of two sixty-five-year-olds who didn't seem to be there for the fishing? He aimed the gooseneck wall lamp to see better the closing chapters of *The Real Adventure* without keeping Joel awake. Phil Kimbley had let him keep the book because no one read that old stuff anyway. "You're an anomaly, Mr. Tyson, if I'm using the right term."

I'm an anomaly, Sean thought now. He marked his place with a forefinger and let the book rest on his stomach. But everyone's anomalous, one way or another, he told himself. That Hindu couple was surely anomalous in this obscure corner of Richland County. Their Kickapoo Gardens Motor Lodge was a characterless block of windows with drawn blinds and numbered doors with plastic chairs out front and only three other vehicles in the lot. Propped up on two flimsy pillows, Sean looked about their home for the coming week. Why had Joel stuck them off there instead of in a nicer newer motel in Richland Center? The walls were spackled in random places, waiting for fresh paint. A heavy old TV sat on a low bureau with a clunky remote and a handwritten list of available cable channels. One surprising touch was the copy of the Bhagavad Gita on the bedside table next to the Gideon Bible.

Sean deduced that Joel had chosen the place not merely to save money but to make every dilapidated farmhouse they'd look at seem quaint and cozy by comparison. He was angry again. He laid the book aside, losing his place because he couldn't find the bookmark he'd tucked between the pillows. Quietly, he edged himself out from the bedclothes. The air conditioner in the rear window was rattling loudly. He needed to assert himself. He slid his boxers down his legs and kicked them off his feet. To his surprise, he was going to wake up that sleeping man over there and let off some steam.

2 When the early sun shone through the off-kilter Venetian blinds, Sean found himself back in his own bed. Joel was staring at him from his with a smug smile. "After last night," he said, "I feel miraculously renewed."

"You ought to be."

"You knew I was only pretending to be asleep."

"I became quite aware of that."

"I liked the sensation of being violated in Viola."

"Very funny, Joel."

Joel's plaintive mood had vanished because they would soon be driving around, checking out properties and maybe narrowing down his list before meeting the realtor on Monday. In the shower, he was soon singing snatches of "Maggie's Farm," so Sean yelled into the misty bathroom, "I'm going to the office for coffee."

"Don't want any," sang Joel under the downpour.

Sean pulled on his polo shirt and slacks and was pleasantly reminded of Owen's outfit and felt rather trim and youthful. He found Mr. S. reading a newspaper in his armchair back behind the desk. He pointed Sean to the coffee urn. Then, the rather heavyset man came around front in his deep-purple flannel robe, carrying a plate of individually wrapped donuts. Sean selected one and said he'd take another to his friend. In Chicago, he'd never have said "friend."

Mr. S. nodded and retreated to his newspaper, but before Sean could get out the door, the curtains in the rear parted and Mrs. S. bustled forth with a small lacquered plate. "No, no, he mustn't offer only donuts. They will keep in their plastics. Here, Mr. Tyson, I have baked genuine Wisconsin corn muffins. You must take them with your coffee. The other gentleman will want a cup as well." She was already pouring it. "And so," she said with an expectant glance, "you are looking to purchase a house here to escape from the city?"

"How did—"

"From Mr. Greenwood's email, of course. I must tell you, we have found it a very congenial area to settle. We can recommend it 110 percent. We brought up our sons here. The eldest was tops in his high school class and took his degree at the campus in La Crosse. The younger is at Eau Claire."

"Congratulations," Sean said and took the second cup.

"Let me hold the door for you. My husband is not as attentive as he might be."

Sean smiled sympathetically toward his fellow male, who didn't look up from his paper.

"You must tell us what you find on the market, Mr. Tyson. At this time, prices are rather low. It is how our eldest could buy into his business."

When Sean made it back to chilly Room Twelve, Joel said, "I turned up the AC after my shower. Oh, good, you brought me coffee."

"And the lady's homemade corn muffins especially for us. So your emails said why we were here."

"Why else would two men spend their vacation in a dumpy motel? Is that mold I smell? The Kickapoo must flood."

"May I turn down the AC?"

Joel pulled on his red Bermudas and Porcupine Mountains T-shirt. He promised to wear long pants for the realtor, but today was too hot and it was only the two of them. Sean intended to remain noncommittal about whatever they caught glimpses of from the road, while Joel's enthusiasms would surely come and go. Nothing Sean could say would sway him.

"I bet my grandmother learned to bake corn muffins, too," Joel said. "Those Indian folks winding up in Wisconsin must feel like my Austrian forebears, trying hard to fit in. My dad used to tell me how it

134

was when he was a kid, with their accents, but he got to grow up feeling American. See, Erastus Quimby never had to feel he wasn't—"

"My Irish-born grandmother did. I'm not all Quimby and Tyson."

"Aw, poor immigrant Shaw-awn. Oh, I mean 'Shah-ahn.' Sorry,
Eileen."

"Joel, you're impossible."

"Just keyed up. Let's hit the road."

« »

On that Sunday, most of Viola was either asleep or up early for
church. Driving through, they saw no one. The little town straddled
the county line between Richland and Vernon, and from misreading
the map, Joel had aimed them further west. Sean chose not to say
anything. When it became clear he'd made a mistake, Joel claimed
he wanted to check out Vernon first for comparison's sake.

"Whatever you say. I'm only the chauffeur."

"Oh, come on, Quimby. Let's have a scenic drive. We could go
as far as the Mississippi."

"Whatever you like."

Joel steered them toward the great river through the rolling fields
of heavy summer green. At one point, Sean noticed a historical
marker beside the road and pulled off to read it.

"What the hell are you doing?"

"It says this is the Black Hawk Trail."

"Oh, Jesus."

"It must be where they fled from the militia. You should be interested, it's your state's history." And Sean read aloud the peculiarly
spaced text:

At Shallow Pond 115 Rods Due
South Blackhawk's 700 Sac
Indians Encamped July

135

31 1832
Soldiers found six decrepit
Indians there and left them
Behind.
Lee Sterling in 1846 found
A handful of silver brooches
There. Hence concluded those
Killed were squaws.

"Jesus," Joel said again, "decrepit Indians!" A smaller sign apologized for the insensitive language from the 1930s when the marker had been placed to honor the centennial.

"Bill Moore would appreciate that," Sean said. He didn't feel like driving on.

Joel leaned out and snapped a photo of the two signs. "I know this means something to you, Quimby," he said in a sweeter voice than usual of late.

Sean sat there trying to envision that rolling farmland devoid of settlement, no roads, only a foot-worn, hoof-worn path through prairie grass. He tried to see seven hundred starving Indians huddling together through the dark night, fearing the white men coming after them. He recalled that Abraham Lincoln and Jefferson Davis had both served in that Illinois militia. When dawn broke, the refugees must have scanned the horizon for their pursuers and kept on going west to cross the river to safety, but some had already starved to death right on the spot where he had parked the little Chevy. When he'd read Gramma's history book, it was his first inkling of what had really once happened on that land of theirs.

"Can we get going now, Sean?"

"Hmm?"

"I know you're doing your dreamy Indian thing, but that's enough for now."

Rather than follow the trail farther to where what was left of

Black Hawk's people had reached the Father of Waters, Joel insisted on heading back east because it was getting toward lunchtime and he remembered a little Czech restaurant over in Hillsboro. They would save the Mississippi for another time.

« »

There was nothing particularly Czech about the restaurant except the dumplings, but Hillsboro got Sean thinking about the books he'd read in high school about Bohemian towns and German towns and Norwegian towns in the Midwest—*My Ántonia, Giants in the Earth, The Good Master*. At the Quimby farm, he'd never known any local people beyond the ones who came to cook and clean. Suddenly, Sean felt alien on the Wisconsin roads. He had a panicky impulse to drive straight to the Kickapoo Gardens, pack their bags, and take the fastest route home to Chicago.

But after lunch, now that they were back in Richland County, Joel began pointing out familiar sights from his youth, and they stopped at a park for a short walk. A long ridge rose above the campground. They followed signs to a water-carved tunnel through the limestone to the ridge's other side, where they found picnic tables and open fields of green and yellow and some of Joel's Ocooch Mountains rising farther off. They had it all to themselves. After his brief panic in the car, Sean felt relieved to stand still on the edge of such open country, though what he said was: "Around here, they probably voted for Governor Walker."

"You have to say that, don't you!"

"Say what?"

"Dwell on whatever's wrong."

"It's what we old lefties do."

"Yes, Karl Marx."

"Come on, Joel."

"Yes, Comrade Lenin."

"Don't be an asshole." But Joel was already walking off on the trail up the back side of the ridge. Naturally, Sean followed, though Joel was storming along at a quick pace and the steep climb slowed Sean down.

At the top, Joel stood waiting for him, still glaring. Sean knew he shouldn't have mentioned Scott Walker, but it did scare him to think of living, even part of the time, in a place where neighbors might want you out of there.

"I see you're in one of your moods," Joel said.

"*My* moods!"

"But look how beautiful all of this is!" Joel held his arm out toward the peaceful land below them as if offering it to his beloved.

《 》

The rest of the afternoon was spent exploring up and down the back roads and through tiny towns called Yuba and West Lima and Bloom City and Hub City. Someone must have once been optimistic in calling a crossroads a city. Or maybe "city" had its original meaning, a civilized place you didn't have to move on from.

Up the gravel roads into Joel's mountains, they did locate several properties he'd noted online. From the roadside it was impossible to tell what they were like, but on the basis of nothing Sean could see, Joel would say, "That one's promising." There were some ugly houses on good land and some appealing houses in dreary dells. The better places weren't for sale. Joel fell instantly in love with one such house. It had eggplant-colored shutters and a front porch swing and sat below a hillside dotted with grazing cattle, apple trees, and wild roses. "What if we lived there!" Joel exclaimed. Sean didn't say so, but he could almost imagine it, at least in summers. There was a shiny Prius out front, which probably meant someone from Madison was up for the weekend. Luckily the property wasn't for sale because, despite himself, Sean might have been tempted.

"You're not going to say anything, are you!"

"Whatever I said, you'd quibble at, Joel."

"So I have to show all the enthusiasm?"

"You generally do."

"Because I'm the impulsive one."

"Right," said Sean.

"Otherwise known as normal," said Joel.

It was their old adversarial pattern. If Sean had been with hunky young Owen, he'd be willingly trying to please, but how long would that last?

Joel decided to save Richland Center for tomorrow, so they circled back up to Yuba for supper. The road sign gave the population as ninety-one, and the town had two churches and three bars. One took up the first floor of a large brick building that must have been built when Yuba had a future. They stepped somewhat timidly inside and found a huge oval bar with four old farmers at one end and, further down, a hugely fat man blabbing about vending machines to the woman behind the bar. No one had given Sean and Joel funny looks, in fact any looks at all. They took stools equidistant from the fat man and the farmers.

The cheerfully buxom barmaid scooted down to ask what she could get them. Joel opted for a Pabst on tap and the deluxe burger with cheese, tomato, lettuce, a slice of baked ham plus onion rings and pickles. "I'm a health nut," he told the barmaid. She thought that was a good one. Sean ordered a tuna sandwich and a diet Pepsi. He caught sight of a scraggly old dude in saggy jeans and a sleeveless T-shirt back in the kitchen.

While they waited, they pretended to watch the sports interviews on the giant flat-screen across the bar. Sean took note of the stuffed moose head on the back wall, the shelves of stock car memorabilia, and the row of blinking flashing video games. "This could be your retirement community, Joel," he said.

"Love it! You gotta admit it's America." The barmaid set down their drinks and asked where they were passing through from. Joel's red Bermudas and Sean's crisp blue polo had easily given them away. "I'm actually from Richland Center," Joel said. "My dad was a dentist there, Dr. Nathan Greenwood, you may have heard of him."

"I bet my mom would've. I'm Inka. That's Czech for 'little girl.' No so little anymore!"

"Who could be, with the food around here," said Joel.

"But I don't eat those deluxes, they're surefire heart attack," Inka said. "You're skinny enough, though." She peeked over at the huge man to make sure he hadn't heard.

Sean was worried that chummy Joel was about to tell their whole story. The farmers still hadn't looked their way. Other sorts of city folk might stride into a small-town bar as if they owned it, but Sean only felt embarrassment. Joel used to tell him he had a case of reverse snobbery.

When the sandwich and giant burger arrived, Sean could only shake his head in disapproval at Joel, who ate every bite. They managed to leave the place without any awkward interactions. Sean credited Inka for having set the friendly tone.

3 The next morning, Sean drove them into Richland Center, but Joel didn't feel like going past the house he grew up in, so they went straight to meet Victorine Forell, their realtor. She was also too young to remember Dr. Nathan Greenwood and, in fact, had only recently moved over from Prairie du Chien. She was an upbeat chatty mom in her late thirties who loved being back at work. Sean couldn't help liking her. She wore a deal of makeup and amply filled out a powder-blue pantsuit of some light synthetic. Sean imagined he'd end up having to defend her style to Joel.

"So, guys, call me Tory," she said, "and let's sit a bit here at my desk so I can get a clearer take on exactly what you're looking for."

On the Formica surface, under fluorescent light, she unfolded a map of the county like the one Joel had been poring over at home. "We prefer north of town," he said, drawing a vague circle with his forefinger. "It's emptier. I used to explore up there as a kid. Our priorities are: quiet road, no near neighbors, and a view of the hills."

"He usually calls them mountains," said Sean.

"The Ocooch Mountains," Tory confirmed, and Sean feared he was losing sympathy till she added, "It's a marketing strategy to lure folks out from Madison. It's an old name on historical maps, though the Ho-Chunk people say we've got it wrong."

Joel gave Sean a self-satisfied smirk.

"I have a feeling," Tory Forell went on, "that you two aren't easily influenced. My guess is you'll know the right place when you see it."

"I certainly will," said Joel.

"You, Sean?" She pronounced it "Shawn" as most everyone did. Back in high school, he had affected the Gaelic accent mark but was soon embarrassed out of signing himself "Seán."

"She's asking you, Tyson."

"What?"

"I wondered if you'll know it when you see it," Tory said.

"I'm not sure what I want. This is really more Joel's thing. I'm open to looking, but I'm pretty attached to Chicago."

"While I'm thinking total retirement from the hell of urban life." Joel gave their realtor a conspiratorial wink.

She sat back, clutched her magenta fingernails to her powder-blue breast and, with a thoughtful expression, said, "One thing I've learned in this business, it's all about psychology. I'd imagined it was financing and inspections and deeds, but no, it's figuring out the buyers."

"We're hard to figure," Sean said. "I haven't figured us out yet."

"It may take a third party," said Tory. She reached her hands across the desk, one to Sean and one to Joel, and gave their hands squeezes. "There's no pressure," she said, even as she held on tight. "You may walk away with nothing. I'm only showing what happens to be on the market. Things aren't moving much. I've got all the time in the world, and if you don't mind my saying so, you're my first male couple, so this could be fun for me. Female couples, one or two, but no men."

"Maybe I should ask," said Sean, "if this is an area where we'd feel—" He couldn't decide how to put it.

"At home?" Tory considered the question. "It's hard to promise, isn't it? People come in all sorts." She straightened up and smoothed out the jacket of her pantsuit.

"I appreciate your saying that," Sean said, because if she'd said they had no need to worry, he'd have lost his growing faith in her.

"We'll be totally fine," said Joel. "I grew up here, for Christ's sake. It's where I belong."

« »

They were driving in Tory's shiny new Ford sedan through what Joel deemed the emptier parts of the county. Three properties were on the day's itinerary, all on gravel roads. Joel wanted to be on a road that didn't lead anywhere people had to get to.

They pulled into a rutted dirt driveway that dipped down toward what Sean would call a gully, but Joel exclaimed, "Wow, and a brook!" There was only a trickle running in it now, but they had to walk across a shaky bridge to reach the log cabin perched up on the other side.

"I'm starting you at the low end," Tory said. "This may tell me what you don't want."

"It's so private!" Joel proclaimed, but his enthusiasm moderated when the moldy smell inside hit his nostrils and the floorboards creaked with every step. "It's definitely doable," he said. Sean kept quiet.

"Now, I suspect the underpinnings are rotted," Tory cautioned, "and my listing sheet says the pump has a small leak. However, it does come with some fine hillside acreage."

"We'd be paying for the land," Sean pointed out. "The listing says, 'Live here while you build your dream house.'"

"I like it as it is," Joel said, but Sean could tell he actually didn't. He was playing a game to get him to push for something more expensive.

"Try this exercise," Tory suggested. "Picture what you'd do here on a humid day with pouring rain and mosquitoes." She gave Joel a schoolmarmish stare. "I'm just saying."

But Joel came back with "Well, we spent last week in an even smaller cabin in the UP and it rained and Sean still wanted to stay another week."

"Because there was plenty to do. Here, we'd only walk up and down the road and get on each other's nerves."

"Let's not waste any more time, then," Tory said. "Now I've got your baseline."

"I could still see it," Joel said while she locked up. They made their way down and across the shaky bridge toward the Ford and more likely prospects. Sean felt a cloud of doom descending on him.

《 》

When they'd set off again, Joel mentioned the sweet old farmhouse with eggplant shutters they'd seen yesterday on a gravel road off Highway D and lamented it wasn't for sale.

"Off Highway D? I don't know that one," Tory said, "but here's something on the upper end of your range with move-in-ability, lots of space, and a great view, plus you can probably talk them down."

"What's the catch?" Joel asked suspiciously.

Sean, riding in the back seat, let them go on talking and hardly listened. Nothing could happen without him. Joel could justify a moldy log cabin as easily as a quaint old farmhouse. Did it entirely come down to Sean's choice? But he'd never agreed to make a choice at all. Tory Forell had saved him from the log cabin, but no wonder, her cut would've been so small. Naturally, she wanted to coax them up the scale. Still, he did like her. She was a reasonable person, unlike Joel, but Sean didn't want them to appear fussy or inharmonious. They were Tory's first male couple, and they'd been too crabby with each other.

"How does all this feel to you, Sean?" she asked out of nowhere.

"You were saying?"

"To have two properties. It can be stressful."

"His gramma had a farm down by the Rock River," Joel said. "A gentleman's farm, that is, but it did go back to his great-great-grandfather who farmed it for real. As a kid, he spent summers there. It's in his blood. He's got to accept that part of himself."

"Is he speaking for you?" Tory asked, turning onto another gravel road and stirring up more dust.

"He generally does," said Sean but, he hoped, in an affectionate tone.

"In every couple," Tory said, "I find there's a spontaneous one and a cautious one. It's the cautious one I pay most attention to."

"Uh-oh," said Joel, "we may have a problem here."

"What I mean," she added quickly, "is that the cautious one won't be trouble."

"Ah," Sean said. Tory was onto something.

"When the cautious one decides, it's solid. The spontaneous one tends to vacillate and wonder if there's something even better."

"Not me!" Joel declared.

"Just my experience, my friend. You wait and see."

Sean wasn't sure if he should appreciate this wisdom or fear what it implied. Something in him longed not to make decisions of any kind. He had always been stubborn, so his decisions stuck for life. That wasn't necessarily a good thing. It seemed that, with Tory, he and Joel had landed in some unexpected form of couples counseling. Joel loved that kind of scrutiny but not Sean, who'd rather go along as he was.

"So it's my cautious spouse you'll have to work on, huh?" Joel asked the woman at the wheel.

"I'm not working on either of you," she said jauntily. "This is what I do for fun. It's why I love my new job. I'm a people person."

"See, Sean, she's one crafty saleslady."

《 》

The next place did have a lovely site, not above a gully but at the crest of a hill between two much steeper ones with rugged limestone outcroppings. The western slope was catching the morning sun, and the eastern one would be glowing golden by sunset. The promised view looked a long way down a green valley with a distant farmhouse and barn, unfortunately new and ugly, but there were acres of grazing land up the slopes and down along a winding stream, so they could ignore those two aluminum-sided blots with shiny corrugated steel roofs. Tory explained that a tornado had touched down a few years back and ripped off the roof and one whole side of the barn and totaled the house. "It's a shame," she said. "I'm told it was a real classic farmstead, old red barn and all."

"Tornados never strike in the same place," Joel said, "so this valley's safe now."

"Where'd you get that statistic?"

"Well, there's not many twisters in these hills anyway, Quimby."

The house for sale was also no beauty, a garrison colonial with fake red brick below and beige vinyl siding above. "Built in '79," Tory said, handing Sean the listing sheet. Joel didn't bother with specifics. He was already bouncing around, checking out the place. "It's in excellent shape," Tory noted. "You'll like the screen porch off the kitchen. It looks out at those great cliffs. A family with four kids lived here till the kids were grown and the parents downsized to town. They left the wall-to-wall carpets and the built-ins plus the fridge."

When they stepped inside, Sean got a comfortable feeling but imagined Joel, already up the stairs, did not. It wasn't at all quaint, more of a suburban tract house in the countryside. A perverse streak in Sean was oddly drawn to its lack of character. He wouldn't feel pretentious there. It wouldn't remind him of the old Victorian he'd grown up in on Cedar Street or of the ancient Quimby farmhouse. Here, the windows were too small, the acoustic-tile ceiling too low, the cabinets and shelves so blond. All the proportions were unpleasing.

He walked into the downstairs master bedroom. It had sliding glass doors out to a wooden deck. Sleeping in there would be so different from their home nest above the loud street. Here, he could walk out in his boxer shorts and sit in the shade with no one to see him but birds and grazing cows, or he could step over to the screen porch and bring out coffee and toast through the kitchen door.

Joel came bounding down the carpeted stairs, saying he could definitely fit his piano up. "Come look, and we'd have our own studies and also a guest room. We'd be able to have guests! We can't have solitude all the time."

But Sean, as he headed upstairs, was thinking how restful it might be with no one else around, sometimes not even Joel. The off-white walls of the four kids' bedrooms had spots of gummy residue where music and movie and sports posters had likely been taped up. That was how sister Mary's boys used to decorate their lairs.

"They say it holds the heat well," Tory was telling Joel when Sean descended. "And in summer, you just open the windows and let the updrafts blow through."

"But I have to say," Joel began in a suddenly thoughtful tone, "to put it politely, it's pretty charmless."

Sean studied the patient smile on Tory's magenta lips. She turned

146

toward him, raising an expectant plucked eyebrow. "I actually like it," he said.

"Charm's not a thing with Sean," said Joel, "despite me being so charming."

"You're both equally charming," Tory said. "And it's hard to see the potential of unfurnished rooms. What's a house but a bunch of different-shaped empty boxes to put nice things in?"

"These shapes don't do it for me," said Joel.

"But you were already heaving your piano upstairs," Sean reminded him.

"Only trying to give the place a fighting chance." Sean wondered if Joel was doing some subtle manipulating, making him defend the ugly house and push for buying it.

Tory clasped her hands again and said, "So we've seen the fixer-upper and the mover-inner. I've set your outer limits. Next, we're going to see the old schoolhouse. I have a feeling about this one. But whatever, I want you guys to sit down, by yourselves, and spend some time thinking if you truly want anything at all. How would you lead your lives up here? How much time would you realistically spend? I'm going to be honest. If you don't see eye to eye, buying a vacation home or, even worse, one for retirement, could be the first step toward divorce. I'm just saying."

"You're scaring me, Tory," said Joel. "And we actually are married in Iowa." But she had only said what Sean hadn't even quite dared to think.

《 》

They stopped for sandwiches at the bar in Hub City to supply, Tory joked, some local flavor. "You city dwellers had better know what you're getting into out here."

"I already took him to Yuba," Joel said. "He survived."

"But will Joel?" Sean countered.

Back on the road, they were driving past fields of corn. Sean got to wondering about cornflakes although he did prefer his oat bran. He recalled that "cereal" derived from Ceres herself, the goddess in the classical myths he'd studied in Mr. Gault's class before getting to *Hiawatha*. That was fifty years ago, but he could still picture himself sitting in the front row, raising his hand with the correct answer. And now, they were going to look at a schoolhouse.

"Each of these small villages had its own back then," Tory was telling Joel in the front seat. "Children of all ages walked to school from the farms. Maybe some got driven over in a horse and buggy. The poor teacher would already be there, stoking the fire, but I bet she gave them a better education than today, despite all the computers."

Sean perked up. She had expressed his own backward-looking opinion. Joel liked to point out the conservative nature of Sean's leftiness, but now he agreed with Tory: "As one who teaches teenagers, I can confirm that my kids don't know squat. I'm ready to quit."

"So you're imagining living up here most of the year?" Tory asked with some hesitation.

"He doesn't know what he's imagining," Sean put in from the back seat without eliciting a retort.

Tory turned the Ford onto rougher pavement past a cluster of houses. Most looked uninhabited. A tall old brick one had lost most of its bricks on two sides, and the lath was showing through. The one-room schoolhouse sat past the vacated settlement on a slight rise at the end of a dirt track in high grass. Tory pulled up beside the simple frame building on its hillock. It was in need of fresh white paint and some new clapboards, but Sean could see the school bell still hanging in the stubby bell tower.

"It's closer to what neighbors are left, but no one would much drive up here. It's got real history to it, guys."

While she fiddled with the rusty lock, Sean surveyed the view and imagined a pack of boys in knickers and girls in long skirts trooping up the hill with their satchels. They had all got up early to help their moms and dads on the farms, and after school some would keep shop at the general store and others do chores at home. They had no idea how much easier life would be for their own great-grandchildren.

With a loud clank, the wide door swung open into a vestibule for coats and galoshes, and then Tory opened a double door into the main room with its scuffy floorboards and tall smudged-up windows. Sean inhaled the dry mustiness that seemed a whiff of the past.

"They closed it down before the Second World War," Tory said, "but later a young couple lived here and put in a simple kitchen and bath in the storerooms behind." She opened a door beside where the teacher's desk must have stood, and Joel peeked in. "And they installed an electric pump for the well and a water heater. The story goes that they lived here into old age. He tended bar where we had lunch in Hub City, and she was some kind of visiting nurse. They had no children. He was long dead, but she passed away recently in a nursing home, and the property has sat empty. It's been on the market for several years. You could get it for under forty, easy, and it comes with, let's see—"

"One acre and the right of way up the hill," Sean said, reading from the listing sheet.

"It's my dream house," Joel said in almost a whisper. Then he began to get excited: "My music would sound great here. I could have quartet nights. And we could put one of those prefab sheds out back for you to retreat to, Sean, when I get on your nerves. We wouldn't want to disturb the architectural integrity of the schoolhouse. We'd be saving it from someone ever bastardizing it."

"I should mention that there isn't much resale value on this one," Tory said. "Then again, the county historical folks might give you a restoration grant. We care about our heritage. Frank Lloyd Wright was born in Richland Center. They're hoping to restore that great old warehouse he designed in town."

"I really love the moldings around the windows," Joel said, "and the wainscoting or wainscoating or however you say it. The dark woodwork reminds me of my parents' bungalow."

Tory suggested they stay awhile and contemplate. She would go out to her car and look at some files. So Sean and Joel stood in the large empty room where once farmers' children had learned all they'd need for a simpler world. Sean kept tasting the musty air, as if it had been trapped there for decades. He forgot the couple living out their long marriage and thought only of rows of wooden desks, attached front to back with tops that tipped up to store schoolwork away.

Joel took a seat, cross-legged, on the worn floorboards in a patch of sun. "Propane wall heater," he noted. "I'm sure there's no insulation. Windows are loose and rattly. Needs some work."

"We could close it up for the cold months," Sean said.

"You're actually considering it?"

Sean was afraid to say anything because he wasn't really considering it, but part of him was dreaming a little. "We'd have to make a pact," he said finally. "I'm not kidding, Joel. A pact in blood. If I were to put my dad's money—"

"It's our money, Tyson, remember?" Joel said from the floor.

"But I'm not going to retire. I'm not moving up here for good. I'd have to come and go. You'd have to drive me to Madison for the Chicago bus because I'd still be working even if you quit your job, which I don't believe you'll do because you love your teaching too much. Maybe you'd cut your schedule somewhat. You could have a dog for company, but it'd have to be small enough for our apartment, too. And I still prefer that seventies garrison house with no charm to this one-room school. And what about down the hill? You want to live so near a ghost town?"

"I saw some junky cars parked and some laundry on a line."

"But Tory's showing us more places tomorrow. We don't have to decide."

"Because you're the cautious one."

"And you understand what I mean about a pact in blood? So you won't change the rules on me? I wouldn't come up here as often as you, no matter what place we might buy. We'd miss each other, our lives would change—"

Joel looked up with hurt in his brown eyes. He took his time before saying, "That sounds like a threat, Sean."

"I'm being realistic." He lowered himself to the floor beside Joel and reached an arm around him.

"But we've lived the way you wanted for thirty years, Quimby! If we don't start fresh now, when will we ever? I don't want to live in the beastly city till I die." He was growing tearful. "Christ, I just realized," he said, wiping at his eyes, "that one of us is going to die before the other one."

Sean let go of him to look into his face, but Joel turned away, so he grabbed those trembling shoulders again and pulled him in closer. He knew Joel said such things without conscious calculation, but they did have their effect. Sean had to stick to his point. "We're not talking about losing each other forever, only how it would feel living apart a lot more." Joel was staring at the sunlight on the floor, so he added, "Perhaps you'd like that?"

"This whole house-buying thing is stupid," Joel whispered to himself, but he went on for Sean to hear: "It's another of my dreams I won't be able to have, like being a real composer, having a real audience. All I've ever had is the Lilienthals and Foxridge Academy."

Sean was on the verge of trying to make up for all of Joel's disappointments by buying him a house in the country, but he caught himself and said, "That's bullshit." Joel wouldn't look up, so he continued: "Here's what I think. We're under no pressure. We've already got one place to live in, which is all most people ever get. I'm not being a lefty, I'm only saying that we have four more days up here. Our gal Tory said we can walk away with nothing. Or maybe something, Joel."

Sean sat in the silence and waited. He knew that Joel didn't want to stop looking, but he also wouldn't truly face the issue of living apart so much. Who was being stubborn now?

Finally, Sean decided to spell out his notion of a pact. "It's slow at the Collective from mid-June to mid-August," he began, unsure of what he might agree to. "I could imagine spending much of the summer months up here. That's my concession. And maybe in the fall, I'd cut back now and then, leave work on some Friday afternoons and go home on Monday mornings. But it's a four-hour drive and who knows how much longer by bus. We have to consider that. And you'd need to promise to come back when it starts to get cold and stay home till it warms up in the spring."

Staring into the sunlight on the floorboards, Joel said quietly, "But I really love this old schoolhouse."

4 All day Tuesday, Tory Forell had meetings with developers, but she'd lined up more properties for the day after. Sean and Joel slept late then drove to Richland Center to check out what Joel called its attractions. Since the Greenwood years, the town had assumed a more prosperous aspect. There was a good bookstore that also sold fine wines and a health food market with freshly baked breads of the whole-grain variety, and some of the antique shops held genuine finds. Joel kept expecting more enthusiasm from Sean, who could only say, "It's that I'm missing the way it used to be. The new stuff seems out of character. Your dad's old walk-up office with the gold lettering on the street door—what is it now? A tattoo parlor."

"Hardly a sign of prosperity, Quimby. But don't worry, this town isn't going anywhere." For lunch, Sean wanted to return to the Mexican place where they'd had supper the night before. "I sure know how you prefer your same old," Joel conceded.

There may have been actual Mexicans in the kitchen, but the

waitress was a local girl named Jaynie, who greeted them with "Good to see you two are up for more!"

After she'd taken their orders, Joel said, "What did you mean yesterday by that pact in blood?"

"To establish the seriousness of the situation."

"But you didn't mean pricking our fingers to sign some Faustian bargain."

"Maybe I did."

"Oh, Quimby, you're so damn—"

"Don't say it."

"Why can't you trust me? We always work things out. We have our different tastes. I've never minded your eye for the boys."

"Sometimes I wonder whose eye for the boys it is. But we may simply have to accept ourselves as we are and that we're not going to change. We should be clear about this and not have to work it out after the fact."

"We always have to work things out after the fact. We can't know till we get there."

Jaynie brought their Tecates. Joel had insisted they each have a beer to defuse the controversy. Sean had asked if he might have his in a glass, so now he raised it to Joel's bottle for a peace-making clink. "It's not that we have to be sure," he said, "but I want us to be clear."

"I'm always clear," said Joel.

"Your idea of 'clear' keeps changing."

Joel smiled across the table, accepting the charge. "It proves I'm adaptable. I'd even go with that ugly charmless house under the cliffs, if you truly prefer it. But I have to get out of Chicago! That's being clear, isn't it? You don't realize how all the people and noise keep me from hearing my music. Gustav Mahler would've understood."

"You said he once lived in New York City."

"Jesus Christ! That was just for one season. Anyway, I've got no Monday classes this fall, so I'll take long weekends to settle things up here. Then, I'll give an extra course in the winter term and only have the choral group in the spring, and I can start moving up. And you'll come for summer, and we'll get a dog. And then we'll see. The school can get some cheap recent college grad to replace me."

During their burrito lunch, Sean allowed Joel to elaborate the logistics of their new life: "Hey, by spring, you might even want to reduce your own hours, Quimby, especially because by then we'll have the dog and you'll have gotten so attached you'll miss it even more than you miss me. Sure, I can phone you in Chicago, but Skyping doesn't work for dogs. They need smells." And on went Joel's imaginings of their life in the old schoolhouse and driving the country roads in their new car or—he was open to it—even living in the ugly house or wherever.

Back in their rental Chevy, Sean wanted to drive them by the old Greenwood bungalow on Fourth Street, but Joel asked him not to. It didn't mean anything to him now and would make him think of his parents being dead. "Instead, let's go back by way of the schoolhouse," he said. "We can pretend we're arriving at our very own place and see how that feels. We've got all afternoon. I'll drive if you're tired."

"No, I'll drive," Sean said. "But then we'll return to the Kickapoo Gardens and take naps."

《 》

They parked at the foot of the dirt track, so they could walk up the way the schoolchildren used to. Some of them might still be living nearby, grandparents now whose offspring had long ago left for livelier regions. Sean stopped halfway to look over the rooftops of the sad little hamlet. He thought he heard a radio playing country music, but Joel hadn't noticed it. He was already at the schoolhouse, peeking in the smudgy windows.

The two of them explored the acre of cleared land. Down the slope behind the building was an overgrown thicket concealing two collapsing outhouses from the old days, one for girls and one for boys.

"Over here's a spot for your private retreat," Joel called from a small height looking out to the cornfields.

"You mean my shed."

"One of those prefabs. They've got windows and window boxes for flowers. You could have a desk and a cot. You could watch Internet porn undisturbed."

"Who says there'd be Internet?"

"We'll get a dish."

"Oh, man, who can argue with Joel Thomas Greenwood!" He stepped up beside him. It was a limestone shelf, a solid flat foundation. He could place the shed with its back to the schoolhouse and look out at only fields and hills and be a contemplative monk in the heart of fertile nature. He would pay homage to Ceres, if he needed a goddess to justify his temporary withdrawal from the world.

Then he thought about the emptiness of the rest of the twenty-four hours. What would he ever do up there all alone with Joel and Joel's music and Joel's dog?

"A dog would love it here," Joel said, taking Sean's hand.

"I was just thinking of your dog," Sean said.

"Our dog, Quimby, our dog!"

"Joel, you always claim to live in the present, but you're predicting all sorts of things we don't have yet."

"Well," Joel said, letting go and stepping back to think before saying, "it's somewhat like when I have an inkling of a piece I want to compose, like when you chose that Longfellow poem for me and I didn't know what it'd eventually sound like, but I got a feel for its atmosphere, the tones I wanted to strike, a vague sense of its shape, what it would have to accomplish. You know?"

It was another one of Joel's unexpected insights. They came from somewhere Sean couldn't quite locate. Mostly, Joel would jabber on about his emotions of the moment, but occasionally he would seem to be reaching deep into his artistic brain and put words to a thought Sean had never heard him utter before. He realized that Joel had a largely unarticulated side that he, Sean, had no access to. Hearing him say such things drew them closer, but Sean was left with an intimation of all that dwelt inside Joel that he could barely understand. So to regain his confidence, he said, "Now, about the ugly house. What tones does it strike in you?"

"Hey, we could drive by there, too, and find out!" He strode over to the schoolhouse and began tapping at various clapboards for rot. Sean followed and tapped a few himself. "See, Tyson, if we got it cheap, we could find a good carpenter—"

"I suppose you also want to drive by that moldy log cabin above the gully where we could build our dream house. Oh, but I forgot, this is already your dream house."

"Pretty much."

"Let's take a walk through the ghost town and see how you feel then," Sean said. They took the dirt track down to what the county map called Quarryville. Sean led the way toward that faint country music.

Joel tilted his head to catch the tune. "It's from that double-wide there," he said, pointing at a half-open kitchen window in which an electric fan rotated.

A woman's hoarse voice was joining the refrain: "Let me tell you how you hurt me, how all your roving broke my heart . . . " Or was it "all your loving"? They stopped and listened.

"Maybe she'll see us and come out," said Joel.

"Your new neighbor."

She did see them, because the torn screen door swung open and out stepped a large woman in an extra-extra-large green-and-yellow Packers T-shirt, which she wore as a dress over what Sean trusted was a pair of shorts. From her back stoop, she said, "Lookin' for someone?"

"We were up at the schoolhouse that's for sale," said Sean.

"Enjoyed your singing," Joel added.

"Didn't suppose no one was around to hear. Sorry about that. See, nobody's here most days, except I saw Fred's motorcycle, so he's over there, likely sleepin' it off." She waved a flabby arm toward the dilapidated house, the only one of two storeys.

"He's missing a lot of bricks," said Joel.

"Fred sells 'em off—antique old brick, people buy 'em for restoration. Not much cash in it, but I suppose it adds up. That used to be the roadhouse. Had the store down below. I can recall it from when I was little."

"Did you attend that school?" Joel asked.

"How old do you think I am, mister! They shut it down in my dad's time. For your sake, I sure hope you ain't thinkin' of buyin'."

"Maybe," Joel said.

"What, the both of you? You cousins or somethin'?"

Sean wanted to claim they were, but Joel said, "No, friends."

"I don't know about two older fellas going in on a one-room house. It'd look sorta funny," the woman said, leaning her bulk against the wooden railing to let herself slowly down onto the grass. She ambled toward them on her thick ankles and swollen feet in flip-flops. "But I don't mean to pry. You from Madison, I bet."

"I'm originally from Richland Center," Joel said. "My dad was a dentist—Dr. Nathan Greenwood?"

"I never go in there. Can't stand towns. I got Fred shoppin' for me when he ain't drinkin'. I'm Mary Peg."

"I'm Sean, and this is Joel." Sean would have held out his hand, but she showed no sign of expecting a shake.

"Anyways, you fellas don't look like cousins. You with those restoration people? Me, I'd let that old shell fall apart of itself, like the rest of Quarryville. You know that big-ass quarry back in the woods? They don't take stone outta it no more. This whole area has had it."

"How many people still live here?" Joel asked, looking around at the five other houses in sight.

"That's Lois and Thad Nowacky's. They keep their place so nice." The sweaty-browed woman stuck a fat finger out toward the only well-groomed lawn and the tidy white ranch house with a yellow Don't Tread On Me flag flying off the porch. "Aw, they're such good folks. Then there's me and my worthless son Richard and, of course, Freddy over there. That's about it. Cosmo comes back once in a blue moon to look after that one." She indicated an unpainted cigar box of a house overgrown with weeds. "No one owns the rest. There used to be thirty-plus residents here, not countin' ex-husbands." She gave a snort, somewhere between cynical and disinterested.

"So it's Mary Peg?" Joel asked.

"Mary Peg Schmitz. That's my second husband, Schmitz, Richard's dad, been dead for some years. First husband was Hooterman. Myself, I'm born a pure Irish Flynn."

"Sean's Irish, too," said Joel, as if to forge a bond.

"Only half," Sean said.

"I'm a hundred percent," said Mary Peg, "but I'm a godless old boozer like Fred over there. It's us against the good folks." She nodded at the yellow flag. The first time around, Sean hadn't caught the sarcasm. "Thing is," she went on, "I believe in live and let live. Lois and Thad Nowacky are funny that way. They got the idea the government's out to take away all their stuff. Shit, I live off the government! What would I do without my checks? You think Richard would support me, the worthless bum?"

This woman was like one of Sean's more troublesome clients, but he resisted taking the counselor role and stood back, trying not to feel responsible for her. Joel must be thinking she'd be part of his new world. "So what's he do, actually, your son?" he asked.

"Nothin'. He does fuckin' nothin'. That's all I can say. If he makes

158

a little dough, don't ask me how, he goes and gets himself another tattoo. I don't know which is uglier, those lizards runnin' up his hairy arms or that ghost skull on the back of his neck. Or the snake on that piss-color flag I have to look at all day."

"So how old is Richard?"

"Now, I'm fifty-one, and I had two by Hooterman, a boy and a girl, when I was still a teen, and God knows where they are now. I didn't get Richard till I was thirty, so I suppose he's goin' on twenty-one. See, Schmitz was a lot older. He was fifty when I landed him. Man, what a mistake!"

It was a good thing Mary Peg hadn't inquired further about the two of them. She was happiest telling her own stories.

"Of course, that bum of a kid seldom shows up here. The thing is, Quarryville ain't much of a real place anymore."

"But why does that 'nice' couple stay?" Joel asked.

"The Nowackys? I call 'em the Wackos. They're paranoid, that's what Fred thinks. They're hiding out from the Feds. Don't expect to get friendly with them, if you're crazy enough to buy that school-house. I knew the old folks that lived there, him anyway. I used to drink at his bar in Hub City. She was what we call a recluse, like the spider."

"Well, we're looking at a lot of places," said Sean, beginning to move along the potholed asphalt. "But thanks for the inside scoop."

"Naw, you wouldn't wanna live here," Mary Peg said. A slight breeze billowed out her Packers T-shirt, revealing huge green gym shorts and far too much pale thigh.

"We'll walk around the block and go on," Sean said.

Joel dawdled for pleasantries, but once the woman had waddled back to her kitchen, he caught up to Sean. "Well, Quimby, there goes my dream of quaint rural life."

They were passing a two-bay garage full of old tires and rusty tire chains. Nailed to the stucco siding was the same yellow-and-Black Bear Wheel Service sign from the gas station Daniel Tyson had patronized in his years as a family man. The bear itself was a mark of Sean's childhood. Its familiar smile was suddenly comforting.

"Which is worse, Tea Partiers or drunks?" Joel asked him.

"Tea Partiers," said Sean, but Joel assured him it was drunks.

<< >>

Sean went gentle on Joel. As they drove on to the garrison colonial, he said, "Don't be hasty. We probably wouldn't have much to do with them."

"But you're used to people like that, Tyson. I teach rich liberal people's kids to sing Handel and Bach and Gilbert and Sullivan."

"You're not going to find much of that up here."

"What about university types from Madison? They've got to be buying country places, too."

"I guess I don't mind Mary Peg myself," Sean said. "She's also what the world's made up of."

"Yes, Mr. Workers of the World."

"Like Grandfather Gruenwald."

"Right, and you're an old Wobbly."

That recurrent quibble had no new ground to explore, so they let it drop, watched the fields go by, and followed with their eyes the ridgeline of the hills. At one point, Sean slowed down not to churn up dust when passing an Amish horse and buggy with its triangular orange reflector.

"I could welcome Amish neighbors," Joel said. "They don't drink, and they're always working."

"Tory may have something better for us tomorrow," Sean said, to get him off his regrets.

"She didn't say, except that there's other prospects."

"But let's not dream too much till we've seen everything. Let's not work ourselves up about the ugly house, either. Keep track of the pros and cons. It's a big commitment you want us to make."

Joel leaned back and yawned, then said, reassuringly, "Only if you make it, too."

It was good to hear that, and Sean warned himself also not to get too dreamy if they sat out on that back deck watching the sunlight shift on the limestone cliffs. He told himself that their little balcony at home was big enough for them, and the late-afternoon light on the brown bricks across the street was as warm as it would be on yellow limestone.

They drove up the gravel drive to the house with its two types of siding and, after peering in the windows at the bare rooms, decided to duck through the barbed-wire fence out back and climb the slope to the west-facing cliff, no longer in shadow. It was a steep trek. The cow paths ran crosswise, not uphill, and they carefully avoided cow pies as they hopped on up, grabbing at bushes and tufts of long grass to keep from tipping backwards. It took more breath away than the Porcupines' more gradual marked trails. Sean felt like his eleven-year-old self as Joel got farther ahead and took a seat on a rocky ledge, but he was huffing, too.

When Sean reached him and sat down, neither said a thing but looked out at the miles of fields and woods and hills. The road wound down the valley, past those new farm buildings, but being so high up, they could also see a road curving along another valley to the north. To Sean, their Chevy looked like one of his Dinky Toys, and the black-and-white splotches of cows grazing were like the rubber ones in his sister Mary's farm set she'd never let him play with. He could picture her in a corner of their back living room, moving her toy herd about while he drove his baby-blue Studebaker and maroon Lincoln Zephyr along stripes in the carpet. Soon, either Sandy would crawl over and mess things up or Danny would stomp in and step on something and blame them for hurting his foot. Sean saw the scene now from his corner of the room as if he were still right there.

When he opened his eyes and looked out, Joel said, "That was a serious climb. I told you these are mountains."

"It's higher up than I thought from below."

"Do this every day, and we'll live into our nineties. I don't care if the house is without charm. It's what we'd do here that counts."

"You're dreaming again," Sean admonished him, yet he knew Joel couldn't help it. It was one of the invigorating charges in their long relationship. Sean did need new experiences, even if it was only trying out a new restaurant, to keep from getting stuck in the mud. But now, what struck him was that the suburban-style house down there was a real house to live in all the year, not merely a summer retreat. If Joel came back around to the schoolhouse, it wouldn't tempt them to move in for good, but if they went for the ugly house, with its red metal roof bright as a valentine heart, it might well be where they would have to live out their lives. "In a way," Sean said aloud, "the schoolhouse might be more practical. That house there has too many rooms to fill."

"Oh Jesus, here we go," said Joel, still taking in the lovely land spread out below.

They went to dinner at the hotel restaurant in Viroqua, the Vernon County seat, and then returned to the cool of Room Twelve at the Kickapoo Gardens. The Satyanarayanans were not in evidence, but there were several new cars out front, though none yet by Room Eleven. They went early to their separate beds. Sean read *The Real Adventure*, and Joel listened to the mp3 file of the *Hiawatha* music that Molly had sent the link for. Then, they each got a good night's sleep.

5 Wednesday morning it was a bit cooler, so they didn't need the AC driving to Tory's office. Joel immediately told her about Mary Peg Schmitz and drunk Fred and the Nowackys, though Sean tried to moderate the tale. Tory agreed that neighbors were a definite consideration.

Sean was beginning to get a sense of the county's geography, even if he couldn't remember what they'd gone past that first day on their own. Now, a Western-style bunkhouse with a horse paddock was up on Tory's itinerary and quickly rejected. Next, she took them farther afield, and there were so many twisty roads that Sean soon lost track of east and west. This had all begun as Joel's deal, but like it or not, it had also become his, and somehow he felt a certain responsibility to please Tory Forell. He wondered where that sweet little farmhouse with the eggplant shutters was, the one that truly might have tempted him.

They wound down a dense wooded valley and then climbed up to a high plateau where the road went arrow-straight through broad fields of corn and sun-yellowed grazing land with no hills on the horizon. A simple frame farmhouse was for sale up there. It would have been worth considering if it weren't so exposed in such treeless flat country.

Next, they went down a precipitous ravine to a well-maintained stone cottage in a shady dell that had the opposite drawback, all hemmed in and dark. Everything they saw that day was in their price range, all were what Joel called doable, but none had the garrison's splendid setting or the appeal of the schoolhouse. A few they even told Tory not to bother opening up.

She suggested they stop in Cazenovia for sandwiches at a place with outdoor tables and umbrellas for shade. As they ate, she gazed at them calmly across the picnic table, seriously contemplating something. "I wonder," she said, "if you're having second thoughts about all this."

"I've always had second thoughts," said Sean.

"But I wonder," Tory continued, "what if we'd seen today's homes yesterday? Maybe you would've been as enthusiastic about them as you were about the schoolhouse. Once alternatives start adding in, it gets confusing."

"I'm not confused," Joel said. "The house under the cliffs is still my number one."

That day, Tory's lips were cherry-blossom pink and her pantsuit grassy green. She'd done something different with her hair, but Sean couldn't tell what. "It's my experience," she said, after they'd finished their BLTs, "that a kind of exhaustion sets in when buyers have been looking awhile. It's not like you're purchasing a living-room suite or even a new car. A home is a whole environment that shapes your life."

"You can always sell it," said Sean, surprising himself.

"Yes, and some make a habit of it. Thank goodness for them, I say as a realtor." She pronounced it "reela-tor," which disappointed Sean. "But you guys don't strike me as house flippers."

"Hardly," Sean said. "We've lived in the same apartment for over thirty years. We've done next to nothing to it, either. You'd have to call it spare."

"I like a neutral space for my music," Joel explained. "It's only our computer room that's cluttered. Sean has his bookshelves jam-packed, and I've got my records and CDs and scores."

"Aha," said Tory, "this helps. I've been projecting a different image of your city lifestyle. You're not the typical male couple I see on TV."

They laughed at that and soon were off, driving to the last house of the day, a handsome solid brick farmhouse from the 1870s. It sat way back from the paved road and might have been possible but for the intermittent roar of traffic.

"Damn," said Joel, "if only it was on some dead end."

"It's too grand for us," Sean said, "but let's look at it, anyway." He felt a need to appreciate something beautiful and old, even if it would never be theirs.

"It hasn't been touched," Tory said. "Local folks don't value these old houses the way they ought. They want all on one level, all the mod cons, central air, and all sealed up tight against weather."

"And they don't want a lot of maintenance," Joel put in. Sean was admiring two huge maples with great thick trunks. "Haven't fallen on the roof yet," said Joel glumly.

"He's a new Joel today," Tory remarked to Sean. "I'm beginning to miss the over-enthusiastic version."

The house was a relic of a lost time—faded wallpapers, worn oak floors inlaid with mahogany, converted gas chandeliers with candle-flame lightbulbs, a stained-glass window of green leaves and red cherries and golden light at the top of the curving staircase. The house was awaiting an earnest young couple from Madison to restore it to the time of their great-great-grandparents. Sean realized he was thinking of Molly and Bill Moore.

"We're wasting your time, Tory," Joel said after touring the second floor.

"None of this wastes my time. It's a chance to see what's out here. Another client may come along who's right for it."

"I hope it's saved from the wrecking ball," said Sean.

As Tory drove them back to Richland Center, with Sean in the front seat for once and depressed Joel stretched out in back, she said, "If you two don't mind, I'm going to do some more investigating at the office. Your job is to think of all these properties, commonsensically, and if I dig up a couple more, we can meet again tomorrow afternoon. I've another meeting with developers in the morning."

"We don't want to wear you out," Sean said.

"Not at all. It's you two that'll wear out long before I do."

"You're like our shrink," said Joel. "I've finally got my spouse into couples counseling."

« »

At the motel, Sean felt it was only polite to go talk to Mrs. Satyanarayanan, who was sitting on a plastic chair outside the office door, reading the paper. Joel slipped into their room for a shower.

"Ah, Mr. Tyson, today any luck?"

"We saw plenty of places. Nothing quite right yet."

"Everything has its downside," she said with what Sean took to be a Hindu spirit of acceptance. She then opened her paper and showed him Tory's agency's ad. "I've been keeping my eyes wide open for you and Mr. Greenwood. Have you seen this lovely estate on the hillside? And what a good price!"

"Yes, we're considering that one."

"You couldn't do better. It looks in tip-top condition."

"Yes, it was very solid, very tight."

"You don't want something old. There are hidden costs. You want to relax in your retirement."

"If I retire," Sean said.

"But Mr. Greenwood said you really must. What is life for? At your age, if you have the savings, stop working. There's no virtue in work per se." That seemed odd coming from a member of the new entrepreneurial immigrant class. "And this one—" Mrs. S. put her beringed finger beside a grainy photo of a small house with a wide deck by a lake in Hillsboro. "It would be so pleasant to sit by the water, and lakes don't flood. The troubles we have encountered with that bloody Kickapoo!"

"But we want to be in Richland County," Sean said. "It's where Joel grew up."

"Sentimental reasoning! But Vernon County has a bit more sophistication, more people like yourselves, Mr. Tyson. We're right on the line. We do all our shopping in Viroqua." Sean wondered what she meant by "people like yourselves" but smiled as if he was flattered. "And yet we are loyal to Richland because it's where my boys got their start, but in the area in which you are house hunting, I must tell you, Mr. Tyson, there are a lot of hicks."

"We'd keep ourselves very private," Sean said. "That's why a lake is no good. Everyone can see and hear everybody else."

"Now, you see, I would enjoy that particularly. I am a somewhat nosy lady, as you may have noticed."

"You're in the right business then," Sean joked, and they parted on a cheerful note. He was surprised at himself for having spoken so decisively about what he wanted to buy, as if he had decided he wanted anything at all. He, too, suddenly needed a shower—and a nap.

Later, they walked all the way into Viola for pizza then strolled about the little town. Sean felt alien there. In Chicago, he would have all of life surrounding him, but here in the quiet, with only an occasional car passing and those few understocked stores and others standing empty or boarded up, he sensed what was happening to America as corporate capitalism continued to crush the little guy. Davey Nussbaum, for all his bluster, was right. But it was doubtlessly too late to fight the power.

"See, there's a nice new public library," Joel called from down the street.

Sean had to agree it was nice and new but said it was probably filled with DVDs and computer terminals.

"Don't be such a crank, Shaw-awn. Give the little town some credit."

"But I don't want to live here, Joel," Sean said flatly.

"Not Viola, necessarily."

"I don't want to live anywhere up here at all." The conviction had suddenly burst forth.

"Now you tell me!"

"It might be fine for a month or two, but I don't want to settle in here and call it our home. You imagine you'll find a congenial community up in these hills. Hell, I'd be more at home with the people here than you! They're not the problem for me."

"But the ugly house—you loved it."

"I didn't love it. It's too big. We've barely furnished our own apartment. I'm sorry, maybe I've played along because I keep telling myself this isn't going to happen."

Joel turned away and pressed his nose against the glass door of the library and peered in. Without looking at Sean, except perhaps in a reflection, he said, "Are you quitting, Tyson?"

"I don't know" was all Sean could say.

"But remember how the world out there is speeding up, and we're slowing down." Joel turned back around and might have had tears in his eyes.

Sean walked toward him and hugged him tight. "I'm not sure if the world's speeding up or breaking apart," he said into Joel's ear. "I do know I want to be with you and not live in separate worlds. The idea of it, Joel—it's something from the past, losing what—"

"But I don't want the Chicago world anymore."

"Though it's being there with me?"

"But our pact in blood, you spelled it all out."

Sean was conscious of being two sixty-five-year-old men embracing in full view of that small Wisconsin town, so he let go.

"I wonder," Joel said, "if Tory could help us talk about it."

"Can't we talk by ourselves? Bill Moore thinks men don't talk enough, though he hasn't tested our sort yet."

"Therapy's too bourgeois for you," Joel said, and they began walking back out of town toward the motel.

"I don't mean therapy," said Sean. "Can't we simply say what we each think it'd be like for us to have different ways of being home together?"

"You start then."

"No, you start."

"I suppose I'm deluding myself again," Joel said. "It's what I've always done since I was a boy." He began to hurry on ahead. Sean didn't want to shout after him up the street, but Joel called back, "You're not exactly undelusional yourself!" Sean looked around quickly. There was no one in sight, no eyes staring out from behind

168

glass. The nearest house had an air conditioner blasting in a front window. When he caught up with Joel, who had wandered down a grassy bank and sat himself down by the gurgling Kickapoo River, twilight was coming on.

"So?" Sean said, standing above him while Joel stared down at the darkening water. Then, Sean took a seat beside him in the dewy grass and said, "We're each somewhat afraid, aren't we? We're older now, and I want to hold onto what I'm sure of, which mostly is you, and you want us to make a fresh start before we get older still. You want to hear your music in the silence. But you want us to be together, too. Aren't we a pair?"

Joel faintly whispered, "Yes."

Sean was considering if there wasn't some crucial difference between them he'd never recognized till now. He hadn't imagined them in such a contest of wills. Sean knew Joel was not going to concede how much he'd miss him or that being alone with his viola and a herd of cows might not be enough for him. He was counting on Sean's caretaking nature coming to solace him. But Sean needed solace, too.

"I bet that muddy old river floods this high up the bank," Joel said. "I don't want us living beside a river that floods. That's why it's best to live up a mountain."

"Oh Joel," Sean sighed, "your mountains! So we're not going to discuss this any further?"

"What's to discuss? I'm holding you to our pact."

"But being apart half a whole year?"

"No," Joel said, "but being sure we love each other even when we're apart. I was sure my parents loved me. You weren't ever so sure of yours. Come on, old Quimby, let's go back to the Kickapoo Gardens."

They got themselves up and walked along as the moon was rising over the cornfields across the road. "Yet there's something in being always together," Sean said under his breath. Joel hadn't seemed to have heard, and Sean didn't say it a second time.

6 He had finished the happily resolved last chapter of his book, where the wife returned from her adventure, an expanded person having found her way to work and love, so it was reassuring if perhaps too easily hopeful. Sean looked over at Joel, who had taken out his earbuds and was staring blankly at the spackled wall above the TV. It was time to sleep.

They each had a restless night. Sean's brain wouldn't stop walking him through empty houses. Once, it was the house of the happy Tyson family, swarming with the four kids and their friends, but suddenly it felt hollowed out and Dad was nowhere and Mom was up in her bed, not to be disturbed. These weren't exactly dreams but unbidden pictures that flashed at Sean's tightly shut eyelids, and he'd turn over again and again and couldn't escape them. From across the room came an occasional sigh or throat-clearing or a fist pounding a pillow into shape. Sean knew not to speak for fear of interrupting the one moment when Joel was falling back asleep.

In the morning, he found only Mr. S. in the office. His wife had gone shopping. Mr. S. handed him two homemade blueberry muffins.

"So she was up early, baking," Sean said to make conversation.

"Indeed," Mr. S. said. "She is a productive woman. I am a lucky man. She takes excellent care. I am not well."

"I'm sorry," Sean said.

"It's the heart. I'm being treated at a first-rate medical facility. No problem." He wrapped his purple robe more closely and shuffled back to his armchair. When another guest came in, he heaved himself up again and Sean made his way out, balancing the muffins and two coffees.

Tory had assigned them the task of assessing the properties they'd seen, so Joel had dutifully made out a chart, listing all the pros and cons and with grades from A to F. He expected Sean to mark it up with his own ratings. "I know you have one single none-of-the-above," he said, "but at least we'll be clear about it. You're the one who wants to be clear."

"What are we doing this morning?" Sean asked. "We can't call her before noon." He was glancing at Joel's chart but wasn't inclined to add his two cents. He found himself entirely drained of thought.

"Hey, why don't you go off for a drive alone?" Joel suggested. "Without me, you might get your own sense of the area. But don't pick up any farm boys!"

"What are you going to do?"

"I'll be fine."

So Sean did take the car and the county map and was glad for the break. He traced his way up Highway 82 to County D and down past A at West Lima to Bloom City, where he took H to Yuba. He considered stopping for a real breakfast from Inka but felt too self-conscious, so instead he followed County C down to Hub City and picked up 82 back to D, where he soon found himself in sight of Quarryville again. No, he wouldn't stop there, either. He drove straight through Bloom City, but this time in West Lima he took A down to 56 and back to Viola. He'd had almost no thoughts during the entire drive. He didn't feel any closer to the landscape now, or any less so. He had simply cleared out his head. He was breathing more easily again. "Everything has its downside," he heard himself say, then opened the door to their room and found Joel pacing around, talking on his cell phone.

"It's Tory," he said. "Tory, Sean just came in. So we'll be meeting you at the park by the ridge, the store there, at one o'clock. You're amazing!" He shut the phone and said, "I've got a surprise for you. I'm not telling yet."

But Sean wormed it out of him. Tory Forell had remembered them mentioning the house with the eggplant trim, though she called it "aubergine." That's what the owners called it when she got hold of them, the ones with the Prius they'd seen out front. Someone in her office knew who they were. Yes, they lived in Madison. He was a physics professor, and they'd fixed the place up as their weekend getaway. No, it wasn't on the market, but the professor had accepted a high offer from Columbia University a year from now, and with their boys off in college, he and his wife were considering selling. They'd have to sell their Madison house, but should they hold onto their country place for a while? Tory had made the case for unloading it now. She could get them a cash offer, no contingencies, and from professional fellows looking toward retirement. They agreed she could, at least, show it and told her where a key was hidden. They trusted her because they'd bought the place years ago from a broker at her agency, but they said not to promise her clients anything. It was so sudden, this prospect of giving up where their boys had spent such happy summer days and gone cross-country skiing in winter.

Sean sat on the edge of his bed listening while Joel paced excitedly back and forth, telling his tale. "Now, don't get your hopes up, Sean," he said.

"Who's getting whose hopes up?"

"All right, but let's both calm down and take it slow."

"I'm calm," Sean said.

"How was your drive?"

"Calm. See how calm I am?"

Joel couldn't stop himself from jumping onto Sean's lap and flattening him back on the bed. Sean imagined he could feel Joel's heart beating, pressed close to his own.

« »

They met up with Tory at the store by the limestone ridge. She was licking a peppermint ice cream cone that went with her pink summer dress. It was the first time she had revealed her rather stocky legs. "I already paid for yours," she said, so Joel marched inside to get them something chocolaty.

"Who are these developers you're meeting with?" Sean asked, to keep at bay his immediate concern.

"It's a new addition on the south side of town. You wouldn't approve, some farm acreage up for sale."

"Good black earth never to be cultivated again," Sean sighed.

"All too true, but I'm making a living."

Joel brought out a dish of Mississippi Mud for Sean and a cone of the same for himself. It was all melting fast in the sun.

"You can leave your car here," Tory said, "and we'll drive up in mine. Ironically, it's on the far side of the hill from that garrison home you're considering. But finish before we get in, so you won't drip."

They hadn't yet discussed what they were about to see. Joel was obviously nervous, and Sean felt somewhat afraid. The tempting prospect had materialized though it might not be attainable. His empty head of the morning was fast filling with too much to contemplate.

There it was, set against a high sloping pasture with a forest on top like a thick head of dark green hair. A dozen Holsteins were following a cow path halfway up, their big heads bobbing, their tails swishing. Somewhere past the peak must be that limestone ledge where they'd sat and looked over into this valley to the north and the eggplant house out of sight under the shelter of its own Ocooch Mountain.

Tory pulled onto the lawn beside a rope hammock slung between tall oaks, the shaded grass strewn with acorns. The house was as Sean had been remembering it, a small reincarnation of Erastus Quimby's homestead down in Illinois. A two-seater wooden swing, like Gramma's, hung from the open front porch ceiling. Gramma still sat and rocked with small Sean there in his earliest memories.

Tory was patting around under a purple window box and pulled out the key to let them in. Joel was completely silent. He must have known to let this one sell itself.

They stepped into a small room with a round table set with burlap placemats and different-colored bandanas in animal-shaped wooden napkin rings at the four places. To the right was a carpeted sitting room with a soft-cushioned sofa and armchairs. Straight ahead, Sean saw the butcher-block counter of a bright modern kitchen and a picture window looking onto the green hillside. "There's also the little room that fits a queen-size bed where the Lauristons sleep, and the boys are up in the loft. Watch out on those steep stairs, Joel. In my business, guys, small is known as cozy."

"We like cozy," Joel called down. He couldn't possibly squeeze his piano up there, so maybe Sean could make the loft his own retreat. He went up as far as a middle step and peered across pine floorboards to a window under the roof peak. In his chest, his heart was thumping, and his temples were beginning to throb.

"I could put my piano where that sideboard is," Joel said as they passed back through the dining room, but Sean said nothing. Tory told them to check out the tiny bathroom off the kitchen and then come out to the screened-in back porch, where there were four wicker chairs and a view of the pasture and a wooden shed at the bottom of the yard. They each took a seat, and Tory said, "I can see you're serious now. What does the cautious one think?"

"I wonder if they really intend to sell. Wouldn't they want to keep it for their sons? It's where those boys grew up."

"It's rather far from Manhattan," said Tory. "The wife wants a summer place in the Vermont mountains."

"You had quite the personal talk," Sean said.

"Our gal knows her business," said Joel.

"But I can't promise anything, guys. They did say, if they decide to sell, they'll work with me." With a twinkle in her eye-shadowed blue eyes, she added, "But I told them, in a slow market, a chance like this may not come again."

"You haven't mentioned price," Sean said.

"They haven't either. If I was listing it, I'd start at seventy. I know that's high, but they'd probably come down to sixty-five."

"Our original limit was sixty," Sean said.

"The money's there," Joel said and then shut up again.

"Who's their cautious one?" Sean asked.

"Emily Lauriston's very excited about moving. She comes from out east. They bought this property because the landscape put her in mind of Vermont. The professor's from Wisconsin. He's more conflicted about leaving, but he said the New York offer would crown his career, so he accepted it."

"Let's walk outside," Sean said, not yet able to say anything for sure, but when he set foot on the soft grass, he began to feel strangely at home. "How much land did you say?"

"Only the one acre. The grazing land past the fence belongs to a farm up where the road ends." She pointed to the outdoor shower and the birdhouses in the crabapple tree and then, beyond, the flowerbed in an old stone foundation, blooming with late-summer zinnias and cosmos. "There used to be a garage here, but it collapsed in an ice storm. Joel, you could maybe fix up that shed at the other end for a music studio."

"He doesn't need any convincing," said Sean when Joel went to inspect.

"He's so quiet today," said Tory.

"Because he's stopped dreaming. He's seen it. What will he do if they won't sell?"

"If I can report that you're extremely interested—"

"You could," Sean said, knowing he was still safe because showing interest was not like signing a contract. But interest, equity, real estate—it was all getting too close.

"Then that's what I'll do," Tory said in her professional voice. "And this time, I don't see the spontaneous one changing his mind."

Joel now came back, elated that the shed had a solid pine floor and could easily be insulated and electrified and there was a window facing the pasture where he could sit and compose like Mahler hearing the alpine cowbells he put into his sixth symphony.

"I'm not sure what he's talking about," Tory said, "but it sounds like a plan."

« »

For supper, Sean and Joel picked up cheese curds, burgers, and malts at a joint in Richland Center. It was only after they were back in their car that they noticed the huge rooftop billboard picturing the governor's smug face beside "We stand with Scott Walker!" They drove off to the town's recreation park and sat on the grass away from baseball games and family barbecues.

By the time they returned to the Kickapoo Gardens, Joel was dead tired. There was a pickup truck outside Room Eleven and a backwoodsy young couple with beers sitting out front. "Need your chair back?" the man asked.

"No, no, we're heading for the AC," Sean said.

Once inside, Joel said, "You're always too accommodating. They took our chair."

"We're not using it. He was perfectly polite. I thought you were in a good mood."

Joel plopped onto his bed and said, "But we'll definitely not get it. Either they decide to keep the house or they ask way too much for your miserly self."

"Miserly!" Sean was already peeling off his sticky polo shirt and khakis and heading to the shower.

"You're so worried about having enough for our old age, Quimby."

"Because who knows what'll happen in this country."

"We can sell Chicago for big bucks. We can live cheaper here."

Before closing the bathroom door, Sean said, maybe for the last time, "I don't want to live up here."

The hot water pouring down and cleaning out his pores conjured up the old bathhouse days of the seventies. Before he met Joel, when he was on the loose and mostly miserable, even when he was with

Floyd, the notion of property, of owning his own place, of owning land, of inheriting something of value or of leaving something of value to someone else—none of that had ever occurred to him. He hadn't yet felt responsible for anyone, including himself. He had encounters in steam baths and rented rooms, and Davey and Andrew hadn't known what he did on nights and weekends. They only knew that Sean, too, was committed to the cause, which was to work against ownership, against property and the power of inherited wealth.

He ran his soapy hands over his body, pretending it didn't look much different from twenty or thirty years ago. To his hands, it didn't feel much different, but a body does change. Property—his thoughts kept turning back to it—property was a permanent thing. If it went down in value, it could also go up, and it was always there. If selected properly, it would surely go up with time. Capitalism counted on that. People had been brainwashed. Property was their charm against ending up as worthless ash. It was the substance of lineage, an actual thing to pass along. Years after death, his dad had drawn Sean back with a hundred thousand dollars.

He soaped what Dad used to call his "equipment." If he didn't want to use it to get children, what was it down there for? Why had it once driven him so? Pleasure, yes, and pleasure could lead to love and love to responsibility. Sean might have been stuck at pleasure but for Joel. Did Joel feel responsibility for him? He didn't often show it, but he'd made himself Sean's for life and that must be evidence enough. Aside from each other, though, they had no one to leave their property to. In a fairer society, where everyone was equally provided for, no one would have to leave property to anyone else, no one would expect an inheritance because the whole community would be the inheritance of all. That was Sean's dream, like Joel's dream of cowbell symphonies on a bright afternoon in the country.

He shut the water off and let himself drip in the misty warmth before stepping out into the overcooled motel room, where his pores would tighten and his skin grow goose bumps. As he stood there, naked and slippery in the shower stall, he thought of that young man named Owen down in Chicago, waiting for a phone call when they got home. Why had he popped into Sean's mind?

The bathroom door swung open, and there was Joel in his camouflage boxers, scratching his chest hairs and saying, "What were you doing in there so long? I desperately need to use the pot!"

« »

Before tucking himself into his own bed, Joel went over to nuzzle up beside Sean and again bemoan the inevitable loss of the most perfect place in the world. "What are the cons? None!"

"Price? An unwillingness to sell?"

"I'm talking about the property itself. It's on a dead-end road. There's all that beautiful pasture we wouldn't have to own, but it'd be as good as ours, ours to look at and walk across. The house may be small, but Tory says it's completely up to code. And it's all so tight and tidy, and it's got that porch in back and my music studio! You'd have the loft to get away from me, and a first-floor bedroom's good for when we get feeble. There's room for a washer-dryer in the kitchen. I measured."

"Slow down, Joel. So what should we do the rest of this week, keep looking, rethink the others?"

"No, it's this one or nothing."

"Nothing?"

"After we've found the perfect place? Tory's calling them again tomorrow."

"You're setting yourself up for disappointment."

"No. We're going to pay whatever they ask. I mean it. We'd regret it forever if we didn't. In the long run, it'll be worth it. Do you want to live in Quarryville?"

Sean would have said he didn't want to live up there at all, but this time he didn't because something in him did want the eggplant house. He remembered how last week he'd sat down in the Porkies by Mirror Lake, sunken in a primeval forest with everything still and quiet, while Joel wandered off to look at the rental cabins, and he'd felt restful and safe and as if he was saying goodbye to something. An obscure feeling had come over him while he looked at the pale, gray water, smooth as glass. Perhaps, without knowing it, he had begun to resign himself to the unknown that was still to come. Well, anyway, he told himself now, the eggplant house wasn't large enough to supplant their real home in Chicago. It wasn't too small, either. He could coexist there with Joel. He'd be reading in the hammock under the oaks or swinging on the porch and hearing a familiar tune from Joel's viola at the bottom of the property. It was the porch swing, when he first saw it, that had drawn him in. Something he had lost in his youth seemed within reach again. It wasn't even the old feeling of rocking beside his gramma at the Quimby farm. It was, rather, the sense of the earth all around under the grass. It wasn't ownership of that particular earth—that was only a legal convention. It was setting foot on that earth, or swinging over it in a hammock hanging between oak trees. It was like the hooves of cattle plodding along a hillside. They belonged there but didn't own it. They were more a part of it than an owner could be. That was the sense rising in Sean's thoughts with Joel lying beside him.

Then, the rumble of the air conditioner failed to mask a sudden moaning from the young couple in Room Eleven.

"They're making babies," Joel said.

"It'd better not take all night," said Sean, and it didn't. Soon, everyone was sound asleep.

7 Getting their morning coffee and muffins, Joel had told Mrs. S. about the professor's house. He reported that she was sure it would be theirs. "You must go meet this physicist," she'd said. It was

how her eldest had bought his motel. The owner had taken a liking to him. It became personal, as all good things must.

That had cheered Joel up, and though Sean advised him not to, he put in a call to Tory's office. The receptionist said she'd be free after her lunch meeting if they wanted to stop by. Now, with a plan of action, Joel decided to take their dirty laundry to a Laundromat in Richland Center so they'd arrive home with clean clothes. And while he did the washing, Sean could go sit in the public library and read.

Sean did need some more time alone. He wanted to think. But coming into town, he first drove them down Fourth Street past the Greenwood bungalow, which Joel had been adamant about avoiding. It looked the same as ever but without the Venetian blinds that Annie used to keep tilted for light but not for being seen. Joel didn't say a word and motioned for Sean to drive on. It must have brought back too much. When they stopped at the library, Joel took the wheel and drove off with the laundry.

At the entry, there was a sign pointing upstairs to a book sale. It was just what Sean needed. Most were decades-old best sellers, thrillers, and fantasy novels, many wrapped in plastic with catalog numbers glued on. Sean quickly identified the books he might want because they weren't so shiny or fat, or if they were fat, they were old and shopworn. Those must've been donated when a grandparent died. There were several Booth Tarkingtons and Hamlin Garlands he'd read years ago. There was a very fat edition of *The "Genius"* by Theodore Dreiser. The quote marks implied the hero wasn't much of a one. There was *Moon-Calf* by Floyd Dell. Wasn't he a well-known radical? The movement had gotten off to such a good start. Sean belonged back then. And there was *Studs Lonigan* by James T. Farrell. He'd read it in college and still had that same Modern Library Giant on his shelves at home. In novels, Sean preferred realistic stories of everyday lives. People were what mattered, people who suffered under the power of the establishment because no one had yet fought hard enough to depose it. His Modern American

Lit course had been all about the crushing of the common people. Reading Frank Norris's *The Octopus* had changed Sean forever. That treasured old paperback was still on his shelves, crammed in with all the other books he couldn't bring himself to donate to the Collective's swap shop, any more than Joel could part with his precious 33⅓ LPs because of the way they sounded on his old turntable. Of course, Sean had read far more books than he'd kept, but he had to own the ones that had mattered most. It was ownership of a nobler kind, wasn't it? He could never be a monk and live in a cell without any possessions. Everyone deserved a reasonable amount of things to care deeply about.

He moved from the fiction shelves to the history section and pulled out a biography of Harry Truman and then one of Khrushchev. There was a picture book on Kennedy, but he skipped that and reached for one on Johnson. My formative president, he told himself. He'd loved Johnson before he'd hated him. Now, he pretty much loved him again. Despite Vietnam, he was the last genuine reformer. Bullshit that Reagan had destroyed communism! That fake Soviet version fell apart by itself, as all corrupt systems must. Or must they? Would ours? Sean wasn't thinking about the eggplant house anymore at all.

On the shelf for poetry, he found a large leather-bound volume, embossed in intricate gold designs, that proved to be Longfellow's *Evangeline*. Someone long dead must have been proud to own such a fine edition. Back then, all schoolchildren knew it. They would've recited bits in the Quarryville schoolhouse. Mary Peg's grandparents surely read it, but what kid read Longfellow now? And why had he cropped up, once again, in Sean's life?

He added the book to his pile and went downstairs to the front desk, where he got the entire lot—Truman, Johnson, Khrushchev, *The "Genius"*, *Moon-Calf*, and *Evangeline*—for three dollars. The biographies were fifty cents each, the novels a quarter, but the poem, because it was so handsome, was a whole buck.

Sean found himself a soft chair in a quiet corner and was soon absorbed in the early life of Harry Truman in Missouri. One day, Sean reminded himself, that innocent little boy would cause A-bombs to drop on Japan.

« »

He was deep in thought. It could happen when he opened a book, just as Joel could strike a chord on the piano and suddenly be somewhere else. And while Sean only studied things, Joel could play what he loved with his own hands. Still, it was significant that certain books had determined Sean's role in life and committed him to finding safe places for people to eat and sleep and feel at home in. It should be unnecessary to keep telling himself that he had been doing his small bit.

The corner of his eye caught Joel coming across the reading room in his Madras Bermudas. "Not more moldy old books, Quimby! Come on, let's get burritos at the Mexican place. I'm starving!"

Later, they made their way to Tory's office and were soon seated back at the desk where their house search had begun. Tory was again in her powder-blue pantsuit, but it seemed softer now with her cherry-blossom lips and nails. She had just spoken with the professor's wife, who suggested they come through Madison and introduce themselves. "Just what Mrs. S. advised," Joel said with a delighted slap on Sean's back.

"But I'm hesitant about you meeting them without me," Tory said. "If they decide to sell, they'll want me to represent them, so it might get complicated."

"We won't make any deals without you," Joel promised.

And Sean asked, "Would it hurt simply to see them?"

"If you could have them sign and send back this agreement," Tory said, "then, well, you see, my job is to help both parties settle at a satisfactory price, but you understand, I'd be working primarily on their behalf."

Joel looked hurt, so Sean said, "It's how it's always done. She'd be our agent only if it wasn't her listing."

"What do I know! I'm a violist."

"A what?"

"I play viola in a string quartet."

"I gathered you were some kind of musician."

"He's also a composer," Sean put in.

"I'd love to hear your music, Joel."

"After I've sent you a CD, you may feel otherwise."

"It takes getting used to," said Sean.

"Is it like classical music?" Tory asked.

"It's more neoclassical modernism," Joel explained, "like an American Hindemith. He was a violist, too. I'm pretty retro for the twenty-first century."

"You don't have to know what he's talking about," Sean said. He was feeling slightly less fond of Tory now but understood why she didn't intend to be cut out of her commission after the trouble she'd been taking with them.

Joel wanted to drive off right then, but Tory wisely arranged the meeting for the next afternoon. "We'll have to cancel our last night at the Kickapoo Gardens," Sean said, "but at least we can spend it at a decent motel."

"And we could hook up with the Moores!"

"Hold on, Joel."

Tory cautioned them not to give up quite on other properties. She reached across the desk to grab their hands and give reassuring squeezes. "House hunting can have awful ups and downs, but I'll always keep trying for you."

That evening, Mrs. Satyanarayanan took credit for their Saturday plan and approved of their early departure. "Naturally, I cannot refund because you have the reduced weekly rate, but I tell you what I'll do. You are members of AARP? I will take five dollars off each night. That's thirty-five total saved."

Without revealing they had resisted all AARP come-ons, Joel told her she was very kind.

"But we are to be neighbors! I am fully confident of it."

Joel said he believed her, but Sean kept his mouth shut.

8 They did welcome the luxury of the Comfort Inn. Sean conceded it was corporate and looked exactly like every other Comfort Inn anywhere in America, but he didn't care. After two weeks of primitive living, he was not going to feel guilty about it. What he really wanted was to be home again, where everything had its place and the sunlight passed predictably from front windows to back and the traffic sounds came and went in a familiar rhythm.

The GPS on Joel's phone was now leading them up the hill above the zoo. When the disembodied female voice told them they had arrived at their destination, they saw a large brown-shingled cottage with a rambling wing extending off one end under the shade of tall trees. The wife, Emily Lauriston, greeted them at the door, and they were immediately "Sean and Joel" when she introduced them to her husband, James. He was handsome in a professorial way, despite his shaggy gray hair, blue work shirt, and old jeans, and the silver-rimmed glasses he kept tipping up and down. "Getting used to bifocals," he said and led them through French doors to a narrow veranda along the back of the house over the bluff. Emily brought out a tea tray and poured the cups and passed around shortbreads. "Some nights," James said, "sitting out here, I hear the roaring of lions. I feel like a gin-drinking British colonial in the African bush, though that's hardly my politics. I suspect I'll miss those roars."

"So you're moving to New York City?" Sean asked, already knowing the answer.

"We are!" said Emily. "It's a big event."

"It was a professional decision," said her husband. "I'd rather stay where I grew up. My grandfather was at UW in French. He worked on Anatole France and Marcel Proust and such authors. This was his house. My father grew up here. It's going to be a wrench, selling it, but there's no way our boys would live here, and with us moving so far from Wisconsin—"

"You could rent it out and then move back when you retire," Sean suggested. He had been struck by the man's evident melancholy. "Or you could rent it for a year till you're sure you want to sell." Joel's shoe gave his shin a quick little kick.

"Oh, you don't have to worry about our dilemmas, Sean," said Emily. It was clear her mind was already made up.

"It's probably best to make a clean break," James said. "It's difficult, but it's better. Emily's lived in my world for thirty-some years, so it's only fair I go live in hers."

"The Columbia housing's wonderful," his wife said, "Riverside Drive with views of the Hudson."

Then Sean said, "Tory Forell, our agent, said you might also get a place in the mountains. Oh, by the way, here's the agreement she wanted us to give you." It had been folded in his back pocket and gotten crinkled. Emily took it and tucked it under the tea tray.

"Vermont, yes, maybe, but enough about us," said James. "We'd like to hear about you two."

Sean could tell, from Joel's alert expression, that he saw this as an audition for his dreamed-of future. Sean himself didn't exactly want to flunk the test, but he also wasn't sure he wanted them to pass it. The professor turned to him first, so he talked about his work, assuming from that quip about politics that James would approve of the Collective. "My college friends and I started it back in '68," he said.

That prompted the question, "You weren't faced with the draft?"

"I got out with my asthma," Sean said.

"But I," said Joel, "simply told them I was a homosexual."

185

"They asked, and you told!" Emily said with a laugh. This was bonding, Sean decided, and when the conversation moved to Joel, it warmed up further.

"Ms. Forell told us you're a musician," Emily said, "but she didn't seem to know what sort."

"Violist."

"And a composer," Sean said. "He's too self-effacing."

"A composer! Tell me." James's melancholy had entirely lifted.

"Imagine a would-be Robert Schumann of the twentieth century," Joel said.

"James plays Schumann a lot," said Emily. "He's an excellent pianist, but he's self-effacing, too."

"You must know Schumann's beautiful, what is it, *Märchenbilder*? With the viola. Do you have your instrument?"

"Now I wish I did," Joel said. "I didn't want to worry about it on our travels."

"You should always have your instrument. I love the viola's moodiness. Recently, I've been accompanying a colleague on the Brahms clarinet sonatas. If you had your instrument, Joel, we could try them in the viola transcriptions. I have to say, Brahms and Schumann are my kind of music."

When they went off into technicalities, Sean turned to Emily and asked politely where their boys were in college. "The artistic one starts at Bennington in the fall, and the scientist will be a junior at Dartmouth. You can guess how pleased they are for a new home base in Manhattan." She lowered her voice and leaned closer to Sean. "I'm pleased, too, but I have to stay cool around my husband. He hates leaving this house. We did discuss renting it, but that meant definitely selling the cow cottage—that's what we call it—but if we're to keep any place in Wisconsin, the cottage makes more sense. Me, I'd like to sell both."

"We don't want to pressure you," Sean said.

Emily leaned even closer, though the other two had disappeared into the house to try out the piano. "James may be a theoretician, but he's also a tenderheart. He's not conflicted about the new job. It's a great late-career move. He's fifty-seven! But he's dealing with a lot of the past right now. He was very close to his grandmother, who lived here into her nineties. Much of the furniture and paintings were hers. We'll take it all east. We brought up our boys here, but at this stage of their lives, they're not yet sentimental. We'll find a country place near skiing in Vermont."

"You're definitely—"

"I grew up across the river from Hanover. My father was a history prof at Dartmouth. Oh, we're a totally academic family. The apartment at Columbia we'd have to sell back at their rates when James retires. No, we'll want our own house in the country to grow old in."

Familiar chords were resounding inside the house. At first, Sean thought they were Joel's *Kinderszenen*, but then he realized they were too strange, and yet he recognized them. They were Joel's driftwood piece. He hadn't heard it in weeks. He told himself he must not know much about music if he mistook it, even briefly, for Schumann. Emily Lauriston was cocking her head toward the French doors. "That's Joel's latest composition," he told her.

"It's lovely," she whispered. Then: "This is so good for James. I'm not musical enough—I just like to listen—but luckily he has musician friends. Speaking of which, I should tell you, we did once give our friends next door, Jock and Mary—he's a waste management engineer—a right of first refusal on the cow cottage should we ever decide to sell. They come up every spring to hunt for morels."

"Oh." Sean felt his stomach drop. This casual bit of news could spoil everything for Joel. He wondered if it also had for him and began to think it might have. "But they may not want it?"

"Most likely not. I suspect it was their gracious way of thanking us for those weekends. But we should run it by them, of course, before we go through your agent. Just so you know, Sean." She fingered the agreement tucked under the tray but didn't pull it out.

187

What could he say? "The thing is that Joel grew up in Richland Center. He really loves the area. His father was a dentist there." As if that gave them a prior claim! Sean had never felt so confused about what he truly wanted. He had always been one to make a decision and stick to it.

"So you both are naturally quite interested," Emily said, leaning back. All of a sudden, she seemed sympathetic again.

"It's by far the most appealing place we've seen."

"Ah, you shouldn't let on. Play hard to get and make us bring down the price."

But Sean's confusion had nothing to do with price. He hadn't thought once about how much they might ask—sixty-five thousand or his entire inheritance. "Well, Tory told us to leave all the negotiating to her."

"I'll let you in on something, Sean. If James wants you two to have it, you will, even if Jock and Mary make a bid. I'm thinking of how, ten years ago, he sold his grandmother's precious old auto to two men from Illinois. Somehow, it made James happy that they were gay. He has the idea that gay men take better care of things. My husband's a quirky one."

Sean had finally seen Emily Lauriston properly. As usual, it took him awhile to register on what other men might see in her, that she was pretty or sexy, that she was beautiful. Emily had large, earnest brown eyes and an elegantly narrow nose that made him trust her. She was a woman in her fifties who was contented with what she had and even more so with what she was going to have. Sean wished he could feel as sure of things.

It sounded like two pianos in there now. They went into the living room and found Joel and the professor, side by side on the piano bench, all four hands going up and down the keys. "It's the Schubert Fantasie, Emily," James shouted over the music. "This is great fun!"

His wife, again, whispered into Sean's ear, "He's going to love all those concerts in New York City."

Joel was wildly happy as they drove back down toward the zoo, before Sean told him about the right of first refusal. "But no!" he bellowed. "They can't! Who are these neighbors? Fuck them!"

"Calm down, I'm driving."

"And James never mentioned it!"

Sean drove slowly past the zoo, pondering how to handle the outburst. "But I could tell he really took to you, Joel. That'll mean something." He didn't want to raise false hopes by passing on what Emily had said about her husband's quirkiness.

"And I thought she liked us, too."

"She did. Those neighbors may well not want it. It was just a courtesy."

Joel pounded the dashboard. "A courtesy! I knew it! That's why they left it up in the air. There's always a hitch that ruins everything."

"Don't jump to conclusions. The Lauristons may not even decide to sell."

Joel turned away in a funk and watched the tree-shaded neighborhood roll by. Sean knew not to say any more.

They found their way back to their motel room and took turns soaking in hot baths and then lay out on their queen beds in fluffy white towels with the AC wafting over them. Eventually, Sean dared to ask what Joel had thought of the professor's piano playing.

"Couldn't you tell? He's a great sight reader. I barely kept up, but then, I'm only a violist."

"Did he like your driftwood piece?"

"Hey, you recognized it! I'm proud of you, Quimby. Yeah, he understood how the harmonies moved. He got it right away. I didn't sing the words. The music has to stand on its own."

"And were you a twenty-first-century Schumann?"

"Twentieth, Quimby. Face it, we're to the twentieth what Dvorak and Tchaikovsky were to the nineteenth, children of the forties.

We're lucky even to have made it to the twenty-first. Tchaikovsky died in '96."

"I'm glad to be a child of the forties," Sean said. "We remember how it was before things sped up."

"But if I'd been born in the 1890s, I'd be seen as a modernist instead of an old fart."

"And you'd be dead."

Joel unwrapped his towel and, naked as a baby, got up to put on clean clothes. He had emailed the Moores, who had returned from Mishe-Mokwa and were to meet them at an Asian restaurant near the Capitol.

« »

"That's where he does his dirt," Sean said. "That's where he defies the will of the people."

The great white dome shone first in setting sunlight and then in shadow as they drove around the square and finally found a parking place on a side street. Sean was apprehensive about seeing Bill and Molly again. They belonged in the Upper Peninsula before the house hunt began. In the original vacation plan, Sean and Joel would now be sitting down to their last dinner at Phil Kimbley's lodge in the knowledge that they had enough money to take such vacations for the rest of their lives. They could even venture into distant lands instead of confining themselves to one single address on a gravel road in Richland County, Wisconsin. But Sean had never been a traveler, had never been to Europe or even to Mexico, and to Canada only briefly at the Soo, so why would he want to start at this late date?

The restaurant had a line out the door, but peering through the window, they spotted the Moores waving merrily from a booth. They pushed their way as politely as possible through the crowd and joined them.

"We would've had you to our condo," said Molly, "but we just got back and it's a disaster area, and this is our favorite meal out."

"It's funny seeing you two out of context," Bill said. "I've been picturing you as tribal elders canoeing off Mishe-Mokwa."

"Sean will take that as a compliment," said Joel.

The four spent some time reminiscing about the seemingly long-ago days by the lake and then let Bill order from the elaborate menu. Neither Sean nor Joel was up on Asian fusion cuisine, but the food turned out to be delicious and not too spicy. Talking about it carried the conversation while Sean kept thinking how they didn't really know these young people. Though they shared the dishes, they each ate whatever they liked best, which for Sean was the more familiar broccoli garlic chicken with cashews.

Eventually, Joel began his recital of their real estate saga. He described each property in too much detail, Sean felt, and was snide about Tory's pantsuits and the bar in Yuba and Mary Peg's blarney, but the Moores were at least pretending to be fascinated by it all. Then he got to the eggplant house and couldn't help but express his anxieties at some length. "It was so perfect. Even Sean had to admit it. Any other place we'd buy he'd carry a big silent grudge about. And now we find out that this damn sewage engineer, or whatever he is, has first dibs!"

To retrieve the lighter mood, because the Moores were surely expecting a fun evening, Sean cut off Joel's whining by saying, more to Bill than Molly, "I bet they sell to us, though. The wife seemed to think the neighbors were only being polite, and she really wants to do a quick deal, so they can buy a place in Vermont. After Joel got the professor playing piano with him, he was winning him over. His wife told me he would really like their cottage to go to people like us."

Joel was wide-eyed. "She said that?"

"She and I had quite a talk while you were banging away in there."

"You didn't tell me that part."

Sean turned to Molly. "I have to watch what I tell him. One way or another, he tends to go overboard."

"You mean you didn't want me to get my hopes up. Jesus Christ, why not!"

"I want us to be steady about this. I'm moving toward it, Joel. And when the professor reminisced about his grandparents, I thought of my gramma and her farmhouse, and maybe that's why I also want to buy that cow cottage."

Joel's brown eyes opened even wider. "You do want to buy it?"

"He does," Molly said. "You two are going to be fine."

"But what if they can't get it, honey?" said Bill.

"Then, they'll be sad together. It's all good."

"It'd be terrible," Joel said, but in that instant, Sean lost all sense of being wary. His innards had shifted, and the tightness softened. He wasn't holding back in uncertainty. The pact in blood he'd asked for wasn't for protection anymore but a kind of harmonious compact. Sean leaned himself back in the booth beside Bill Moore, who was scraping up his Vietnamese noodle dish, and appreciated Molly sitting composedly across from him, even her New Age-iness and what she'd said about being sad together. He had always assumed that if one of them was sad, the other's duty was to cheer him up, and when one was overly happy, the other should try to tone him down. But soon, they would be old men. Why keep fretting about balancing the good with the ill? Why not dip down together into sadness? After all, they couldn't know which one of them would die first. If they were lucky, they could be happy together till then. But Sean knew this was all a psychological oversimplification.

Across the table, holding Molly now by the wrist as his ally, Joel said, "So you'll let us outbid this Jock person?"

"We'll see if it comes to that." Sean noted the pleased smirk on Joel's lips. He hadn't seen him look as contented since they swam in the Big-Sea-Water up north.

192

"I love that Molly," Joel said, when they were back in their Chevy. "She's got us figured."

"Bill sure didn't say much. And he's researching if men go silent! He's his own best subject."

"It's not Molly's fault. She's naturally engaged. Your Bill's a prig."

"These one-way streets have me all screwed up now. Where's your GPS, Joel?"

Sean didn't want to reveal his own new peaceful state of mind. He felt it there inside himself, but it'd be undermined if made evident to Joel. Instead, they'd go on in their accustomed fashion and, meanwhile, wait for chance and luck. James Lauriston would have to decide to sell, then the neighbors would be given a shot, and if it went as Emily seemed to think, they would set the price and Tory Forell would call. What the professor had said, seeing them out the door, was that he liked the idea of Joel's viola serenading the cows on the hillside. "They wouldn't be your cows," he said, "but they won't know that. They'll moo back. They make their own music, the way my lions do." Perversely, Sean had thought of Chicago traffic and imagined what James would have to hear, living in New York City.

At the motel, when they got into their separate queen-sized beds for a good night's sleep, Joel said, "I'm going to send an anonymous threatening letter to those sewage people."

"No, you're not."

"But I'd like to."

"And you won't."

"How about a nice pleading letter saying we need the place to save our marriage."

"Our marriage is safe."

"So you're just going to wait?"

"We're going home tomorrow, and I'll be back at work Monday, and you'll go back to school soon, and you'll be practicing Brahms with the Lilienthals."

"Or Schoenberg."

"But what if, on our way down, we stopped at my sister's? I haven't been there in months."

"Your sister's not so fond of me, and you don't approve of the North Shore scene."

"She likes you perfectly well, and it's not about the North Shore. You wouldn't even look at your childhood bungalow."

"Because the Greenwoods don't live there now. I don't like to think about it. You go wallow in your past, if you want to."

"I don't plan to visit the old Cedar Street house. I just want, I don't know why, to see my sister. We only talk by phone. You don't have a sister, Joel. You don't know what it's like."

"I don't even have cousins. I'm all alone in the world except for an old Quimby. You don't know what that's like, either."

After thirty seconds of silence, Sean said, "Do you want some company over there?"

"Maybe one quick squeeze."

Sean felt his way across in the dark and under the covers and spooned him awhile, chastely and sleepily, then tiptoed back to the other bed.

PART FOUR

1 They were back in Illinois. Driving slowly down leafy Sheridan Road, Sean sensed a different air. It was the lake, he figured, a freshness, probably imaginary or maybe the first touch of autumn sweeping in. Joel was sleeping. At least, he had his eyes closed and was tucked against the headrest. He had not been pleased about stopping at the Aherns'. He always took their friendliness for condescension, not so much because he was Jewish but because his dad had been a small-town dentist. Back when he met Sean, he'd picked up no hint of his Tyson world. He'd taken him for a lower-middle-class state-college man doing good work for underprivileged city folk. That was still how Sean wanted to be seen.

They crossed the town line, and the turn for Mary's was coming up. "We're almost there," Sean said with a tap on Joel's shoulder.

"Home?" Joel yawned and stretched. "Oh, no! Jesus, I forgot. Do we have to, Shaw-awn?"

"She's expecting us."

"You commit us to so much shit without considering me. You know how creeped out I am by the castle."

It did have a crenellated limestone tower at the crotch of its pseudo-Tudor wings. Sean pulled up the circular drive and stopped at what Joel called the portcullis, the studded mahogany front door. Reluctantly, he followed Sean up the front steps. They didn't even have to lift the knocker because the door swung open, and there was Mary, barefoot in shorts and a DePaul T-shirt, her auburn locks now back to brown and a bit longer. "My fellow heirs!" she exclaimed, kindly including Joel in the plural.

"Let's not talk about it," Sean said. He gave his sister a hug, while she firmly kissed his cheek.

"Yet!" she said. "But I want to hear about your trip and the properties you saw. Trev and I haven't decided what to do with our own little windfall. Maybe a time-share in St. Croix where we can golf? Or Turks and Caicos? Definitely nothing in the South. No Fort Lauderdale! I understand it's totally gay now. How about you two buying Dad's place off the Villalbas!"

"Slow down, Mary."

She was giving Joel a sisterly hug and then leading them out to the back deck with its retractable awning and kitchen-sized gas grill. "You'll stay till Trevor gets home from the club? I told Keith and Charlotte you were coming. Devin and Polly are out on the lake, but your favorite grandniece may show up. You two don't realize how important you are for Quincy's hipness quotient."

"If we're all it takes—" Sean began.

"Oh, you!" Mary pressed him into a rattan chair at the glass-top table where she'd already set out a tray of cheese and pita chips and pointed Joel to a chair on the sunny side. "Cold beers?" She went to the bar fridge and brought them frosted glasses and bottles of Leinenkugel. Joel's antipathy to the suburban style of life somehow never showed when he was invited to take part in it. He'd only complain before and after. He was watching thirstily as Mary poured out his beer and had a slice of Gruyère ready on a chip.

"Eat cheese or die," he said. "Wisconsin state motto."

"Really? Oh, he's joking. I knew it," Mary said, pulling up a third chair between them. "We don't see enough of you boys. So let's hear the whole story."

Joel deferred to Sean. He must've known that his own enthusiasm would only make it more difficult for Sean to stick to his willingness to buy the eggplant house. Now that they were back in Illinois, the whole trip did seem dreamlike to Sean. Was there really a small farmhouse in a Wisconsin valley that could be theirs? If they lost it, would he live forever in deep regret? But as he summed it all up for his sister, he did it rationally and calmly, as if nothing might work out because of the first refusal business, and besides, there was no rush. They might, after all, decide not to buy anything and simply rent different places each summer to escape the city.

"On the other hand," Joel finally butted in, "it's going to happen even if I have to shoot a sewage engineer." He set down his emptied glass.

"Let me get you another Leiny," Mary said. "I like your attitude, Joel."

"Waste management," Sean said quietly.

"Well, his days are numbered," said Joel. He took a first sip off the second icy glass Mary handed him.

"Sean?"

"Still nursing mine."

She poured herself one more and sat back down. "So what do you think? Our next project is a pool. I don't know why we've put it off so long. It means a higher fence across the back, but who wants to look at the Vogels, anyway? Now, when you drive out through the village, Sean, you'll see they've painted our old Cedar Street house a muddy green. I loved growing up in that house, such a handsome old Victorian, and now I'm in this fifties showplace. So nouveau! But it sure is cushy. Love the sunsets out here at cocktail hour. We're spoiled."

Having entered his sister's world, straight from their sojourn in the North, Sean felt more than ever the great chasm between her life and his. Joel might be content with his beer and cheese, listening to Mary carry on, but Sean wanted to get back to their apartment in its world of all sorts of people. Mary had stayed in the town they grew up in, had found herself a great provider of a husband and had two sons she could pamper. But Sean had been determined to lose all of that. And there she sat, his little sister, luxuriating in her opulence, chatting away with the small-town dentist's son, eager for details about possible second homes in Wisconsin.

"And, Sean, I do wish Devin hadn't taken Polly out sailing. As a

197

broker, she could give you tips about circumventing that first refusal. It all comes down to moolah, and you've got it, brother."

"On a related subject," Sean said, "what do you think our younger brother will do with his?"

"I know one thing. Sandy doesn't want your Collective involved."

"It was just a suggestion."

"He's been talking to Danny, who's coming out to meet with Dad's firm. I don't suppose you'll try to see him?"

"It's been a couple of years."

"He's your own brother, Sean. He's approaching retirement. And he's made big changes. I'm sworn to secrecy, but for one, he's not drinking."

"I am drinking," Joel said merrily.

"Two is your limit, Joel."

"Yes, Mr. Tyson, sir."

"You two! Oh, I hear Quincy!"

Out the door came the rising tenth-grader Sean hadn't seen since her middle school graduation. She was a long-legged blonde, tanned and trim in white tennis shorts and low-cut top, startlingly more adult than the girl he remembered. "Uncle Sean!" she practically sang, "and Uncle Joel, yay, yay!"

When she had settled down with a greenish Odwalla smoothie, her grandmother said, "Look how pretty she's gotten, and here I am in my slobby fortieth reunion T-shirt. But it's Sunday, and it's family, so who cares?"

"You're looking good, Grandma. When I'm sixty-three, I hope I'll look as good as you."

"Was that a compliment?" Mary asked Joel.

"Oh, Grandma, of course," squeaked Quincy.

Sean glanced again at her cleavage, the most grown-up part of her. In his day, boys never got such glimpses, even on the beach. Despite having a sister, a mother, and a grandmother, he had never been that curious about the female body.

Quincy had lots to tell about her summer and a boy she'd been playing tennis with named Benjamin. Joel asked for details, which she gave with blushes and giggles, but Sean turned the conversation toward school. "Do they still do the sophomore mythology course?"

"I don't think they call it that, Uncle Sean. I think we're doing global studies."

"That's pretty much what it was," he said, "everything from the Greeks to *Hiawatha*."

"We're definitely doing native peoples' creation stories," Quincy said. "I'm supposed to have done summer reading, but I haven't yet."

"Too much Benjamin," said Mary.

Because he'd been thinking about it in Wisconsin, Sean said, "The one I loved most was the myth of why we have spring, the one about Ceres. She's where we get the word 'cereal.' She was the goddess of the harvest. She had to wait for her daughter to come back from the underworld before she'd plant the crops. Myths are the way people used to make sense of nature. Now, thankfully, we have science, but they're still wonderful stories."

"You should've been a teacher, Uncle Sean."

"I'm a teacher," said Joel, "but I'm fixing to call it quits."

"Oh, no!" Quincy moaned. "You're too young to retire, aren't you? I don't want you or Uncle Sean ever to retire. I brag about you both all the time. I've been telling Benjamin about you getting married in Iowa. He thinks gay men are cool, but luckily for me, he's into girls."

Suddenly, Sean remembered he was again in range of that young man, Owen, and had no idea what he was going to do about it.

« »

Having told their real estate saga to the Moores last night and that afternoon to Mary, and then to his nephew Keith and wife Charlotte when they dropped in later, Sean felt it turning into its own kind of mythical tale about things that happened in another time and place. Keith and Charlotte, fresh from a Sunday dinner with her parents, showed mild interest, but Joel had grown more enthusiastic with each of Sean's recitations. Charlotte, a blousy chub of thirty-three, looked quite formal beside her T-shirted mother-in-law. She and Keith were still in their church clothes though he had loosened his tie and draped his sport jacket over the back of his chair. Sean had never much liked Keith. He was the cool-headed nephew, while Devin had some of their mother's oomph.

"Uncle Keith," Quincy said, "did you have Mr. Turner for English?"

"Joe Turner. Good teacher. Just starting out when I had him. Took over for Gault. That old man was scary!"

"I loved Mr. Gault," Sean said.

"You had him before he went batzoid, Unc Sean," said Keith.

"Did he really?" Quincy asked.

"Did he ever!" said her grandmother. "Parents had to meet with the headmaster. Gault took a leave in the middle of the semester, and in came Joe."

"I've always thought," Sean said cautiously but determined, "that Mr. Gault helped me not to be a Christian. No offense to Episcopalians, Charlotte, but the things we studied in his class got me doubting. In a good way. He taught us that people everywhere have always made up these incredible stories they somehow convinced themselves were actually true."

"You liked the Ojibway ones," Joel said, as if to tone Sean down.

"But there's a difference between liking and believing."

"The thing is," said frustrated Quincy, "what I wanted to say was, it's Mr. Turner's son Benjamin I'm going out with now. We were playing tennis, and I was going to bring him over, but he had to lifeguard at the Club. I mean, his dad's not a member, but he's got a summer job there, and I wonder what it's like being a teacher's kid and living around here."

"His parents were pretty well off, Quince," Keith said. "You knew them, Mom. Didn't old Prof Turner teach at Northwestern with Unc Albert?"

"This is amazing!" said Joel. "I had a Professor Turner for History of Mathematics, the course for dummies."

"It's a small world," said Charlotte, her first real words of the afternoon.

"Older people are always talking about who they knew back when," said Quincy.

"You mustn't mind us, dear," said Mary.

"No, Grandma, but I was wanting to ask because Benjamin and I are getting serious, and I don't want the money issue to come between us. I mean, he has to have a summer job lifeguarding!"

"And you should have a job, too," Mary said. "I sold beachwear at Old Orchard when I was your age."

"I mowed lawns," Sean said, "before your crews of undocumented Mexicans." Joel could have one-upped him but mustn't have wanted to seem the poor kid.

Mary threw up her hands. "And what it cost to bring up two boys!"

"Come on, Mom," said Keith, "Devin and I never deprived you of a thing."

"Well, you can thank your father for that."

"And it hasn't kept me from making my own little pile, either, Mother."

"So, Uncle Keith," said Quincy, "do you and Aunt Charlotte plan to ever have kids?"

"You don't ask such questions," said her grandmother. "But I will ask you, then, if you and young Benjamin Turner are being careful *not* to have a kid."

Charlotte's pink cheeks went slightly red, and Keith said, "Mother, you're so bad!"

"See," Mary told Sean, "you've entirely avoided this battle of generations."

"It's no battle, Grandma, it's fun. I love hanging out with my family. I just wish my parents would get off the lake and pick up Bradford at softball and come over so, for once, we'd all be together, the great uncles, too. I wish Benjamin could meet the rest of you. You'd really like him."

"And is there any other subject you'd like to talk about?" Mary asked, but the grown-ups already knew the answer.

« »

Trevor called to apologize that he was going around another nine holes, and Sean did want to get home to unload and return the rental and prepare for work the next day, so they drove off after fierce hugs and kisses from Mary and Quincy, light hugs from Charlotte, and Keith's hearty handshakes. Joel had been buoyed up by the visit he'd claimed to dread, while Sean felt sunk in the past. He let Joel babble on about the difference between Tysons and Greenwoods, about public schools and private, about busty girls and lifeguard boys—to him, North Shore life was at best satirical.

To make up for having been driven past his own childhood home, Joel insisted they head out by the newly mud-green Cedar Street house, onto which Sean's inner eye had to superimpose the dusty yellow clapboards, white cornices, and charcoal-gray shutters of his youth. He saw again his mother's stockinged feet, pacing the living-room carpet by the green corduroy couch where he lay. He saw the tempting file cabinet in his father's study. And further back, he saw Mary's farm animals and his long-lost maroon Lincoln Zephyr rolling its tiny rubber tires along the stripes of the back living-room rug. He even saw baby Alexander in his mother's arms and heard the slaps and thumps of Dad and Danny playing catch out on the driveway.

"You're not listening," Joel said.

"I'm pretty beat," said Sean. "I want to get home."

When, at last, back on their balcony in the canvas chairs with takeout panini from Lo Grasso's, Sean confessed he didn't want to think about moving away from there to any cow cottage or schoolhouse or garrison under limestone cliffs. He wanted to stay where they were, forever.

Joel didn't say a word but shot him a disbelieving stare, his lips open, his eyes wide.

"I'll probably feel better tomorrow," Sean said.

"It's from seeing Cedar Street," Joel said. "You get like this after being up there. Look, it's somebody else's house now. Your family's gone." He began staring across the street at the wall of three-decker brown-brick buildings. "So if you don't want to buy the eggplant house," he said, as if talking only to himself, "then we won't, even if we could. It's your money, it's your decision. I can have my dreams, but mostly they're about us. That's how Dr. Nathan would talk. 'Your mother and I,' he always said. 'We' this, 'we' that. I don't remember either of them referring to one without the other. They never said to me, 'I love you.' It was always: 'We love you.' That probably made me weird."

"It's weird that you call him Dr. Nathan."

"Because everyone did. I don't know why not 'Dr. Greenwood.' Kids at school knew me as Dr. Nathan's son. Lots of them, he'd filled their teeth. I only once heard a lady call him her Jewish dentist. Without too many Jews around, I suppose it didn't matter much."

The sunlight had been moving up the brick-pillared porches across the street. The top one would soon be in the shadow of their own building, and a slight chill would descend with the twilight. Sean was glad he'd said what he said and that Joel had made it all right, at least for now.

Later, when he was squeezing the books he'd bought at the library sale into the shelves in the middle room, Sean found himself pulling out the tattered paperback of *Jennie Gerhardt* to peek inside the back flap and make sure the phone number hadn't magically disappeared. Then he took the heavy Truman biography with him to bed to read beside Joel, who had already fallen asleep.

2 Sean was happy back at work. He answered his colleagues' questions about his two weeks off with a brief tale of hiking and canoeing and driving around Joel's home turf for sentiment's sake, making much of the refreshing idleness and giving prominence to the Satyanarayanans and Mary Peg without mentioning Victorine Forell or the Lauristons.

Neither Andrew nor Davey knew of his inheritance, and he might never tell them. They had brought him into a world of people barely getting by, despite working hard at two or three jobs and bringing up four or five kids alone or living with some drunk they had to escape from. Sandy Tyson might have been one of them, but none of Sean's people had a suburban sister to lean on or would ever inherit a hundred thousand in stocks and bonds.

Sitting at his desk awaiting his first client, Sean put down his paperwork, took off his reading glasses, and remembered way back when a sweet-faced teenager from out east had stepped anxiously into his old office in the storefront. He had some Irishy name and was an obviously guilt-ridden runaway Catholic gay boy. All he needed, he'd said, was a roof over his head. Sean figured some older man had kept him awhile and then kicked him out, though all the boy said was that he had nobody and he sure wasn't going to go talk to some creepy old priest again. With all of Sean's many cases, why had this one come to mind so vividly? A rush of feeling was sweeping over him, almost as if his mother were still alive, and he wanted to pound on his desk or get up and open the window to the street and yell out that religion ruined people's lives so stop believing all that crap and act like human beings, for Christ's sake! It was the sort of thing Davey and Beth used to do in their yippie days. Sean himself never quite yelled during protest rallies but mostly stood in the crowd quietly showing support.

That was back when he'd lost touch completely with his Tyson cousins. These days, he heard about them all from Mary. She'd forward emails and links to blogs, but Sean never followed up. He wanted to be free from ancestors and the generations to come. He didn't feel sad about it. He never even thought about it except now, remembering that runaway kid and wondering what became of him. Sean had placed him in a rooming house in Uptown. He was nearing fifty now, if he was even still alive. Those were the gay boys that died back in the eighties.

Elise knocked on the door frame. "Quiet day, Tyson?"

"No one scheduled till ten."

"You seem depressed."

"Depressed?"

"Maybe your vacation was great, though I don't see why you can't go south in the winter instead, but you don't seem rested and revived like you should."

"It's the transition, I guess."

"Or a sign to consider cutting your hours?"

"I love the work. I've been at it forty-plus years. It's what I do. It's harder to gear up, is all."

"It's not that I'm trying to hustle you out, but—"

It was still haunting him, the memory of that homeless teenager standing nervously before him, shifting from foot to foot and scratching an ear. Not that he knew the whole story, but it wasn't only Sandy the boy reminded him of. It was some aspect of his younger self.

"Tyson?" Elise snapped her fingers to bring him back.

"Ms. Ilg!" Franklin called from down the hall. "Your nine-thirty is here."

"Shit," said Elise, "just when I was getting at the Sean Tyson nobody knows. Hey, didn't I hear something from Andrew about Joel wanting to retire to the country?"

"Yeah, and who'll pay for it!" That just made it harder to acknowledge the inheritance when Joel sooner or later got his way.

« »

That afternoon, having helped a single mother work out a payment schedule for her subsidized housing, Sean stayed at his desk in his cramped little office with its wall map of the city and framed prints of old-time street scenes with trolleys and horse-drawn cabs. His parents had been born at the very end of those days. His mom came from a neighborhood like that, and where his dad was raised had been more a village than a suburb. It made sense that he chose the shy Catholic city girl he'd met at a dance party for new inductees. The coming war gave him some social leeway, and then perhaps it was in the army, with all those other men, that he couldn't hold back what he'd hoped to suppress by marrying quiet Eileen Dermot. The notion gave Sean an inkling of sympathy for his dad. And he remembered Mom sending him off to seventh-grade dancing school, saying maybe someday at a grown-up dance he'd also meet the right girl so it was important to master the foxtrot. Mom had thought she was still Dad's right girl. How humiliated she must've been among the North Shore mothers when Dad went off with his man friend. An inkling of sympathy, this time for Mom, slipped into Sean's thoughts, but soon he sent both inklings shivering down his spine so he wouldn't have to contemplate them anymore.

And yet, tears were welling now behind his eyelids. He had to remind himself he was at his desk, presumably examining a pile of printouts. He reached thumbs and forefingers up under his reading glasses and wiped his eyes dry, blinked, and looked over in time to greet his next client, another single mom, this time white, with three little children trailing behind.

"I'm Mr. Tyson, come on in. Here, have a seat, Ms. Dunwoodie. Hi, kids, there's enough chairs for you, too." The smallest one hopped onto his mother's lap. "I've gone over your application," Sean explained, "and there's a number of good options to consider."

The woman hadn't spoken yet, the children hadn't made a peep. For all they knew, Mr. Tyson was the government. It wasn't like the old days at the storefront, when he'd tied his long brown hair back with a bandana, worn granny glasses and a blue work shirt and jeans, and the applicants had seen him as some mellow hippie helping them out.

« »

Joel had taken the bus out to Foxridge Academy to put his classroom in order and photocopy his new piece for the choral group. When he and Sean sat down to a quick spaghetti-and-meatballs supper with salad out of a package, they told each other their days. Sean said nothing of his periods of daydreaming nor of Elise pushing him to cut back, and anyway, Joel did most of the talking. He'd met with Vincent Hill, the drama teacher, to coordinate plans for the annual opera. "It's about fairies taking over parliament," he said. "Remember when we did *Iolanthe* in '96?"

"Why doesn't Foxridge do something American for a change?"

"You're such a chauvinist, Quimby. But it's got great music and a lot of vocabulary they don't know. These kids today think of fairies as actual fairies, like in Victorian times. It doesn't mean queers the way it used to. They're into all this moronic fantasy shit."

"What's for dessert?" Sean asked.

"Check the freezer. But at the finale, the whole boys' chorus actually turns into fairies. Back in '96, they were afraid they'd offend me with their snickering. We didn't even have a GSA yet, but they surely suspected me. You really don't remember? And that slender lad who was a fairy only down to the waist and sang that song about

207

the class system? You approved, Tyson. The tune goes: 'I might be as bad, as unlucky rather, if I'd only had Fagin for a father!'" He stood up to take a bow then went to wash the dishes. "Fagin, of course, was an old Jew, but I had Dr. Nathan for a father, so I'm normal."

"When I hear a song," Sean conceded, "sometimes it comes back to me." But decades of those productions tended to run together. Joel would come home from rehearsal singing the songs all over the apartment. Last year, there was the one that went: "Fill the bowl with Lesbian wine, and to revelry incline!" It was a catchy tune, and the kids loved singing "Lesbian" loud and clear. Sean still hadn't gotten it out of his head. "But why was that boy a fairy only down to the waist?"

"Because his father's a mortal. That's the whole plot. Remember, you wanted the kid who played the part in '96 to be a fairy from the waist down instead."

Sean couldn't stop wondering if he should call up Owen tomorrow. He wanted to sit down with someone he knew nothing about and who knew nothing about him. Joel was chattering on about Vincent Hill's ideas for the sets, but Sean only pretended to pay attention.

3 When Thursday came around, Andrew Stone stopped by Sean's office first thing and took the client's chair. "Remember your old pal Mr. Thorp? Well, Mrs. Markovich called, that big fat Croatian, and even her mean self can't take him anymore. He went on a bender and got to yelling that she was some kind of nasty old Serb. Talk about insulting! So now he's out on his sorry ass and bound to show up here again."

"Please don't send him to me, Andrew."

"No way. He went on about you worrying your mother sick with your drug addiction and how you refused him decent lodgings with his own kind."

"Franklin gave up on him, too."

"If he comes, I'll handle him. He doesn't seem to mind black men, but he figured Franklin was a Mooslim and you were one of those fags."

"Fancy that," said Sean.

"Well, there's the deserving poor and the undeserving. It's not for us to treat them differently. We decided that, when we began. Brush up your Marx." He swatted Sean on the top of the head and did a sashay out the door.

Sean was left counting the minutes to five-thirty when he would leave the safety of the Collective and go meet Owen in Boys Town at a quiet café. He feared running into Floyd Griffin but didn't know another place to suggest. When he'd called him, Owen at first sounded confused, then it hit him: "Oh, Sean, yeah, wow, you called, cool, man, I'd really like to see you. I didn't know it was you. I'm at work, out of breath, sorry, wow." It had gone something like that. Sean had tried to sound calm, but his hand holding the phone was shaking. Owen could've forgotten him, or said he couldn't get together now but thanks anyway. That might have been better. Instead, they were actually going to meet and be sitting down to drinks together, himself and that somewhat peculiar young man.

It was sticky late August in the city, no lake breeze, no clouds to the west. The sun was casting shadows halfway across the street, but the opposite side shone all yellow. From the shade, Sean noticed Owen in crisp khakis and, this time, a white polo emphasizing his tan. He was waving eagerly in the sunlight. Sean crossed between slow-cruising cars and shook his hand as he might shake an applicant's, but Owen's extra-firm grip held on for several seconds, the brown bicep tight in the white sleeve. His irregular features—bent nose, blinking eyes, mouth in a crooked-toothed grin, and deep-dimpled chin—were odder than Sean had been picturing them. Owen's floppy light-brown hair was cut short now, so there was nothing to soften his face in the bright late afternoon.

"I never expected you'd call," he said. "I figured never to see you again. I mean, with my new schedule working nights, but Thursdays I'm off, so Thursdays are good for me."

"This morning, I thought I'd caught you at work."

"Oh, that was because today I was subbing."

They were standing outside the café. Owen was bouncing foot to foot nervously, or perhaps he was keyed up with too much excitement. He was worse than Joel ever was. "So this is the place," Sean said. "You been here before?"

"I don't go out much, I mean, I go out, but it's mostly on walks and things."

Sean imagined he knew what "things" meant but was afraid of taking everything this young man said the wrong way. Maybe Owen was an entirely inexperienced creature. Sean shepherded him toward a back table so passersby like Floyd wouldn't spot them and Owen wouldn't be distracted by the street.

"Did you have a nice vacation with Joel?" Owen asked, as if the Joel part was over now and Sean was out on his own.

"You remembered his name."

"I'm good at memorizing. I have to remember my trainees by name. It builds their confidence. Fat ones, thin ones, young ones, old—I associate names with bodies. I'm body-oriented, as you can tell. I work hard on my whole frame."

It was his first flirtatious remark, and it excited Sean. He felt the thumping of his heart.

"You're in good shape," Owen said, "for being near to my dad's age. I mean, if he was alive, he'd be sixty."

"I'm sixty-five."

"Wow! I thought you were like mid-fifties. I usually can tell from working closely with bodies. Of course, I haven't worked with yours yet," he said with a lopsided grin.

A skinny tattooed waiter in a loose tank top asked what they were drinking. Owen wanted a cup of black coffee. Sean happily avoided a beer and ordered iced tea.

"I caffeinate too much," Owen said, "as you can probably tell. Don't worry, I'm not on speed or anything. I work in the health field."

"You were also taking accounting?"

"The new schedule screwed that up. Can't take night classes."

"That's too bad," Sean said but told himself, as long as he was kind, he wasn't responsible for this fellow.

"Don't worry," Owen said, looking across at Sean with wide eyes as if to read his mind. "The thing is, I'm having good times. I'd like to share some with you."

Sean only thought to say, "Well, here we are."

"You told Joel?"

Sean avoided the question by saying, "He's at his quartet rehearsal."

"He's in a band?"

"He plays viola in a string quartet."

"Oh," Owen said with some enthusiasm. "I like classical stuff. They end the day with it at the health club after all the hip-hop. It's to chill out at closing. Man, all that hip-hop and salsa and what have you, it can be a bummer. I try tuning it out, but it's to gas up the trainees."

The pale waiter with his arms and shoulders entirely tattooed brought their drinks and halfheartedly took their orders for wraps and salads. Owen seemed really hungry. Sean said it was his treat, but Owen didn't want it to be like that.

"Like what?"

"Like me being taken out. I'm thirty-two. I make good money."

"I didn't mean it that way," Sean said, ashamed or hurt or maybe just embarrassed.

"I know," said Owen. "You're a solid kind of guy. I bet you could calm me down some."

"In the sense of—" Sean presumed he meant by going to bed together, as if it was already the plan.

Owen shrugged his wide shoulders. "I could tell when I'd watch you on the El. I can tell about people, men anyways. Most of them I don't trust. I always lived by myself, ever since high school downstate. I can't deal with roommates or like a boyfriend. I'm pretty much a loner."

Maybe that was what this was about. Owen needed to talk about himself with some solid older man he could trust. It wasn't about sex at all.

"But when I bumped into you that night down the street here," Owen said, "it was like great. It's okay, isn't it, I mean between men. I mean, Joel wouldn't mind?"

"About?"

"You know, us sharing good times."

Suddenly, their food was there and Owen took a few big bites into his wrap, roast beef and horseradish, and Sean bit into what the menu called a Caprese—mozzarella, pesto, and tomato, his favorite combo. He and Joel would get them at Lo Grasso's, but this one wasn't quite as thick and tasty.

"It's not because of my hypothesizing," Owen said at last. "That was something I said, I mean, I thought it, but it wasn't the reason I said hi on the El. It was sort of interesting, that's all, the thing about my dad. You could come over to my place when we finish eating, huh? I don't have anyone over that much. I don't do that online stuff, not me."

Sean was still unsure of what Owen expected. And what could he ever tell Joel, who right then was playing his Shostakovich or Mozart or maybe Schoenberg with the Lilienthals and Sheila Bowden. Was this how things started breaking apart, or had it already started when Joel got the bug about Wisconsin? Sean squinted at his watch as if to see if he had time, but of course he had. Joel wouldn't be home before ten.

212

"I'd like to see where you live, Owen."

"It's only one room because I'm saving to actually buy. It's through the service entrance. You come in the alley, so it's way private. It's a few blocks over."

"I thought you didn't live near here."

"I had to move."

Sean stupidly imagined Owen showing up at the Collective and Davey Nussbaum placing him in a cheap basement room, but Owen didn't know what Sean did for work. The event to come, whatever it would be, had no connection with their daily lives. They really knew nothing about each other. Across the tabletop was a younger more muscular body, and the person inside it was hard to figure out. The touchingly odd face, shifting at times to being almost handsome, was puzzling, but the body made its own sense. It was asking to be helped calming itself down.

《 》

He couldn't think it through while it was happening, but Sean went over it again and again on the bus ride home. He hadn't been confident he'd be up for it, but he had been, and then some. Owen's features had softened in the dim light from the alley. The hard muscles of his arms and chest and back were silky under Sean's fingers, the hard-rubber bottom and thighs, too. Owen must've shaved himself all over the way bodybuilders did. To the touch, he was like the models in Dad's magazines, despite their handsomer faces. Faintly lit, Owen's open eyes had stared up at Sean, while his supple body squirmed in rhythm beneath him. Sean could forget his own age and home, forget even Joel, though now on the bus he had to decide how much he would tell him or if he would tell him anything at all. If he did, maybe Joel would stop being so pushy about retiring and listen to him for once. With Owen, Sean had felt no pressure to do what it turned out he wanted to do.

213

Afterwards, he couldn't tell what the naked young man beside him was feeling, but when he'd dressed and they were standing, Owen in only a towel, at the service door out to the alley, Sean had draped his arms around the broad back and hugged him tight and thanked him for the good time. Owen nodded, somewhat sadly, and said, "So Thursday nights, I'm free. You can call. Only if you want to. I'd understand. I won't bother you, I promise." Then, he shrugged and closed himself in behind the door.

At his own apartment, key in hand, Sean had yet to decide whether to confess, but inside there wasn't a light on. Joel wasn't home, the message machine wasn't blinking, and there was nothing on Sean's cell. He went to take a hot shower so as not to smell of Owen, but all Owen had smelled of was smooth slippery skin.

Sean got in bed in a fresh T-shirt and boxers but didn't pick up the Truman biography from the bedside table and instead reached to the lower shelf for *Evangeline*. He leafed through the old volume, looking at the engraved illustrations, then read the first lines. He had come to "*Ye who believe in affection that hopes and endures, and is patient,*" when he heard Joel's key turning and felt suddenly full of what Andrew Stone would call Catholic guilt. He closed the dark-blue cover of the beautiful old book and laid it on the bedside table.

"Hey, I'm late, sorry. I didn't even call. It got so heavy after we practiced, I was too upset." Joel was standing in the doorway, holding his viola case.

"Are you all right?"

"I suppose, but—" He set the case on the floor and came around to his side of the bed and crawled up next to Sean. "See, first I got them to play through my driftwood piece, no words, just strings. It sounded so good. We went over it three times. Sheila didn't even say it was too Vaughan Williamsy. You'd claim you liked it, no matter what, but the Lilienthals liked it, and James Lauriston had liked it, and their opinions really mean something."

214

"Sorry for not meaning anything," Sean said, but Joel was going right on.

"Then, we got into the argument over the Brahms or the Schoenberg. It looks like Sheila might win. We agreed to work up both, and I'm to ask if Irene Wilson could do the solos. Sheila feels it will link Mozart's dissonances to the eventual breakdown of tonality."

"Joel, but what are you upset about?" Sean stretched an arm out to draw him closer.

"Well, they wanted to know about our trip, and I'm afraid I got too revved up over the eggplant house and too worried because of the first refusal thing, and I said we might end up in the schoolhouse instead. And then I made the big mistake of asking if we could try singing my Longfellow piece, I mean, singing it a cappella. I'd brought the copies. I took the tenor line, which was high for me, but when we got to 'Their lives thenceforth have separate ends,' the soprano cut out because Rebecca was choking up, and then she started to cry, and Art went and hugged her and Sheila gave me a pissed-off glare and said I'd asked for it—didn't I have any idea how they felt about me moving away?"

Sean was holding Joel tighter and tighter and letting him nuzzle up into his armpit.

"It's your fault, Sean Quimby Tyson!" came a muffled grumble. "Why did you have to give me a poem about growing old and everybody drifting apart and never being one again?" He lifted his hand and beat firmly on Sean's chest, but Sean only squeezed tighter.

So they lay in silence awhile. It was not a time to confess. Sean felt reprieved. If Joel never knew what he had done with Owen and it never happened on any other Thursday, it would soon be only a sweet memory, a last touch of youth.

"How did the evening end, Joel?"

"Well, of course, Rebecca was chagrined and apologized, and Art said it was because they never wanted to lose me, their favorite

215

violist in the world, and I promised they wouldn't, I'd come back regularly enough to keep the quartet going, and I told them how you didn't want us to move at all. You'll be glad to know, Rebecca said, 'Good old Sean!' We laughed some and it was a bit better, sort of. At least, before I left we hugged, the Lilienthals and me, and I said maybe nothing would change anyhow, but Sheila had gone back to fold up the music stands and put the scores away, so I only waved to her. I could see how pissed she still was."

"I'm glad your music made Rebecca cry," Sean said. "I'm sure it wasn't simply the words but the way you put them in harmonies. Isn't that what music should do?"

Joel didn't say anything, but Sean could feel the body next to him tremble slightly, then quiver, and heard a soft whimpering. "I didn't mean to," Joel managed to say.

"But it's good that you did. It's what was true."

"I feel so bad. We might as well call Tory Forell tomorrow and give up on the whole thing."

Sean knew that wouldn't happen, but he squeezed Joel closer anyway. He wasn't about to say they could even buy the schoolhouse if it came to that, but somehow his seventh-grade Marxism had popped into his head: "From each according to his ability, to each according to his need."

4 When Sean came home from work on Friday, Joel reported on several emails. Molly Moore wanted to know if anything was happening on the house issue, and there was one from Phil Kimbley wondering if they were keeping those two weeks in August 2012 because, if they sent a deposit now, he'd reserve Chibiabos for them at a ten percent discount. There was also an e-card from Mrs. S. at the Kickapoo Gardens Motor Lodge, sending "greetings to our new neighbors we hope" with a link to their son's motel in Illinois. And Joel had, in fact, phoned Tory Forell, not to withdraw from the field

but to see if there was any news. There wasn't. She thanked him for sending his CD, which was certainly different, she said, but in a good way. "I bet she only got through one movement," he said. He'd written back at length to Molly, and to Mrs. S. he said they'd be sure to let her know when they found something.

"You mean *if*," Sean said.

"But as for Mishe-Mokwa," Joel went on, "I said I'd have to talk it over with you but hoped we'd be able to. So what am I going to tell him? We could reserve it and still cancel and pay the fee. It'd be nice to see the Porkies again and do some other trails. I wonder if the Moores would be there."

"I'd be afraid to spoil our pleasant memories," said Sean. "And we may be busy with other matters."

"Like fixing up the schoolhouse."

"Joel, what's this new gambit of yours?"

"My backup plan. I can't stand the tension."

"As for me," Sean said, when they'd sat out on their shady balcony, "I got email today from Danny. He is indeed coming to see Dad's lawyers. He says he wants to set up something for Sandy. Sandy wouldn't let me, but he doesn't seem to mind Danny. And Danny wants us to get together downtown. He says he'll be with someone, and I got a feeling it isn't Libby."

"Us get together or just you?"

"I'd rather you came."

"I'd rather I didn't. You brothers should have your heavy talk without me."

"But this 'someone' will also be there."

"Shaw-awn, I really don't want to."

"All right."

"But you want me to."

"It'd be better for me, but I don't want to put you through it, if you don't feel like it."

"I don't."

217

"All right."

"Phew," said Joel.

They leaned back with their ginger beers and cooled off, though it didn't quite feel like summer anymore. Sitting outside, above traffic and pedestrians, always comforted Sean. They'd lived in that apartment so many years. He knew every brick in the pillars holding up the third-floor balcony, where no one ever sat out unless they were having a party. Parties never bothered Sean, any more than Joel's music caused their neighbors to complain. People left each other alone. Up in the country, they'd have to know everyone. Their comings and goings would be monitored. Cars would pass so seldom that each one was bound to signify something. Sean was entirely contented with anonymous city life. Already in '68, he had claimed it as his own. He was doing useful community work, and in his nighttime explorations back then, he found other young men who wanted him to take them to bed. It was like being fifteen again and running naked in Gramma's meadow in the moonlight, that powerful sense of freedom. Some men he saw only once or twice, but then there was Floyd, till Floyd began seeing Mick as well and those two were getting into the whole mid-seventies scene. Sean felt more comfortable hanging out with Davey and Andrew after work, talking about Watergate or the war or, later, Jimmy Carter. But then it was Floyd Griffin who dragged him to Joel's birthday party and, surprisingly, into a happier world.

And there sat that same Joel Greenwood beside him, all these years later, on their little cement balcony. It was home and love and, even still occasionally, sex, not like sex with Owen, but that was only once, and a second time, Sean was sure, wouldn't go as well.

"So about the schoolhouse—" Joel left the word hanging in the evening coolness.

"Yes?"

"Well, I don't think Mary Peg and those 'Don't Tread On Me' folks should be the deciding factor. It's such a historic building, and

218

you wouldn't feel you had to come up as often, because it's not like a real house. It'd be more of a vacation place for you."

"Not for you?"

"But I don't mind living simply. All I need is my music and open fields and the Ocooch Mountains."

"You say."

"I need a simpler life, Sean." Because he hadn't called him "Quimby" or "Shaw-awn," Joel was clearly being serious.

"You live simply enough here," Sean said. "So do I. It's not that we have people over or go out on the town much. I've got my books and the couch to read on and our bed. You've got school and the quartet, and I've got the Housing Collective."

"And your Internet porn," Joel said, "and the boys by the lake."

"And what could be simpler than that!" Sean teased back. "And look at our apartment. Anybody else, after thirty-plus years, would have tons of stuff lying around."

"Because you never wanted to have stuff. You don't think you deserve stuff. How could you have more stuff than your underprivileged clients! Hey, isn't your big fundraising dinner coming up?"

"But I don't want stuff. I don't care about stuff. I don't even keep the books I read unless I really loved them. Most I take to our swap shop."

"Fundraising do-gooder Sean Quimby Tyson. Let's go inside. I'm getting chilly."

"It's a whiff of fall," said Sean.

Nothing was resolved. He was willing to wait and see what happened with the first refusal before another fight, but evidently Joel had decided they were buying something, regardless. Sean headed back to the living room, where Joel had gone to play something familiar, harmonious, lovely. Oh, it was Chopin, the raindrops. He didn't stay to listen. He went into the bedroom, lay down, grabbed his reading glasses, and picked up *Evangeline*.

The famous old poem, which he'd never before gotten around to reading, was about two young lovers exiled from home, from Acadia. The British renamed it Nova Scotia and sent them wandering off in opposite directions, she by sea down to Louisiana, he west along the Great Lakes to the Mississippi. That was all French North America before the United States pushed itself westward. Sean thought of the many names, from Detroit to Des Moines, Ardennes, Des Plaines, Vincennes, St. Louis—the Midwest might have taken a different course and none of them would be speaking English. They wouldn't be Quimbys, Tysons, Dermots, or even Greenwoods. They'd have other bloodlines, other names. They wouldn't be themselves at all.

Joel still hadn't come to bed. He'd played more Chopin and what Sean knew was the dependable *Kinderszenen*. Then the music stopped, but there was no soft sound of approaching footsteps. The two of them were in their solitary meditations, at least Sean was. He laid the handsome old volume across his stomach and snuggled his head deep into the pillow. He had promised he also wanted to buy the farmhouse with the aubergine trim. If that fell through, he had secretly allowed himself to imagine their life, part-time, in that old Quarryville school. He'd even walked himself through the ugly new garrison colonial of fake clapboards and brick. He'd pictured the morning sunlight on the western limestone cliff and on the eastern one at sunset. But was it only idle dreaming? Even the hundred thousand dollars he had coming to him seemed an insubstantial fantasy. If Rebecca Lilienthal had been brought to tears by Joel's choral piece, why hadn't he been? He would be losing much more, but he hadn't quite believed it yet.

He was always like that, Sean told himself, he'd always been like that. He would hunker down and wait to see what would happen next. Those years when he was fifteen, sixteen, seventeen, eighteen, he'd held his dad's secret close inside, didn't think it over, wouldn't ponder what it really meant, even about his own young self, and then he'd gone off to Kenyon College, and when the secret came out, he couldn't admit he'd already somehow known it but had put himself on Mom's side till she found out about him, too, and then he'd hunkered down again. He'd always been like that, Sean kept telling himself, and he was still like that now.

He was staring at the gray ceiling, streaked with yellow street light through the slats of the blinds. What was Joel doing out there? He needed him in bed so he wouldn't feel lonely. For so long, there had come no change in their life together, and he had never wanted one. It had never seemed much of a question. In their fifties, even after turning sixty, they had seemed to have plenty of time ahead. They had hardly thought of failing health, of aches and pains, of fading memory. Ten years ago, they had felt as young as ever. Ten years from now, though, at seventy-five, they surely would feel the difference. The whole Ocooch Mountains thing of Joel's must be about escaping age, he decided. When you start something new, you feel young again. Joel acted younger every time he started a new composition, but Sean had nothing like that in his life. Yet he'd felt young in bed with Owen, whose body in the dark seemed no younger than his own, or rather his seemed as young as Owen's because they were moving as one body and he lost track of who was who.

He stretched his arms above his head, straightened his legs out under the sheet, and curled up his toes. He yawned deeply, expanded his chest, flattened his stomach where the book lay, and every muscle felt tight and strong. Then, out there, he saw the bathroom light snap on and heard water splashing in the sink. Joel was humming a tune he didn't recognize, but once they were both in bed together with the lights out, Sean wouldn't be able to see, or even feel, how old they had both become.

5 The weather warmed up, as it usually did in September. Joel declared a beach day and began packing a lunch while Sean retrieved their beach towels and blanket from the fresh laundry and stuffed them into his backpack with that fat old book *The "Genius"* because he didn't want to risk getting sand in the binding of *Evangeline*. "What should I bring for you, Joel?" he called into the kitchen.

"I don't intend to read. I'll take my music and plug myself in, and you won't have me interrupting your story."

Sean stopped at the full-length mirror on the back of the bedroom door. He looked at his knobby knees and pasty thighs and pale feet in leather sandals. He slung the pack over his back and squinted to see himself as he once was, persistently a remnant of a past era. Who wore cutoff jeans anymore? Who'd wear a ragged plaid flannel shirt to the beach? He'd carried that pack to work for years before Andrew convinced him a shoulder bag would be a little more professional. But going to the beach, Sean could be his old sloppy self.

Now Joel appeared in his trim red Bermudas, Porcupine Mountains T-shirt with the bear on it, and the insulated bag slung over his shoulder. They made a funny enough pair, heading out the door into the sunny day.

It was only a few blocks to the lake. Lots of strollers, coming or going, nodded or smiled, some with preoccupied city faces. Sean tried to stick close to make room on the sidewalk, while Joel walked with the bag swinging off his shoulder, bound to knock against somebody. But they made it across traffic and through the underpass and up to the grass by the ash tree. "Let's opt for sand," Joel said. "It's the last gasp of summer."

"You'd miss the lake, wouldn't you?" Sean asked, after spreading out the pale-blue blanket.

"I can handle missing it," Joel said. "It's not going anywhere. And with me out of town, you'll be down here checking out the company whenever you like." He peeled off his T-shirt and lay down on his back, his chest hairs glistening.

Sean, too, felt sweaty from the walk on hot concrete, but there was a light breeze, and when he unbuttoned his flannel shirt, he sensed the sweat drying up off his bare skin.

"You look like an old hippie," Joel said. "If only you'd get stoned, it'd be so much easier to deal with you. You wouldn't be so worried about our future."

"And you wouldn't be so worried about who I'm checking out."

"Who said I'm worried?"

"But," Sean began, wondering how best to put it, "how would you feel if I did check someone out? Seriously, you only work up these scenarios because you think I'll never act on them."

Joel was scanning the bodies spread across the sand, lots of out-of-shape middle-aged white people with splotchy red or dried-up leathery skin and a sampling of chubby brown Latino families, a subdued black contingent, and some raucous Asian teenagers. "I don't see David Foster Wallace," he said. "Sorry, Tyson."

"As if I'd stand a chance."

"Maybe that intellectual young dude is in search of a wise old mentor."

Sean only sniffed. He was getting uncomfortably close to Owen.

"Or," Joel said with a leer, "a daddy."

"Just what I need!" Sean snapped, to shut off the conversation. He reached into his pack for The "Genius" then used the pack as a pillow to prop up his head.

"DFW boy would be so impressed with you reading that moldy old tome." Joel was scratching his stomach hair as if conjuring up how else to make trouble. Sean knew there was no way he could confess now about Owen. It would hurt Joel too much. Instead, he would let himself go on being kidded, confident in Joel's devotion. Despite Owen, he was also confident of his own devotion to Joel.

After a while, his arms were getting tired holding the heavy book over his head to block the sun, and his reading glasses kept slipping down his perspiring nose. He set the book on the blanket, turned onto his stomach, and asked Joel to smear him with Age Shield. He leaned up on his elbows and tried to keep reading while Joel rubbed in the cream. It was a longtime familiar intimacy that had lost the erotic stimulus it would have if it was Owen massaging his back. Exactly the same action could have such different effects. He remembered his mother slathering his prepubescent self with old-fashioned suntan lotion down at Tower Road Beach and how he'd loved the feeling of his skin absorbing all the heat of the summer sun.

The novel wasn't holding his attention. It kept jumping from one thing to another too quickly for him to sink into its world. Maybe he didn't feel like reading at all. He rested his head on his crossed forearms and closed his eyes. Joel finished up with the backs of his legs and said, too loudly over the music playing in his ears, "Your turn to do me."

So Sean pulled himself up to a squat and leaned over the prone figure in red Bermudas. Little stray hairs that hadn't been there before had emerged on Joel's back, like the hairs Sean had noticed proliferating in his ears and nostrils. Their bodies were at a new stage—the stiffer joints in the mornings, a slight unsteadiness of step, fainter night vision, all the signs of time and change. Slowly, fondly, Sean worked his cream-covered palms over Joel's pointy shoulder blades, all the way down to the hairy patch at the base of his spine. This is an actual person, he told himself. For all his solid flesh, Owen was still only an image.

« »

They did dip into the lake, slowly, and agonizingly when the water reached the crotches of their shorts, but it was much warmer than Superior. They wouldn't be going in again before next summer. Once they were all the way under, it wasn't so bad. All colors of bodies, all sizes and shapes, were splashing around them, a crop of screeching children close to shore, a few vigorous swimmers farther out along the chain of floats marking the bathing area.

After they came dripping back on land, Joel led Sean past two young men for him to check out, a thirty-ish couple much like themselves thirty years ago. "Which one's your choice?" Joel asked, back on their blanket. He was retrieving his mp3 player from where he'd zipped it inside the insulated bag.

"I have to choose?"

"It's your game, Shaw-awn."

"They look inseparable, Joel, sorry."

"Oh, Quimby, I keep trying to cheer you up."

"I'm cheery."

"But I can tell something's on your mind."

"So you really want me to have a quick fling with some attractive fellow. Then what?"

"You'd have gotten it over with."

"It?"

"Being sad."

"That's not what I'm sad about, not that I'm sad, anyway. I'm somewhat tired is all."

"You're sad. I can always tell."

"Maybe about my brother coming from Ohio."

"No."

"Or maybe about the first refusal thing."

"By the way," Joel said, "I wrote to Lauriston."

"You didn't tell me."

"He's my professor pal. Mostly, I wrote about music. I've been practicing those Brahms sonatas." He reached for the player and tried to stick the buds into Sean's ears. Sean wriggled but then, suddenly, his head was filled with a piano and viola at full volume.

"Turn it down, Joel!" He yanked out the plastic doodads.

"Jesus, calm down."

"Why didn't you tell me you wrote him? I thought you're set on the schoolhouse."

"But we still hope for their cow cottage. No Tea Party neighbors or fat Mary Peg."

"Maybe we should just go with the ugly house," Sean said.

"Good, I'll call Tory as soon as we get home."

"Okay," Sean said, to call his bluff.

"I will."

"Go ahead."

"I mean it."

Sean propped his head back on his pack and peered out through his toes at the horizon. He would say nothing more. He knew Joel was still holding out for what he truly wanted, and he also suspected they would have some sort of second home in Wisconsin before the snows fell.

6 He was waiting between the lions on the steps of the Art Institute. That new friend of Danny's intended to make something of her first trip to Chicago and had dragged him to look at the famous paintings, *The Blue Guitarist, La Grande Jatte*. Her name was Phyllis Vaughan. She was very much Danny's junior, and to Sean's huge surprise, she was a black woman from the Caribbean. As arranged, he had joined them in the gift shop, but they went on browsing for so long that he volunteered to meet them outside.

He was gazing across Michigan Avenue at Orchestra Hall with the names of Joel's favorite composers, except maybe Liszt, carved in stone above the tall windows. In Sean's days with Floyd, they'd gone to Thursday evening concerts together, and he had felt mostly bored till it got to the loud parts. Then the music sent a strange charge through him, a kind of bodily attentiveness where everything tingled. Floyd always had snobbish things to say when it was a piece he didn't think much of, or he'd bitch about a guest conductor or some star soloist. With Joel, the few times they sprang for tickets, it was a pleasanter experience. Joel wasn't as critical, but he surely knew more about music than Floyd Griffin. He loved every minute of it and would grab Sean's elbow at the loudest parts. But it ended when Joel got to shepherd a select group of Foxridge kids on Friday afternoons as part of their music history class. "You were never that eager to go," he'd said, but Sean did somewhat miss his times in that old hall over there. The only concerts he heard now were by the Lilienthal Quartet or Joel's students, which he did enjoy but never could let the music take over because Joel was up there to be proud of.

Finally, Danny and Phyllis came down the steps with plastic sacks, no doubt containing the same Picasso and Seurat souvenirs Mary had bought for her daughter-in-law's party. "So!" Danny said, taking charge. "Sorry for holding you up."

"No, it's a beautiful day. I needed the fresh air."

"Your lake is all sparkling today," Phyllis said. "It has an almost tropical color, doesn't it, Daniel?"

"In Cleveland, we don't go to the lake much," Danny said, "but we do see it from our eleventh floor, a flat gray sheet is what it mostly looks like."

Sean hadn't picked up any sign of his old drinking problem. Danny's face wasn't as puffy or red as on his last visit. He looked trim and businesslike, as did his new friend in her rather severe unsummery business suit.

Danny still hadn't said anything about Libby or the girls. He was proceeding as if no explanation was required, and Sean wasn't going to ask in front of Phyllis. He suggested they have lunch at a quiet little café where he'd been with their sister when she told him about Carlos Villalba's obituary.

"Quite appropriate," Danny said. "Goodbye, big lions! They're what I remember most about coming downtown as a kid. And the Field Museum, of course. I remember those little winglike things on the corners of the roof. I don't know what you'd call them architecturally."

"You should see the new public library," Sean said. "It looks like it's about to take off with those giant griffins on top. It's named after old Mayor Washington."

"See, Chicago's in a lot better shape than Cleveland, brother. But, you know, I couldn't live here. Too much of my past. You know?" Sean certainly knew.

When they were seated in the cool air-conditioning and the very same Osberto came to take their drink orders, Danny said he'd have a diet Coke or Pepsi, whichever, and Phyllis asked for lemonade. Trying not to show surprise, Sean said he'd have a lemonade as well. It was nice, ordering again from Osberto, who probably hadn't recognized him.

"Yep," Danny said, "I'm totally off the sauce. It's thanks to Phyllis. See, Sean, it was a choice between being axed so close to retirement or getting my act together. The colleagues came down hard, took me bodily into treatment, but it was Phyllis here, that's how we met, she's really why I did it. Six months now."

"Wonderful," Sean said. "Does Mary know? She didn't tell me anything."

"Oh, we talk all the time. I admit we intentionally keep you out of the loop. That's for not being on Facebook! If you were, you'd know everything, and Mary wouldn't feel so constrained about passing on family news. I suppose it goes way back, your secret life and all, but we're well past that, aren't we? I mean, by now."

"Families can be complicated," Phyllis said. "I don't know a family that isn't."

"Even the good ones," Danny said. "Maybe they're even more complicated when they do stick together and drive each other crazy."

Sean decided to say, "Is that what happened with you and Libby?"

"I wondered when you'd ask, brother."

"But Mary didn't say anything."

Osberto brought over a tray with their drinks, and he was looking curiously at Sean, as if he'd seen him before but wasn't sure. When he'd gone back to the kitchen, Danny leaned across the table and said, "So, Sean, I can tell he's gay from the way I caught him looking at you."

"Oh, Daniel, what do you know?" Phyllis said.

"I'm glad I still attract the fellows," Sean said as self-deprecatingly as he could.

"You're still a handsome guy, little brother. Look at me with all these wrinkles. That's from losing the weight, and now that extra skin's still hanging around." Phyllis leaned her head on his shoulder and gave his cheek a pinch.

"But Mary doesn't know?"

"About Phyllis? Sure, but I told her in confidence. Sandy doesn't know yet. Tasha and Kendra are on board with it. They've got their own lives now."

"They're impressive young women," said Phyllis. Funny, Sean thought, how Mary had been sitting there in an African-print blouse with big gold hoops in her ears, and here was Danny's somber black friend with straightened hair like the First Lady's.

They ordered seafood salads—"See, we're watching our weight, brother"—but Sean chose the Reuben sandwich.

"Ah," Osberto said, "you are brothers?"

"Last time I ate here," Sean told him, "it was with my sister, not that you'd recall."

"Ah, yes, I do because she cried and you gave her big hugs." He grinned toothily but didn't linger and went on to let the next booth order.

"What was she crying about?" Danny asked, as if he couldn't imagine Mary crying.

"She'd shown me the obituary. It was the line about being life partners and their many dear friends. Dad's other life—"

"I'm into my other life, Sean. I hope someday Tasha and Kendra won't be crying about that."

"You're still in their lives," Phyllis pointed out. "They have their dad back."

"Oh, thanks, Phyl, for reminding me. That's the most important reason for us to get together here, brother. Well, I've been meaning to apologize, you know, to make amends, face to face. It's the step I'm at. I'm making amends with Sandy, too."

"And you're going to help him to—" Phyllis began when their salads arrived. Osberto was sorry the Reuben would take a bit longer.

"That's okay," Danny said. "I'll be doing all the talking, so I need a head start. Man, I'm a whole new animal," he added when Osberto had gone. "Can you tell?" It was all so fresh and exciting to him that Sean couldn't help but be a bit wary of the change.

And once the fat juicy sandwich had arrived, his brother did do most of the talking. Sean soon learned more about his marriage than he'd ever known. He'd always assumed Libby was the put-upon one, but Danny said she began bitching about him right from the start. He always went into things with open-eyed enthusiasm. "It's what made me good at sports," he said, "whereas you were so cautious. Hell, I guess cautious wins out in the end. You and Joel seem pretty much okay, right? But, man, I sure hadn't got a hint of the control freak I'd teamed myself up with. We waited on having kids then figured they'd help us out, so we tried, but Libby sure could be one hell of a bitch."

"Daniel," Phyllis said, "it's not about her."

"I know, I know, I've learned something, Sean. It's a relief not to be doing the blame thing anymore."

Sean found himself liking Phyllis. Danny was going on to explain how she was an administrator at the facility where his colleagues had stuck him to dry out. She'd been through it all herself, a way of coping with her first marriage, but she'd been sober for seven years. He gave Phyllis a pat on the arm. "But you're not allowed to date when you're an in-patient. Very strict about that. So the day I get out, I give her a call, and what do you know, here we are! Anyhow, it's about time I listened to you. Mary tells me you're buying a place in Wisconsin?"

"We are" popped out of Sean's mouth. "But it's a matter of which of the ones we've looked at."

"There goes the inheritance! So you're retiring? Me, I'm not retired yet, sixty-seven and going strong. Hell, I couldn't afford to, except now, with this major influx from the dishonored dad—"

Having wiped the Russian dressing off his fingers, Sean set his napkin on the table and looked quizzically across at his big brother.

"Yeah, well, you have to admit he dishonored his proper role. I'm not saying it wasn't for the better. For him, I mean. It sure wasn't good for Mom or Sandy, but us olders, we handled it, Mary and I, anyway. You, I have to say—I'm not criticizing at this late date because I was pretty much of a shit, too, but I got past it sooner. You never got past it. Not that I ever again felt as close to him the way I did as a kid—tennis and golf and setting off fireworks and all that good stuff."

"But Sean had his unique reasons, Daniel," Phyllis said in the helpfully calm voice Sean tried to assume when talking to clients.

Osberto came to clear off and ask about coffee and dessert. Danny said, "Go ahead, splurge, brother, I'm paying."

"We're splitting the bill," said Sean.

"I'll let him pay the tip," Danny said with a conspiratorial wink at their waiter. They each only ordered a coffee, and after Osberto left, Danny leaned across the table and said, "You could leave him your cell number, Sean. I can tell he's available."

"Oh, Daniel!" Phyllis scolded. "You realize, Sean, he has a heart of gold, but he loves to make trouble."

"I do not! I'm demonstrating to my dear brother that I'm cool with his lifestyle. My girls helped educate me, didn't they, Phyl?"

"You're going to love getting to know them, Sean."

"When we all descend on you in Wisconsin!" Danny added. "So when will you move up for good?"

"No, no, we're not leaving Chicago. Wisconsin is more Joel's idea of a getaway from the city for weekends, and he gets summers off. I can come and go."

"You know what Phyllis and I are doing with our dough?"

"*Your* dough, Daniel," she said.

"We're buying a motorboat to buzz out to our place in Put-In Bay. No more ferries. You did know I had that little cottage out there on the island? In the divorce, Libby gets our house, I get the cottage, and I've already moved into Phyl's high-rise condo. See the news you miss from not friending me on Facebook?"

"Phyllis," Sean said in the spirit of a fond brother-in-law, "do you realize what you've gotten yourself into?"

She leaned back in the booth, threw an arm around Danny's once broader shoulders, and said, "After my first husband, I can honestly say I'm ready for this character."

"Oh, that's another thing," Danny said, elbows on the table now, "we're getting married as soon as I'm a free man. I'm robbing the cradle. She's only forty-three!" He held out his right hand for a shake. Sean grabbed on and felt he did, indeed, have his older brother back, but it might prove somewhat exhausting.

« »

Danny and Phyllis weren't meeting Sandy till five when he got off work, and Danny wanted to walk through Grant Park and see the fountain again. He didn't care to see the big silver Bean at Millennium Park. He didn't even want to look behind at the vastly enlarged skyline. He wanted to see what he remembered.

Leaving the café, Sean had waved back at Osberto, whose eyes fixed on his, longer than out of mere politeness. Danny was closer to the truth than he knew. Sean was not unlike Trevor Ahern, eyeing the waitresses at his country club. Mary was probably right about men when they got older. Was it a sex drive or more of a response to what you were losing? It didn't usually lead to action. It was an instant thing Sean couldn't put a name to, but it was largely harmless, so why think twice about it?

In the park, Danny was striding ahead while Sean strolled peacefully beside Phyllis. "I'm very glad he's found you," he told her.

"I'm glad I found him," she said with a modest smile. She was stockier than he'd noticed at first, but she had a certain ease about her that made him comfortable. "You know, Sean, I've watched so many men struggle with the problem, and I can discern when it's more circumstantial than inevitable. I truly believe Daniel's got it in him to start anew."

"I hope so, for your sake. And for his, of course."

She took his arm in hers and said, "It's time you two became brothers again. All those years, he didn't want you to know what a failure his marriage was. Of course, it wasn't all Libby's fault. You know that. But he didn't want anyone in the family to know and especially you, because of you being with Joel. It was his pride. He and Libby kept up a front for their girls, too. He wasn't going to do to them what your dad did to all of you."

"He didn't even tell Mary?"

"Just hints, I imagine. But she was the first he told about us. I can't wait to meet her. We're taking the train up and spending the night before she drives us to O'Hare Monday morning. We've talked on the phone. We even Skyped. She's a lot like Daniel, the talkative sort. And what's Sandy like?"

"There's really an actual job he's got now?"

"At the zoo, just custodial, he told Daniel, nothing with the animals. I guess he's had his struggles with addiction, too."

Danny had stopped on the path ahead because he'd seen Buckingham Fountain bubbling and then suddenly shooting a splendid spray high in the air. "Phyl!" he called. "You should be here after dark with the colored lights." When they caught up to him, he said as if deep in memory, "One summer night, Mom and Dad brought me downtown for a show, *Flower Drum Song* or some such, and Dad drove us through the park, and I can still see those colors gushing out everywhere. It was only for a minute driving by, but it has stuck in my mind. Like fireworks at Gramma's. Remember the Catherine wheel at the end of the diving board? Hey, now look over there. I can see the little wings on the Field Museum. And that's the Aquarium, and out there's the Planetarium. School trips! Shit, how it all comes back!"

《 》

When Sean had recounted all of Danny's surprises, Joel wished he'd been there. The sensible Caribbean girlfriend, the sobriety, the stupid jokes and vivid memories—Joel, for the first time ever, said he regretted not having a brother.

"You've inherited both of mine," Sean said. "Sandy prefers you to me anyway, and Danny's going to come visit you in Wisconsin while I'm down here paying the bills."

They were taking in the last of the day out on their balcony. The bricks across the street were shining like red gold. "Maybe if he brings this Phyllis," Joel said. "What island's she from?"

"Saint something, I can't remember. She has just a trace of an accent. She's been an American for years now."

"And I thought Danny was a racist sexist drunken pig."

"He was never exactly racist or sexist, Joel. He was a loudmouth jock. It took him a long time to deal with Dad. They'd been so close. He went through a lot of women before Libby, but I'm sure he wasn't the whole problem. Whoever is?"

"Certainly not me, Tyson."

"Well, you're sure strong-arming our retreat to your imaginary mountains."

"They're real, Shaw-awn."

"They're imaginary right now. You've dreamed up our life there, but it doesn't exist yet."

"So what? Phyllis can't be sure Danny will stay off drink. He didn't hesitate to spend his inheritance on a motorboat. Loosen up, Sean! Jesus Christ! Even Sandy's sort of shaping up."

234

"We'll see." Sean pushed himself slowly up and out of his canvas sling chair.

"And I've got to go back to school this week!"

"Good, you'll have other things to obsess about." Sean went inside to begin fixing dinner.

7 They had returned to their regular routines. September was always the busiest month at the Collective, and whenever a new semester began, Joel got charged up with a new crop of students and new music to rehearse and casting the opera and catching up with all his co-teachers. He hadn't yet tried out the driftwood piece, but he told the choral group he'd written something over the summer especially for them, and they were psyched, he said. Sean got thumbnail sketches of each kid in his advanced class, the ones he'd be taking to the Friday afternoon concerts. Sean, in turn, had told Joel about the deluge of folks looking to find better housing before the cold weather, but his stories never had quite the same effect. "It's all so depressing," Joel said, after hearing one particularly sad case of an Iraq War vet, so Sean caught him up instead on Andrew and Elise and that Franklin was saying he was already burning out. "These wimpy forty-somethings," Sean said. He got the expected dubious reaction when he told Joel about Davey's involvement with a new protest movement against the top one percent.

A couple of nights later, in bed after turning out the light, Joel said, "Do you realize that, if you counted the entire population of the earth, we ourselves would be in the top 1 percent?"

"Maybe top two," said Sean, "but still."

"And we're going to have a second home, as Tory calls it, and your brother's got one already, and he's buying himself a yacht."

"Not a yacht."

"And your sister's putting in a pool, and Sandy's getting an actual paid-for apartment. I bet he'll go out with Nussbaum occupying the streets. It'll do him good."

"Unless he does something crazy and gets hauled off to jail."

"At least he'll be part of something. You're so lucky, Tyson. Your whole family's entering a happy new phase."

"Yeah, right."

"And I'm going to shove you right along with them."

Lately, Sean had been thinking a lot about these things. Long ago, he'd given up on being part of a happy family. True, he had his reasons, as Phyllis had said so sympathetically. But here was Joel, lying beside him in the dark, dreaming of their own new phase in his so-called mountains. No doubt he was imagining music and solitude and cows mooing on a hillside and being away from Sean, who could visit, who would visit, and Joel would get all he needed of him, but Sean needed Joel there beside him every night or he might find himself seeking out Owen in his basement room or even inviting him over when Joel was in Wisconsin, and that would be terrible. He didn't want to take care of Owen and his worked-on body with that strangely passive person inside it. It was silky and smooth and like hard rubber and in need of what Sean could never truly give. Or was that only an act? He'd stood by the door, wrapped in his towel, leaving it all up to him.

Joel was already asleep. He had a way of drifting off and then waking with a start and blaming Sean for keeping him from his one chance at a good night's rest. Joel was scraggly and fuzzy and lumpy in places, and he always smelled like Joel. Sean would know him in the dark. They were the same age, on the same gradually sloping path, going at pretty much the same speed, though Joel's was erratic and Sean's was steady. They were so lucky to have each other. But that sleeping man there could manage without him for weeks at a time, for months even. Joel could lose himself playing his viola, be his whole self in the pieces of music he made up out of nothing but what was in his ears. He could wander restfully for miles in his hills, never lonesome because he'd be surrounded by his countryside, no city streets, no people of strange sorts with messy lives and fears and mistrusts and disappointments. Sean worked daily with such people, trying to help them, but "It's all so depressing" Joel had said. He didn't want to hear about it.

There was no passing traffic down there out the open window. It was an oddly silent moment for ten o'clock at night in Chicago. Sometimes that happened. The city stopped moving, stopped calling back and forth. Its sirens were silenced, its loud radios turned down, its lights shut off. Only the one streetlamp shone dimly beyond the drawn blinds. No puff of a breeze rattled the down-turned slats. Joel was breathing in a regular slow rhythm.

Sean had started to cry tears. He felt them on his cheeks. He didn't want to lose all of that, that one and only home, that ever-present man beside him. He was afraid something was coming to an end. Was it his own stubbornness? He wiped his cheeks with the backs of his hands, then he grabbed the bedspread and pulled it up to his chin. They would also soon be tucking in a blanket, and then they'd be extracting the fat comforter from its plastic bin under the bed and spreading it over the top, and instead of edging away from the heat of Joel's body, Sean would nudge himself closer so they could both keep each other warm.

« »

A few days later, he had given up on The "Genius", and Evangeline was getting too upsetting—all that absence and exile—so Sean had picked up the heavy biography of Lyndon Johnson and dipped into the middle pages. It took him back to his college days when all that was happening. Strange how what had seemed so current hadn't taken long to become historical. And yet, stretched out on the couch while across the room Joel was practicing for quartet night, Sean decided that Johnson remained his notion of a president. All those that had come since never seemed the real thing. He must've associated LBJ with Dad, the way they'd each broken faith with him. He also had no other dad but Dad.

"What's that you're playing, Joel? It doesn't sound right."

"It's the Schoenberg that Sheila's foisted on the Lilienthals. It's actually beautiful when you get to know it."

"I don't think I'll like it."

"You can't tell from just the viola. I have a lovely tune that opens the third movement. And wait till you hear the soprano come in. Irene's glad to do it, she says, if we can tolerate her old-lady voice."

"She's no older than us, is she?"

"Voices get older sooner, but she's still got it. When I went to the department, the secretary said she was in a practice room, so I stood outside and heard her singing Hugo Wolf's *Kennst du das Land* full voice. Besides, the Schoenberg needs character more than bel canto. She says she still has her high notes."

"I suppose it's about things breaking apart?"

"It's about feeling breezes blowing from other planets."

"Other planets don't have breezes, Joel."

"It's Expressionism! Jesus Christ, Sean, you're such a literalist."

"How would I know," Sean said and went back to 1966, his own historical moment, without a father, with less of a family, with a new set of friends in DeKalb and a new purpose slowly forming through his classes and in late-night discussions with Schoener and Nussbaum and Stone. They didn't know, for sure, if they would ever set up the Collective they'd been dreaming of. The others didn't know that Tyson had a secret crush on Nussbaum, didn't know what thoughts he held close, lying awake in his narrow bed in the room he shared with Stone. They didn't know that one of them would go to Vietnam and get killed. All they knew was how much the imaginary future mattered. Why didn't it scare me back then? Sean asked himself. The future scared him now, and there was so much less of it.

"And here's where the voice comes in," Joel said. "Sheila says it's the moment in music that says goodbye to the past. But so what if he cuts out tonality for a while? He still ends up in F-sharp major!"

"I don't know what you're talking about, Joel."

"Oh, Quimby, it's so frustrating living with a musical idiot."

"I know what I like."

"Typical refuge of the idiot." Joel made a deep grunt of mock despair and picked up his instrument to play something that sounded sad, but also beautiful. "Schoenberg!" he said. "Opening of the third movement. Sheila's going to have her way." Then the phone rang. "It's probably her," Joel said. "I emailed her that Irene's up for it." He laid his viola carefully in the velvet-lined case at his feet and hurried into the middle room to answer. "Who?" Sean heard him say, and then, "Oh, yes, hi, how are you doing?" And then, "We're both good. I was just practicing the Schoenberg Second for my quartet's fall concert. It's still pretty rough."

Sean let the heavy LBJ biography down to the floor and cocked an ear.

"So what's the news?" Joel's eager voice asked. Sean could tell he was suddenly nervous. It was either Tory Forell or James Lauriston, probably Lauriston since Joel mentioned Schoenberg. Sean sat up, then stood and tiptoed in his socks into the hall. "You've decided to?" Joel said, as if catching his breath. "We've been hoping . . . No, they do? Oh, no! But it seemed so iffy!"

Sean's heartbeat was heavy in his chest, and his fingers had begun to twitch as though they needed to hold something.

"I know you did. But it was so perfect for us. It's what we've been dreaming of, all this time."

Sean stepped into the middle room. Joel held the phone away from his ear so he could listen in, but he didn't put it on speaker.

"What if we could offer more?" Joel said. Sean could tell he was trying hard not to sound desperate.

The professor's distant voice kept saying how sorry he was, how sorry Emily was, too. "We really wanted you two to have it, but Jock and Mary are holding us to our promise. It's been their dream, as well. We had no idea! We thought it was only a politeness between friends, you know, for all our country weekends. Of course, we do like them a lot, and they've decided to get out of Madison for good, downsize, retire, slow way down."

"So have we!" Joel almost squealed. Sean stretched his arm around him and squeezed. He saw tears filling those wide brown eyes. And then, suddenly controlling himself, Joel said, "How much are they offering?"

Sean barely heard Lauriston say, "It's a fair offer, and we did promise them. I'm really sorry it took me so long to decide to sell. I know I've put you through a wringer."

"And Tory Forell is handling it?"

"Well, we may be calling on her to help with, you know, the details."

"Oh, Jesus!" Joel said, now truly crying, so he passed the phone over and slipped out of the room.

"Hello, James, Sean Tyson here. It's sad news for us. I mean, we do have other options, but your cottage was ideal, especially for Joel and his music. I'd do anything to get it for him. No chance of them changing their minds?"

"I'm afraid not, Sean. I did make a case for you, but they've come out with us so often, hunting morels, cross-country skiing, summer weekends weeding the garden and cooking big meals. Jock said they always thought of it as their surrogate country house. I didn't realize it when we promised them. I'm really sorry. They're good people, though. You'd like them if you do buy a place out there and get to know them as neighbors."

"Oh, dear" was all Sean could say. How was he ever going to make up for this? Joel was off in the bedroom, and it sounded as if he was pounding the pillows. So Sean said, "I could offer a lot more, if that would persuade you. I've come into an inheritance. I'm not used to spending this kind of money, but—"

"I wish, I wish," said the other voice on the phone. "We should have been clearer from the start, but it's so hard for me to leave everything here behind and venture off into the unknown. We're selling the Madison house, too. It's so expensive to buy in the East, and Emily wants a place in Vermont. The boys are all for it. But I'll never be inside these old walls again. I'm a creature of habit. No more roaring of the lions!"

Sean couldn't help but feel close to this James Lauriston. They were facing the same prospect. But Joel wouldn't understand, and he certainly wouldn't want to make friends with Jock and Mary when he finally resigned himself to the schoolhouse or the ugly house on the hillside. Sean asked the professor to call if anything miraculously changed his neighbors' minds and said as friendly a goodbye as he could. "And give my best to Emily," he added before hanging up and going to their bedroom to deal with Joel.

《 》

Sean no longer knew what he wanted for himself, if he wanted anything at all. In one sense, he wanted nothing or, at least, nothing new, nothing to change. But he saw how sad Joel was, as if his future had lost its promise. And yet how stupid that was! Not being allowed to have his notion of a dream house hadn't deprived his life of all meaning. Joel could be a most annoyingly spoiled child. But somehow, Sean always managed to forgive him and do whatever he could to make him feel better. The odd thing was that, at a certain point, Joel would move past his sorrows and find the next all-absorbing desire and leave Sean lamenting what they'd both lost.

That night, after the professor's call, he had promised and promised and promised they would get themselves an even more perfect place up there in the Ocooches. They could even buy that first moldy log cabin above the gully and, for the price of the eggplant house, tear it down and have a new cabin built to suit their precise needs. This vision brought a temporary calm as they lay, cuddled close under the blanket Sean had pulled up over the two of them. He couldn't help thinking that this sixty-five year old in his arms was an overgrown adolescent, but he didn't mind. All he wanted was to get him past the crisis and steel himself for the next phase, whatever it might be.

On the next morning, at the breakfast table, Joel begged him to come to the Lilienthals' that night. After Rebecca's tears last week, Joel didn't want to be there without him. Besides, Irene Wilson would be coming to try out her part, and she'd love to see Sean. They could announce the loss of the Lauristons' farmhouse, and Sean could reassure Art and Rebecca that he wasn't about to let Joel disappear into his ancient mountains.

At lunchtime, he stepped out of the office to get himself a sandwich, so he told Andrew, but he also intended to make a call to Owen. Before last night, he'd been idly contemplating meeting the young man on another quartet night, but he could keep the temptation alive by apologizing for being too busy this week. Yet he didn't know if Owen was counting on him to call. Sean might be only one man of many circling through Owen's basement room.

"Yeah?"

"Owen?"

"Oh, Sean, hey, your name came up. I was afraid you'd call. I've got to sub tonight at the club. I wish I could see you, though. Usually, Thursdays are good."

"I've got to do something with Joel, anyway," Sean said, "but I wanted to—well, I'm sorry not to have called sooner."

"I wouldn't have known before yesterday about subbing. So maybe next week, huh? It was so good seeing you. I felt sort of lonesome after. I don't guess you could come over now?"

"You're not at the health club?"

"I'm going in later. Would it take too long to get here now from work?"

"I'm afraid I have an appointment in half an hour," Sean said, though his next client wasn't due till three. "It's very tempting. I wish I could."

"I just woke up before you called," Owen said with a yawn. "I'm about to take a shower."

Sean's blood was pumping fast at the same time he felt silly, standing on the sidewalk by the corner store with so many people walking by. He held the phone closer and tried to appear businesslike.

"So I'm naked," came Owen's sleepy voice.

"I can easily imagine."

"And now I'll have to go into work being all horny and such. Darn!"

"Owen, you're a tempting young man."

"I'm just available, is all," he replied, rather wistfully.

Sean said he wished he was available as well, but he had to get back to his desk, and he promised he'd call the next time he could. Owen promised he wouldn't bother him, which strangely made Sean want all the more to see him again. He closed the phone and, as soon as he hit the air-conditioning of the corner store to get a ready-made tuna sandwich, realized how much he'd been sweating.

8 He got off the train in Rogers Park and caught sight of Sheila Bowden with her cello descending from the Evanston bus. "Well, if it isn't!" she said. "Welcome to Round Two of the Lilienthal Debates." They set out in tandem along the sidewalk. Her aluminum instrument case was equipped with wheels, so it bumped along ahead of her like a baby stroller.

"Wouldn't it be easier to pull it behind?" Sean asked.

"But then I couldn't keep my eye on it."

"What do you do if it snows?"

"Take cabs. Now, Sean, Joel emailed about losing the dream house, so you needn't fill me in. My only concern is what can you do to tone down that blithering fool boyfriend of yours? He's so foot-in-mouth with Art and Rebecca. You're supposed to be on the job."

"After all these years, I've given up trying," Sean said.

At the next curb, Sheila stopped wheeling while they waited for traffic. She seemed shorter and not as round as he'd remembered. He noticed those delicately small fingers gripping the neck of the shiny silver case and now pushing it on. "All the Lilienthals need," she said, "is assurance that their honorary son will show up most every Thursday from now on, except for summer vacations."

When they reached the opposite curb, Sean said, "I'll make that a condition of buying the schoolhouse, if that's what's next."

"And kick him tonight if he gets into one of his spiels. Besides, Irene Wilson will be there. We've got work to do." She pushed her cello case on down the sidewalk of the Lilienthals' leafier street, where the trees were already beginning to show a bit of yellow. Joel must have been emailing her extensively because she went on about him reading *Hiawatha*, and she knew about their hikes in the Porkies and exploring Black Hawk country and how he had played four-hand Schubert with the professor in Madison. Sean began to wonder if Joel had come to mean as much to the cellist, in her windless cat-furred basement, as he did to his mentors, the first and second violinists.

Despite the house's closed windows, Sean could hear Irene warming up inside. Art came out and helped bump the cello up the steps, through the front door, and down the hall. Rebecca was at the piano, playing chords for Irene, but they stopped in the middle of a scale and came to welcome Sean with hugs. But where was Joel?

"I don't expect you'll much like this music," Rebecca said, "but it's important to Sheila's thesis, so the Brahms is out. You'd have preferred it."

"I'm ready for anything," Sean said.

"He's a good sport," said Art.

"So are we," Rebecca added. "Here, let's sit awhile and await our

244

tardy violist. I don't know, Sean, if he mentioned my little crying jag last week, but I assure you, we simply want you two to be happy, wherever you wind up." She led him to the couch and plunked him down between herself and Irene. Art and Sheila took their usual armchairs.

"It's great to see you again," Sean told Irene. "You sounded beautiful. I didn't want to interrupt."

"Just getting the old voice going," she said. "You'll hear plenty more, if you can stick it out. I suspect, if this concert comes off, it'll be my farewell public appearance. It was awfully kind of Joel to dredge up his aging classmate. I will, henceforth, limit myself to teaching."

"Where is that boy dawdling?" Sheila said.

Sean imagined Joel didn't want to find himself awkwardly alone with the Lilienthals before the others arrived. He'd left it to Sean to smooth things over first.

"This is a departure for me," Irene went on. "I'm not a twentieth-century soprano." Her long brown fingers with shocking-pink nails brushed lightly across her lips, as if to seal them. Sean had always found her enchanting, somewhat of a priestess, but he knew his inclination toward black people was its own form of prejudice and could be traced back to his mother's "dumfree" song and sharing off-campus quarters with Andrew Stone out in DeKalb.

"She's underselling herself, of course," said Art.

"No, but seriously, Art, after Mahler and Wolf and Strauss, I'm done."

"Richard Strauss didn't die till 1949, my dear," Art reminded her. "You've sung his *Four Last Songs*."

"In younger days," said Irene. "I'm at an age now where they'd be more appropriate, but I couldn't manage those long soaring lines. Still, it's comforting to think I was already four years old when he wrote them. I was alive for that last great romantic effusion."

"But," said Sean, "in the twenty-first century, people can still be romantic, can't they?"

245

At which point the doorbell rang, the front door opened, and Joel barged in with his viola case, puffing short breaths. "Sorry I'm so late. I got hung up at school with the Chorus of Fairies. They're going to be adorable. Oh, good, Sean's here. Hi, lovely Irene, let's start."

« »

At first, the viola did have a real melody, but then it all began to sound muddy to Sean's ears. If Joel hadn't told him the song was about breezes from other planets, he would never have guessed it. Irene's voice, on its own, might have been beautiful enough, but the quartet was wrapping it in off-pitch harmonies, or so it seemed to Sean. Then it got screechy and her voice with it. He kept his eyes on Irene's face, her pink-shaded lips, her broad mouth wide open to hit those unexpected notes, her gaze intent on the musical score she held in her long fingers.

Sean wondered if he'd made that remark about still being romantic in order to stand with the Lilienthals and their Brahms and their long-lasting marriage and to solidify their sense of himself as loyal and true and loving. He'd wanted them, Sheila too, to think of him that way, yet on his lunch break he'd made a call to Owen, and even if he'd not planned to see him, he hadn't wanted to give up the possibility of some future Thursday night. He had a better reputation with the Lilienthals than he deserved. Joel was the true romantic who threw himself whole-heartedly into things. Sean was watching him now, deep inside his strange music. There were five of them together, making that music with its unpleasant sounds and these incomprehensible German words pouring from Irene's expressive mouth. Joel had called it expressionistic, and Sheila said it was about things breaking apart, breezes from other planets, something new in our world, but Sean couldn't hear it. His thoughts wandered to Owen, to the sight of him stepping out of his shower and toweling off his silky skin. Had the music led him there, or was Owen's image his escape from the unpleasant music? He never could concentrate on music as itself. It wasn't like a novel, where he'd forget he was reading and, in his mind, see only what was happening on the pages as he turned them.

Art called out for them to stop and try that part once more. Irene asked the others to give her a moment. She ran a forefinger over her score, marking a beat with her other hand. "Yes, I've got it now," she said. "How am I holding up, Sean? Not too croaky?"

"Not croaky at all. I love hearing you sing."

"As opposed to us playing, Quimby? Don't worry, you'll get used to it."

"It's definitely from another planet," Sean quipped.

"No, that's the next movement. This one's the Litany. Didn't you like my opening solo?"

"I'm fretting about my two-octave leap coming up," said Irene.

So Joel had avoided reviving last week's upset. Music-making could smooth over anything.

《 》

Walking over to the El afterwards, having waved to the Lilienthals at their door, and to Sheila, stuffing her instrument case into Irene's black Saab for a ride back to Evanston, and to Irene as she pulled away from the curb, it seemed Joel had a confession to make. "I wasn't actually rehearsing the girls' chorus, Sean. I was phoning Tory Forell about our future plans. I've been thinking we should drive up again, not this weekend because it's Parents Night at school, but the weekend after, so we can reconsider some things. Maybe there'll be new listings. And, you know, it's September. Tory says sellers are anxious to unload before the market goes dead and they have to wait for spring."

Sean was gazing up at the sidewalk trees with their clinging leaves, yellowish in the glow of the streetlamps. "Wait a minute," he said. "What?"

"And this time we could stay at a decent motel. Mrs. S. wouldn't have to know."

"What weekend?"

"Not this one—the next."

"But our fundraising dinner's that Saturday. I told you."

"I don't think you did."

"Joel, it's been on the calendar."

"But you didn't remind me."

"I have to be there. It makes or breaks the Collective for the year. We can't be away."

"But the weekend after that, Tory's got a realtors' conference in Milwaukee. I could maybe go by myself?"

Sean had stopped at the next street. There wasn't any traffic, but he didn't want to cross. He looked closer at the man standing beside him, viola case in one hand, a tenuously hopeful twist on his lips. Sean humphed once and began to cross.

"Don't be that way," Joel said, following and grabbing at Sean's elbow with his free hand but failing to slow him down.

"I'm not being that way. You're being that way." Sean picked up his pace and was newly aware of his firm footfalls on the cement. "You've always gone to the fundraiser with me." He was unsure if Joel could hear him.

At the end of the block there was plenty of traffic, so they stopped again, and Joel said, "I'll stay home then. It's only, if we're really going to do this, we should have a second look before winter. I wouldn't decide anything without you, I'd just report. It's not as though anyone cares that I'm at the fundraiser. We never sit at the same table. Who'd notice?"

"But you're so good with the old ladies, Joel. And there'll be some Foxridge parents and old alums with big bucks. Davey counts on you."

Now they could cross, and the El tracks were in sight. "I do want to help," Joel said. "I suppose we could go up later in October. It's just that I'm so antsy. I can't stop thinking about the—you know." He gave Sean a sad-eyed look when they reached the other curb.

Because Joel hadn't run it by him before calling, Sean feared he and Tory were conniving to pull him into a quick deal when there was no reason to rush. Next spring, there would be more listings, and why buy a house only to shut it up for the cold weather? But because it was how he tended to handle impasses, what Sean said was: "All right, you go up by yourself. I don't want an antsier Joel on my hands than I've already got."

"No," said Joel, the way he expected he might, "I'll stay and go to your fundraising dinner. I owe you that, at least."

They left it there for the moment, and on the train, Sean had no trouble choosing someone in Joel's game, because the car was full of college boys heading down for the Thursday-night kickoff of the weekend they used to have to wait till Friday for.

« »

At breakfast, Joel seemed to have forgotten Tory. Instead, he was getting anxious about his eleven o'clock chorus rehearsal, when they were going to try out the driftwood piece. "Either they'll object that it's depressing or they'll like it for that. You can't tell with kids. They act cool and hip, but underneath they're sentimental slobs."

"It's not depressing," Sean said. "It's real and sad. That's not the same."

"Reality doesn't do it for them, Quimby, but I think they'll enjoy singing the dissonances, the way their ears vibrate when the notes get too close, like when we did the Gesualdo."

Sean didn't remember which that was, but he nodded as if he did and said he couldn't wait for their fall concert. That reminded Joel that he'd be home later than usual on Friday because the music history kids had their first excursion to Orchestra Hall and had to be returned to Foxridge before he could get home. At the door, heading out to catch his bus, he mumbled to himself, "I guess I could go up next weekend on my own, though it'd mean missing the dinner."

Sean decided not to have heard that and turned up the hot water over the dishes. He yelled, "Bye, Joel, have fun," before twisting the faucet off to hear the front door click shut.

Later, on the El, it occurred to him that if Joel would be calling their realtor, he might call up Owen. On Parents Night he had planned to visit Floyd Griffin, but why not see Owen instead? Besides, he'd be seeing Floyd next weekend at the fundraiser. Would Owen be at his health club on a Saturday night? His schedule always seemed to be changing. Much of what that young man said seemed questionable. He could send him a noncommittal text, but what if Joel somehow retrieved it from his phone? That was how most infidelities came to light nowadays.

At the office, Andrew hadn't brought in donuts because he was the liaison to the volunteers organizing the big event and had to run out to a meeting. Davey was off, and Elise had called in sick, so Franklin and Sean doubled up on appointments. In the free quarter hour Sean had counted on to call Owen, a fax came from his dad's lawyers that required signatures to complete the transfer of funds to their AmTrust branch. For the first time, Sean regretted having a joint account. But Joel had always trusted him, and he had always trusted Joel, who had a slightly lower salary. They had never quibbled over shared expenses. They each spent modestly and hated shopping for anything but necessities. Unlike Floyd, whose apartment was cluttered with wobbly antique furniture, frayed oriental rugs, and what he called his *objets d'art* on every dusty surface, Sean and Joel preferred inexpensive simplicity and tidiness. Yet now, with his signature alone, Joel could go ahead and rearrange their life together.

Sean's fifteen free minutes must have passed, because an elderly and quite large black woman in a shabby full-length camel-hair coat had shown up at the door dragging a banged-up brown leather suitcase. "Mr. Tyson, I'm Mrs. Webster. I meant to see Miss Ilg, but she's sick and the man sent me down here because he's got somebody else up front."

"Yes, I'm expecting you, come have a seat, Mrs. Webster."

She shuffled to the client's chair and barely squeezed herself between its padded arms. "I like your pictures," she said, pointing a thick finger at the street scenes of Old Chicago. "That was back in the horse and buggy time. My grammy used to make whinnies and clop-clops for us kids so we'd know how it was in her day. We've sure come a long ways since, thank the good Lord."

"We have," Sean said, "but I fear we still have a ways to go."

"That's the truth," said Mrs. Webster, sounding short of breath, "but I'm one of the lucky ones. I can bear witness to that. You see, I've come into a small sum of money, and I'm here so you can find me a quiet, safe place of my own with private kitchen and bath and conveniently located. When I spoke to Miss Ilg over the telephone, she assured me she'd find me such a place if I wasn't in too much of a hurry. There might be something in a property up there in Rogers Park with a partial lake view."

"Yes, I know the building, Mrs. Webster. It has several nice subsidized units. It's old but solid and very clean. Let me check the listings to see what's open." Sean scrolled through his files to pull up the particulars.

"A partial lake view would provide just the right touch," the elderly woman said, quite self-possessed. "I don't need much space, but I need restfulness. Where I'm at now isn't exactly secure, if you know what I'm saying. No, I'm looking for safe and quiet in my declining days. I've earned it, haven't I? Way back, I began as a seamstress. Whoever has a seamstress these days? Recently, I've been taking care of old folks in their homes, folks older than I, bless their hearts. Here's the form Miss Ilg sent for me to fill out—Emma Jo Webster, age eighty-five, my Social Security, the address of my last employer for reference."

"It's all in good order, Mrs. Webster," Sean said. "Let me make this call."

She did turn out to be one of the lucky ones. A small sixth-floor studio had come available, and there was an elevator, so she needn't worry about stairs, and being that high up and facing east, it had more than a partial view over the four-story building next door. She'd see the sun come up out of the lake each morning and the moon each night. "It's semi-furnished—bed, dresser, table and chairs—and has a kitchenette but only a shower in the bathroom."

"Oh, I couldn't heave myself up out of a tub, anyway," the old woman said.

Sean was happier than he'd been all day, happier than last night or the day before. He couldn't remember when he'd felt as calm, not since sitting by Mirror Lake in the Porkies. He'd given Mrs. Webster even more than she'd hoped for. He pictured her rising before dawn, sitting by the one window, and waiting for the gray lake to turn silver as the sun rose.

He called and got a very satisfactory reference then went over all the paperwork and faxed it everywhere it had to go. The Collective had excellent relations with that management firm, having sent them only their most reliable clients. Sean pulled a folding chair up on her side of his desk to go over the payment schedule and show her the bus routes. She thanked him many times over and said she'd be sure to write him a note when she was settled. As she tugged her old suitcase behind her out his door, Sean imagined it held all she owned or, at least, all she could never bear to part with. A Salvadoran couple with a baby was waiting patiently in the hall for the next appointment.

There was no time the rest of the day to call Owen. Sean sensed that his impulse of the morning, when he was angry at Joel, was waning. Still, before he caught the train home, he stood in the doorway of a boarded-up warehouse and pushed in the numbers he'd long since memorized. There was no answer, and it didn't go to voice mail, only rang and rang. He was somehow relieved. But waiting up on the platform, he felt a buzz in his pants pocket and quickly answered.

"Hey, Sean, it was you. I was out of range momentarily. Your name came up. Wow, I didn't expect you'd call. So what's up?"

Sean stuttered explaining that Joel had to be at school Saturday evening and, if Owen didn't have plans, they could maybe get together, if only for a short while.

"Me have plans?" said Owen. "I never have plans. Saturday nights can get lonely. Only thing is, I work till ten, and I'd have to get home and clean up and you probably can't stay out late, huh?"

"Probably not, it's Joel's school thing."

"Bummer," said Owen. "Maybe I could switch hours with someone."

"No, no, there'll be other chances," Sean said quietly into the phone. He decided not to say that next weekend Joel might be going to Wisconsin. He was unsure now why he'd called Owen at all.

He heard that wistful voice he didn't know what to make of say, "Only if you want to," and then the southbound train roared in.

《 》

Sean started grilling the salmon steaks as soon as Joel bounced through the front door shouting that he was starving. There he was, beside him, with a hug and a smack-of-a-cheek kiss, saying he'd had an exhausting but fabulous day. They'd been late to the concert because the school's new van driver was a dork. They had to wait in the lobby for the first piece to end, but it was by some Italian composer Joel didn't think much of. Then they had to squeeze past two silver-haired old ladies on the aisle to get to their seats in time for the flute concerto, which the kids thought was awesome.

"But what about your choral group this morning?" Sean asked.

"One moment. First, I have to tell you about the concert."

"You're all keyed up," Sean said, flipping the steaks to the skin side.

"I've been humming the Tchaikovsky all the way home. I tend to forget about Tchaikovsky. My parents had 78s of the Fifth. It was probably the first symphony I ever loved. They also had the *Pastoral* and the *Prague*, but when I was four or five, I'd make Dr. Nathan put on side twelve of the Tchaikovsky and I'd march around the house like a little *tsarevich*."

"You still do," said Sean. "But how did the kids like your piece?"

Joel had perched himself on the stool by the sink and was tapping out his march on the Formica. "DUM-da-da-DUM-da-da-DUM-DUM! You'd recognize it, Quimby. I told you, my kids are sentimental? That lovely second movement that sounds like 'Beautiful Dreamer,' da-da-da-DUM-dah, you know? Astrid Flanagan had tears on her cheeks. I'd heard she broke up with her boyfriend."

"Slow it down, Joel. Do you want fresh baby spinach or frozen petite peas?"

"Cook the spinach. Anyway, it took me back to when music started for me. What did my parents have? A Victrola and one shelf of albums—highlights from *The Land of Smiles* and *The Gypsy Baron* and good old schlocky Viennese waltzes, but I went more for the Mozart and Beethoven, and then LPs came in, and they let me choose one a month for the family at the record shop. Can't buy records in Richland Center anymore."

"Okay, now," Sean said, having heard those stories of Joel's musical childhood many times before, "tell me about the choral group."

"Yes, but I just have to say, guess who I bumped into at intermission? Floyd Griffin! A year ago, he switched to Friday afternoons. 'To join the retired demographic,' he said. The kids thought he was a hoot. You know how Floyd gets. He was so snooty about the Ibert concerto and even snootier about Nino Rota. 'Movie music! What was Muti thinking! Good thing you missed it.' Floyd was acting it up for the kids, but that did make them feel better about being late. Oh, and I told him you didn't have a date for Saturday night, so he wants you to drop by and he'll fix dinner. Call him."

"A date!" Sean scoffed, but he couldn't help imagining what he might have been doing instead of visiting Floyd.

"Now, are you ready?" Joel hopped off the stool to hug Sean at the stove. "They loved my music! They loved it! They really loved 'who was changed and who was dead.' At their age, they love being morbid, because it doesn't mean anything to them yet."

"They sang the whole thing?"

"Well, sort of. I mean, I pounded out downbeats for the changing time signatures and played the chords, and they muddled through right to the end."

"That's great, Joel, congratulations."

"Well, we only really worked on the opening stanzas."

Sean flipped the steaks to peel off the crispy skin and flipped them back again. He swirled the baby spinach around in the other pan as it softened and curled up and shrank, the whole package reduced to two small servings. Then he poked at the red potatoes in the toaster oven to see if they were done.

"I need a real beer," Joel said, rummaging in the fridge. "Don't we have any? Jesus Christ, all we've got is your ginger beer."

"*My* ginger beer?"

"It's only because of you, Shaw-awn. I'm going to start keeping real beer in the house. I liked that Leinenkugel your sister served. 'Have another Leiny!'"

"Joel, you are really wired tonight."

"It's been an amazing day."

"Set the table."

"Yes, sir, any other orders, sir?"

"Yes. Calm down."

"Not possible, sir."

"Well then, pass your plate and I'll dish out your grub, boy. I have a feeling you called Tory today."

"Oh, shit, I forgot! I got so busy. I'll call her tomorrow. What am I supposed to say, Quimby? I mean, am I going to drive up there or not?"

"You're coming to the fundraiser with me," Sean said with a stern frown that he knew would have no effect on whatever it was Joel was intent on doing.

9 On Saturday, back from brunch at Lo Grasso's, Joel decided to email Tory instead of bugging her by phone, most likely to keep Sean from eavesdropping or butting in. Later, before checking his own mail, Sean opened Joel's and read: "Would you recommend I come up next weekend rather than wait for when Sean can, too? I don't want to risk losing out to another buyer, and I'd love to be able to get a start settling in before it snows." It was clear what answer was expected, but none had come yet. Sean opened his own mail, and there was a surprisingly long letter from Mary—subject: Brothers.

"All right, Sean. It's truly time, after Danny's great visit, for you to reach out to Sandy. He's in his new place, I got him a smart phone, so you can use any of the contact info below. I helped with furnishings. It's a small studio in Uptown. You may know the building from stashing poor folks there. Baby Alexander's sixty! Yikes, how does this happen?! He loves the zoo. He should've been working with, or at least near, animals all along. Remember how he'd tell people he grew up on a farm and wanted to go back? Anyway, he's off all substances except his prescriptions, and Danny even met with a counselor for him. Danny's a whole new man, too. Phyllis is some prize! Trev and I are definitely visiting them next summer at Put-In Bay. You and Joel should come. They've got plenty of room. We'll drive you out with us, and Sandy, too. We're the old folks now. We need to hang out with each other. When was the last time us four kids got together?"

Sean couldn't remember a time when there wasn't one of them missing, himself or Danny or Sandy, and the three boys might not have been in one place without Mary since they were in school. Quickly, he wrote her back, promising to follow up, and then decided, why not, to call Sandy right then. If he was going to Floyd's for dinner, he could see his little brother on the way.

"Dammit, how does this fucking thing work?" was what he heard first.

"Sandy? It's Sean."

"What the fuck? Who? This stupid thing—"

The phone went dead, so Sean tried again. It rang and rang, but finally Sandy's voice came on, less muffled and frantic. "So who's this?"

"Your brother Sean. Mary gave me your number."

"Oh," he said. "See, I'm at the zoo. When people call, you have to tell them where you are because you could be anywhere. I don't like the implications. The world is fucking up big time. Luckily, the animals don't know it. That's why I like working here. I can be in their world instead."

Sean wondered if Sandy was simply talking to some random listening ear, but he let him go on about animals awhile before asking when he'd be getting home.

"After I do the monkeys."

"When's that?"

"Around four. I don't really know."

"You don't have a quitting time?"

"There's certain chores that must get done, Sean."

So he did know who he was talking to. "Because, Sandy, I'll be near your new address later, and if you're not busy, I'll drop in."

"It's pretty slick. Mary got me all this trendy shit for the kitchen and, like, towels and sheets and rugs, and basically a new mattress and a super-comfy armchair to read in because, here's the amazing thing: the old gent that went gaga left behind a shelf of major books I intend to read—philosophy and poetry and Greek drama, like the *Oresteia* and shit. Danny told the relative who was throwing stuff out to leave them behind since I lost all my own."

"Nice," Sean said. He felt a twinge of jealousy that Danny had contrived to do for their brother what he had spent his working life doing for people he didn't know. "But can I come by?"

"I wouldn't mind. See, Mary thought I should have you and Joel over."

"He's got a meeting at school, but he'll want to come next time."

"Yeah, well," Sandy said, "I'm heading on to the monkeys now. You can come by later. I'd rather you brought Joel, though. Remember him playing 'Lay, Lady, Lay' when we got the inheritance? He sounded just like Dylan. Warning, my buzzer says 'A. D. Tyson' but it won't open the door. I have to come down to let you in."

« »

When Sean got there, he waited several minutes after his first buzz, so he pushed again. Perhaps Sandy had forgotten and was wandering about or sitting on some park bench haranguing whoever passed by. But then the door swung in, and Sandy stood there, shirtless and scrawny, tangled wet gray hair dripping onto his sunken chest. "I was in the shower. I smelled like the zoo."

Sean followed his bare feet up two flights of linoleum-tread stairs to a landing with four doors. Wet footprints led out from the open door of Number Twelve. Ahead, Sandy had grabbed his Blackhawks sweatshirt off the floor and was thrusting his skinny arms into it. When his head popped out from the neck, he was staring hard at his brother. He didn't pull up the hood.

258

"You've got good light here," Sean said. The room was very clean and showed Mary's touch, colors coordinated, soft yellows and greens. Sean turned to the set of shelves full of old books.

"I'm going to read them all, sitting right here in my groovy new chair. Remember Mom's sleeping porch in Lincoln Park? Sometimes, I walk by there and look up at it. Remember me out there reading my *Zarathustra*? '*O Mensch, gib acht!*' See, I've been going to the Internet to learn German. Mary showed me how to get everything for free."

"That's great, Sandy." He had sat himself in his comfy armchair, so Sean pulled up a kitchen chair to sit near him.

"See, there's no English equivalent of the word *Mensch*. You have to say 'human being' and that's not exactly poetic. It's from Zarathustra's *Midnight Song*. If you said, 'O Man, take heed!' it'd be inaccurate as well as sexist. Women are *Menschen*, too. It's the kinder side of humans, what we'd call humane, though it's really more like animals. It's the good soul. They use it in Yiddish, as in 'Joel's a real *Mensch*.' I bet his parents used to say that. Brecht's play *The Good Woman of Setzuan* is really the *Mensch*, but they translate is as 'woman.'"

Sandy was sitting there with his long knotty fingers twitching and the sunlight bright behind him so his face was in shadow. Sean squinted to see him better then scooted his chair over to one side. What were those pale staring eyes seeing—his brother? Or would Sandy regale any unsuspecting person with the same lecture?

"I say Zarathustra's *Midnight Song* every night before I go to sleep," Sandy said. "Now I'm doing it in German, because that's what it really says. 'Sorrow is deep, but delight is deeper.' Don't you believe that, Sean? However deep your sorrow, there's something that's even deeper. The German for it is pronounced *loost* but not plain 'lust' like Americans mean it. It's more like being on a high. Not craziness, not like I get sometimes, but steady, calm, always there, deep inside, you know—delight."

"A driving force?" Sean asked hesitantly.

"Not like being driven, it's not compulsive, it's not hyper, it's how I'm trying to steady myself."

Sean hoped the job and the apartment hadn't set Sandy on another upward spiral. This talk was a danger sign. He might easily tip over into his old rage. It had happened many times before. "You're a student of philosophy," Sean said. "You've always been the family intellectual. I wish I had your questing spirit."

"You have it," Sandy said. "You're not in touch with it, that's all. Joel has it, because he's a creative artist. If you weren't with him, you'd be such a dull dude." He was leaning back in his armchair, grinning. The sunlight caught his acne scars. There was a faint smile on his lips that might be a sign of brotherly affection.

Sean couldn't think what else to say, so he nodded self-deprecatingly.

"You're so closed up always, Sean. I don't mean to hurt your feelings because, I mean, you've done lots of good things for people. Besides, questing doesn't mean you have to get anywhere."

"But you're here now," Sean said. He wondered if Davey or Andrew had ever placed anybody there. He was sure he'd never worked with the building himself. It was somewhat upscale for the Collective. It was Dad's money and Danny that got Sandy there. He hadn't wanted to go through Sean. He'd sooner have gone to a shelter than turn to his do-gooder brother.

"I'll probably stay here awhile," Sandy said. "But I have an idea of moving out to the country. I'm sure to find a cheap room in one of those little towns near Gramma's farm. There's plenty of weird cats like me, living alone above storefronts on those empty main streets. Now that I'm clean, I don't need Chicago."

"There's drugs in the country, too," Sean said. "It's supposedly worse out there."

"But I'm clean now, Sean!"

There came the first hint of his anger, or maybe the first hint was when he'd called him dull, so Sean decided to say, "I'm sorry I wasn't more part of our family, Sandy. I wanted to be, but I couldn't."

"Have you always been faithful to Joel?" Sandy asked out of nowhere.

"Why do you say that?"

"Mary thinks you two act like you're still in your twenties. You don't ever seem to grow up, she says. You're fancy-free is how she puts it. It weirds her out. She's the responsible one of us because she's got kids and grandkids. She doesn't resent me with my other problems, but she resents you, Sean. She says you don't know what it takes to raise a family."

"She's mostly kidding," Sean said. "She likes to rib me and pat herself on the back."

"I don't think she was kidding." Now Sandy was leaning forward on his blue-jeaned knees, staring too close to Sean, who felt it coming: "You did to the rest of us exactly what Dad did. You acted like you were mad at him, and then you went on and became like him. At least he left us his money."

"I did offer to help find you an apartment."

"Some crummy flophouse for homeless losers. I know what your Collective's all about."

Sean stood up to avoid the stare and, shaking in his legs, stepped over to the bookshelves and held on to steady himself. "We find decent housing for single moms, Sandy, and for old people and people who've lost their jobs."

"You wouldn't have found me a place as decent as this."

"I wanted to help set you up with regular payments."

"Danny already did that. Mary got me all moved in here. It's not like charity from some bullshit Collective."

Sean recognized it was pointless to defend the work he did. It was their rule when facing disgruntled clients. Sandy might be his brother, but he was also slightly crazy. For all his philosophical studying, he couldn't be reasoned with. Sean found himself responding more as a professional than a brother. He was determined not to ramp things up, so he said, "I'm sorry if I didn't put it the right way. I didn't mean it as charity. It was only because I figured that my familiarity with the housing situation—" But then he added, "Between brothers, it wouldn't be charity. It would've been out of love."

"Yeah, sure. Besides, it took Danny like half a day to figure out the fucking housing situation."

"May I get myself a drink of water?" Sandy was silent, but when Sean had filled one of Mary's unbreakable French café glasses from the tap, he turned and saw the hood up over his brother's head, hiding the straggly hair and shading the staring eyes. Sean sipped and looked out the nearest window at the distant skyscrapers. Finally, he said, "I also wish Joel was here. You like Joel more than me, don't you?"

"Mom didn't trust him," Sandy mumbled into the neck of his sweatshirt.

"But you do."

"He's all right. You didn't answer yet if you were faithful to him."

"Of course I am," Sean said, knowing that, despite Owen, it was true.

"You better be," said Sandy. "I got shat on by too many women, so I know what it does to a person. Mary thinks you gays don't have the same ideas about having an affair as moms in the suburbs."

"I don't know why Mary's unloading her gripes on you, Sandy. We've each got enough gripes of our own."

"I need a nap now" came from the hooded figure hunched in the armchair by the other window. "You should probably leave."

"We'll do better next time," Sean said. "I'll bring Joel."

Sandy slowly raised a knobby-knuckled hand in what Sean took for the peace sign. He could tell that Sandy was regretting his outburst but wasn't capable of apologizing for it.

"I'm glad you like your job so much," Sean said as he turned the doorknob to go.

"The animals help," Sandy said. "Look into their eyes and you leave the whole human race behind."

« »

There was no welcoming committee on Floyd Griffin's front stoop, so Sean rang his bell and waited for the click to let himself in. Floyd was leaning over the banister on the top landing. "Someday, Sean, I'll be too fragile to climb those stairs and have to move to an elevator building. How's the breathing? Take it slow, rest halfway."

"I can make it."

"You were always young for your age. Since eleven, I've been old for mine. I was initiated too young, but that's what camp counselors were for, weren't they?"

"Not at my camp."

"Oh, right, at your camp you initiated each other."

"Some of us did."

"But not poor little asthmatic late-blooming Sean Q. Tyson. And here you are now, hardly out of breath." Floyd embraced him with his long skinny Oxford-shirted arms and presented a bony cheek for Sean to kiss.

"Where are those boys of yours from the first floor, Floyd?"

"Gussying up to go out dancing. It's Saturday night. Remember Saturday nights? Come on in."

It was too chilly to sit out on the deck, so Floyd led him into the living room, chock-full of handsome rickety old furniture, none of it inviting. Floyd valued the look of a thing over its function. In his years with Mick, in their previous apartment, he'd given his unassuming partner free rein in one room only, and that was where the comfortable couch and chairs were relegated. After Mick's death,

263

Floyd had distributed them among his neighbors and moved only the antiques into his new place. He'd told Sean he simply couldn't look at that ratty old couch without seeing Mick lying on it, enervated in his final months of life. Floyd had suffered a loss Sean could scarcely comprehend.

He took the least precarious chair, a wooden rocker with, thankfully, a needlepoint throw pillow on the seat. Floyd balanced briefly on the stiff-backed horsehair sofa's arm before offering the usual lemonade to accompany his own last G and T of the season. "Tomorrow, I switch to bourbon and water, and I wrap the deck chairs in a tarp and roll up the awning—my fall rituals." He made his way to the kitchen from where, over the clinking of ice cubes into tall glasses, Sean heard, "So how's the country boy's efforts at relocating you to the sticks?"

Sean rocked the chair, which creaked worrisomely, so he steadied it to a stop. "Joel wants to go up next weekend to reconnoiter, but I've got the fundraiser."

"And I'll be in attendance signing over a generous check," said Floyd, sitting back down on the narrow sofa, and the old friends raised their glasses to each other. "He can be terribly irresponsible, that boy," Floyd said.

"I gather you saw him at Orchestra Hall."

"With a charming troupe of teens. There was one particular stunner who's to play the fairy shepherd. We really must go, Tyson."

"It's not till November."

"I expect to be alive." Floyd often joked about life and death, age and illness, subjects Sean was careful to avoid. "And you do know, I'm quite fond of your Joel, but I can't imagine living with him. I suppose you can't imagine living without him."

"I'm trusting we'll strike a compromise," Sean said. "Joel likes to overplay his enthusiasms. He'll calm down. By the way, I stopped at my younger brother's new apartment. He's in much better shape. I have to credit Mary and Danny. Sandy wouldn't let me help him out. He always took money from Dad, but me he still has trouble with."

"Families! I'm the oldest survivor of mine. Benefit of being an afterthought."

"Joel's the only survivor of his."

"Even less complicated!" Floyd got up to draw the heavy musty curtains across the windows facing the deck, where night was falling. Sean noticed how gingerly he stepped, how slightly stooped he was, and how he had to fuss and fiddle with the tangled curtain pulls. When he crossed the room, the glow of the table lamp made what little hair he had appear almost blond again. It was odd to see a face, known from late youth to early age, and now to glimpse, within the likeness, what had once been so familiar. "I've made a delicious bouillabaisse," Floyd called from the pantry. "You lads don't take any more effort over cuisine than decor. You and I never could've lived together. Mick was a splendid chef, but you two can't be bothered to fry up a burger. I will say this for Joel Greenwood: his pupils adore him. He absolutely mustn't give up teaching. Whoever adored me like that at work?"

« »

When crumbs of the baguette speckled their placemats and they had slurped their last spoonfuls, Floyd went to boil water for Sean's mint tea and fix himself a drop of Grand Marnier. Sean pushed the cane-seated chair back from the tippy pedestal table and gazed through the candlelight at the wall of books opposite. Floyd's retirement, he knew, was made up of much reading, much theater and music, a quiet neighborhood pub in winter, a sidewalk café in summer, and the occasional intimate encounter. He had many friends and acquaintances of his own age and some younger devotees like those two downstairs. It was a pleasant life, but Sean couldn't picture himself like that. He wasn't social enough, he didn't care to go out

265

much, but what would his retirement be, away from the city bustling about?

Floyd set a delicate cup and saucer before him and took his own snifter to the other side of the table. Before his host could launch another topic of conversation—they'd been arguing about the Occupy movement—Sean remarked in a casual tone, "I wonder if you've ever noticed a muscular young fellow in the neighborhood who wears pressed khakis and tight polo shirts. Last time after I left here, he stopped and chatted with me on the street because he recognized me from my commute."

"Tallish, crooked nose, sharp chin, a bit gawky?"

"Sort of lopsided face but nice-looking."

"He stopped and talked to you? Tyson, you devil! I never have your luck."

"Nothing happened then, I promise."

"If it's the young lad I'm thinking of, he's been somewhat of a fixture lately. He strolls up and down, around the block, and gets picked up pretty frequently, I'd guess. There's something old school about him. Fifties physique model? He's probably a hooker, but who knows. And you didn't take the bait?"

"He was friendly enough. He gave me his number, but I said I had to get home."

"But you took his number."

"Well, he gave it to me." So far, everything Sean had said was true.

"He must be into oldsters," said Floyd. "Did he ask if you were 'generous'? That's the code. Tyson, you're such a straight arrow!"

"He walked with me to the bus stop and gave me one of those manly hugs."

"And you still have the number."

"It's written down somewhere. I forget—" Sean didn't want to lie, but ever since Sandy's question, he'd been contemplating his own unfaithfulness and now regretted mentioning Owen.

"Anyhoo," Floyd said, "he's likely to have every disease in the book. Young ones think, because we have the meds now—oh, if only Mick had hung on for two more years, he'd be sitting over in that chair or, well, I suppose we'd still be in the old apartment. His room would be full of his crap, and we'd both be sleeping in my room in there—" He pointed and then recalled himself. "I mean, in my room in the old place. I can't believe it's been nearly eighteen years! Remember those tall windows down to the floor, with the wrought-iron railings outside so nobody could fall out, and the lake out across the Drive—fuck, it was a good life!" Floyd swirled the snifter and breathed in, then sipped and added, "Eighteen years, Sean. The latter part of life goes very fast, laddie."

"So I've noticed."

"Because we've done all the growing that once marked time. Now there's only cataclysms, death, disease, moving to Wisconsin. Don't let Joel Greenwood drag you off there, Sean. Take your summer trips up north, go south in the winter. Mick and I always took two weeks on Sanibel, enough to relax and get sunburned."

"Not great for my skin cancers."

Floyd gave an impatient stare and resignedly shook his skull-like head. Sean wondered if he cooked only for guests and otherwise subsisted on cheese and crackers and drink.

They left the table and returned to the stiff-backed horsehair sofa with refilled teacup and snifter. "Now if you happen to come across that number—" Floyd began.

"What number?"

"The gawky muscleboy's."

"I don't know where it is."

"I'll never reveal how I got it. Look around for it?"

"I wasn't intending to call him," Sean said, as if to help himself resist the temptation. It would be wise to seal Owen up in an unspoiled memory. It couldn't possibly go as well a second time.

They went back to talking about times past, and Sean didn't leave Floyd's till almost eleven. He feared he'd bump into Owen on

267

the way to his bus, but he made it safely home to Joel, who had just returned from Parents Night.

"Nothing like appreciative Chicago rich folk, Quimby. My kids provided the evening's entertainment, selections from the opera. Handsome Willy knocked their socks off with his big song about social inequities. Ironic, in front of that crowd!"

"That's the boy Floyd took a shine to."

"Floyd Griffin is shameless. I hope he fed you well." Joel was stripping off his suit and tie, wandering down the hall out of earshot.

"I do worry about him," Sean said, traipsing after. "He seems so much frailer."

"He got old, Shaw-awn. I suspect we look the same to him. You've always liked old people. Now's your chance to be one."

《 》

After breakfast, it came out that Joel had indeed arranged to meet Tory on Saturday and had reserved a rental car for Friday morning and a motel for two nights, maybe three. He was in his jogging shorts and headed out before Sean had a chance to react. So that Sunday morning, he fell into a low mood, indoorsy and sedentary. Joel might go for a run in the crisp air, but Sean felt the weight of time passing and soon had stretched himself out on the couch with nothing to read or listen to, only the front windows brightening with the sun above the eastward rooftops and puffs of autumn air through the open windows along the side street. He heard a car whir slowly by, but it was some while before the next one. He did hear the murmur of two voices down on the corner, but then they separated and called back and forth from opposite sides of the street going different directions. He couldn't make out what they said, only their inflections up and down, like chattering birdsong. Then, quiet. He listened closely and caught the hum of traffic out on the main drag

268

and the blaring of a distant horn, the hiss of bus brakes. No sounds came from 3-B above or 1-B below, nothing from across the hall. The Filipino children downstairs were so well behaved, their parents so proper. The lawyer couple up top hadn't thrown a party in months. He didn't know their first names, though he did know Mia in 2-A from their brief polite chats by the mailboxes. He thought of Floyd's livelier building and his neighborhood with its tempting street life and then of Owen's basement room off that alley, dark and airless. Owen wouldn't have every disease in the book! He'd supplied Sean with lube and a rubber from the shoebox under his bed where he kept such items. He hadn't asked for anything. He didn't expect anything now. He was so awkward and blinky and melancholy for a young man in such fine shape. Sean wished he knew why he was that way, wished he could be generous to him, but knew he shouldn't, mustn't, wouldn't. If he and Joel were to move to Wisconsin, he would never run into Owen again. Thinking of Joel up there on his own next weekend, by himself, alone, hoping to settle where they'd live together into their old age, made Sean terribly sleepy. He lay on the couch in the sunny breezy living room, eyes closed, on that peaceful Sunday morning with Joel out jogging, and let himself doze off as another car thrummed by.

He woke when he heard Joel come stumbling in, breathing huffs and puffs, and heading straight to the shower. Sean didn't want to get mad at him. It wouldn't do any good. They were on a path leading to their lives thenceforth. He would have to accept whatever came of Joel's jaunt up to Richland County.

"But what about the Friday concert kids?" he asked when Joel came up the hall, rubbing himself down with his bright-blue bath towel.

"It's not every week or we'd bankrupt the school. But I do have to reschedule my choral group because I plan to get an early start."

"Quartets the night before?"

"Want to come?"

"I'll skip this week. I may have to stay late to help with the fund-raiser." He was allowing himself to consider calling Owen one more time.

"Sorry I'm going away, Sean."

"It's all right." Sean rolled over onto his other side. He really didn't want to talk to Joel right then.

"I can tell it's not."

"You missing the dinner is nothing compared to you moving to Wisconsin."

"Us moving," Joel said. "Half the year. I'll go up in the spring, and you'll come for summers and long fall weekends. We have our Faustian blood pact, remember? And I've promised the Lilienthals to stick with the quartet. I even promised to write a new piece, maybe that two-cello quintet for when Clara comes home."

"I bet you haven't told anyone at Foxridge yet," Sean said.

"I sort of told Vincent Hill. It's fine with him because the opera's in the fall, and he's doing the senior play in the spring, Chekhov's *Three Sisters*. Oh, Jesus, I'm so sick of the academic calendar! Aren't you sick of the Collective yet? You've been housing people for over forty years, Quimby. You've done enough good for the world."

Joel scrubbed his wet head with the big towel then dropped it to the floor and jumped, naked, onto Sean and started tickling him. He got the giggles and slapped Joel's ass. "I should put you on a leash, boy."

Joel then lay still and said, "Speaking of dogs—"

"Uh-oh."

"Well, Vincent gave me a great tip. There's a greyhound rescue website for, you know, retired racers. They're only two or three years old. They're docile sweet dogs. His neighbors have one."

"Too large for an apartment."

"No, they grew up in kennels. They simply want to lie about and rest. No more competition."

"But you wanted a big floppy sheepdog."

"Greyhounds sound easier. I want a dog to lie around with, like this." He squirmed his bare self tightly up beside Sean.

"But you have me for that," Sean said.

10 On Monday, Sheila Bowden called Sean at work to invite him over for pizza in her underground den. "No Joel!" she announced. "How about tomorrow at six? It's time for us to have that talk."

Sean had been dreading it, but he couldn't put it off. And he was curious to see where Sheila lived. The next day, he left the office early and caught the train north to Evanston. He followed her detailed directions past where the old Coronet Theater used to be. Dad would give Mom a break once a month and take all four kids to see Margaret Rutherford as Miss Marple or Terry-Thomas in some goofy British comedy. One time, Mom had taken Sean alone to see Greta Garbo in *Camille* because Dad didn't want to go. It was embarrassing seeing that old movie with his mother. He remembered a lady behind them whispering to her husband, "I wonder what she was thinking, bringing that boy to this!"

Sean turned down several quiet streets and soon found himself in front of a rather gothic Victorian house, grand but in need of paint and hemmed in by overgrown bushes. He'd imagined Sheila in a brick apartment block with no greenery. He took the cracked cement walk around back, located her unmarked door down three steps, and knocked. Sheila opened up, saying what he later learned was: *Hereinspaziert in die Menagerie!* "Something in German about a menagerie," he told Joel, who identified it as the first line of the opera *Lulu*. "Sheila loves her little quotes."

The den did smell like a zoo, and there was a mess of papers and books on tables and chairs and clothes strewn about. Two tortoise-shell cats appeared, huge fluffy creatures mewing and whipping their tails and staring at Sean till he stroked them.

"The fatter one's Qusay," Sheila said, though Uday looked nearly as large. "They're such thuggy kitties, aren't they! Let me take your nice corduroy jacket so it doesn't get covered with fur." She hung it on a high hook next to an array of her own outfits beyond the reach of her cats. Sean noticed the cello case leaning in a corner behind a folding chair and music stand. There wasn't much floor space for her to set up and play. The saggy couch, draped with various fur-coated blankets, offered no obvious spot to sit on. "You're not allergic, are you, Sean?"

"Not to cats."

"Or dogs? Joel wrote about the retired greyhound you're adopting."

"He sure keeps you informed of his every whim."

"Oh, I know all about your beloved. We do Facebook now. But I confess, once again I've got you here on false pretenses. You're afraid I'm bent on probing your family history, but this time it's Joel I'm concerned about. Do you feel he's verging on some kind of minor breakdown? By the way, I've ordered half pepperoni, half eggplant. The kid knows my door by now."

Sean glimpsed three empty pizza boxes stacked up in the kitchenette beside unwashed cups and bowls and plates teetering on each other. He thought of Owen's utterly bare basement room and couldn't decide which of the two was the most depressing.

"I'll have more light when the landlord takes out the air conditioner for winter." Sheila was bustling about, removing blankets and patting down cushions. "This old house is full of oddballs. There's a slow-witted young man upstairs with a pet duck. In warm weather, he puts it outside in a pen, but I think he sleeps with it at night. My own dumpy flat is an illegal unit, so I get it dirt cheap. Some fine family once owned the place, but now it's a repository for lost souls."

"I hope you're not lost, Sheila," Sean said and took the end cushion she indicated.

"But isn't it the perfect environment in which to theorize the breakdown of tonality?" She piped one of her shrieky laughs.

From his seat, Sean could see into a small inner room, its narrow bed piled with pillows and quilts where a cat was now proudly nesting. "But, Sheila, I thought your dad was—"

"Yes, I had quite the cosmopolitan childhood beside the Seine and the Danube, not to mention the Potomac. Life among the think tanks! Well, certain extravagances aren't sustainable when alcohol's involved."

"But your mother?"

"Mother Number One, dearly departed. Mother Number Two saved herself in time and got out. Poor Mother Number Three—but by then I was at Oberlin—well, she stuck it out to the bitter end."

"So this is why you're fascinated with—"

"Duh!" Sheila squeezed herself beside him, displacing the other cat. Sean wasn't sure which one it was. It jumped up behind her and nuzzled her neck, purring loudly. "But I don't intend to explore our comparable family collapses. I must talk to you about the present crisis."

A sharp knock on the door caused both cats to leap off their respective perches and scoot under bed and couch.

"Could you get that, Sean? I'd have to climb over. I've paid for it electronically. Aren't these new phones remarkable?"

Sean swung open the basement door and took the very warm box from a pimply-faced white boy in a muscle shirt. He said, "This is for my best bud Sheila."

"Hello, Clayton," she called from behind the books piled on a table that seemed to serve as her desk. "*Je t'adore*, which is French for 'shut the door.' *Auf wiederschauen!*" Returning, Sean spotted her laptop under the scattered photocopies and musical scores. "Grab us two Bud Lights from the fridge, Sean. You don't mind our laps?

There's no other option. And better bring some ersatz napkins, and can you find two reasonably clean plates?"

He balanced beer cans, plates, and an almost depleted roll of paper towels atop the pizza box and lowered himself next to Joel's cellist pal, wondering what to expect next.

"Cheers!" she said, clanking her Bud Light to his. "You're my first dinner guest, Sean Tyson. I shall never let the Lilienthals see this dump, and I don't want you squealing to Joel, either. I'd hate for them to think they had to rescue me from my squalor. I choose to live here, and I'm entirely at ease underground. I emerge quite respectably into the world up there. I have my students, I have my colleagues, I have the quartet, I have a salary with a health plan, and most of all I have my theories. Here, pepperoni or eggplant?"

"One of each, please."

The cats reappeared and hopped onto the back of the couch. The fatter one, Qusay, if Sean remembered rightly, made himself into a softly vibrating neck pillow for Sheila while Uday slunk back and forth behind Sean. "You could pick him off a pepperoni," Sheila suggested, so he cautiously held up a greasy little disc, which the cat first pawed at and then snatched between its jaws and slipped away into the bedroom.

"Excellent pizza," Sean said, hoping to stave off any unwelcome revelations about Joel.

"Back to the topic at hand," said Sheila. "You weren't with us on the night your beloved had us sing through his valedictory choral work. I admit it was quite lovely, if a tad neo-English-madrigalesque, if you catch my meaning." She piped a gentler squeak.

"I can't say I do, but go on."

She gave him a fondly condescending shake of the head. "You're a doll, Sean Tyson. Anyway, my point is, Rebecca took it badly. So did Art, though he's not one to go all weepy."

"But isn't that what music's for, to touch the emotions?"

"Ah, yes, and it's a mark of Maestro Greenwood's peculiar

274

genius that the expressive harmonies he found for those devastating words could draw such tears from an old lady. It's what I meant by 'valedictory.' He's not only abandoning the Lilienthals. Your Joel is contemplating the brevity of life. What do I know? I'm not yet forty. But his setting of that poem and his mania for leaving town are one and the same. That's what he emailed me at two a.m. after Parents Night."

"But he was all charged up when he got home."

"With Joel, 'up' is not always the best thing. You must know that. His mind gets racing. He told me you fell peacefully asleep and he sat up for hours worrying over a remark you made about the two of you looking old."

"But he's the one who said it! I'd had dinner with my friend Floyd Griffin, who's looking sort of cadaverous lately, and Joel said we probably look the same to him."

"Well, either way, it set him off. He had confessed his secret appointment with your Wisconsin realtor and figured you were furious. And at Parents Night, one of his boys performed a song that made him feel guilty for criticizing all the work you do for poor people while he indulges himself composing music no one really wants to hear, and on top of that, he's looking old. All the same, he's going ahead with his dreams and causing Rebecca to weep, and he's messing up your stable life together and thinking he's a terrible person."

"Why am I always the stable one?" Sean had to ask. "Why do I have to hold it all together?"

"Someone usually tries to. But it can become an unavoidable sequence when things get going like this. That's my whole doctoral thesis."

Sean was wiping his greasy fingers with a torn-off paper towel. Sheila passed the pizza box to offer a third slice, so he lifted out another eggplant. She plucked off a pepperoni disc for Qusay, still purring against her neck, then Uday galumphed in with a demanding meow, so she plucked off one for him, too.

"And now," she went on, "with your beloved venturing off into strange dissonances, you want to impose a tone row on him as a form of serial security blanket!"

Sean heard it as "cereal" and had no idea what she was talking about.

"But I'm not much interested in the tidy twelve-tone system. In music, at least, I prefer to study the periods of unexamined freedom when the rules are breaking down."

"You think Joel's having a breakdown?"

"Oh, it might only have been some passing midnight terrors. Your beloved's a volatile character. But he's best when he isn't up against rules. His own music never went twelve-tone. Each new piece he writes, he has to feel his way. Call him spoiled, if you like, but maybe you can still let him go on up there to Wisconsin by himself for stretches of time without you."

"Yet back when we had brunch, Sheila, you said my job was to stop him from deserting the Lilienthals. Now you're saying I have to let him move away?"

"Because now he's promised to stay with the quartet," she said, "and he's promised us a two-cello quintet for Clara's visit next year. You see, over these past weeks, I've altered my analysis. I hadn't realized you were so fearful of the new. But there's twelve months in a year. You could give some away. Is it all because of your father having left you?"

Sheila had turned her cat-shrouded head toward him, a fluffed-out tail hanging down across her near shoulder and twitching perceptibly at the tip.

"My father?"

"Let's talk about him," she said.

For an obscure reason, Sean was willing to. Sheila had coaxed him into her confidence. He was the sole person she had allowed within her sanctuary and now had made him her co-conspirator. She was such a delicate-boned round little compact thing, but her disorderliness did puzzle him. There was that profusion of blankets and quilts and khaki pants and blouses in off-whites and browns and grays and muddy greens, skirts an awkward length that hit the calf, scarves and shawls of various shapes and shades, plus fuzzy hats and mittens along a high shelf. The papers piled on tables and chairs were stacked every which way, bent and curled and yellowing. Sean wondered if her doctoral thesis was anything more than an excuse to collect endless evidence to ruminate on forever. There must be scads of musicological detail behind what, to Sean, was simply a statement of an obvious fact that he had discerned in Joel pounding out increasingly painful harmonies on the piano at home. Maybe it went back to that dissonant quartet by Mozart where, significantly, Sheila's cello supplied what she'd called the organizing principle. Was it she, not Sean, who was trying to hold it all together? Not by the evidence of her living quarters.

With the greasy plates set on the random piles of musical scores on the nearest table, Sean settled back into the couch cushions and accepted the other cat, Uday, onto his lap. He was one heavy kitty. Sean cautiously stroked his ruff till he yowled, but then a steady purring began, vibrating against Sean's groin, a hypnotic element of Sheila's impromptu analytic session.

"You loved your father," she said, "but you never felt he loved you."

"He loved my older brother, Danny. They'd play catch out in the driveway."

Sheila continued: "You loved your mother, but she didn't love you enough to get past the betrayals, your father's and then yours."

"I wouldn't call mine a betrayal."

"But taking it from her point of view."

Sean nodded, though none of this was news. "Walking over here," he said, "I was remembering going alone with her to the movies at the old Coronet to see Greta Garbo as *Camille*. Dad said it was too old-timey romantic, but Mom wanted to see it again."

277

"Your poor mother."

"I was the only one who would go with her."

"Which brings me back to you, old fellow. Why haven't you given yourself more freedom?"

"What?" Sean turned to look at the somewhat catlike face of Sheila Bowden, fat Qusay's tail now encircling her throat like a necklace.

"You see evidence spread around here of my own freewheeling. I got tired long ago of tidying up after my father. Fuck tidiness, say I!" Sean expected a piping shriek, but none came. "Aren't you tired, Sean? Wouldn't you like to sit, now and then, on a grassy pasture in the sun and listen to the mooing?"

"You're working for Joel now," Sean said in a playful tone. "I thought this was about me."

"But I am working for you, Sean. Your needs happen to coincide with your beloved's, that's all. You both have to learn to spend some time apart and not fear it. The time will come when one of you will no longer have the other." She had said it as a simple truth, which it surely was, but it was also the inconceivable unknown.

So Sean argued back: "All the more reason not to be apart now."

Sheila shifted her shoulders to shrug off the cat and sat up straight as it yowled out of the room. "I wonder how your father felt when he took himself away from his wife and kids, from you, Sean."

"How could he possibly have done it?"

"How did you possibly take yourself off from him?"

"How did my mom take against me being with Joel, and even before Joel—against me and Floyd, or me and what she had no idea at all I was doing?"

"Unanswerable questions," Sheila said in a most casual tone. She was smoothing out her dark-gray linen skirt that had ridden up above her knees, so she pulled it down but didn't try to get up off the saggy couch. Sean remembered her saying she wouldn't be able to extricate herself from the sling chair on their balcony, being broad of hip and short of leg. He remembered her accompanying Joel in his viola sonatas while he himself remained out on the balcony and each sonata added more wrong notes, more offbeat rhythms, right up to the sixth, the music for those plague years he and Joel had passed safely through. "You're thinking?" Sheila murmured.

"It isn't death I'm thinking about," Sean said, surer of what he meant. "It's what's in the poem I gave Joel, the lines about the first slight swerving of the heart. It's when you realize you're alone even now, and your oldest friends no longer know the same things you do, the way you once thought you all did. I won't ever understand Joel, and he won't understand me."

"But no one understands anybody!" Sheila exclaimed. "It's the wise person who accepts that. You can't do anything but adjust. A baby expects to be the center of attention. Slowly, it learns otherwise. Ah, but this is elementary stuff. In my many years of Viennese-style psychoanalysis, I learned it's only in the particulars that you get anywhere. Let's see. Your beloved Joel portrays you as a staunch Americanist. You object to his school putting on British comic operas and German chamber concerts and gloomy Russian plays. In analysis, such are the nitpicky quirks one starts with. What is it about being American? Off, Uday, go join your fat brother in the other room." The cat didn't choose to move. "Stubborn feline! But you see what I mean? If I say your father didn't love you, that's a meaningless generality. What's it made up of? The feel of those scurrilous magazines in your trembling young paws? The sounds from the driveway of a baseball smacking into a glove? The questions—how did he possibly do it? how did you?—must remain unanswered, but dig into your old associations, that's what you have to do. You're a different sort of egg from Joel. He bounces along, feeling every moment, measure by measure."

"But you said he was having a minor breakdown."

"I wanted you to recognize his current state of mind for what it is. Remember, Joel's adoring parents never denied him a thing. He always got what he wanted. He got you, didn't he?"

"Is that a compliment?"

"Meant to be," said Sheila, "you're such a doll."

It was pitch black outside the high narrow window, the left-hand one without the air conditioner. There was only the dim ceiling light now, glowing from above a dusty glass shade, dotted with what looked like dead flies. Sean, but not short Sheila, could reach up and dust it off, which he was tempted to do when at last he stood and deprived the cat of his warm lap. It seemed an appropriate moment to depart.

They threaded their way through the clutter to the illegal apartment's anonymous door. "Thanks so much for dinner, Sheila."

"You won't go telling on me now."

"I didn't even let Joel know I was coming. He supposes I'm setting up for the fundraiser at St. Anne's Parish Hall. Episcopalians, naturally."

"My father was a Scottish Presbyterian," Sheila said. "How do you like them apples?"

"You're a most original person, Sheila Bowden." Sean pulled open the door, but outside when he turned to wave goodnight to the low doorway, he saw in her face, struck by a beam of moonlight, something of the old breaking-apart world across the sea that somehow meant so much to her and to Joel.

« »

Sean couldn't pretend he had been at the Parish Hall setting up tables. He had gone, last minute he said, to Evanston for pizza with Sheila. Luckily, Joel was so preoccupied with school stuff that he wasn't as intrigued as expected. Not that Sean would have revealed Sheila's attempt at analysis, but he might have broken his promise and described in gross detail the disaster area she inhabited. However, he only got as far as her greeting him in German with the line Joel easily identified, before he had to hear all about Vincent Hill's set design for the Arcadian landscape ("very like the Ocooches," he said) and the huge hassle of rescheduling the choral group to Thursday so they could tackle the Brahms motet and give "The Fire of Driftwood" another try. To deter himself from further relating his evening, Sean did slip in the good news from Andrew Stone that over a hundred people had reserved seats for Saturday night, which meant the economy must be coming back, at least for the donor class.

"So you won't miss me there," said Joel as he stepped into the shower. Soon, from behind the rush of water, came a familiar refrain: "Fill the bowl with Lesbian wine, and to revelry incline!"

Climbing into bed, Sean felt strangely distant from the man he'd lived with for more than thirty years. When Joel emerged, smelling of soap and minty mouthwash, he did ask if the cats were as monstrous as Sheila portrayed them and received confirmation. "I won't pry deeper," he said. "I'm glad you're being cooperative with my favorite cellist. Say, did she tell you about my idea for the scherzo of my new string quintet? There's this amazing eleven-tone row when Iolanthe rises like a Rhinemaiden from the stream. Just because our scale has twelve notes doesn't mean you can't use only eleven, inverted retrograde and all."

"She did say something about twelve tones, but it was lost on me."

"Poor old social worker Quimby."

"But, Joel, one thing—don't mention you know I went there tonight. I promised I wouldn't tell you."

"Sheila loves her conspiracies," said Joel, pulling up the covers on his side of the bed. "But the fact is, she wrote me about her plan yesterday on Facebook."

"Still, don't tell her I said anything."

He promised not to, leaned over for a kiss, stretched his arms

281

above his head and let out a cowlike yawn, and they both switched off their bedside lamps.

A blast from a car horn woke Sean in the middle of the night. Joel grumbled once, turned over, and went back to snoring. Sean had been dreaming of something unsettling, maybe Sheila's muscle-shirted pizza boy or the one who slept with a duck, but more likely it was an embodiment of Sean himself, searching for a precious thing he'd misplaced but couldn't remember what it was. He had been on the verge of locating it when the honking car pulled him from his slumbers.

While Joel snored on, Sean's half-awake mind took to going over and over the things Sheila Bowden had spoken of. Did Joel indeed always get what he wanted? He wanted to be a well-known composer, or at least respected for his art by those few whose opinions counted in the long run. The long run—the phrase throbbed in Sean's head. What would all that matter after they were gone? What did it matter even then? But it did seem to matter to Joel. He hadn't always gotten what he wanted, he was embittered by that, but why must Sean be the one to make up for it? Sheila would say he took care of Joel instead of taking care of himself. Yet Joel claimed not to need therapy because he'd figured himself out at puberty and decided he was normal. Sean had never felt normal, but therapy was too bourgeois for him. In a properly communistic society, where everyone got free psychological counseling, he would happily participate. And if everyone had decent housing—

No, I always do this, Sean's drifting thoughts told his brain. He pulled the blanket up and tucked it in tight against the cool draft from the half-foot of open window. He shunted politics aside and meandered back toward Sheila Bowden. She hadn't understood what he meant by "the first slight swerving of the heart." He should feel sorry for her. She had, as far as he knew, always lived by herself. She'd never had what Sean had now and would surely have for years to come. And also he had a sister and brothers and old friends like Davey, out occupying the streets, and Andrew, setting up tables without him, and Floyd in his Boys Town aerie, and he had their own too-tidy, almost paid-off apartment, and an inheritance ...

His whole body was growing foggy with sleepiness. Now the steady rhythm of Joel's snores was lulling him into dopey incoherence. What dream doors would be opening up for him next?

11 Wednesday, a chilly autumn air shaded by clouds. Sean didn't feel much like talking at breakfast. Joel might have pushed for more about his evening at Sheila's, but he was getting away to Wisconsin and must have decided not to risk a squabble. The two were oddly polite to each other over cornflakes and pomegranate juice.

There was a staff meeting at the Collective to congratulate Andrew on the prospects for the fundraiser but also to discuss what to do about Davey Nussbaum's possible absence if he were unable, or unwilling, to leave the barricades, as Sean put it. Traditionally, it was Nussbaum who rallied the donors to the cause, but Elise Ilg and Franklin Malik nominated Sean as substitute master of ceremonies should he be needed. Andrew, after all, had done enough work. Reluctantly, Sean agreed and began dreading the prospect. He was much more comfortable speaking one on one.

That night, Joel was again preoccupied, this time with preparing for the opera rehearsal and his small choral group and then quartets, all in one day. Rescheduling had meant cutting into soccer practice for some of the kids, but Foxridge did put art before sport, while academics went before all. "They're not going to like the Brahms motet," Joel said. "Puts my piece in a better light. Poor Brahms—and after we bumped him for Schoenberg! Oh, and Irene's coming again tomorrow. Sure you don't want to be there?"

"Not with all we've got going on at work, Joel."

So each of them returned to his own world. Sean got into bed to get back into *Evangeline*, but it was so sad to read of separated lovers searching for each other over the wild Midwest. Sean knew, from leafing ahead to look at the illustrations, that they would be reunited only when Gabriel Lajeunesse was dying.

Joel came into the bedroom, cheerfully humming something that hardly seemed a tune. Sean held his hand up because he was at a poignant moment in the poem, but Joel wouldn't shush and hopped in beside him, said he loved him, gave him a quick cheek kiss, and rolled to his side groaning, "Go to sleep, I'm exhausted." And shortly: "Could you please turn off that light! It's keeping me awake."

In the morning, Joel had to go in early for a teachers' meeting. He had left by the time Sean stepped out of the shower and felt a premonition of life alone, of waking to a silent apartment and eating a solitary breakfast. It might be relaxing for a day or two, maybe a week, but it would soon turn too quiet and how would he know when to fix dinner or go to bed?

On the El, Sean dutifully located the most appealing choice, a lanky tousle-haired youth holding onto a pole with one hand and an e-book with the other. It might be a novel by David Foster Wallace or some other favorite of the intellectual young, but judging by the goth T-shirt and tight jeans, it was likely a fantasy thriller. Now that Wallace had joined the company of dead Midwestern authors, Sean might give him a look.

Settled back behind his desk, after coffee and donuts, he felt his cell phone buzz against his thigh. Joel would be between classes, but the number Sean recognized as Owen's showed up on the little screen. Luckily, the first client was late. "Is that you, Owen?"

"Oh, hi, I didn't mean to bother you at work. I hope it's okay. I know you're pretty busy, but hey, so it's Thursday, and I was thinking maybe I could see you."

"Let me see, I'm not quite—"

"They cut my hours, and it's really a downer. My landlord wants me to do some things I don't exactly care to do, so I may have to move."

Sean waited for a few seconds, uncertain what to decide.

"Hey, are you still there?"

"I was looking at my calendar. Are you all right, Owen?"

"I'd love to see you, like maybe after your work, or on your lunch hour maybe?"

"I don't have much of a lunch hour today. Um, well—"

"We could meet for just a bit. It doesn't have to be at my place. I'd sort of like to talk to you."

So Sean said he'd find him at the café in Boys Town at six, and right then a neatly dressed man in his late thirties showed up for his appointment. Sean shut the phone and pointed to the closest chair. "Hello, Mr. Kramer. Nice to meet you." They shook hands firmly, and Kramer said to call him Sam. He'd been out of a job for a year and seven months, his wife had given up on him and gone back to her folks in Kansas, he couldn't keep up the mortgage, so he was dumping the condo and needed a cheap place, any place, it was only himself, he didn't expect much, they'd been waiting to have kids but now they never would, the whole plan he had for his life was shot to hell.

"I'm sure we can help you," said Sean.

《 》

Joel did call during his free period while Sean was searching websites to familiarize himself with the latest listings. Apparently, rehearsals were going great. "The boys love the big March of the Peers, you know, 'Bow, bow, ye lower middle classes!' It lets them be the men their rich liberal parents have taught them to hate. And all of them loved the double chorus of Peers against fairies. I had to explain 'hoi polloi.' They had it confused with 'hoity-toity.' But now I have to switch moods quick for my choral kids. You can't say Longfellow isn't American, Quimby. And Greenwood's a full-blooded American composer."

"You sure are hopping today," Sean said.

"It gets to me, hearing all this music coming to life. And I'll force the Brahms on them the way Sheila forced the Schoenberg on us. '*Ich fühle luft von anderem planeten,*'" he sort of sang.

"What the hell was that?"

"Air from other planets, Sean. It's weirdly related to the driftwood fire. It's also about friends fading away, like ghosts, but then it goes mystical and transcendent. Your Longfellow's sadder because he leaves us hopeless. He's saying, 'That's all, the long-lost ventures of the heart' . . . and poof!"

"'The first slight swerving—'"

"Yes, but then toward the end it gets worse, remember: 'the long-lost ventures of the heart that send no answers back again.' Jesus! I spent days on those two lines. I couldn't work the retrograde thing because no answers could come back at all. See what I mean?"

"And isn't there a line about the leaves of memory?"

"'The leaves of memory seemed to make a mournful rustle in the dark.' That one was easier. Of course, I didn't imitate rustling leaves, but I got it right. You'd be surprised how bright major chords can sound mournful in that context."

"I'm eager to hear it."

"Four weeks to our fall choral program, six to our quartet concert, eight to the opera!"

"And somewhere in there you're looking to buy a house?" Sean had not intended to mention it, but out it had come.

"Well, I do best, Quimby, when I've got a hundred things going on at once."

Sean had a feeling all this jabber was to deflect from what was, in truth, happening between them.

Realizing he had yet to tell Andrew that Joel wouldn't be at the dinner, Sean found his old college roommate at his desk and gave him the bad news.

"But I seated him with those moneybags Foxridge alums, Tyson! We're counting on Joel's schmoozing skills."

"Put him on a leash and drag him in," said unhelpful Elise on her way back from the ladies' room.

"Can't," said Sean, "he'll be up in Wisconsin."

"Wait a minute here," Andrew said. Perturbed, he ran a hand over his shaved head. "Is this still about him returning to childhood?"

"Unacceptable," said Elise.

"Joel's determined we're buying a summer place up there."

Franklin was leading a client out the front door and must have heard Sean's voice rising. "Up where?" he asked at Andrew's door.

"He's rented a car for tomorrow," Sean said in a calmer tone. "The realtor can't make it next week, and then Joel's in the thick of rehearsals and claims that, since sellers want out before winter, we'll get a good deal, so it's now or never."

"That Joel of yours!" said Elise, shaking her head.

"Up where?" Franklin asked again.

Andrew leaned back in his desk chair, arms crossed behind his scalp, and explained: "Tyson has been worrying over this from before their vacation. Greenwood thinks he wants to go back to where he came from. Sounds like a late-life crisis. And who's expected to pay for it?"

"Well," Sean said, pausing to think it through, then: "Comrade Nussbaum wouldn't approve, but if you'll keep it to yourselves, I'll confess I came into a small legacy from my family, and property is cheap in Richland County."

"How small? How cheap?" Franklin asked.

But Andrew took over. "So it's all your money! I pretty much assumed so."

"Well, Dr. Nathan did leave Joel enough to take a bite out of our monthly payments, so we're sort of even, and I do make a bit more than he does, paltry though it is."

"Spend it while you can," said Elise. "You're entitled. I've been urging you to retire for months now."

"You've been shoving him out the door," Andrew said. "Why aren't you shoving me?"

"Because you're not as depressed as this one. Look at him." Elise slung a motherly arm over Sean's shoulder, which tensed him up.

"I'm not depressed," he said, "and I don't want to stop working. I'll maybe arrange a part-time deal like Davey's. But we're absolutely keeping the apartment. And Joel's not serious about quitting teaching. He just gets this way. It would be mainly for summers."

"So you're joining the second-home set," said Franklin.

"You've got the Thumb," Sean reminded him.

"Leila's parents do."

"Someday it'll be all yours."

"And a very upscale place it is, the Thumb."

"Have you seen the Ocooch Mountains?"

"Guys, guys," said Elise, "you should each get a winter time-share in the South like Patsy and me."

Andrew tipped himself forward. "But what am I going to do with those Foxridge alums? And what if Nussbaum gets tear-gassed or locked up? Tyson, you've promised, you have to pull us through, you hear?"

"One last time before you vanish into the hills," Elise added.

Sean glared at her and said firmly, "I'm not retiring. I'm not even ready to cut back. I'm not vanishing anywhere."

"Hang in, brother," said Andrew. "We'll all be out of here soon enough, and I don't want to be the last of the old guard. Let me say something, everybody. Maybe we'll pull in a record sum this time around, but don't you know this shit we do can't keep up with what all's going down out there? We can't even afford a receptionist anymore. We'll be forced to go city or county, maybe even fed. We'll be subsumed in some nasty bureaucracy. What, our ballet-dancer mayor expects joints like ours to save his sorry ass? It's a new century, comrades."

"The wise old man speaks," said Franklin.

"Maybe he speaks truth," Sean said. What Andrew Stone was predicting had long been at the back of his own mind.

"Elise and I have more hope, don't we, Elise?"

"Yeah, we're still in our forties."

"Youngsters!" said Andrew. "Now get outta here, all of you. I got work to do."

« »

There stood Owen, tapping his fingers along a lamppost and shifting from foot to foot. He was wearing his usual pressed khaki slacks and a soft green polo that tightly gripped his biceps and chest. Why would a gym cut the hours of a specimen like that?

"Oh, I didn't see you, Sean. I was looking the wrong way. Hey, so how's it going? How was work?"

"I'm somewhat overscheduled lately. It was all right."

"I don't even know what you do," Owen said, blinking nervously and not quite meeting Sean's eyes.

"I'm in a kind of social services office."

"Oh, man," said Owen, "I sure could use some social services."

"Do you want to go in and have a coffee or get something to eat?"

"Sure, sure." He stopped tapping the post and said, "Oh, I didn't even shake hands. I'm a little out of it today." He gave Sean a superstrong grip and then held the door for him.

"But you're looking as good as ever," Sean said when they'd sat at a table by the window. He hoped Floyd or, worse, his boys downstairs wouldn't be walking by.

"What if that's all I've got?" Owen asked.

"I don't think so, Owen."

"My landlord says it's not enough. He wants other stuff."

Before Sean could ask what he meant, the same skinny tattooed waiter came to take their orders. "Only two black coffees? That's it?"

"For now, I guess," Sean said. "Sure you don't want a wrap, Owen, or a pastry?"

"No thanks."

"Oka-a-ay," the waiter whined and slouched off.

Sean was going to ask about the landlord when Owen said, "See, I don't seem able to keep jobs. I try too hard. Is that it?"

"I wouldn't think so."

"It's probably happening all over," Owen said, "them laying people off and downsizing, and when you've got no seniority—but if you keep losing jobs, you never get seniority. It's fucked, excuse me, I mean, I'm getting so discouraged."

"And what about your landlord?"

Owen bent his head down, as if embarrassed, and wouldn't look up. His brown hair was growing out nicely again. Sean would have liked to stroke it and reassure him. "Well," Owen whispered and then waited a second.

"Whatever it is, you can tell me."

"What it is, is I get my room free, but I was, you know, supposed to let him do me, like, whenever. It wasn't so bad, but then he had, I don't know, some weird ideas."

"Is he a lot older?"

"I'd say he's about your age, or I mean the age you look to be."

The coffees came, set down by tattoo-covered arms. Sean called after the kid for two slices of the peach pie.

"But I don't—"

"Look, Owen, I can at least pay for pie." Sean was considering telling him about the North Side Housing Collective. It would be wrong of him not to, but it felt risky, even though he'd come to trust

290

Owen's discretion, or wanted to. Yet he wasn't sure. What Floyd said about him cruising the blocks was slightly troubling, but what was his own job for if not to help?

"But, see, it's sort of awkward, because what I was hoping," Owen began, then sipping his coffee and nervously blinking over at Sean. His face was so appealingly lopsided and craggy. It had the particular charm of being not quite handsome, but almost.

Sean had barely caught what Owen had said too quietly, so he cocked an ear and leaned closer across the table.

"I mean," Owen said, "I'd have to put down a security deposit and one month's rent, maybe two they sometimes want, and the thing is, like it isn't the coffee and pie, it's more like me asking if you could hypothetically lend me, like, approximately nine hundred or something till I get a steadier thing going."

"Oh," Sean said, "Owen—" He hadn't expected it but told himself he should have. "But you know," he said, his mind telling him not to, "there's city agencies that help people find affordable housing."

"I wouldn't like going to the city."

"Or private ones," Sean dared to say.

"I'd rather go to a friend." Owen blushed at his last word, red rising up his smooth tan cheeks. "I know, you have Joel to be with, and we only did it that once, but we could again or as much as you like. It's that I've been getting a feeling you're not exactly into it, I mean, even once in a while on the side? I guess it was a one-timer, huh? That's fine with me. I didn't bother you, did I? Joel doesn't know, does he?"

"No," Sean said.

"I'd never tell him, I promise. You can totally trust me."

"I do. You're a good person, Owen."

"I'm sort of a hot mess."

"You don't look like one," Sean said and then felt bad he'd brought it back to the body when this young man needed to be more than that.

The pies were placed more gently, along with the check and, this time, the curl of a smile. "Whenever you're ready, bro."

"That boy knows me," Owen said.

"He doesn't seem to."

"He came on to me once. I don't go for scrawny young guys with tattoos. Do you?"

"It's certainly the look around here these days."

Owen sighed and dug into his peach pie. Sean watched him before tasting his own. Owen might have preferred a roast beef sandwich.

"So you don't have to be sorry if you can't help me out," Owen said between bites.

"But an agency—"

"I don't feature getting welfare."

"But a private agency."

"Or a handout," he said, suddenly gruff. "I'd pay it back." It was a glimpse of the Owen that wouldn't submit to his creepy landlord. Floyd may have been right about him hooking, but he did have some limits.

They ate in silence. Owen stared out the plate-glass window at passersby. Sean figured he must recognize a lot of them from his nightly meanderings, and they probably recognized him. He could well have many so-called "friends" to approach with his request. Perhaps he'd already done so. He might be stashing a plentiful sum under his mattress. What could Sean fully know of him? That basement room was so bare, but it might not be his only home. He might use it only for assignations. No one lived that sparely and wore clothes from Abercrombie. Maybe he slept in some penthouse with his landlord. Or he could've made up the whole landlord story to appeal to Sean's moral sense. My moral sense? Sean asked himself. He counted on having one, but now he leaned across the table again and, with a tremor in his voice, said, "It's that I don't have that kind of money, Owen. My salary's not great, and I have to plan for retirement, and there's cuts in my line of work, too. I might have to go part-time. And Joel's only a music teacher, so you can imagine, we're mostly month to month."

Some of this was true, but he had left out the fact of his dad's trust. He told himself he mustn't get further entangled with that strange young man there, still staring out the window.

"I'm so sorry, Owen. I wish I could help."

"Even a short loan? It wouldn't have to be so much." Outside, a middle-aged man in a light overcoat strolled by and spotted the two of them. Sean thought he gave a brief nod as he passed, but nothing had changed in Owen's unblinking eyes. "So maybe I won't be seeing you again?" he said like a sulky child.

Then, remembering, Sean said, "I made you think of what your father would look like if he'd lived, didn't I? Is that what this is about?"

"Not really," Owen said, still staring out. "It was sort of a line, I guess. I had the idea you'd like it." He turned, at last, and smiled his off-kilter smile.

Sean saw suddenly that Owen had stopped seeming desirable. One feeling had left and another come in. Right then, he wished he could simply write out a check for a thousand dollars and get it over with, but he said, "You really should go to a housing agency, Owen." After forty years at the Collective, he could usually tell the genuinely needy from the scammers. He wasn't sure about Owen, though. Was it pride that kept him from seeking public assistance, or did he, in fact, not need it? Had he ever taken those accounting classes he talked about? Did he even work at a gym? Maybe he merely worked out there. And where did he actually live? But Sean was confident he'd never show up at his office.

He put down a twenty, which left the waiter a largish tip. Owen said, "Thank you. I guess maybe I'll go back downstate if I have to. But I promise I won't call you again."

"You're a kind and considerate person," Sean said. "You'll find something."

"I liked it with you."

"I liked it with you, Owen."

"You've still got it. I'll always remember you."

"I'll definitely always remember you," Sean said and knew he would.

"If you see me around, you don't have to say hi."

"Of course I'd say hi."

"But if you're with Joel or somebody."

They had stood and were heading to the door, which again Owen held open and then, when it shut behind them, stuck out his hand. Sean shook it with both of his and said, "You're very thoughtful, Owen. I feel bad I—"

"It was too much to ask for. I'm sorry." He walked quickly away, across the street between passing cars.

Floyd had asked Sean to dig up Owen's phone number for him. Maybe he should. But he thought it through and decided not to. It wouldn't do either of them any good.

《 》

Quartet night ran later than usual. They had to get Irene's part in shape because she wouldn't be free to rehearse again till right before the concert. "But she has it down now," Joel reported. "She can do anything with that amazing old voice. She says, for this one last time, she's going to let it fly."

"Let's get to bed, Joel. You're leaving here early."

"And I have to pick up the car. Are you still glum about it?"

"Not especially," Sean said on his way into the bathroom.

"Hurry it up, Quimby. I'm going to shower and shave tonight to save time tomorrow."

Later, Sean was almost asleep when Joel came tiptoeing in then stubbed his toe coming around the bedpost, which snapped Sean out of a half-dream.

294

"Sorry, sorry, it's dark in here."

"I wasn't sleeping."

"You were pondering."

"Sort of."

"Mulling it all over in quimby fashion. It's going to be all right, Sean."

To move off the subject, Sean asked, "How did 'The Fire of Driftwood' go today?"

"It's taking shape. They can hear it as a whole now. I'm adjusting the dynamics."

"You love your teaching, Joel," Sean said into the darkness. "You'll never quit." He'd brought the subject back, despite himself.

"But I'll be ending on a high note! And I'll do an extra course this winter, so all I'll have for spring is the choral concert. I'm figuring on reviving my old Carl Sandburg settings—you chose those poems—and then the *Hiawatha's Wedding* part of the Coleridge-Taylor. Black composer, Ojibway subject—perfect for that school! My boy Willy I told you about, I think he can handle the tenor solo. We've been working on his upper register."

"I bet you have."

"No, Tyson, that would be you. Anyway, it's a lovely song. Chibiabos sings it at the feast. Remember our cozy log cabin named for him? 'He, the sweetest of musicians.' That's me, isn't it?"

"Sometimes the sweetest."

Joel scooched himself over to be spooned. Sean pulled him close while Joel returned to dreaming up their new life in Richland County but finally conceded, "This assumes I find us a place you agree to."

"It's up to you, Joel."

"No, it's up to both of us."

"That's what you say."

"And I mean it, Shaw-awn."

They lay entwined awhile, and then Joel twisted himself around

295

to press a soft kiss on Sean's neck before yawning and rolling back to his side of the bed. His breaths soon were coming steadily.

Open-eyed, Sean lay awake on his back. Now that summer had passed, the closed blinds were covered by heavy lined curtains for warmth and little light crept into the room. Sean imagined he was floating, lying on his back in the Big-Sea-Water, pushing his bare feet off the sandy bottom and gazing up at white clouds and blue sky and sensing the Great Spirit everywhere, all places, all times. "Fancies floating through the brain"—a line from the poem he'd foisted on Joel. But there never had been a Master of Life smiling down from those clouds with love and pity on his wrangling, quarreling children. We're alone down here, Sean reminded himself, so it's up to us. He'd gone and left Owen alone, too, when he might have helped. Even if Owen hadn't actually needed his help, still he could've helped him. The young man had walked away from him too quickly, crossed the street dodging cars then disappeared around the block, and Sean had barely got a last glimpse of him. We each of us need at least some kind of help, don't we? he asked himself, lying in the dark, and he was the one able to give it, but he hadn't. He waited a long while that night for the comfort of sleep.

PART FIVE

1 Joel was packed up and out by eight o'clock. He'd be back Sunday night, or maybe Monday if he needed more time. He usually had Mondays off, anyway. So three nights apart, thought Sean. He couldn't recall the last time they hadn't spent the night under the same roof. It must've been the summer Joel went up to help his mother after Dr. Nathan's death, or was it later, when Annie Greenwood herself was dying?

It was worrisome to have Joel driving off alone. He was so distractible and got directions confused, made crazy left turns, wouldn't have change for the tolls. Sean had to trust he'd get there without him and find a decent motel and call him at work as soon as he was settled.

Joel didn't call till late afternoon. Sean had been nervous all day but wasn't about to make the call himself. If something had gone wrong, he'd have heard. He was trying to stay cool about it, but when at last the cell buzzed, he pushed the wrong button and disconnected the call. Joel redialed and got him. "You won't believe it," he said.

"What?" Sean said too anxiously.

"It's nothing bad. Well, maybe about the schoolhouse, but I went straight out to Quarryville and guess who I saw?"

"Mary Peg Schmitz."

"No, no, but remember her saying that now and then someone named Cosmo came back to clean up around his place, that unpainted cigar-box house with all the weeds? But his name's not Cosmo, it's Kasimir! Mary Peg never heard it right. Kasimir, Johnny Kasimir, 'Kaz' we called him. He was one of the farm boys I knew. I told you."

"Kaz?"

"Johnny Kasimir. He's sixty-four and potbellied."

"He's the one you used to fool around with?"

"One of them. And he's got seven grandchildren! And he lives in Richland Center and can't seem to sell that little house he bought when he first got married. He says no one will buy in that shithole of Quarryville. He was out whacking weeds in a T-shirt with his belly out over his belt. Not the slender kid I once knew. He comes there sometimes with his buddies to hunt and fish. He's a housing contractor. The old Kasimir farm's long gone. I sure do remember that hayloft!"

"I bet you do."

"Kaz and me, we did just about everything."

"Okay, Joel, calm down, I don't need the details. You saw the schoolhouse again?"

"But it's out of the question. Not that we'd want Kaz's place, either. He says the Tea Party couple, the Wackos, they're scary folks. There's bad blood between them and that Fred in the house missing its bricks. It's Evangelical Christians versus the lawless drunken motorcycle dude and his fat lady friend. And the Wackos don't like Kaz because his weeds are up against their lawn, and they've got guns to ward off the Feds, he says. After I told him I've been with you all these years, he said what the Nowackys hate most is fags. Well, he said 'gays.' He's a solid guy, John Kasimir. You'll like him. 'We sure had fun back in the day,' he said, but we didn't pin it down any more than that."

"Joel," Sean interrupted because he'd seen a client waiting outside, "be quick. The schoolhouse is out, and have you got a motel, have you met with Tory?"

"Tomorrow morning. I'm at the motel now, but I'm going to Kaz's for supper and meet his wife. He'll be a great guy to help with repairs, whatever we buy."

"I have to see the next applicant. Call back when I'm home."

"We can Skype," Joel said. "I've got to see evidence of my old Quimby. I want you here with me. It's no fun without you."

"It's very strange," Sean said, and they said quick goodbyes with no reciprocal "I love you" from Sean, who had beckoned to a pale young woman who looked lost and scared.

« »

They were about to close up. Franklin and Elise had already left, but Sean found Andrew in his office shuffling papers. "What's new from Nussbaum?"

"He's still making trouble at the LaSalle Bank or, I forgot, the Bank of America it is now. We may never see him again. But I got a text. Typical." Andrew lit up his phone and passed it across his desk for Sean to read: "Totally psyched! Amazing what we talk about here. Planning on tomorrow but not sure. Cool?" Sean grimaced, and Andrew said, "So I texted back 'cool.' What else can we do? You have to step in, Tyson, but if Nussbaum does show, you'll do Joel's bit at the Foxridge table. They'll be predisposed to a faculty spouse. Oh, and you'll be pleased. I got an email from Mary Ahern, saying they cleared their schedule last minute and will be there."

"I bet Trevor found out one of his associates is coming."

"I bet it's your sister's power of persuasion. She tried to entice your little brother to join them, too, but he isn't up to it."

"He's philosophically opposed to all charities," Sean said. "At least, he's opposed to mine."

"So I put her and Trevor with Elise and Patsy. They'll squeeze him dry. As for that old beau of yours—"

"Put him by you, Stone, and he'll write out a nice check."

"Excellent. So I'm going back one more time to the hall. Want to come?"

"I've got to be home to Skype with Joel."

"Sit a minute then," Andrew said. He ran his palm over his shaved head as if in preparation for a serious talk. "What's happening with you two?"

From the client's chair, Sean looked across at his old friend. They'd shared a shabby room in DeKalb before Andrew knew Sean was gay, before Sean had had any such experiences and had sunk his romantic yearnings into daydreams of that unavailable scruffy Davey Nussbaum and made of Andrew Stone his steady best friend. Davey was with Beth, Andrew was on and off with Maxine, and Tommy Schoener was getting into Buddhism. In some sense, Andrew was still Sean's best friend. He could talk to him for real. Joel had ways of avoiding reality and reducing all of Sean's worries to his quimbiness.

"So speak," Andrew said.

"Okay. This summer I chose a poem for Joel to set to music for his choral group. I chose it because it touched me in some way I didn't understand. It's odd how you can read a poem like that, and it gets you to feel things you haven't yet felt from experience. It's preparing you, because when you get to that place in your life, you recognize it as if you'd already been there. I never knew I'd feel separate from Joel, not know who he was inside. We've been together over three decades, half our lives, the best half, by far the best. I've been at home with myself at last."

Sean waited to catch up to his thoughts, and Andrew said, "And at home with Joel."

"I thought we were both there for good," Sean said.

"But now he wants to change, what, your geography?"

"Geography's not just your place on a map, Stone."

"But he doesn't want to change you. I'm sure he loves you as you are."

"He wants to move me into his world and expects me to be the same person." Sean had bowed his head and was staring at his khaki-clad knees. He couldn't let Andrew keep catching his eye.

"You're afraid to stop working, Tyson."

"I like working, it's what I do."

300

"I'm afraid to stop," Andrew said. "I'll admit it." Sean didn't look up, so he went on. "I need the money, of course, but I hardly get to see my grown-up little girl anymore, and my people are all gone. A few ladies make time for me here and there. I take my night courses to exercise the old brain. I'm always studying. That's pretty much it. I don't imagine I'll team up with anyone again. Oh, maybe with some old lady down the hall when I wind up in a retirement home. I'm not griping. I'm doing fine, but shit, man, make the most of Joel. A peaceful life in the country amongst poor white folks, hell, I couldn't do it, but you still have Chicago to come back to, and we'll hang out like we used to, won't we?"

"I'm not used to sleeping alone," Sean said.

"At our age, Tyson, it isn't like we need it every night. You'll come to prefer your very own bed."

"We haven't been apart for one night since his mom died."

Andrew put his elbows on the desk and leaned in closer. Sean could see he wasn't going to let him off. "You know it's not about falling asleep, old pal. It's about Joel wanting something you don't want. Till now, you didn't know he wanted it. Back there in college, I remember hearing about how your daddy ran off with some man to be queer together, and how your momma hadn't suspected and neither had you, so you had to look after her, and I didn't know the half of it, did I? You have a thing about secrets, Tyson. Are you afraid Joel Greenwood has something else going on up there in Wisconsin?"

"Not unless it's a potbellied carpenter he fooled around with in high school."

"The thought crossed your mind, though. What's a potbelly at our age if the rest still functions?"

"That's not it," Sean said. "It's about Joel getting what he wants."

"I sure know what that's like. Maxine wanted most everything. She'd say, 'What kind of well-educated black man these days sticks himself in a low-pay go-nowhere job when he could be a bank manager or something?' Oh yes, and she had a point. But I didn't have the ambition. I've been happier doing our kind of work. If there were more people like us—remember Schoener saying stuff like that? To him, ambition was the root of all evil."

"I wonder, Andrew, if one reason we've stuck with this so long has been for Tommy. How could we give up what we'd all planned together?"

"Till they take it away from us, man."

"And you think they will."

"Amazing we've held them off this long, Tyson."

"So what are you studying on your nights now?" Sean asked. He didn't want to get back to the talk about secrets. He'd never told Andrew about finding Dad's magazines, but Joel had told the quartet, and Floyd Griffin knew. Who knew how many people did! But Mom never knew, Mary didn't or Sandy, and not Danny, either. He'd kept it from all of them, and even from his old best friend.

"Right now," Andrew was saying, "I've got a course on the Age of Reason—Voltaire, Rousseau and that crowd, the Rights of Man, plus Tom Paine, Sam Adams, Jefferson and his slaves, all that. The eighteenth century didn't get us very far. But what's this poem you gave Joel? I remember you reading us poems and stories in college. You were always feeding us stuff from your American Lit courses."

"I probably read it to you back then, Longfellow's 'Fire of Driftwood.' It was all underlined in my anthology. In the margin, I'd scribbled 'Wow!' Stupid college kid. But I didn't recognize it when I found it for Joel."

"Oh, one last thing about him," Andrew said. He was leaning closer again. "Listen, Tyson, accept it, you'll never know what goes on in that screwy head of his, but some fine music comes out of it. That's more than either of us can say. I've heard him play. I've got those CDs of his. I listen to them, not so loud as to annoy the folks next door, because it's an acquired taste, but over the years I've acquired it. Leave it at that, Tyson. You'll never understand him or stop him from doing what he does. He's an artist. And he'll surely never understand you. We're only hanging around for at best another couple of decades, so make the most of it." He shuffled his papers into a neat stack and came around the desk, pulled Sean up out of the chair, and gave him the sort of hug lefty men all gave each other back in the flower power days.

« »

Sean had often come home to an empty apartment, but he'd always known that Joel would be there after a teachers' meeting or an evening event at Foxridge or from playing quartets. This time, Sean knew he wasn't coming home that night or the next night and maybe not the next. When Joel had gone up to tend Annie Greenwood, his absence hadn't troubled Sean, but this time it did. He was having supper with those Kasimirs. That was fine in itself, but it was the first step in returning to the haunts of his youth, where Sean would have no place. He'd never expected Joel to hang out back on Cedar Street with those goof-off brothers down the block who used to act like juvenile delinquents from Chicago. He and Joel did once rent a car to drive out to the old Quimby farm. By then it was a nursing home. They'd stopped beside the road and walked along the wire fence, with its NO TRESPASSING signs, to the meadow of those quiet afternoons spent reading by the weedy creek bed or that one night of running through the long grass, naked under the moon and stars. They had not returned since. Sean didn't want to overlay his own past with images of old people in rocking chairs up on the terrace where Gramma once sat, shelling peas and shucking corn.

In their empty apartment now, he set his shoulder bag down and stood awhile staring at the Ravinia posters, one between the windows, the other above the couch. Joel still spoke of those concerts with wonder. He had seen Paul Hindemith himself conduct his Concerto for Orchestra and Stravinsky conduct *Petrushka*. Joel had never forgotten how, when old Igor got the march music bouncing

303

along, he had rested his baton on the podium and flipped through the score till it came time to pick up a fresh beat. And Joel had sat in the front row, right below tubby bald old Paul and could almost have touched his shoe, so close was he to his fellow violist. There was also an American composer named Wallingford Riegger he'd talked to at Orchestra Hall after the old man's Fourth Symphony. Dr. Nathan had had a dentists' convention in Chicago and brought along teenage Joel, who was not about to shy away from walking right up to meet a famous composer and praise his music.

Sean had heard those stories often enough. What if he, young Sean Tyson, had met James T. Farrell or Upton Sinclair? As a boy, he did get to see Carl Sandburg recite his poems and sing folksongs with his guitar, but on a stage far away, an ancient mythical figure with bright white hair.

He might as well make himself something to eat—kielbasa, salad, and a roll. And when that was done, he had to wait for Joel's call to set up the Skype session, which would be late, if he and Johnny Kasimir got talking of old times. What did Mrs. Kaz know about them fooling around in a hayloft?

Sean lay down on the couch and gave *Evangeline* another try up till he reached these lines:

> *So came the autumn, and passed, and the winter, yet*
> *   Gabriel came not;*
> *Blossomed the opening spring, and the notes of the*
> *   robin and blue-bird*
> *Sounded sweet upon wold and in wood, yet Gabriel*
> *   came not.*
> *But on the breath of the summer winds a rumor was*
> *   wafted*
> *Sweeter than song of bird, or hue or odour of blossom.*
> *Far to the north and east, it said, in the Michigan*
> *   forests—*

There, Sean had to stop. Michigan forests—he couldn't read on. He knew what would happen after the lovers found each other again, but he didn't want to know for sure.

He got up stiffly, as if feeling his age for the very first time, and went into the middle room. Having gotten only so far with Truman and Johnson, and passing over *Moon-Calf* for a day when he wanted to believe a made-up story again, he pulled out the book about Nikita Khrushchev, who'd once been as nearby as Iowa, admiring the corn when Sean was a boy. He was fascinated with the man and had wanted so badly to see him in the flesh, but Dad wouldn't drive him over from the Quimby farm. "You sure have some funny ideas about communism, young fella," Dad said.

Sean lay down again, intending this time to finish a book he'd begun, but first, he thumbed through the photos. It came back to him, the jolly fat man holding up the ear of corn, or gleefully pounding his shoe on his UN desk, or sourly disapproving of Shirley MacLaine's can-can in Hollywood, and looking grumpy with Nixon in the model kitchen. Then the phone rang, so Sean staggered out to the hall to catch it in time. Joel was in his rental car on the way back to the motel. The Kasimirs were early-to-bedders, but he'd tell more at exactly nine o'clock after he got the Wi-Fi code from the receptionist.

《 》

Sean was in the middle room where sometimes, with the door closed, he'd sit watching X-tube. Now, with a click, there was Joel and, in a corner, a tiny Sean that Joel was seeing full-screen in Wisconsin. They both spoke at once, stopped, there was a slight delay, then Joel said, "You're not mad at me, are you?"

"Why would I be?"

"Because I'm up here missing the fundraiser and seeing Johnny Kasimir after all these years and having fun without you. I was afraid you'd be going out looking for boys."

"Oh, sure," Sean said with barely a thought of Owen.

"But instead, you're the safe stay-at-home Quimby I love so much." On the wall behind Joel hung a woodland scene, traditional motel art. Sean couldn't make out much else but the trim on a pillowcase and Joel's wispy gray curls and his chin in need of a shave, his upper lip as well. It was stretched out in a happy grin.

"You've had a few beers with the Kasimirs."

"Well, it's Wisconsin, Shaw-awn."

"How was Mrs. Kaz?"

"Franny's adorable, a big blousy babe, cooked us up a feast, piles of hash browns with gobs of applesauce, and two fat greasy pork chops apiece. Good Jewish meal."

"Your diet will go to hell if you move up there."

"You'll have to come keep me in line."

Sean made a face at the little camera eye and asked, "What do they think of us being a couple and you buying a place?"

"Us buying," said Joel. "It's all great. We can meet for beers in Hub City when he's working out there or get deluxe burgers in Yuba. I'll be seeing Tory tomorrow and going over any new listings, and on Sunday, Johnny's coming out with me to look at things and give estimates on him doing repairs or rehabs. He's the man!"

"Cool it, Joel. You're out of control."

"But no more schoolhouse. It's sad, I loved it, but I don't want us to get shot. You look tired, Sean."

"I was reading on the couch."

"Don't worry, Kaz and Franny are entirely fine about us. They know some gay men up here. He's doing work for two guys with an antique shop in Spring Green. They just bought that handsome old Victorian house we saw with the maple trees. Did I mention that already?"

"Joel, I don't know a thing."

"It's because I'm so excited being back. I almost feel you here with me seeing it all. Driving around today, I was talking to you out loud. 'Look, Quimby, what do you think of this one?' You're with me even when you're not."

"Definitely the easiest way to deal with me."

"You're still mad, I can tell."

"No, worried is all. I'm trying to stay open-minded."

"But I love it up here! My soul lifts. It spreads out across the land. I hear music coming to my ears. '*Und die Seele unbewacht will in freien Flügeln schweben . . .*' The *Four Last Songs*. My heart gets beating fast. Oh, I got the sweetest email from Rebecca and Art—well, it was from Rebecca, but she signed it from both. They wanted to wish me luck finding the perfect place and promised to drive up next summer with their violins and bring Sheila and her cello so we can play quartets amid the cow pies. And Clara's flying in from California the weekend of our fall concert! I wrote back saying the first piece I compose in Richland County will be that quintet for all five of us. It's back to normal with the Lilienthals, Sheila Bowden, too. They understand."

"They don't have to live with you."

"Oh, Shaw-awn. Then you can stay in our shoebox apartment and we'll Skype occasionally." Joel's brown eyes were glaring at him from the screen. Sean checked out his own little face in the corner. It looked droopy and wasn't saying anything, but then the large face of Joel said, "I seem to remember we made a pact."

"We did."

"So what's the problem?"

Sean was surprised at himself saying, "I already miss you, and it's not even been one day. I've been reading about Nikita Khrushchev and thinking about being a lonesome little seventh-grade commie."

"Poor old you."

They were looking at each other's picture, two snapshots but for the blink of an eye or the crook of a lip. What if that were the last time I ever saw him? Sean asked himself. His stupid fear was at the heart of it all.

Joel promised to call or email, or both, after he'd met with Tory and had a notion of what, if anything, would work for them. The ugly house was still tops on his list. His piano would fit up the stairs, Sean could have his own study for porn watching, they'd have the deck out back to follow the sunlight from western cliff to eastern, they'd hear distant moos from down the valley. So what if the house had no charm!

Sean explained he had to be at St. Anne's Parish Hall early tomorrow to help Andrew with final arrangements. "And I may have to substitute for Davey, so I should make a few notes. The Aherns are coming, and Floyd."

He got a feeling that the virtual Joel in there wasn't quite paying attention, though he did say, "Sorry to miss seeing my old alums, but you'll explain."

"If I'm not at the head table."

"What?"

"I just told you I may have to emcee if Davey's in jail or something."

"In jail?"

"Never mind, Joel. Go to sleep and dream of haylofts."

"You're mad again."

"No, but it's too weird talking like this. If you were here, I could maybe get you back under control with some tough love."

"That'd be nice," Joel said.

So they said cheerier goodbyes and I-love-yous, and then Joel disappeared into cyberspace, as did Sean from Joel.

2 The Parish Hall of yellow limestone stood beside St. Anne's Church, also limestone, on a well-shaded street in Lincoln Park. Sean walked through shiny wet fallen leaves while golden and orange ones came drifting down about him in the dry breeze that had followed the morning rain. He had the notes he'd struggled

over for hours now tucked in his breast pocket along with the tie he'd have to put on later. He wasn't used to his squeaky dress shoes that came out only for the annual fundraiser and for funerals, but the last of those was Uncle Albert's at Northwestern two years ago. Vegetarian Aunt Sue was still alive. Mary often went to visit her. Aunt Elizabeth had died several years after Dad, and Uncle Ted died way back of lung cancer. Sean's own generation's turn was coming up.

He didn't like churches, but the new priest at St. Anne's had made the Collective her parish's special cause, so Sean was grateful for this one. Andrew had seen him coming and was holding open the heavy oak door. He thanked him for being there early to help and led him down a corridor of Sunday school classrooms and past the day-care center into the empty Parish Hall. Andrew had already set the dozen round tables, each designated by a plastic number sticking out of a centerpiece of dried autumn flowers. In keeping with their mission, the dinner was meant to be festive but not lavish, so the red tablecloths and napkins were of paper and the place settings came from the Parish Hall kitchen. They began carrying the metal folding chairs out of the storage closet and distributing them, ten per table. The wooden chairs at the head table on the dais would hold only board members and the emcee, and there was a lectern waiting for either Davey or, if it must be so, Sean.

He complimented Andrew on his job arranging the tables and then asked, as casually as he could, "You haven't heard from Nussbaum?"

"Not even a tweet. He's either doing something clandestine or getting hauled off for it."

"I did write up some notes in case."

"Don't stress out, Tyson, you'll be fine." Andrew clanked open another chair. "It's a tough day for you, maybe, with Joel away?"

"He was supposed to call by now." Sean patted his chest, felt the lump of his tie and notepad, and realized he hadn't transferred his phone from the windbreaker to the sport coat. He was always misplacing the damn thing, but of all times!

"Here, call him on mine," Andrew offered. "If he doesn't pick up, tell him to call back or email. I never forget my devices, Tyson."

Joel didn't answer, but Sean left a message, both hoping and fearing he'd hear something before the board members arrived for their predinner meeting. He and Andrew went on unfolding chairs and then divvied up the place cards to follow the seating chart.

"You've got the Foxridge table," Andrew said. "But Beth will take it if you have to stand in for her maniac husband. Do you recognize any alum names?"

"One or two, sort of."

"I'm putting your sister here," Andrew said from table ten, "and Trevor between Elise and Patsy. I'm going to sit by old Floyd at table eleven, as you suggested."

"He'll appreciate the attention unless there's a handsome youth on his other side."

"Not likely in this crowd. But notice how I've not gone boy-girl-boy-girl the old-fashioned way. Of course, people will switch cards and sit wherever they prefer."

Working the other side of the hall, Sean asked, "Say, Stone, what became of that bothersome old crank Mr. Thorp?"

"He never came back. I understand he's in some county facility, drying out."

"He took me for the druggy son. At least druggy's not as bad as faggy."

"You said it, man." Andrew did one of his brief sashays in his sharp new Italian suit and bright-yellow tie. "Too bad sister Mary couldn't bring your brother, though. I'd like to see the little stoner," he said, circling a far table, planting cards. "Oh, my phone buzzed. Yep, it's Wisconsin." He held it out to Sean, who quickly crossed the hall.

"Jesus Christ, Quimby, how could you forget your phone! I tried calling, I really did, but I was out with Tory checking on some miserable backup places like that shabby log cabin we saw the first day, remember, the one with the footbridge, but the ugly house is by far the best. It'll be perfect for us with those expansive views, and it's move-in-able—carpets, appliances, only needs basic furniture, but we're minimalists."

"We'll think about it, Joel." He looked at Andrew, who had raised a finger to indicate he'd be back then left the hall. Sean wished he'd stayed.

"But here's the deal, Sean. There's a family that's made a very low-ball offer. The sellers are holding out for more but told Tory they won't be able to hang on past Halloween. We could offer fifty-five and settle at fifty-seven-five. Tory can't reveal what the low offer is, but when I proposed fifty-five, she said that might do the trick. It's below our top of sixty, and it's such a fantastic setting, and the house is solid and has all those rooms."

"It's perfect for a family," Sean said.

"But, Shaw-awn, we'll be a family when we get our greyhound. I'm naming her Lucy Greyhound after that novel you made me read about the small-town girl pianist."

"*Lucy Gayheart.*"

"Greyhound, Gayheart, whatever."

"Wait a minute, Joel. Who is this family that made the offer?" Sean's voice was echoing in the empty room. It sounded shaky, but Joel's took a steadier tone.

"What difference does it make?"

"They might be needing a bigger house."

"You mean how many kids do they have? A dozen, I don't care. They'd be strewing plastic toys all over the hillside and leaving rusty fridges and washing machines and junk cars on the front lawn."

"Joel, stop it." Sean pulled out the chair intended for Floyd Griffin and, weakening in the knees, sat down.

"This is real estate, Tyson, not charity. You worry about one family, but what about the family that's selling? They deserve the best price, don't they? That's how it works, Comrade Khrushchev!"

"Grandfather Gruenwald might disagree."

"But you don't know anything about either family! The low-ballers could be a front for speculators putting out cheap bids to make a killing. If our Faustian blood pact comes down to your vague sense of economics, which is actually a cover for your stupid guilt about every fucking privilege you've got, Jesus Christ, get over it!"

Sean waited to answer and listened to those heavy breaths coming from inside Andrew's phone.

"Well?" Joel finally said.

"We see the world so differently," said Sean sadly. He felt tears welling up, so he pressed his eyelids with thumbs and forefingers beneath his glasses and then looked up at the plastic number eleven stuck among the dried flowers of the centerpiece. It struck him as odd how it consisted of two number ones, a one and another one. It made him think of summer camp, when he'd heard those rumors of things that went on in the twelve-year-olds' cabin, things his boyhood had no words for.

"So?" Joel's voice said through the smooth little gizmo pressed to his ear.

"I won't agree to the ugly house," Sean said. "You promised we'd only buy what we both agreed to."

"Do you want me to find out more about the low-ball family? They could be totally undeserving and beat their children and need a hillside hideout to do their thing."

"Come on, Joel."

"Do you want me to find out?"

"It wouldn't matter."

"But you took such a liking to its lack of charm. I was the reluctant one. We went back and climbed that steep hill below the cliffs and sat and looked down across all that pasture land. You loved being up there."

"Still," Sean said, "I don't want it. Some family needs it."

"God dammit, Jesus Christ! You always say I'm impossible. It's you who's impossible this time. Fuck it, I'm hanging up."

Sean knew better than to call back right away. He went out to the corridor and found Andrew inspecting the kids' drawings taped up in the day-care center. There were a lot of haloes and crosses in them. "You didn't have to leave, Stone. I sort of wanted you to hear."

"Some things a man has to handle alone. But you can give me all the dirt now."

They sat at the head table, hierarchically raised above the rest of the hall and adorned with a large vase of fresh autumn flowers at either end. The lectern was marked with a brass medallion of St. Anne, mother of immaculately conceived Mary. Sean's mom had returned to a faith in such things and believed her second son was persisting in the sin of her ex-husband. Who came up with such horseshit? Sean asked himself.

He repeated Joel's arguments and then his own. Andrew's only comment, with an arm slung around Sean's shoulders, was: "Isn't it you that's the undeserving one, Tyson?"

Sean thought it through and said, "It's not me. It's some poor family in Richland County. I don't care if they're no good. I don't know what they can afford, but fifty-five thousand is more than we'll take in tonight to help house poor people down here."

"I'm hoping for an even fifty," Andrew said. "We've got some high rollers coming. Let's finish with the place cards and take your mind off Greenwood."

« »

First came shy Leila Malik to be of help till Franklin got there. She was a self-effacing dark-hued woman Sean had always found sympathetic. They chatted awhile about her grown children. There was

313

nothing more to be done before the arrival of the caterers and the kindly parishioners who'd volunteered to wait tables.

Appearing from the kitchen, Andrew said, "I gave you table six, Leila. Just be your usual charming self."

"You know I'm a terrible conversationalist, Andrew."

"But you look lovely. All you have to do is pretend interest in what's said. It's likely to be about their summer travels or their brilliant offspring at the best universities. If they realize you're Lebanese from Detroit, they'll be especially nice."

"Oh, Andrew."

"Be glad I didn't put you with lawyers. They're for Patsy to fire up. I wish I had a spouse of my own to enlist, now that Sean's has finked out."

"Franklin told me."

When the board members started filing in, Andrew sequestered them in a Sunday school room where he'd stashed some half-decent wine and cheese for their private meeting. Next, the catering crew, half a dozen energetic young folks of various races and genders in black T-shirts and jeans, hopped from a van in the alley and began unloading. Then a few older Episcopalian ladies showed up to be instructed in how to serve. And soon, more came. Andrew was rushing about but stopped when Franklin lugged in the unwieldy charts he'd been compiling at the office. They set about duct-taping them to the bare plaster walls below the high-up gothic windows.

Elise and Patsy breezed in, arm-in-arm. Sean couldn't tell which one of them yelled, "Keep it low-tech, boys!" And suddenly, there was Beth Nussbaum, in one of her preserved sixties getups, striking a pose on the dais. He went over to ask after Davey. She was worried sick. "He hasn't texted or called, typical of him to forget everybody but himself. And you always found him so admirable, Tyson. I hope it's finally dawned on you that he's a wackjob."

"You old hippie, Beth, you've even preserved that flowery hat."

"My party outfit," she said. "I'm evoking the founding spirit of the North Side Housing Collective."

Eventually, Sean had a chance to snag his old roommate and ask if he could check for email on his laptop. Nothing had come to "andrewstone46," so Sean logged in to his own account and found he had unread mail from the Lilienthals: "Dearest Sean! We're truly sorry to miss your big dinner this year, but we've sent a contribution in support of the cause. We so admire the work you all do. And, Sean, also for how thoughtfully you've been managing the other housing issue closer to home. Our Joel is a continuous challenge, isn't he, but we do love him—and very much you, too. As ever, Art and Rebecca"

Sean closed the computer and put it safely back in Andrew's briefcase. They'd risen to Joel's challenge, the Lilienthals had, but he wasn't too sure about himself.

He had no time to dwell on it. He sat down at the head table and tried to revise his notes while people were hurrying about. The volunteer ladies were filling the taller glasses with ice water and placing the salads just as the prospective donors began to arrive. Sean's mind was racing. He ripped some pages from the notepad to put them in a more logical order. He should renumber them, but he'd even forgotten his pen.

Reverend Dunhill came by to reintroduce herself. She was a cheery red-cheeked woman with a clerical collar that would have shocked his mom, not to mention the rainbow flag pinned to her jacket. After some pleasantries, Sean asked if she happened to have a pen he could borrow. She pulled one from an inner pocket and let him get back to his preparations. "But remember, Mr. Tyson," she said with a chuckle, "you're preaching to the choir."

While the guests were searching for their seats, the board members came trooping in, followed shortly by the ratty, bluejean-jacketed, gray-bearded figure of Davey Nussbaum, red bandana wrapped around his thinning tresses. He called out, "I made it, everybody!" People turned, some knowing who he was, others

315

puzzled but amused. Beth ran over to give him a kiss, and Sean, deeply relieved, stepped down from the dais and took his humble seat at the Foxridge table. He swiped away Beth's place card and retrieved his own from his now empty breast pocket.

"Michaelson," said the large middle-aged man to his left. "And that's Mrs. Michaelson on your other side. We decided to flank our hostess who just left. You weren't at the school in my day, Mr.—" he glanced at Sean's card, "—Tyson. On the soccer field, I was known as Mad Dog Michaelson. Guys thought I was a dumb ox, but I've ended up doing rather well, haven't I, toots?" His wife gazed affectionately past Sean at her satisfied mate. There was an attractive younger man seated beyond her who looked somewhat familiar. His place card read "Gerald Katz."

Through the still-circulating crowd, Sean spotted Floyd Griffin by the kitchen, chatting up a caterer in a very tight T-shirt while Andrew kept beckoning him to table eleven. From across the hall, Elise was waving at Sean then gesturing frantically at the Aherns' empty seats to either side of her, but Sean could only hold up his palms in a shrug and shake his head. Mary was generally late wherever she was expected to be.

"Mr. Tyson," said the youngest alum at the table, "Gerry Katz, Gerry with a G. I doubt you remember me. I was in Mr. Greenwood's choral group. We sang his Sandburg songs. I'm sorry he couldn't make it. My senior year, I was Strephon in the opera. You probably saw it."

Sean leaned forward to see past Mrs. Michaelson, who obligingly pushed her chair back a bit. Was this once the boy Joel had made such a fuss about? He would be thirty-two or three by now. "I'm sure I did," Sean said. "I see all of Joel's productions."

"I hear they're doing *Iolanthe* again this fall," said Gerry, "and I'm definitely going. I wonder who's taking my part."

"Joel had to be up in Wisconsin this weekend or he'd have been here. You should email him, Gerry. He'd love to hear from you."

"I'd really been hoping to see him tonight," said the young man.

"The school does breed loyal alums," said Mrs. Michaelson. "Our three boys all went, and now we've got a granddaughter at Foxridge. My husband was on the board, weren't you, toots?"

"I served my term," said the former Mad Dog.

Practically everyone was seated when the last guests appeared, a county liaison to HUD, about whom Sean had mixed feelings, and her date or colleague, an earnest-looking fellow he didn't recognize, and there, at last, came Mary and Trevor Ahern, hustling hectically toward Elise's waving arms. They didn't see Sean, who tried to catch his sister's eye but knew the moment would come soon enough.

« »

Reverend Dunhill had stood at the lectern to give a nondenominational blessing of the evening's meal, then everyone dug in. When the Episcopalian ladies came to remove the salad plates, they took orders for fish or tofu stir-fry on rice while the black-clad caterers poured white or red jug wine into the stubby juice glasses the Parish Hall's kitchen had provided. The Michaelsons stuck to their tall ice waters, but Sean opted for red, now that he wouldn't be speaking.

"That's Tom Luft, Class of '74 like me," said Mr. Michaelson, pointing across the table. "Hey, Tom, this is—" he checked the card again, "—Mr. Sean Tyson. Now what exactly is your position at the school?"

"Faculty spouse," Sean said.

"His partner is Mr. Greenwood, my music teacher," Gerry Katz explained.

Michaelson took that in stride and then went around the table, pointing and asking for everyone's name and class. "We're Foxridge parents," said an older woman. "Our Phoebe was Class of '89."

Sean tried to link names to faces, but with all the tales of

317

schooldays past, he didn't get to say much on behalf of the Collective. He'd leave that to Davey after dessert.

No one seemed to mind the hippie food and wine. Good spirits and volubility spread around the hall, reminding Sean of Sylvie's hearty suppers in Nokomis Lodge with Phil Kimbley beaming at all his assembled guests, Cinder at his side. Gerry Katz had much to say in praise of Mr. Greenwood, who'd introduced him to the great music that had enriched his life, he said. That was what the arts were for.

"Yep," said Michaelson, "but don't leave out sports. You got to have both. Am I right, Luft? Now, Tom was the worst soccer player ever, but you played, didn't you, Tommy boy? Sure, sometimes he'd forget there was a ball in play and get dreaming up some new money-making scheme. He's quite the Internet entrepreneur now, aren't you, Tom? See, Mr. Tyson, we've all made ourselves good lives, and it's come time to give a little back."

"My parents died last year," said Gerry. The men's faces around the table went stony, and the women murmured sympathetically. "They left me more than I need. You know, Mr. Tyson, when Mr. Greenwood was coaching me on my song about the 'tipsy lout through the city sneaking'—see, I remember it to this day—well, he got talking about luck and how some people plain never get any. 'I might be as bad, as unlucky rather'—"

"'If I'd only had Fagin for a father,'" said Sean, astonishing Gerry Katz. "Joel's always singing things around the apartment."

"Who's Fagin?" asked Mad Dog Michaelson.

"You know, in *Oliver Twist*," Gerry said. "He's the miserly old Jew, not like my own generous Jewish dad, who left me so comfortably off. Mr. Greenwood taught me that when you perform in front of an audience, you have to believe in the words. Singing that song was the first time in my pampered life I understood what having bad luck could do to a person."

"Are you still in theater, Gerald?" asked a lady, Class of '62, whose name Sean couldn't retrieve.

"No, I work at a health clinic on the South Side, but I'm not an MD," he added in deference to the two doctors across the table. "Mostly I do drug and alcohol rehab."

Mad Dog raised his water glass. "I'll drink to that!"

Immediately, his wife changed the subject. "I've been urging Steve to join the board here. What does one have to do to propose oneself?"

Finally, Sean could do some promoting. "I'd be glad to put his name in. We need all the help we can get."

《 》

In the lull before the custard and cookies were brought out, Mary came by Sean's table to give him a tight hug and apologize for their late entrance. "It was sheer hell getting Trevor off the golf course on such a balmy afternoon. But this is all so fun, brother. Elise is a real peach, and that Patsy sure knows how to make tracks with Trevor. He's loving every minute. Of course, he's always had a thing for lesbians."

"And waitresses at the club," Sean said. No one was listening to their conversation because Michaelson was holding forth about the pack of Republican idiots running in 2012. He didn't think much of the new mayor, either, but he was an Obama man right down the line. He came back fiercely when one of the doctors expressed reservations about the Affordable Care Act. Gerry Katz's eyes zoomed back and forth between the two combatants. Mrs. Michaelson seemed anxious.

Sean caught most of this while Mary chattered on, but he did whisper to her that he was so relieved he didn't have to take over for Davey. "But you would've been so great, Sean. Damn, I wish it

319

was you." She hugged him again. "Sorry I couldn't drag Trev away from his latest crush, but he said he'll catch you after the speeches." And off she went.

There was to be only one actual speech, but first the newest board member introduced herself and thanked St. Anne's for supplying the hall and the excellent wait staff, thanked Cosmic Catering for the deliciously original repast, and thanked all the loyal supporters who'd come to celebrate the North Side Housing Collective's long history of service to the community. Then, the chairman of the board, serving his final term, called on the devoted, overworked, underpaid staff of the NSHC to stand, one by one. "And don't hold back your applause! Mr. Franklin Malik—Ms. Elise Ilg—and the founders themselves: Mr. Sean Tyson—Mr. Andrew Stone—and now our featured speaker, fresh from the streets—and we got quite an earful over dinner!—Mr. David Nussbaum."

Davey sloped over to the lectern, totally the old hippie, the absolutely least formally dressed person in the room, and yet, to Sean, the embodiment of all his youthful ideals. He could still picture the long blond locks, the smooth chin, the bright eyes now going cloudy. Sean's own eyes misted up at the sight.

"Good evening, folks," said the scratchy voice. Davey coughed, cleared his throat, placed his hands out on the lectern, and said, "This woman at my side—we squoze her in here with us notables— she's been my partner in crime for well over forty years, and all that time, she's kept the faith, as you can tell from her retro fashion statement. Take a bow, Beth."

She stood and waved the peace sign with each outstretched hand. The assembly gave her a rousing cheer.

"But we did lose one of us four founders," Davey said, "to the war in Vietnam." The hall went silent. "I don't suppose anyone here but us oldies knew him, Tommy Schoener, who came here with us other recent grads of Northern Illinois University—" From somewhere in the hall came a loud whoop. "Right on! We came to Chicago in that revolutionary year, 1968, and cooked up this project. We were young and unwise and didn't know diddlyshit about the ways of the world. But Tommy was our visionary, and Sean was our scholarly resource. Andrew was the practical one—and, by the way, he organized this big feed tonight, didn't you, pal! All this week, I got so many of his goddamn tweets because I've been shirking my responsibilities. Take another bow, Stone! I love you, man."

Andrew hopped up briefly and sat right back down. Floyd Griffin gave him a fond slap on the back.

"Yes, and I, the undependable one, I'm not sure I've been good for much of late, but back at the start, I suppose, I was our firebrand. One of us had to be. And now, what is it, an overdue midlife crisis or a last-ditch hedge against mortality? I don't usually look this grubby. You'll have to excuse me. I've been down in the Loop. I've been sounding off outside some banks. I've been occupying what should rightfully belong to all of us. Some of you tonight may find what us folks out there are doing offensive, or counterproductive, or just plumb naive. And here I am, asking for your contributions, so I don't mean to turn you off. But I simply had to join a movement that's spreading all over the country. When I saw young activists and old radicals and nice plain ordinary folks who've felt the outrage, I had to join in. What's wrong with the richest country in the world that it expects a bunch of fucking old idealists to find housing for its people? I'll tell you the truth. I wish the Collective didn't exist. I guess I'm asking you all to do whatever you can, politically, to put us out of business. Okay, I'll admit, I'm an old-fashioned socialist. I want our ostensibly democratically elected representatives to do their job and stop handing it over to shoestring operations like ours or to what they like to call the faith-based community. What about the whole fucking community of everyone in this city! Hear that, Mayor Emmanuel?"

The hall had gone silent again. Sean couldn't tell if people felt uplifted or uncomfortable. He glanced at Gerry Katz, whose long-lashed eyes were riveted on Nussbaum.

"And how about our whole corrupt state of Illinois? How about the so-called centrist politicians that rule us from Washington? Centrist, my ass! It's a con job, folks. They're bought and sold. Okay, yeah sure, all of us, and I include Beth and myself, we're pretty well off when you consider the miseries of the whole planet. I don't mean to insult anyone here for having a disposable income. Please, dispose of some of it here. For Christ's sake, we totally need your dough!"

Steve Michaelson grabbed Sean's elbow, leaned close to his ear, and said, "That bloke is one crazy motherfucker. Sign me up!" But Mrs. Michaelson looked somewhat distressed, and across the table, Tom Luft was frowning into his empty custard bowl.

"You have to forgive me." Davey was growing hoarse. He cleared his throat again and went on in a softer voice. "You have to forgive me. I've been charged up all week out there, camping out, eating crap food, washing in some tub. But I wish each of you could come down and see it. If it really is 99 percent of us, or let's be conservative for a moment, 95 percent, hell, make it an even 90, but we're talking three hundred million Americans. We can do this! I haven't felt this charged since we marched on old Mayor Daley and the racist pigs at the Democratic Convention. Obviously, I didn't exactly prepare this mess of a speech."

Finally, laughter arose, table to table, and Mad Dog's wife gave Sean a hesitant smile.

"I hope Reverend Dunhill will understand," Davey said, nodding her way and getting a friendly nod back. "Because I trusted the spirit would move me. I probably fucked up. But when I see how honest working people are losing jobs to overseas, how what I call not-free trade is all rigged, and the prison business is booming, and our city schools have gone to shit and what are we going to do if our kids don't know anything? And everybody gets conned into thinking they have to buy so much useless stuff! Now I'm getting depressed. There's times I'm about to quit in despair. Don't you guys get like that sometimes? Is it only because I'm getting old and losing it? Is

322

the power out there too huge to fight against? Damn, I'm ending on a downer. Maybe I'd better stop."

He looked over at Beth, who said for all to hear, "That's my beloved husband, everyone!" She stood up beside him and leaned against his shoulder. "He may drive me up the wall, but he always means well. That's what it boils down to, meaning well, right?"

"You got it, babe." Davey tipped back the brow of her flowery hat and kissed her on the lips. Most of the hall applauded, and Michaelson held his fingers to his teeth and let out a piercing whistle. Davey sat down, hidden by the lectern, and Beth took her seat alongside him.

The chairman of the board motioned to Reverend Dunhill, who ascended the dais to close the ceremony. "I will leave you with one simple thought," she said. "Speak truth to power, whatever your truth is, and the truth itself shall set you free." To Sean, it was something Schoener might have said in the old days.

« »

Milling about afterwards, the guests found their way to the people they wanted to talk to. Mary pulled Trevor through the crowd toward Sean, who didn't feel like getting up yet. Gerry had gone to try to meet Davey, and Steve Michaelson, his wife in tow, had stepped around the table to argue with his old classmate, Tom Luft, the worst soccer player ever.

"Sean, Sean, Sean!" squealed Mary. She hugged him hard, saying, "How I wish Sandy had heard all that! He would've eaten it up, every word. Wow!"

"Hi, Trevor," Sean said, getting up to shake his brother-in-law's thick-fingered hand. "Was that a bit too much?"

"Naw," said Trevor, "you think I can't take it? Look, old blowhard financial types like me, we're realists. Everything's always on the table."

323

"And he's writing you a healthy check," said Mary.

"Anything for your little sister, brother Sean. Besides, I prefer to choose where I put my money and keep it out of the government's filthy claws. Indeed, that was quite the show, yeah, the whole shebang—those punked-out caterers, the nice old white ladies serving the grub. I looked over those charts on the wall. I can see the operation's in tight straits. I also see the good work you all do."

"Trev loves charts," Mary said. She'd worn that African-print blouse again and those hoops in her ears in hopes, Sean imagined, of bonding with the African American contingent she'd assumed would be in attendance. Of course, it was, but of necessity in modest numbers.

"We've got to be heading home now, Mare," Trevor said. "I've been on the links all day and I'm beat."

"Did you know anyone at your table, Trevor?" Sean asked.

"No, but I tell you, that Patsy is a firecracker. She had me by the balls."

"Trevor!" Mary squawked. "That's enough. We're outta here. Bye, brother. I trust Joel's finding you quite the country estate today. Elise told me the whole story. She says you're a tad reluctant. True? But you've got the funds now. Leave this madhouse behind!"

"Come on, Mare. Vamoose."

"Oh, I invited Quincy but, needless to say, she had a date with her Benjamin. That's love. So you and Joel come up and see us soon and email me pictures of the new place."

Sean kissed her cheek, and away went the Aherns. Then he felt a tap on his shoulder and turned to see a much overweight elderly black woman he was startled to recognize as the client he'd placed successfully a week or so ago. "Mrs. Emma Webster," she said.

"Yes, of course, I didn't spot you earlier. Which table were you at?"

"Other side of the room," she said, "but I want to thank you personally, Mr. Tyson, for what you did for me. Every morning, when I look out my window and see the sun rise out of the lake to bring me one more day, I remember to bless you. You may recall I came into a small sum of money, so I'm in a position tonight to make a modest contribution." She passed over a properly filled-out check for a hundred dollars.

"Goodness, Mrs. Webster, are you sure you can spare—"

"Only a small offering. Now, quite frankly, Mr. Tyson, I was appalled by your sloppily dressed colleague. I'm not holding it against you. I'm sure you would've delivered a much more appropriate speech."

"I might've had to, if he hadn't shown up in time."

"What a shame," Mrs. Webster said and added with a sly twinkle, "You ought to have barred him at the door. And why did he have to go use all that rude language? I doubt the lady preacher made much of him, either. Well, I won't keep you."

Sean took his seat once more. He felt wrung out. When the crowd had cleared, he'd go reassure the Nussbaums and help Andrew dismantle the tables, and he might get the scoop from Elise on his brother-in-law or take down the posters for Franklin, who had to get Leila home. There sat Patsy, intensely engaged with other lingering lawyers, and Floyd was back in the kitchen, making himself useful among the young. For now, Sean waited. He loosened his collar and pulled off his tie. He wanted no responsibilities at all.

3 When he finally made it home Saturday night, he checked right away for messages. Joel's voice on the answering machine said, "Where are you, Shaw-awn? You can't have left for the dinner already. I'll call your cell." He located his cell phone in the pocket of his windbreaker, draped over the bedpost. Again, Joel's voice came on. "Where are you! This is nuts. Sean, I have an important proposal. Jesus Christ! Pick up. Call back when you get this." But there was also a text that had come in later. All it said was: "That's it. I've had it. I'm not talking to you."

So Sean had a bad night. Reading about Nikita Khrushchev couldn't take his mind off how his heart felt hollowed out, sunken, pounding emptily beneath the covers. He turned out the light and tried to sleep, turned it back on and tried to read, gave up and turned it off again. There was a late party going on in the converted school across the side street. He'd thought it was all retired people over there, but somebody was sure having too much fun.

At dawn, Sean got himself up, put on his robe and slippers, and went to the balcony. It was chilly out there, still in shade, but he sat in a canvas chair and tried to think but couldn't quite. He knew Joel's bad temper would fade. He knew they would talk soon. Through the years, they'd quibbled and squabbled and eventually worked things out. Reassured, he went back inside to warm up. He lay down on the couch and somehow fell into the sound sleep he'd sought all night long.

When he woke, sunlight was shining, cars were rumbling by, voices were floating up into his ears. And the phone was ringing. No, not the cell, the cordless. He'd left it by the bed last night in case Joel should call. He fumbled around in the dark-curtained bedroom and found it in time. Before he could speak, a voice that wasn't Joel's said, "Good morning, Moses. Calling to see if Aaron's off dancing around those golden calves up there."

"Oh, it's Sheila? What are you talking about?" Sean sat himself against the pillows and pulled a blanket over his bare legs.

"Isn't he in Wisconsin? That was his plan after quartet night."

"That's where he is."

"You're on your own. I'll meet you at that scrumptious breakfast joint down your block, if you need a friend."

"Thanks, Sheila, but you would have a long ride on the Sunday schedule. I'm waiting for him to call. How are the cats?"

"Don't avoid the issue, Sean."

"No, really, I appreciate it, but I'm fine. We had our fundraiser last night. I've been sleeping late."

326

"I would've been there if I had the spare change, but as you saw—"

"Of course not. It was for people with thick wallets like my brother-in-law."

"How much you pull in?"

"I imagine I'll find out at work."

"Joel back tonight?"

"Maybe not till tomorrow."

"So how about dinner at a quiet restaurant of your choice?"

"I do appreciate it, Sheila. Maybe after he's found his perfect place and I need advice."

"Listen, Sean, I've been deceiving you. I happen to know he's already found a place that your politics won't let him have. Remember, we're in constant radio contact. And now he's gone out with his old chum, the contractor, and isn't planning on talking to you before you come around."

"And you're calling to give me a push?"

"Oh no, I'm not taking sides on this one. I was only thinking you might need someone to talk to. Ouch, Qusay, stop kneading my knees! Scram!"

"Sheila—" Sean didn't know what else to say because he didn't quite trust her anymore.

"All I can do is offer," she said. "I don't want you fellows breaking apart over this."

"But I've heard you're fascinated with such things."

"That's for my beastly thesis. It's about what's already happened when you can't do anything about it, like tonality or the Austro-Hungarian Empire or your dad."

"So what's your advice, if you're on both of our sides?" Sean knew he sounded abrupt and doubtful.

"If I say it, you'll assume I'm in Joel's corner."

"But say it."

"I don't know about this place he wants. He sent photos. It's completely without charm, but he says you liked that aspect of it.

It's your ethical objection he's not buying into. He thinks it's bogus. Myself, I don't. It's you all over, Sean Tyson. But what I wonder is if there's any price at all you'd feel ethical about."

"It's not the price," Sean said. "It's that we'd be cutting out some-one's family. I want something no one else wants."

"There's got to be a lot of that up in those ersatz mountains of Joel's."

"That's your advice, to keep looking?"

"That was my advice to him, too. And I told him, whatever you buy, if he deserts the Lilienthals, in my book he's toast."

《 》

Sean felt curiously reprieved. Nothing need happen quite yet. He went to make some breakfast and a cup of coffee to wake him up. He didn't want to wait home all day for a call, and Joel was driving around with Johnny Kasimir anyway, but he didn't want to leave the apartment, either. He would go back out on the balcony, now that the sun was up over the buildings across the street, but first, he drew open the heavy bedroom curtains and tilted the blinds, got dressed in flannel shirt and jeans, pulled his slippers back on, and yanked the windbreaker off the bedpost.

He had poured a second cup of coffee and was halfway up the hall when he thought to check email. In any case, he should respond to the Lilienthals, but when nothing came up, he figured he'd wait. Joel wasn't going to email or text or talk to him at all that day. The last time he'd seen Joel's face, it was staring out of that screen from a motel room so many miles from home.

In the crisp fall morning air, sitting in his chair with his steaming coffee, Sean was invisible from the sidewalk, and the balconies across the street were too shady for anyone to stay out long. He and Joel liked morning sun and evenings in the cooler air. They had chosen the best side of the street. They were so anxious signing the mortgage because they'd only been together a short while. But they could always sell, Dr. Nathan had explained. It might seem high right then, but just wait and it would come down in time. Don't ask why, he'd said, but that was how this damn capitalism they were stuck with worked. Their payments would eventually seem like chicken feed, and they could borrow on their equity if things got tight. As, in fact, they had done. Sean missed Joel's steady old dad and his attentive mom. What if he'd had a mom and dad like them? He didn't much miss his own parents, or if he did, it was only for how they'd seemed to him in his childhood. That was so far back. He couldn't recapture how good it once felt to a wheezy, scrawny, studious boy to be at home with them on Cedar Street.

He sipped the hot coffee and let the sunlight warm him. He might walk down to the lake shore, but he would have to see people, and he didn't want to encounter anyone right then. He didn't want to talk to anyone but Joel, who wouldn't call or write, and Sean wouldn't call or leave a message for him. He'd have to wait. He did try to reconsider the ugly house under the cliffs. Joel had a point about what the sellers also deserved. They'd brought up four kids there, they had needs as much as the low-bidders. Or maybe, after all, it was the amount of money he'd have to withdraw from the bank. The money did matter. He wondered how hefty a check Elise's Patsy had wormed out of Trevor Ahern. Davey's speech, all told, might have hurt the cause. Sean would have wanted to say the very same things, but he knew he wasn't brave enough, or as foolhardy. Instead, he would have enumerated all the good work they did and told stories of actual cases. He'd assembled notes on a bunch of them, including Emma Jo Webster's, never imagining she'd attend. Would she have stood up and said, "That's me!" and sung Sean's praises to the crowd? He'd also compiled notes on Franklin's statistics and was planning to point to each chart on the wall and elucidate it. But that would have been boring. He was no Davey Nussbaum. Yet he might've done all right because he had believed in the cause ever since reading Marx in seventh grade. Either way, though, he wished Joel had been there. If he missed anyone in the world, it was Joel.

« »

Sean whiled away the afternoon, daydreaming, dozing in the chair as the sun rose above the balcony's pine-plank ceiling out of sight. He conjured up vanished scenes, erotic and otherwise, and got nowhere in his aimless puzzlings. When he grew too cold, he traipsed back inside, washed the dishes, checked the phones in their charging stations, and went to the middle room to write Rebecca and Art. There was an email from Joel. Stunned and a bit afraid, Sean took a seat at the desk and read it through slowly, not daring to scroll quickly ahead.

Dear old Quimby,
I say Quimby because I'm communicating with your gentler side not the fearsome Tyson of last night. I don't know how you'll take this, but here goes. Okay. I drove around with Kaz. I showed him the eggplant house that will never be ours, and he said it would've been ideal, but we didn't look long because there were folks out front, not the Lauristons so I'm guessing they were the first refusers. I admit they looked pleasant enough, but fuck them! So we kept on driving. There was that shady stone cottage down in the dreary dell (no way) and that farmhouse on the open heights (no way) and a couple of new listings Tory showed me as well as, remember, that log cabin on the hill above what you called a gully and I called a brook but today Kaz called it a crick. All right, so he insisted we get out and have a gander. "Live here while you build your dream house." Remember? Don't worry, we won't need to build a dream house. Kaz came up with a plan to make one out of what's already built. I recalled Tory had found the key tucked on a beam below the front porch. So we went in and poked around, and the mold wasn't so bad in the cooler

weather. He said he could jack up the whole thing and run new sills on pillars and insulate underneath and ventilate and replace the rotten floorboards around the leaky pump. The rest is sound. The cedar-shake roof's still good but could use more insulation. I'm sending all these details because I'm not talking to you right now. And I don't want you fussing at every little obstacle. So listen: Kaz can replace the pump and upgrade the pipes and electric and build a screened porch off the back. I know there's only one small bedroom (cozy!) and a big room for everything else, but my piano won't take up much wall space. I promise not to bang on it too much. Mostly, I'll play my viola on the hillside, and you'll be reading out on the front porch in a hammock we'll sling up. Kaz says he'll shore up the footbridge. You'll probably say it's to cross the River Styx, but for me it's the Rainbow Bridge to Valhalla. See how operatic I'm feeling about our new life? And there's plus or minus ten acres, mostly up the hill, which faces south, so we won't have to do more than sit and watch the light creep down from the crest each morning and creep back up in the evenings. So what's the deal? Tory says we could get it, as is, for well under thirty, and Johnny says he can do the whole job for no more than fifteen. Let's say fifty thousand max with fees and taxes and unknowns. It's in the works, Sean. I wrote a check for $1000 in earnest money and handed it over this afternoon. The cabin's been sitting on the market for two years. The owner moved to Florida. We won't be displacing a soul. And we'll be employing Kasimir Contracting, if you're worried about the working class. Kaz can start as soon as we close. He'll get it done by Thanksgiving. He needs what Governor Walker would call "the jaab." Okay, I'll compromise. We'll shut it down for winter this time, drain the pipes, lock it up, but I'll be back up in the spring and only come down once a week for choral rehearsals and quartet nights, and you'll take a bus up some weekends. I know it's a lot of driving, but I'll have some kind of car by then. I have such good memories of our Chibiabos cabin in the UP with Phil Kimbley coming by with his old dog for a chat. And we'll have Lucy, our greyhound, and there won't be enough room for Danny and his lady friend, so they'll have to stay in this cushy motel I'm at in town. And the Moores can come out on day trips. Are you furious? But it was our pact, and when you sit on that front porch and look out across the narrow valley with the day lilies along the brook back in bloom and the wooded hills I call the Ocooch Mountains, you'll know I did good by you. Sleep on it overnight. Tory won't deposit the check before tomorrow afternoon, and we can even forfeit the thousand bucks, if it comes to that. I'll love you anyway.—Joel

For a spell, Sean sat on the rickety desk chair, trying to take it all in, but he couldn't. He would at least answer the Lilienthals' email, which he read again to calm himself and then set his fingers on the keys and replied:

Dear Rebecca and Art,

Thanks so much for your contribution. Andrew Stone will be sending out formal acknowledgments for tax purposes. I missed you both. The event went well but got a bit rowdy when my old friend Davey Nussbaum took the podium. No damage done, I hope. Thanks also for mentioning my home front. The challenge continues, so it's reassuring to know you both understand what it's been like. Looking forward to your "Dissonant" concert!

Love, Sean

And then he got up and went to lie on the couch and find out if he could think better there. At first, it was only the new fear that Davey's rant might have cost them next year's HUD money. He worried so much about people's housing. He always had.

But what came to him next, lying on the couch, was an almost forgotten chilly night in the forest at summer camp. He was sitting cross-legged on pine needles with his cabinmates around a fire of blazing logs, while the older boys, in the loincloths and beaded moccasins they'd sewn in crafts period, danced the Indian dances they'd been taught. Their pale skin was painted with bright stripes of all colors, and what yearning small Sean had felt, what loneliness he hadn't yet understood—

"Poor Mom," he found himself whispering into the couch cushion. Yes, he'd been lying once like that on the couch at home when she told him about Dad, her stockinged feet pacing back and forth before his squinting eyes. He'd already known the secret. He'd been holding it tight inside himself since he was fifteen. Mom would never know he'd known. The Cedar Street house had already begun to break apart.

He turned onto his back to stare at the ceiling as the coming evening faded it to gray. Joel will always be happy, he decided, and I'm a great part of his happiness. He thought of the performances he would soon be attending, those dark quartets and "The Fire of Driftwood" and the "Fagin for a father" song in the opera, and all the while, Johnny Kasimir would be putting the log cabin in good shape in time for Thanksgiving. But in the spring, they would be spending more time apart. He would sleep alone, read alone, take the El to work and stupidly play Joel's choosing game despite himself. He would visit Floyd and have suppers with Andrew. He'd take the Northwestern up to Mary's or have Sandy over for hamburgers. And he would hop a bus to Madison now and then, and Joel would pick him up in a little Chevy with a gentle greyhound riding in back. They'd drive off into the hills where Joel belonged and he did not and would not. He couldn't fathom why that was, what form of exile it would be, an exile from what? And so he stopped mulling it over and got up, switched slippers for shoes, put his windbreaker back on, and struck out to walk about his city as night was falling.

Joel Thomas Greenwood was not the sort of person to think things carefully through, either. That's not entirely the case, because he did think carefully about every note he put on paper, every note he played on strings or keys, measure after measure, counting through time. But in the rest of his life, he tended to leap ahead on impulse. An impulse had drawn him thirty-two years ago into a lifelong love. His enthusiasms came fast, and if they worked out, they lasted. If they didn't, they were gone and forgotten, as was the ugly house and the one-room schoolhouse before it, the eggplant house before that, and now he was enthusiastically onto the log cabin. This one might be about to stick.

Sean Quimby Tyson was the sort of person to hold onto old things a long time, to hold them deep inside, but strangely, he also didn't think about those things carefully enough. He simply held them. He had never once thought of leaving the Housing Collective. Somebody had to do the work not being done for the common good. It was a prepubescent conviction, but he had held onto it because he believed it ought to be true. His beloved thought it was bullshit. It didn't matter. They wouldn't live long enough to find out what world history yet had in store.

But one day next spring, the piano in the corner of the front room would be gone, also the oak music stand and chair. No sequence of odd chords would waft down the hall to a half-asleep man in a bed much too wide for him alone, no mournful viola notes would serenade the night. But how could two men grow old together in a two-room cabin on a gravel road in hilly country with no more work to be done?

On that October evening, no answer came back at all, yet their blood pact would be honored. Something deep inside each of them had agreed upon it. They had been sitting on sunlit floorboards in a musty old schoolhouse in the dying town of Quarryville, surrounded by ghosts. Those warm floorboards had been scuffed by generations of farm kids' clunky boots and high-button shoes while they reckoned sums and recited poems they would soon forget and solved useless equations they would never have to solve again.

JONATHAN STRONG was born in Evanston, Illinois, in 1944 and has lived in Massachusetts and Vermont since his college days at Harvard. His first book, *Tike*, appeared in 1969; *Quit the Race* is his sixteenth novel. He has taught writing at various colleges for forty-seven years, thirty-six of them at Tufts University, where he continues to teach.